THE
LOST
ORPHANS

BOOKS BY ELLIE CURZON

A Village At War Series
The Ration Book Baby
The Spitfire Girl
The Wartime Vet
Wartime Wishes for the Land Girls

THE LOST ORPHANS

ELLIE CURZON

bookouture

Published by Bookouture in 2025

An imprint of Storyfire Ltd.
Carmelite House
50 Victoria Embankment
London EC4Y 0DZ

www.bookouture.com

The authorised representative in the EEA is Hachette Ireland
8 Castlecourt Centre
Dublin 15 D15 XTP3
Ireland
(email: info@hbgi.ie)

Copyright © Ellie Curzon, 2025

Ellie Curzon has asserted their right to be identified as the author of this work.

All rights reserved. No part of this publication may be reproduced, stored in any retrieval system, or transmitted, in any form or by any means, electronic, mechanical, photocopying, recording or otherwise, without the prior written permission of the publishers.

ISBN: 978-1-83618-568-0
eBook ISBN: 978-1-83618-567-3

This book is a work of fiction. Whilst some characters and circumstances portrayed by the author are based on real people and historical fact, references to real people, events, establishments, organizations or locales are intended only to provide a sense of authenticity and are used fictitiously. All other characters and all incidents and dialogue are drawn from the author's imagination and are not to be construed as real.

Catherine: For Rick, the very best there is, and for Mum, Dad, Debra and Stephen, with love. And Pippa, you'll always have my heart.

Helen: For Sheila, who was evacuated when she was only five years old.

HISTORICAL NOTES

In the early days of the Second World War, hundreds of thousands of children were evacuated from British towns and cities to the relative safety of the countryside. But many returned. One small group of those runaway evacuees in London's East End decided to do their bit and help protect their city, risking their lives for the war effort as the Blitz raged. They caught the imagination of a country in its darkest hour, and became known as The Dead End Kids. Night after night children as young as ten took to the streets as bombs rained down, putting out fires and rescuing those who were trapped. Two of these fearless children were killed whilst on duty, but the Dead End Kids went on with their dangerous mission. These brave children are the inspiration for the Blitz Kids.

PROLOGUE
ELSIE

London, January 1941
Moments before the bomb fell

The shrieking wail of the sirens got right into Elsie's head and rattled about her skull. It sank into her teeth and her bones and made her heart hammer. There was no way to hide from the howling, even in an air-raid shelter. And after the siren, the planes would thud overhead, and the guns would go off.

As for the bombs, they were the worst of all. They made the whole earth shake.

Elsie ran along the uneven, icy pavement. She was only eight, and small for her age; it was so hard to keep up with the running, jostling figures that hurried along the freezing, dark Whitechapel street. She hadn't had time to button her thin blue coat, and her dark green scarf trailed behind her.

Some of the crowd that had swallowed Elsie were from the orphanage, like her brother, Jack, and their friends. Others were locals who had left their warm houses to run out into the cold for the safety of the nearest Underground station. The few lampposts were shaded for the blackout and shone narrow strips of light onto the cracked pavement, so that all Elsie saw of the hurrying crowd was a knitted hat here, the shoulder of an overcoat there.

Her red knitted beret was sliding off her short, dark blonde hair as she ran, but she couldn't adjust it. She held tight to the little grey and black dog who was struggling in her arms, terrified.

Elsie had found Pippa hanging around the orphanage. The nuns didn't allow pets, but the little dog had come to find her in the yard where Elsie and the other children played.

'Elsie, come on! We've got to get you to the shelter!' Elsie's older brother, Jack, urged. He held out his arms. 'Give Pips to me and run for it!'

Elsie shook her head defiantly. She wasn't going to let go of Pippa, even though carrying the dog slowed her down. She wouldn't let go of anyone, not today, when her friend Rob had been buried in the cemetery only hours before. She glanced up at the sky as the searchlights strafed the darkness, and saw one of the barrage balloons that hung high above London, its anchoring cables designed to entangle enemy planes.

'Give him the dog!' shouted her friend Connie, who was heaving for breath. 'Elsie, come on!'

I'm not letting her go, Elsie thought. She couldn't say anything out loud any more.

'Ned, look after Connie!' Jack shouted as the crowd surged around them. He glanced up to the dark skies, where the silhouette of planes soared across the moon. 'I'll stick with Elsie!'

Ned shot him a sharp salute and called, 'Will do, squire!' Then he grabbed Connie's hand, even though she was years older than him. 'Come on, Con!'

Connie glanced back at them, her eyes wide, her face pale apart from the red of her scar. Elsie knew she should have kept up with her friends, to get to the Underground station as fast as she could, but Pippa needed her.

A man in a flat cap accidentally barged into Elsie as he ran past, catching her arm with his elbow, and she lost her balance. She tried to grab the air with her gloved hands and, in that awful moment, her arms were no longer a cradle for the little dog: Pippa jumped free.

Elsie opened her mouth wide to gasp, but no sound came out, only steam in the icy cold air. She stopped in the middle of the pavement, trying to see where Pippa had gone, but all she saw was a crowd of people – women holding babies wrapped in blankets, elderly couples with their walking sticks, men carrying suitcases. They buffeted against Elsie as they plunged past, rushing to the shelter.

Elsie started to elbow her way through the oncoming crowd, heading back the way she had come. She could hear Jack calling for her and for Pippa, but she didn't turn back.

Then she spotted Pippa nimbly dodging through the tide of people, back towards the orphanage. She was just out of reach, and Elsie tried to call for her, but she couldn't. Her voice had fallen silent the moment she'd realised she might never see her mum again.

She kept going, even as she tensed at the sound of the planes passing overhead. The ground beneath her feet shuddered as a bomb hit somewhere.

She followed Pippa down the side street that led to the orphanage, the dark, gloomy building looming up ahead. As much as she wanted to run away from that awful place, she wouldn't leave Pippa.

The little dog darted through the open gate and across the cracked, weed-filled yard at the back of the orphanage, into the outhouses. There was an old washhouse there, where Elsie had played with Pippa for hours, pretending it was washday with Mum, and now the dog disappeared through a gap at the bottom of the door. Elsie hurried after her.

The planes were louder now, and another sound joined the racket, a high-pitched whistling that grew louder and louder.

Elsie had just grabbed for the handle of the washhouse's door when the entire world fell apart.

Everything went black. She tried to move, but everything hurt. The door was on top of her and she tried to push it, but it wouldn't budge. It was heavy, so heavy. And there was dust. Smoke.

Would she die here, all alone? Like everyone said Mum had, when the bomb had hit their home. There'd been nothing left. Just a crater and broken bricks. She must've been scared; she must've cried.

Elsie shivered as tears poured down her face. Jack had been following her; had he made it as far as the yard? What if the bomb had fallen on him too? He couldn't die, he couldn't leave her all alone in the world.

Pippa had to be close by, and yet Elsie couldn't hear her barking. She wiped her cheek, and felt the scrape of grit against her skin from her fingers. Had the last few things left to her been snatched away?

Somewhere, there were screams and the rattle of guns; the world shook again as another bomb fell close by.

In the darkness, she gingerly stretched out her hand and tapped the door that lay above her, hoping someone might hear her.

ONE

Bethnal Green, London, August 1939
A year and a half before the bomb fell

Early that morning, Elsie and Jack caught the train to the countryside with Mum to go blackberrying. It was something they did every year.

On the train Jack read *Robinson Crusoe*, while Elsie stared out of the window at the city flashing by until the buildings fell away and the fields filled her view. Mum had worn a summery red and white gingham dress with a straw sunhat on her blonde hair. Elsie had brought Ginger, her ragdoll, which Mum had made for her when she was a baby. She had orange wool for hair, and black buttons for eyes, and kept slipping from under Elsie's arm as she reached for the blackberries. In the end, Ginger had ridden in the basket so that Elsie wouldn't lose her.

They'd walked up and down the sunny country lanes, Elsie trying to keep up on her little legs until Jack picked her up and sat her on his shoulders, where she perched as she plucked the plump, dark fruit from the thorny hedges. Elsie picked one berry for the basket and one for herself, and was full up by the time they got to the station to catch the train home. Her arms and legs ached, and her skin felt warm from the sun, but she was proud of the heap of blackberries in Mum's basket. When Jack thought nobody was watching he tried to sneak a berry for himself, until it turned into a game, with Elsie trying her best to catch him out every time.

They arrived back at their terraced house in Bethnal Green, in the East End of London. It stood near Victoria Park, where she and her brother often went to play with their friends. Elsie had been born in the house, and her brother too. She never wanted to live anywhere else.

In the narrow hallway was a photograph on the wall of Elsie as a baby in a frilly dress, Jack sitting beside her, wearing a huge grin. On the floor was a rag-rug, made by Mum from colourful fabric scraps of old clothes; she had woven memories into it with her slender, nimble fingers.

'Hello, Dad!' Elsie called. She poked Ginger's face round the edge of the door to the front room, before peering after her.

Dad, in his shirtsleeves, was sitting in an armchair with his feet on a stool. A shaft of sunlight that came in through the net curtains made his dark, neatly oiled hair gleam. He had his nose in the newspaper and didn't seem to notice her at first. He looked like he had something on his mind; he often did these days. All the grown-ups were worrying about Germany.

Elsie didn't understand. She remembered the prime minister coming back on a plane, waving a sheet of paper and saying there was peace. Could the prime minister have been wrong? Elsie didn't like the thought of war. She'd seen all the names on the memorial from the last time everyone was fighting. Would even more names be added to it? Dad always said that if the war happened, he'd give up portering and join up to fly a plane. Would he be safe?

'We've got loads of blackberries!' Elsie told Dad, and he looked up from his paper and smiled back at her.

'And we would've had even more if Jack and Elsie hadn't kept eating them.' Mum chuckled, dimples showing in her cheeks. She stroked Elsie's hair. 'I might've had a couple myself, of course.'

'Just one or two?' asked Dad with a smile that crinkled his eyes.

Jack wandered in and threw himself onto the sofa, his book clutched in his hands. He looked towards Dad's newspaper and asked, 'What's the news?'

Leaving Dad and Jack to discuss the headlines, Elsie and her mum went into the small kitchen at the back of the house, with its window overlooking the yard where the laundry hung on the line between Dad's tomato plants. Jack had left his library books on the kitchen table, and Elsie moved them to the dresser. Mum's best china, painted with cheerful pink flowers, was on display on the dresser's shelves.

Mum made a pot of tea and Elsie took two cups through for Jack and Dad. Then it was time for Mum to use her magic to transform the blackberries. Elsie brought bags of flour and sugar down from the shelf in the larder, and Mum went through the cupboards, bringing out bowls and pans, sieves and spoons.

Mum tied a blue apron round her slim waist and helped Elsie put on her small one. Elsie loved helping Mum in the kitchen, watching the concentration in her blue eyes as she measured the ingredients, the sugar catching the light as it fell from the packet into the bowl. Mum did her best to feed the family, even though Elsie knew that times were hard.

She had come downstairs one night after having a bad dream about a fire that had spread across the whole of London, and she and her brother were trying to put it out with buckets of water. She had overheard her parents in the front room, talking in hushed tones about money. Elsie knew they did their best to keep a roof over their heads, Dad working all day as a porter and Mum doing shifts behind the till at the chemist's, but they weren't rich like the people who lived on the other side of London. They didn't have a car, and they certainly didn't have servants. They only went to the seaside once a year, for a short holiday. And yet, Elsie wouldn't have swapped her life for someone else's, because she and her brother were loved and their home was filled with laughter.

As pans bubbled on the hob, filling the steamy air of the kitchen with delicious scents, Elsie stood on a chair to watch Mum making pastry. The kitchen table was white with flour and in the middle of it was a circle of dough that Mum was flattening with her rolling pin.

'Is it my go now? I want to help!' Elsie hopped up and down on the chair with joy at the prospect of rolling the pastry for the blackberry tart. There'd be blackberry jam, and blackberry crumble, and blackberries with cream as well.

But in her excitement she lost her footing. Her heart lurched as she slipped off the chair.

And yet, she didn't fall.

Mum caught her with her floury hands, encircling her in her soft arms, and Elsie was safe. She leaned against her and grinned up at Mum's gentle blue eyes.

Chuckling, Mum dotted a dab of flour to the end of Elsie's nose and went on rolling the pastry.

She'd always be safe, as long as Mum was there to look after her.

* * *

Now

A tear worked its way down Elsie's cheek as the memory of that afternoon of blackberry picking melted away.

There was something she needed to remember, and yet she couldn't. It was as lost as her voice.

She could barely move, and she didn't try to wipe away the tear. Her head hurt, and she coughed again, trying to clear her lungs of the brick dust that had been kicked up by the bomb. Her mouth was all gummed up.

She was so thirsty and tired. Her eyes were closing and she couldn't fight it.

TWO
LISETTE

London, 1941
Moments before the bomb fell

Lisette shifted as she tried to get comfortable on the hard platform of Whitechapel Underground station, pulling her dark red winter coat tight around her. She toyed with the fringe of her black, knitted scarf as she tried to push away the memory that came to her every time the air-raid siren sounded. Of waiting in the shelter for her Tom, her Monsieur Anglais. The man who never arrived because he hadn't reached the shelter in time.

So many lives had been lost. And still it went on, raid after raid, and still, by chance, Lisette survived. She had thought Tom would be safe in the Ministry of Information's film unit; his background as a film editor meant he hadn't been going off to fight. Instead, he'd made shorts of airmen answering the scramble bell, and reels that showed the public how to put out incendiary bombs.

But she'd been wrong; he hadn't been safe at all.

She couldn't bear to think about her luck running out like

Tom's had, and yet she wondered why she should be spared when his life had been taken. She didn't even know what had become of her mother, dear Maman; Lisette had begged her to leave Paris, but then the Nazis invaded and it was too late. The borders slammed shut, and she hadn't heard a word from Maman since.

Lisette tried not to let the sadness consume her because, when she sang on stage, the audience were there to be entertained, to be transported from the shortages and air raids and fear for just one night. They watched Lisette, tall and slender, her long hair turning golden in the lights, but they didn't know how hard it was for her to smile when her heart was full of ash.

She should've been used to the bombings by now; they came nearly every night. She was safe from the air raids if she was at Jasper's, the basement nightclub in Soho where she worked, but when she was anywhere else in the city, like she was this evening after visiting a friend, she had to run to find shelter. The nearest Underground station was usually the best place to go, and many of them had been turned into subterranean towns, with canteens, and dormitories full of bunk beds.

Up and down the platform, tired people in their winter coats and scarves were stretching out for the night. Some had come prepared with a small picnic, and others had brought blankets and suitcases with them. Next to her, a silver-haired man and his wife had closed their eyes, trying to get what sleep they could, while others chatted quietly in small groups.

The air in the station was warm, like it always was, with a smell of metal, grease and dust, and the scent of all the people who were sheltering, a mixture of lavender talc and men's cologne, pomade, sweat and sour milk.

Far away in the tunnels, Lisette could hear the distant clatter and hum of trains over the rat-a-tat of the anti-aircraft guns and the sudden echoing boom of a bomb landing somewhere in the city above their heads. It would be chaos up there, a hell that she couldn't bear to think about.

On the wall opposite Lisette, on the other side of the tracks, a poster showed a rosy-cheeked girl standing in front of a sunny, rolling field, declaring, *For a healthy, happy job, join the Women's Land Army.* She wondered how many city girls saw that poster and dashed off as fast as they could, unable to stand another night sleeping on the hard floor of the Underground platform surrounded by crying babies and others' snoring. But despite the dangers and the discomfort, Lisette couldn't bring herself to abandon the city that had welcomed her when she'd arrived from France. It was the city she had made her home, and where she had loved her Tom.

But no matter how bad it was above ground, it was far worse in France. She treasured the last letter she had received from Maman. She had no idea if her mother was safe, if her cousins and aunts and uncles had survived. Every awful news story that leaked out – the refugees mown down, the young French men forced to work in munitions factories in Germany, swastika flags flying along the Champs Élysées – she cried, picturing her family, her neighbours, the whole nation of France.

'Here's a welcome bit of class in glamorous Whitechapel! Mademoiselle Souchon, as I live and breathe!' said a gravel road of a voice.

Lisette, disturbed from her sad reflections, looked up to see the bulky, well-dressed figure of a man who smoked so much it sounded like he was gargling tar. He had a fur coat over his shoulders, revealing a sharply cut suit, and the light glinted off his large gold watch and the ring on his little finger. He was the best-dressed person in the station, even though underneath that veneer, Lisette knew, was the sort of man it was best to keep away from.

And he was addressing Lisette.

'Mr Mahoney,' she said. His bulk had cast a shadow across

her. She didn't want to say his full name, not out loud. *Toe Mahoney*. It was best not to dwell on how he'd got that name; Tom had told her one night and she'd thought he was joking. Until, with a shiver of horror, she'd realised he wasn't at all.

Mahoney lifted his hand and took off his hat in a gesture of politeness. His other hand remained unmoving in its black glove. Lisette had heard that there was no hand in that glove at all, that it had been lost somewhere along the way, but she didn't know if that was true or just part of the legend. Legend followed Toe Mahoney around, but it was no legend that this was the man who ran the East End.

'Me and Ma Mahoney, God bless her, seen you giving your show last week,' he said. 'And Ma said you was the best she'd seen since the war started. And she's seen Gracie Fields. Thank you, mademoiselle, for giving her something to smile about. She ain't had much to be happy for since she lost my brother.'

'I am pleased she enjoyed the show,' Lisette replied. She did her best to smile, even though Toe Mahoney made her nervous. She'd come down here to be safe, and now another danger was pursuing her. Not that he'd do anything to her, there were no rumours like that. And yet he hadn't got to be the king of the East End without breaking a few bones; an aura of threat hung around him like the fug of cigar smoke. But even a gangster who dripped in gold jewellery could lose a relative to the war. 'I'm sorry for your loss.'

Lisette was aware that her conversation with the gang boss had attracted attention from other people sheltering on the platform. It was hardly surprising; Toe Mahoney was something of a celebrity in these parts. At her words of sympathy he shifted his bulk in his polished correspondent shoes, then cleared his throat with that same gravel rumble.

'Well, that's decent of you to say,' he replied. 'He went down with HMS *Glorious*, did our Wally, but not before they gave the Krauts on the *Scharnhorst* something to think about. It ain't much of a tonic though, miss. He was a good lad. Twenty-three years old... I don't think I was ever as young as that.'

Lisette swallowed. Hardened though Mahoney was, he was still visibly upset about the loss of his youngest brother. 'Just a boy,' she said. 'But he did a good thing. When I think of my family in France, I—'

Suddenly, cutting through the muffled sounds of war above their heads, came voices. The high, sweet voices of children singing, the acoustics of the Underground station making the sound echo around them. They sang 'You Are My Sunshine', and the sleeping couple next to Lisette opened their eyes, smiling as they looked around for the singers.

'Oh, ain't that sweet!' the lady said, nudging her husband.

And it was. Even though the children shouldn't have been in London, their voices made Lisette's eyes fill with tears. Toe looked in the direction of the song, holding his fedora to his breast as he listened.

Walking along the platform were two children, holding hands. One was a grinning boy, about nine years old, with large, hopeful blue eyes and a head of golden, curly hair. He held out a cap in his free hand and his grateful audience dropped in whatever coins they could find. Beside him was an older girl, about fourteen or fifteen. She was at that awkward age, not yet an adult, but no longer entirely a child, wearing an Alice band to hold back her shoulder-length brown hair.

Lisette found herself staring at the angry red scar down one side of the girl's face. She forced herself to look away, and yet their sweet voices drew her attention back. They both had the dusty, worn look that so many people in London had these days, their winter coats held together with darns and their shoes needing to be reheeled. But added to that, the children looked pale, their faces pinched with hunger.

Times were hard and food was scarce, but couldn't these

children's parents send them to the countryside with all the other thousands of evacuees, where they'd be safe and fed?

They were only a few feet from Lisette when they reached the end of their song. Addressing everyone on the platform, the girl said, 'We're raisin' money for the orphans. Like our mate, poor Rob. We said goodbye to him today.'

The little boy nodded. His huge eyes brimmed with tears and his lower lip trembled as he offered around the soldier's cap that he carried, shaking the coins in his cap. 'He went up when that van exploded in Spitalfields. God bless him, he was my best friend.'

Around Lisette, people were tutting and shaking their heads. She'd heard about Rob from her friend Tilly, who she'd been visiting in Whitechapel. A lad, all of twelve, who was killed when a van had exploded outside Spitalfields Market. And yet, there were rumours. *They say he was stealing petrol. Well, what do you expect if you muck about like that?*

Lisette took some coins out of her pocket. 'Here,' she said, reaching out towards the children. 'Take this, buy some food.'

'God bless you, pretty miss,' said the little boy. Then he blinked up at Mahoney, who had replaced his fedora on his head. The gang boss took a wallet from inside his fur coat, the gleaming leather bulging with the enviable contents. A life of crime clearly did pay. He laid it in his unmoving gloved hand, opened it and thumbed through the contents. 'Please, Mr Mahoney,' the boy said, 'we come from St Mary's Orphanage. If you can spare a few coins, sir, it'll mean the world to us.'

'You're with them nuns, ain't you?' Mahoney had already selected a coin, but when the little boy nodded to confirm the name of the orphanage he winced and shook his head. Then he looked into his wallet again and Lisette got the distinct impression that he was increasing his donation. Lisette had never heard of the orphanage but, if it made even Toe Mahoney pause, it must be a sorry sort of place. He selected his donation and dropped the money into the little boy's cap, to a chorus of impressed gasps from his audience. 'You an' me might have a little chat, son, eh? You know your way around the East End?'

The boy nodded. 'I do, sir!' he said brightly. Lisette's heart blanched at the sight of the sweet little face, the child too trusting of a man like Toe Mahoney.

'I've seen a lot of you kids doing the running for the black-market boys.' Toe dropped another few coins into the hat. 'I want to know who's pulling them strings. Something's changed in this manor and I'm looking out for who's behind it.'

'I'll ask around, Mr Mahoney!' the child offered, glancing into the hat with his wide blue eyes. 'There's a lot of work going fetching and carrying. That's what Rob was up to when he— someone paid out for a proper nice funeral for him though. Least he got a decent send-off.'

But children shouldn't be talking about funerals and decent send-offs. They shouldn't even be thinking about such things.

The lad swallowed, his thin throat bobbing. Mahoney added one more sprinkling of cash to his collection, then ruffled the boy's curly hair. 'Now you don't let them nuns get their hands on that, son. And if they try, you tell them it come from Toe Mahoney. But don't you forget; I want to know what's been going on in these parts lately. I'm hearin' it all over town and nobody's talking.'

'I'll dig around. And God bless you!' The little boy beamed. He gave his companion a nudge. 'Say thank you, Con!'

The girl standing beside him smiled at Mahoney, her scar puckering. Lisette wanted to find a policeman to tell him that the children were involved in goodness knew what. But what could she do if they were in the care of the nuns? Not that there was much evidence of any caring.

'Thank you, sir,' the girl said, and gave a curtsey. 'Bet you'd all like another song to take your minds off—'

Lisette felt it before she heard it. Everyone on the platform was hurled sideways, and half a second later came an almighty boom. The children lost their footing, and without thinking Lisette reached out to catch them. Shrieks ran through the crowd and a baby wailed in terror; a pitter-patter of mortar rained on them from the ceiling.

Then there was silence. An awful, dense silence. Her heart in her mouth, her arms round the two, thin children, Lisette closed her eyes.

THREE
LISETTE

Now

'That was a big one,' the silver-haired man sitting next to her whispered. 'God help them, poor bleeders. I just hope it's not Balham all over again.'

Lisette forced herself to open her eyes and released the children from her arms. The station looked just as it had before. It wasn't Balham again, at least not here. Balham had been awful, nearly seventy dead when the bomb exploded in an Underground station and burst through the sewer where six hundred people had been sheltering.

But she could hear a dreadful metallic whining noise echoing down the train tunnel. Her stomach twisted painfully as she realised a huge bomb had landed nearby.

At Lisette's side, the little boy had clamped his fist round the cap he was carrying, gripping the money it contained tight. He was staring up at the ceiling as he murmured in a small voice, 'One of the sisters was at Balham. They reckon she drowned in the tunnel when the bomb went through the sewer.'

His lip trembled again and he glanced towards Lisette. 'She was a mean old bird.'

Mahoney had been knocked to the floor by the impact, his hat flung from his head down onto the tracks. 'Somewhere just took a hell of a knock,' he growled. 'It's time we gave bloody Adolf a taste of it!'

Lisette gave the boy a wobbly smile, and said kindly, 'Then she won't come back again.'

'She said it was sinful to wash with warm water,' Connie told her. 'I suppose it serves her right!'

'I wish a bomb'd drop on the orphanage,' the little boy whispered to Lisette. 'But only if the sisters are still in it, knocking back the gin.'

'Ned!' Connie scolded. 'You can't say that. Where the heck would we live if there weren't no orphanage?'

'You should go to the countryside,' Lisette answered. 'It would be better than here.'

Ned shrugged. 'I got sent out and come right back again,' he said. 'Least with the sisters, you know they're cows, but you've got all of London to knock about in. Out in the countryside, I was stuck with a cow of a farmer's missus and there weren't nowhere to go except fields. So I packed my whatsits and come back.' Then he grinned. 'And I brought my gang, the Blitz Kids, with me!'

Lisette tried to hide her astonishment. He was very young to have a gang, and anyway, she thought, it was extraordinary to think of evacuees coming back to London and naming themselves after the very thing they'd been sent away to avoid.

'The Blitz Kids, eh? Once a Londoner, always a Londoner,' said Mahoney proudly, dropping another donation into the little boy's cap for his efforts. 'I've got work for lads who know their way around. No more trekking the Underground platforms when you run messages for Toe Mahoney.'

'Whitechapel born and bred!' Ned replied. 'I've been with the sisters all my life. They ain't got no prettier in all them years neither.'

Lisette remembered the various convents in Paris, with their high, windowless walls and sense of utter calm in the middle of the city. Her cousin Mirabelle had shocked the family when she decided to take vows. Lisette had visited her, speaking to her through an elaborately carved grille. She couldn't see much of her, just an impression of black and white in the shadows. But she couldn't imagine Mirabelle being cruel to children if she'd been sent to work in an orphanage.

'They're mean,' Connie told them. 'They said God punished me with this' – she gestured to the burn on her face – 'because I'm vain.'

'That's dreadful!' Lisette replied, her blood boiling. 'As soon as this raid is over, I will come to this orphanage and I will tell them what I think!'

Mahoney nodded; Ned watched him for a moment, then nodded too as Mahoney told Connie in a fatherly sort of way, 'You don't listen to them nuns, you got a lovely face, and a cracking voice on you too.' He jerked his thumb towards Lisette. 'You need to talk to this lady here, she sings songs for a living!'

Connie turned to Lisette, her eyes wide with amazement. 'You're a singer? Well, blow me down with a—'

Her last word vanished, silenced by the blast of another bomb that was so loud and so close that it echoed and echoed inside Lisette's head and sent tiles crashing down from the station's ceiling. Lisette held the children tight.

'Flippin' heck, that was close!' a young woman further along the platform declared.

'That must've been here, in Whitechapel,' Connie said, her voice hushed. Suddenly her tone was vivid with panic. 'Oh, no, what about Elsie and Jack?'

Ned was already pushing the contents of his cap into the

pockets of his threadbare coat. He put the oversized cap on his head and told Connie with the determination of someone four times his age, 'I'm going up top. You stop here, Connie.'

'You ain't goin', Ned. You're too little.' Connie wriggled out of Lisette's embrace and got to her feet. 'I'll go.'

Lisette couldn't believe what she was hearing. Every bone in her body locked up. They couldn't go outside. Tom hadn't got to the shelter in time, and she'd never seen him again.

'You're not going anywhere,' Lisette said firmly, 'not in an air raid!'

Ned sprang to his feet and took Connie's hand. 'Come on then,' he said. 'You ain't ever goin' to do as I say anyway! Blitz Kids stick together!'

Lisette couldn't believe it. Were they brave or stupid?

But suddenly she was standing, even though she didn't want to leave the station and go outside, where bombs were crashing through the night sky onto the city. And yet the thought of these two hungry, neglected children risking the air raid alone made her heart quail.

'Then I'm coming with you,' she said, trying to keep her tone steady as a voice shouted inside her, *what are you doing? Stay where you are!*

'You're havin' a laugh!' Ned replied. 'You should hang around for the all-clear, but we've got mates out there!'

And with that, he and Connie were darting along the platform. They were fast and nimble as greyhounds, weaving through the crowd and springing over those who were still hoping for a few winks of sleep. Lisette followed, running in her heeled boots that'd seen better days.

Her heart raced. Not just from the effort of running along the crowded platform, but from the prospect of what lay outside: the chaos, the fires, the ruins. Tom would have wanted her to stay where it was safest, and yet she knew she couldn't abandon the children.

She nearly tripped over a suitcase and received a furious, 'Oi, you!' in response. But she didn't stop to apologise. Every second counted. She couldn't risk losing sight of the orphans as they raced towards the surface, where fire rained down from the skies onto London below.

FOUR
LISETTE

Lisette picked her way up the immobile escalators, where more people were sheltering uncomfortably, huddled on the wooden steps. Ned and Connie were far ahead of her, but she was determined to go after them, even though her palms were sweaty with the increasing racket of guns and planes and the smell of burning.

By the time she had reached the top of the escalator, Lisette's legs felt like wet string. She could barely stand. She shouldn't be doing this; she didn't even know these children. Why on earth was she going after them?

Now was her chance. She could turn round, go back down to the platform and wait it out until the all-clear sounded.

She stood, her hand braced against the curved wall, her heart hammering. Tom hadn't been in the shelter. He'd died, straight away, they'd said. He hadn't suffered.

And yet those children. Those poor, motherless, fatherless, children. No one cared for them. People gave them coins, but who had tried to stop them from running into the bomb-ridden streets? No one. Except Lisette. She was all they had.

Strength returned to her; she swallowed down a lump in her

throat and carried on, running through the unlit ticket hall. The children were at the door to the station, trying to force open the sliding metal grille that opened onto the smoke-filled night, as a man in an ARP uniform hurried towards them.

'Stop that, you hooligans!' he shouted. 'Do you want to kill us?'

'We've got mates out there!' Ned bellowed, the angelic little boy from the platform nowhere to be seen now. He seized the grille and shook it hard, eventually succeeding in opening the heavy gate just enough to be able to slip through. As he squeezed between the grille and the wall, he gave a departing cry to the ARP warden of, 'And put that bloody light out!'

Connie laughed as she followed him. The sound was shocking to Lisette. How could they laugh as they left a shelter in the middle of an air raid? Didn't they know they might all soon die?

'Come back here!' the man shouted, shaking his fist. Then he noticed Lisette as she ran up to the gate. 'These your kids, are they? They ought to be in the countryside!'

'I'll go after them,' Lisette said. Everything around her seemingly shifting and unreal, she followed them, leaving the relative safety of the station and heading into the darkness.

Except it wasn't entirely dark. It was like a painting of hell that she'd once seen in a gallery. The darkness, in various shades of black and grey, glowed with the intensity of fires that licked up against the ruins. Bullets from the anti-aircraft guns flew like shooting stars and the searchlights were bright columns of light against the night sky. But no hellscape before had featured planes, their engines thrashing against the air as another bomb fell, shaking the ground beneath Lisette's feet.

'Ned, Connie!' The smoke caught in Lisette's throat as she called after them. She had no idea where she was as her eyes struggled to adjust to the darkness.

'What you doin' coming out here?' Ned was running back

towards her, dodging the rubble that scattered the street. Something had been hit, but Lisette didn't know what. All she could make out were the collapsed buildings around them, consumed by flames that Ned and Connie didn't seem to see. 'Stick with us or get back down to safety, but you can't just bloody stand there!'

He had such an old head on those young shoulders.

Tom, I'm sorry, but I think you'd understand. You would have gone with them, too.

'I'm staying with you,' Lisette told him. Connie waited further down the street, broken glass glittering on the pavement like diamonds around her feet. 'I'll help you find your friends.'

Because there were more of them, children like Ned and Connie, hungry but brave, abandoned to this hellish night.

'It's this way,' Connie said, as she swung her tatty, home-knitted scarf over her shoulder. She pointed towards the other side of the street, where Lisette could see nothing but ruins blurring into the smoke and the fire-studded darkness.

'I reckon the orphanage copped it,' Ned admitted. 'Bloody lucky everyone was out!' Then he set off running again, shouting, 'Elsie! Jack!'

Connie joined in, calling the other children's names. Lisette, not knowing what else to do, joined in, even though the names were unfamiliar.

'Elsie! Jacques!' she called. Her English always slipped into her native French when she was unnerved. They ran over the smashed pavements and through the debris, Lisette completely ignorant of where they were headed.

Ned was already up ahead, still yelling the names. His head was snapping from left to right, the flames lighting up his young face as he looked for his missing friends. Lisette couldn't bear to think of what would happen if the pair hadn't got to a shelter and had been caught up here when the bomb landed.

A shudder suddenly ran through her, as a memory forced its

way back to her. Tom's face, appearing as they'd pulled back the sheet on the stretcher so that she could identify him. He was lying so still. The breeze caught his hair and for a moment, just a moment, Lisette had thought they were wrong, that he was still alive. She'd grabbed the sheet, shouted and cried, and a policeman came and dragged her away.

As she followed Ned, she knew that in the ruins that lay either side of them, where flames roared up where roofs had once been, where empty windows stared like unblinking eyes, there might be people lying there, like Tom. Still and pale, as if they were sleeping. But they would never wake up again.

'Elsie! Jacques!' she kept calling, the words ceasing to mean anything, just sound that battled feebly with the racket of the air raid all around them.

'Help us!' Lisette could barely hear the voice over the sound of the mayhem that had gripped Whitechapel. She saw Ned freeze up ahead, his head lifting as he tried to hear the desperate cries. 'Please!'

Lisette strained to hear. 'Is that Jacques?'

Connie shouted through hands cupped like a megaphone. 'Jack, we're comin'!'

'The washhouse!' Jack shouted. Lisette could hear the frantic panic in the young man's voice. 'Elsie's trapped! I can't get her out!'

'We're on our way, Jack!' Ned dropped his head against the heat and took off running, until the smoke swallowed him up.

Lisette paused, looking up and down the street, hoping to see a fire engine or an ambulance or someone who could help. In the distance, she heard a bell ringing as the emergency services rushed through the air raid, but there was no one nearby.

She carried on, following Connie in the direction that Ned had gone in. A wall ran alongside the street and, further along, a huge pile of bricks was collapsed in the road. Lisette clambered over it, almost turning her ankle in her haste, and found herself in what had once been a yard.

She stood, frozen to the spot, as she took in the sight of a mountain of rubble, the spiked remains of shattered walls trying to hold it all in.

A building had stood here once. A place of refuge for children. But there was nothing left here now except desolation. And the shadows of three little figures in the ruins.

FIVE
ELSIE

Waterloo Station, London, September 1939
A year and half before the bomb

It felt like a day trip, but it shouldn't have really, seeing as Dad wouldn't be going home with them. He looked smart in his RAF uniform, and Elsie felt so proud holding her small hand in his large one as they headed to the railway station to wave goodbye. She kept picturing him sitting on an enormous paper aeroplane, a giant version of the ones he made with Jack.

All the way up the escalator from the Underground train, Elsie read the recruitment and government information posters that had replaced most of the adverts for plays and cigarettes. *Join the ATS* caught her eye. It showed a lady with red lipstick, her head turned aside with all the glamour of a film star. She ignored the poster that told families to evacuate their children to the countryside. She didn't want to leave Mum on her own. When her eye fell on a poster of an airman, with the warning *Careless talk may cost his life*, a shiver went through her. That could be Dad. But he'd come home, he would. He had to.

The station was so busy, filled with men and women in uniform, lugging their kitbags over their shoulders. Elsie kept ducking – she was just the right height to be caught by the bags as they swung past her face. Some of the people in uniform looked relaxed, smoking as they leaned out of the railway carriages, chatting to their families on the platform, while others stood awkwardly in their new, unfamiliar clothes.

Jack looked smart in his Sunday best, striding along proudly beside them. His eyes were wide as he took in the sea of uniforms and Elsie saw him swallow, then he told Dad, 'I'm going to join up too when I'm old enough. I want to do my bit.'

'You've a few years to go yet,' Dad said with his familiar smile. 'Hopefully this'll all be done and dusted by then. Besides, you can do your bit here. I need you to look after Elsie and your mum.'

Jack gave a very serious nod, his brow furrowing as he glanced at Elsie. When he met her gaze, the sombre expression lifted and he smiled. 'You can count on me, Pa,' he promised. With a wink he told them all, 'You heard, I'm the man of the house now!' But Elsie knew her brother and she knew when his happiness was forced. And now, as they were saying bye to Dad, his anxiety was all too obvious to her.

Elsie drummed her fingers on her gas mask box. She had tried the horrible thing on and it was so uncomfortable. But she knew Jack would make her wear it.

'Jack's in charge,' Mum said with a playful grin, and patted his shoulder. 'Although that doesn't mean you can leave your greens.'

Among the men and women in uniform, Elsie saw groups of children carrying suitcases. They had parcel tags tied onto their coats. Some of them were laughing and joking, but the little ones were crying for their mums. They were going off to the countryside, but Mum said it was all right at the moment; they didn't have to go yet. Elsie was fine with that. As long as she could lie on the sofa in the evening with her head on Mum's lap as she read her a story, that was all she could ask for.

Dad put his hand on Jack's shoulder and turned towards him. It was like looking at two versions of one man, one still a boy, the other a father, and when Jack met Dad's gaze Elsie saw love and pride and concern battling in his features.

'It's going to be all right,' Dad told him kindly. Then he looked to Mum and Elsie and promised with a smile, 'I'll be home before you know it.'

The departure boards clattered overhead and Dad glanced up, reading the destinations. Jack looked up too, following their father's lead. When Mum also lifted her gaze to the boards, Elsie saw the concern in her face. It was gone in a second, replaced by a smile for the little girl when their gazes met.

'Right, time to say see you soon,' said Dad, leading them towards a waiting train, his arm still round Jack's shoulders. It seemed as long as the whole station, every door standing open to admit the men in uniform. 'No goodbyes for the Taylors. Just a see you soon and a big I love you!'

Elsie and Jack and Mum circled Dad in a huddle and clung on tight. But the station was so busy, with so many people hurrying by, buffeting into them, that their hug soon broke up. Mum was holding a hankie tight in her hand.

'See you soon, Dad!' Elsie said. 'We love you!'

'Give Hitler a wave from us,' said Jack. 'Right before you drop a hundred-pounder on his rotten old head!'

Dad hugged Mum tight, then threw his arms round Jack, who gave a laugh and said, 'Give over!' Then he stooped and picked Elsie up, holding her tight.

'I'll see you soon, little lady,' Dad murmured. He kissed her cheek, then bundled her into Mum's arms. 'I'll see all of you soon. And I love you something fierce!'

She watched as other men dressed in the same blue as Dad swept by, and up he went into the carriage. The door shut behind him and, when he leaned out of the window with the other men from the RAF, Elsie felt like her heart would burst with pride.

She looped one arm round Mum's neck, and with her other hand she waved to Dad. There was cheering, singing and laughing. But Elsie couldn't join in.

Finally a whistle blew, the last door slammed shut, and the train began to chug out of the station in a billow of smoke as Jack came to stand beside them, waving his hand in wide arcs.

Elsie watched Dad for as long as she could. She didn't blink, trying to take in every last bit of him so that she would always remember him. He became a figure in blue waving out of the window, disappearing into the distance as the train took him away.

And that was the last time she had seen him, before the letter came. Before Elsie and Jack found out that he'd gone missing over enemy territory. He didn't even know what'd happened to Mum.

* * *

Now

As Elsie drifted in and out of consciousness, she held on to the tiniest of hopes that she might see her father again. As memories of her parents swirled around her, there was something buried in her mind that she couldn't dig out. If only she could remember what it was... but when she tried to recall it, all she saw was darkness.

Sometimes in the orphanage, when she felt very sad, it seemed as if her parents were close to her, even though she couldn't see them. She felt it again now, and was sure they were outside her brick tomb, just on the other side of the door that lay above her. Couldn't she hear them? And was the door lifting now? Wasn't that her father's hands she could see, prising it open?

The light coming in was so bright. Elsie closed her eyes.

SIX
LISETTE

January 1941

Through the smoke, Lisette could see a boy, rail-thin in a winter coat that looked too small for him. He was balancing precariously on a pile of bricks that once had been a building, frantically picking up pieces of rubble and hurling them away: bricks, chunks of lead guttering, slates from the roof.

Lisette squinted against the sharp, sooty air. Looming up beside the boy was the remains of a perimeter wall, which didn't look as if it would be standing for long. One of the bricks dropped down and smashed only inches from the boy, but he didn't seem to notice the danger. His attention was fixed entirely on his Herculean task. Ned and Connie were there beside him, grabbing at the bricks with their bare hands, hurling them away as they called out for Elsie.

'Come away from there!' Lisette called. But they didn't acknowledge her. Fighting her urge to run back to the shelter, Lisette clambered onto the ruins to pull the children back. The sharp end of a wooden rafter caught in her stockings, but she let it tear the precious nylon. There was no time to worry about that. *Jacques, this must be Jacques.* 'Jacques! It's dangerous, that wall's going to come down any second!'

The smoke stung Lisette's eyes and scratched at her throat as she tried to catch the young man's hands, but he snatched them back and dug once more into the rubble. His thin hands were filthy, skin scratched and torn and bleeding as he clawed at the bomb debris, his shoulders heaving with sobs and exertion. She tried desperately to breathe despite the smoke that choked her as she burrowed through the debris alongside the children.

'It isn't coming down!' Jack snapped, dropping to his knees and digging into the broken masonry. At his side, Connie and Ned were just as desperate in their efforts, none of them afraid for themselves but focused only on their trapped friend. 'Elsie, I'm here! Can you hear me, sis? Give us a knock or a cough or something!'

'Elsie!' Connie shouted. 'Give us a yell!'

But how could anyone hear anything in the noise of the air raid? The planes were still thudding overhead, chased by the anti-aircraft guns, and every so often there was the *boom* of yet another bomb dropping. The sound of fires roared nearby, and the ones that went through gas mains were even worse, setting off more explosions.

And yet, for all the noise, she could hear something. Tapping.

Jack gave a choked cry. 'I'm here, Else. I told you I wasn't ever going to leave you, didn't I?'

But it wasn't over yet. More bombs could still fall as the raid continued, and, while the little girl might still be alive, she could be badly injured.

Lisette hurled bricks aside and threw roof tiles to the ground. Her neatly manicured nails snapped as she picked up a broken length of wooden beam, and dust rose from the debris, making her cough. Her hands were cut and stabbed with splinters. She winced, struggling to see in the dust-ridden, smoke-filled darkness, but she barely registered her own discomfort, all her thoughts fixed on the little girl who had been buried alive.

Another nearby crash shook the earth, but the little band of rescuers didn't pause. Sirens blared, searchlights sweeping the sky where the Luftwaffe and the RAF battled, but all of Lisette's attention was on the fractured ground below her. Somewhere beneath what used to be a building was Elsie.

Ned was the smallest of the rescuers and he wriggled down into the space they had created, scooping up the debris in both hands until he rapped his knuckles hard against something wooden. 'You under here, Else?' he asked. 'Give us a knock, mate!'

Lisette's heart seemed to stop beating as she strained to hear a reply.

And there it was. A knock. Then another. Then, after a moment, as if Elsie had been gathering strength in her tiny safe spot under the rubble, there came a tirade of knocks.

Connie laughed with relief. 'She's all right! The door fell on her!'

Jack grabbed for the wooden beam that Lisette had discarded and jammed it beneath the edge of the door. As he did, the brick wall above them sent a shower of masonry dust down onto them and Ned glanced up, shielding his eyes against the debris.

'Come on,' Jack instructed, following his friend's gaze until he returned his attention to the beam with new determination. 'I'll lever it up, you lot lift it. Elsie, when I say go, you get ready to wriggle out, sis.' Then he took a deep breath and put all his inconsequential weight against the beam that was beneath the door. 'Go!'

The sudden movement threatened the unstable wall, but Lisette tried not to think about it. They'd be quick, and Elsie was in one piece. She'd be free in no time.

The beam creaked as Jack levered up the door, and Lisette

was at Ned and Connie's side as they grabbed the edge of it and heaved it upwards. Suddenly, a small figure, so grey with dust that she was almost a ghost, squirmed out from under the door. She took a huge, heaving breath of air, her arms spread, and suddenly Lisette was cheering with the children.

'We saved her!' Lisette cried with joy and relief. Jack gave a choking sob of relief and exertion as he let go of the beam and the door clattered back down.

'Bloody hell, Else,' he gasped. 'You gave me a right fright!'

A clatter of bricks caught Lisette's attention. She looked up, eyes wide with horror, as she saw the remains of the wall drunkenly pitch and sway.

It's going to fall.

'Out of the way!' she yelled to the children as she dived for Elsie and wrapped the little girl in her arms. She collapsed to the ground, cocooning Elsie against her as the avalanche of rubble plummeted down, sending her plunging into oblivion.

SEVEN
ELSIE

Paddington Station, London, June 1940

'But we don't want to go!' Elsie wailed, as they hurried into the railway station. It was like saying goodbye to Dad all over again, except this time they wouldn't be going back to their home in Bethnal Green. She was gripping Mum's hand tightly, while in her other hand she clung on to her ragdoll.

'It's going to be fine, Elsie, I promise,' Jack assured her. He tapped the label that was attached to his coat, bearing his name and his birthday as well as the address he was leaving behind. 'I'm going to be with you all the way and we'll be in the countryside. It'll be like living in one of your Beatrix Potter books!'

Elsie was trying not to burst into tears. Mum would stay in London, Dad was on his airbase, and she and Jack would be in the countryside. The whole family would be split up.

Around them, she was aware of the men and women in uniform again, but they weren't chipper like when they'd said goodbye to Dad. She'd seen a sailor on crutches as they'd walked up to the station, and soldiers with their heads bandaged. Dunkirk, that was it. All these young men must've escaped France just in the nick of time. But it meant that London wasn't safe any more. They couldn't stay, everyone said so.

'You've got Jack with you,' Mum said, as they paused to look up at the departure board. Elsie heard a tremble in Mum's voice as she went on, 'When you get to the village, you two hold on tight to each other. Don't let them send you off to different billets. And when you get home, we'll get you the puppy you've always wanted.'

'Can't we stay, Mum, please?' Elsie begged her. She gazed up at Mum through blurring tears. Her mum blinked at her as if she herself was trying not to cry. 'If the siren goes, we'll run to the shelter as fast as we can, I promise!'

'The countryside's going to be full of animals and fresh air,' Jack said, but Elsie could see tears glistening in his eyes too. Her big brother never cried though. 'I bet there's some lovely big sheepdogs for you to play with too!'

'I... I suppose so.' Elsie's voice was almost a whisper. She was only a little girl. And little girls never got to do what they wanted. No matter how much she cried, they'd have to be evacuated. 'And you'll come and visit, Mum. Promise?'

Mum bobbed down to her level, stroking Elsie's arm. Her blonde hair cascaded over her shoulders, and the light that came through the station's glass roof made the wax fruit on her straw hat shine.

'Of course I will, when I can. And we'll write letters, won't we? It's good practice for your spellings.' She stroked Jack's arm, too. 'You and Jack will be together, and he'll be looking after you, just as he always has, because that's what good big brothers do.'

Jack nodded. He dashed the back of his hand across his eyes. 'I promise,' he assured them. Then he gave a shaky smile. 'We'll come back as proper country bumpkins!'

'And I'll be a Land Girl!' Elsie told her, cheering up. It

wouldn't be so bad, would it? Fresh air, and animals. Mum would be at home, looking after the house so that when they came back, and Dad, too, they could all be together again.

Elsie wrapped her arms round Mum and hugged her tight. She caught the scent of her; a perfume that smelt of flowers, which always seemed out of place in London.

'I love you, Mum,' she whispered.

'I love you, too,' Mum replied.

EIGHT
ELSIE

Now

She curled into the embrace, forgetting for a moment where she was. The orphanage was a bad dream, and she was back home again, in Bethnal Green. The kitchen smelt of blackberry jam and the pans rattled on the hob. She'd slipped but Mum's arms were round her, protecting her. Her mum, who—

No. Mum was gone. And their home, too. And instead, she was in the arms of an unknown woman who had flung herself on top of her as the wall had come crashing down.

She wasn't moving. Wasn't breathing. Elsie had only seen her for a moment, her rescuer with the long hair and the elegant clothes. Just for a second, she had thought it was Rita Hayworth herself, stepping down from the silver screen to save her.

But it couldn't have been. It was just a dream, and now, whoever she was, the kind lady lay unmoving.

Why did the war take everyone that Elsie loved? Her mum, and Rob, and Dad was missing, and now this lady who had come out of the dark night to protect her, only to be killed as well. And where was Pippa?

She could hear her brother's voice again and those of their friends, but they seemed very far away. Her nose and mouth were full of dust and dirt, and she could see nothing but the darkness beneath the rubble. Pippa was gone and Mum was dead and now, Elsie thought, she would die too, beside the lady who had tried to save her.

'It's going to be all right,' a voice said suddenly. Elsie heard it clear as day, as clearly as she heard her brother call her name again as the darkness lifted and she blinked up into the face of her rescuer. 'Hello Elsie, I'm Mr Wyngate.'

She wondered how he knew her name, but her brother was there, and her friends, too. They must've told him as they dug them out.

She looked up at a man in a hat and an overcoat, like a private detective she'd seen in a poster at the cinema. His face was mostly in shadow, but she could see a square jaw, and the glittering of his eyes under the brim of his hat. Behind him, the searchlights stroked across the dark, smoky sky.

She'd never seen a man like him before outside the cinema. Maybe they really could step down from the screen to save people after all.

Elsie opened her mouth to speak, and yet her throat was still dry, still paralysed. She lifted her arm, stretching her hand out to him, to this strange and exotic man. He reached out and seized Elsie's hand in his own, but not like the sisters did, clutching with a fierce, bony grip. Instead, Mr Wyngate twined his fingers gently with Elsie's just like Dad used to. Then he gave a small smile and said gently, 'Let's get you out of there.'

With that, he reached his other arm round Elsie's waist and scooped her out of the rubble.

'You're safe now,' he murmured.

Elsie clung to him, her grubby hands tight on the lapels of his overcoat. The fabric felt so soft. He smelt so strange, like a fresh morning, but with spice in it. Was that cologne? She stared into his dark gaze, and rested her head on his shoulder. She felt safe with him, despite how unusual he seemed.

She turned to look back down at the lady, and tears squeezed their way out of her eyes and ran down her dusty face.

She was lying on her back, unmoving, her eyes half open and still, one leg twisted behind her. Her arms were crossing her body as if she was still holding on to Elsie.

'Dunno who she is. She followed us from the tube station,' Connie told Wyngate, her voice hushed. 'Helped us dig our mate out. Then that wall come down and she flung herself at Elsie and... Is she gone, Mr Wyngate?'

Wyngate glanced back at the woman who had sheltered Elsie. He set his jaw and said, 'Not if I have any say in it.' Then he turned his gaze back to the children. 'Don't run away. I promise you can trust me.'

'We'll hang about, sir!' Jack reached his arms out to take Elsie from Wyngate and she let herself be handed over to her brother's care. Wyngate immediately began to make his way back towards the lady, but Jack clung to Elsie as tight as a rock in a flood, whispering, 'Oh, Elsie, I love you, you little terror.'

Elsie sniffed, and burrowed her head against Jack's neck. She hoped he knew that meant that she loved him too, because she couldn't say the words out loud. Then she lifted her head and scanned the ruined yard, wondering where on earth Pippa had gone.

There was no sign of her; no floppy black ears, no little paws. And Elsie couldn't hear Pippa's bark, the cheerful one she always gave when Elsie came out to play with her.

Pippa had run into the washhouse. Was she safe? Was she somewhere under the piles of bricks and rubbish? She was so little, she could squeeze into a tiny space and easily wriggle out again. Maybe she had a hiding place somewhere, and she was there right now.

As she looked over, she caught sight of the lady again. She

was so still, like one of the nuns' statues of Mary, as little clouds of dust still rose from the fallen wall, and smoke billowed across the ruins where the orphanage's yard had once been.

'Are you a policeman?' Connie quizzed Wyngate as she stood with her arm protectively round Ned's shoulder. 'Only you ain't got your uniform on!'

Wyngate was standing beside the lady, his back to the children. It was as though her rescuer didn't even hear the guns or see the dogfights, as though the bombsite was something he saw every day.

'I'm not a copper.' Wyngate swept off his coat and bundled it round Elsie as she cuddled to her brother. It was warm and soft.

He wasn't a copper, but Elsie didn't care who he was. He'd saved her, hadn't he? No one had saved Mum, or Rob. And maybe he could save the lady.

Wyngate turned back to the lady and gently took her gas mask box from where it was tangled round her arm, then he stooped to lift her into his embrace. It looked like the drawing in Elsie's picture book when the prince lifted Sleeping Beauty from her deathbed, but there was no spinning wheel here, no castles either. When her arm fell lifelessly to her side, Elsie saw Ned flinch back. Nothing usually scared Ned, the boy who'd been born on the streets, but he drew closer to Connie, then reached up and gripped her hand.

Wyngate knelt and settled the lady gently down on the door that had sheltered Elsie when the building fell. He glanced over his shoulder and addressed Connie and Ned. 'Run down to the road and flag down the ARP; tell them we need an ambulance and we've got a casualty who's receiving mouth-to-mouth. Come straight back here when you've done it.'

'Got you!' Ned said. He paused only to pat Elsie gently on her elbow, then he and Connie darted away in search of help. As they disappeared into the smoke, Wyngate gave Elsie and

Jack a nod that she knew meant it was going to be all right, just as he'd promised. It had to be. Then, without another word, he bowed his head and put his mouth to the lady's.

Could he breathe life back into her? Elsie gripped Wyngate's coat, so much warmer and softer than her own tattered one. He was breathing for the lady, and pressing his hands against her chest.

Elsie hoped for a miracle among the ruins, in the racket of guns and bombs. No one had been able to save Mum, but perhaps, for this lady who had risked her life to save her, a miracle would happen.

'Come on!' Wyngate barked gruffly, before he dropped his mouth to the lady's again. Jack was watching too, his gaze fixed on the pair of them as he clung to his sister, his own breath held. Elsie could see tears in her brother's eyes, unfalling but glistening in the searchlights as he tightened his embrace.

Wyngate pumped his hands on the woman's chest again, his voice fierce, 'Just one damn breath!'

NINE
LISETTE

She jolted awake, her lungs suddenly filling with air. She had no idea where she was. Who was this man, pressing his mouth against hers? Was it Tom? The wall had collapsed on her, on Elsie... was she dead? Was she with her Monsieur Anglais once more?

But her spinning thoughts were sliding into place one by one, and she remembered the children, and the yard, and the bombed-out orphanage.

Lisette put her hands on the man's broad shoulders, and stared back at him. Even though her vision was blurry, she knew him from somewhere. How could she forget a face like that, with the strong jawline, and the dark eyes, or his broad shoulders?

'Where is the little girl?' Lisette pleaded, her voice rasping as she began to breathe for herself.

'She's safe,' was all he said.

Lisette sighed with relief. But she ached all over. Everything hurt. Where had she seen this man before?

'You saved me,' she whispered. 'But who are you?'

'Mr Wyngate,' the man replied. 'I'd usually introduce myself first, but time was pressing.'

'I'm Lisette. Mademoiselle Souchon,' she replied with effort.

Suddenly, a man shouted, 'What's going on here, then?' His voice echoed around the ruins of the orphanage.

Wyngate looked over his shoulder and called, 'Wyngate, Ministry! I've got two casualties, one who needed resuscitation. We need an ambulance.'

There was something commanding in his tone. He sounded like the sort of person no one would ignore. What ministry did he work for?

Lisette turned her sore head just enough to see a man in a tin hat with ARP painted across the front raise his hand in acknowledgement. 'There's none nearby, sir! It's a hell of a mess tonight!'

'I can get a motor goin' for you!' Ned offered. 'Don't need no key, neither!' The little boy turned that angelic gaze on the ARP warden. 'You wouldn't tell nobody about one little hooky motor when there's a lady and a kiddie who need the docs, would you, mate?'

'Well...' The warden paused, seemingly in thought. 'Take it. Just make sure you bring it back and put it where you found it. And be careful, won'tcha? We don't want you getting hurt like poor Rob.'

There it was again, that name. Rob. The boy who'd blown himself up stealing petrol. He'd been like these kids, fending for themselves, without an adult alive who truly cared for them.

Wyngate gave a sharp nod. 'For tonight, you're officially working as an agent of the Ministry,' he told Ned. 'Go and requisition us a car. And make it a nippy one.'

'Yessir!' Ned saluted with such force that he nearly knocked his military cap off his head. 'I'll be back before you know it!'

Wyngate turned back to Lisette. As he spoke, he took off his jacket and laid it over her like a blanket. 'How do you feel?'

'Everything hurts,' she admitted. 'I can't move.'

'I'll carry you.'

But despite her pain, she felt relief. And she felt a hunger. Not for food, but for life. *Her* life, which had nearly ended tonight.

'Is she all right?' Jack asked, his voice filled with concern. He took a few steps forward and Lisette saw that he was carrying Elsie, who was swathed in a dark greatcoat that must belong to the man who had rescued them both. 'You saved our Elsie's life, miss.' And he buried his face against the little girl's hair, stifling a sob.

She'd never saved anyone before. She couldn't get her head around it. Lisette, a singer in a Soho nightclub, had saved a child's life.

Her gaze wandered from the little girl, caked in dust and debris, to the stranger who had brought her back to life. *Wyngate*. He'd breathed for her, pressed and pressed against her heart until it had started to beat again.

'I got you a right nice motor, Elsie!' Ned called from the edge of the rubble. 'My favourite girl's only riding to hospital in a bloody Rolls-Royce!'

Elsie grinned. But she didn't say anything in reply.

'Cat's got your tongue, has it?' the ARP warden said jovially. He'd come closer, picking his way cautiously across the bombsite, and patted Elsie's shoulder.

She stared back at him, her eyes large and fierce.

'Elsie don't talk,' Jack said protectively, taking a step back. 'She will one day, but she don't just now.'

She hadn't called out from under the rubble when they'd tried to dig her out, Lisette recalled. How strange, for a child not to talk. And yet in her short life she'd lost her parents and lived here, in this dreadful place that was now nothing but broken bricks and shattered roof tiles under the screeching sky. No wonder she'd fallen silent.

'All right, lad, I'm sorry to hear that,' the warden apologised. 'Let's get you all into the Roller, then. Mr Wyngate, I'll give you a hand with the lady.'

'You've done your bit, Warden,' Wyngate replied, lifting Lisette easily into his arms. 'I'll take it from here.'

TEN
ELSIE

The whole street looked like it'd been flattened, and the ARP man cautiously headed off, weaving his way through the fallen bricks and shattered glass. All the roofs were gone, and only some buildings had any floors left. Flames licked up inside the ruins, jabbing out through the holes where windows had once been. Still the planes flew over. Still there was the distant crash and bang of bombs falling.

Elsie barely recognised the street. But she *did* recognise Toe Mahoney's fancy black Rolls-Royce, drawn up at a haphazard angle at the kerb. She'd seen it before, when he cruised the streets of Whitechapel in it, handing out sweets to the children. Where he'd got them from, Elsie couldn't imagine. He'd looked like a gangster from a film, his hat at an angle, while the aniseed twists and Everton mints sparkled in the air as he'd thrown them.

'You're goin' to hospital in style!' Connie said proudly.

Ned gave a firm nod. He reached into his pockets and brought out handfuls of money. Elsie had never seen so much.

'Look how much cash Mr Mahoney gave us down in the Underground,' he said. 'He don't like nuns neither.'

Wyngate frowned at the sight of the money as he opened the door.

'Mr Mahoney's very generous,' he said. He opened the passenger door of the enormous car and leaned into the vehicle so he could settle Lisette. Elsie watched with wide eyes, as though she was back at the pictures with Jack and their friends as the heroes saved the day. 'Don't get too close to him.'

Once Lisette was safely in the car, still covered by Wyngate's jacket, he turned to look at the children.

'I'm going to take Elsie and her friend to the hospital and I want you all to head to the shelter,' he explained. 'Take the key to my flat and go there after the all-clear. I'll meet you there once the doctors have taken a look at her. It's in Spitalfields, by—'

Elsie clung to Jack and he shook his head. 'No way, mate,' he said. 'Elsie and me stick together. Connie, Ned, you two take the key and do as Mr Wyngate said.'

'But what if you never come back?' Connie asked him, forlornly. 'What'll me and Ned do?'

Elsie nodded. She didn't want her friends to vanish into the bomb-filled night. What if another bomb fell, another building collapsed, another wall tumbled down on them?

Lisette stirred. It looked like she was still hurting as she slowly lifted her head to speak. 'Go to the shelter. Be safe.'

'No can do,' Ned replied. 'I nicked – sorry, *requisitioned* – this motor, so I can't just hand it over. I've got to stick with it. And Connie can't go on her own, so that means we all stick together. Sorry, Mr Wyngate, them's the rules.'

And Wyngate smiled a tiny smile. He gave a nod and said, 'Get in the car then.'

Elsie smiled back at Wyngate. He had a nice sort of smile. He didn't smile very much, so when he did he must be happy.

Connie cheered as the four of them clambered onto the leather seats. 'Well, this is la-di-da!' she announced.

Jack slipped in beside Connie and settled his sister down on the soft leather seat with Wyngate's coat safely cocooning her. When Ned climbed up to sit beside her and closed the door after him, she spread the coat over his legs too.

'You all right now, Else?' Ned asked kindly. He reached over and took her hand in his. 'I'll bet Pippa had to run off 'cos she's got to help Mr Churchill do something really important. She'll be back when she's saved the day.'

The idea of Pippa being somewhere in the ruins terrified her, but she would've found somewhere safe, Elsie told herself.

The Rolls-Royce was luxurious, but it wasn't a gentle ride. The air raid was still going full tilt, and around them there was nothing but mayhem.

The flames from the fires lit up the night sky. The car bumped over debris and the hoses that the firemen had laid across the road. Some of the rubble was so big that Wyngate swerved across the road to avoid it, and it was like being on a ride at the fair, except Elsie was frightened and clung onto Jack. The car rattled and the ground shook as another bomb landed somewhere, close. She closed her eyes tight for a moment.

There was all that racket still, of the planes and the guns, and ahead of them two searchlights met and caught a white shape in their beams, like a handkerchief, that drifted down from the sky. A parachute. A pilot who'd baled. Seconds later, there was a dreadful din, a horrible whining, wailing noise, and a plane that seemed to be flying through a ball of fire came hurtling down through the sky. It smashed head first into a warehouse just a street away, straight through the roof.

'Bloody hell,' murmured Ned, turning to gaze out of the window. Elsie hadn't known Ned all that long, but it was long enough to know that not much surprised him. Yet she felt his grip tighten on her hand. He looked to Elsie and said, 'Did you see the parachute, Else? I reckon that's just what your dad did, you know. He's in a farmhouse in France, tucking into a right stinky cheese!'

Jack nodded. 'I bet he is too, Ned. He'll have parachuted out just like that; he'll write when he can.'

Elsie swallowed. Ever since the letter had come from Mum, telling them Dad was *missing in action*, she had thought of him still alive somewhere. There was something important about what had happened to her parents hidden in her memory, locked away with her voice. Would she ever remember it?

Machine-gun fire hammered away nearby, and the bullets arced over the road, into the sky.

'Exactly, he's in a farmhouse,' Connie said, raising her voice over the boom of another bomb. The road shook from the impact, and the car nearly jolted onto the pavement. 'Only he can't find a stamp to put on the letter. But he's all right, I know it. And as for us, I can sing, Ned's got his jobs with Toe Mahoney. We'll be fine!'

Elsie watched the silhouettes of Lisette and Wyngate, cast against the flames that lit up the night sky. The two adults had looked at each other just then.

'See, maybe I *do* know a few things about the wide boys around Whitechapel these days that Toe Mahoney'd like to hear,' Ned said. 'There's a new boss in town and he's mopping up the business. Me, I'll work for whoever's paying, and I'll tell Toe whatever I find out about the new bloke and all. But it'll cost him!'

'And that'll keep us fed,' Connie said confidently.

'Don't fall in with those men,' Lisette said. 'They only care for themselves. It's not a game.'

Jack nodded, as sensible as ever, 'Mum and Dad always told us to keep away from those sort of people, Ned. They're not our friends; look what they did to Rob!'

'But all that cash!' Connie exclaimed. 'With Ned's dosh and mine, we could put ourselves up at the Ritz.'

Ned shook his head. 'No way. What've I always said to you, Con? I'm saving up, see, for a nice house that we can all live in. All four of us and Pippa, and no rotten nuns or any of that rubbish. And Rob would've been there and all! And I'll tell you, Miss Lisette, there's good money running for them wide boys. And right now, the money's better than ever!'

Elsie had heard all about Ned's plans. The two of them had drawn the house they'd live in when Rob was out carrying packages and messages back and forth for the men in nice suits. They sat side by side on their threadbare bedcovers by the light of a candle, scratching out their dream houses on wrinkled paper bags with the pencils Jack kept sharpened with his penknife.

They looked like the home that Elsie and Jack had shared with their mum and dad, a world away from the place where they'd found themselves. She didn't know where he kept his stash nor where Rob had hidden his, though she had a suspicion that stash was now part of Ned's.

'Little Ned,' Lisette rasped. 'Those men are gangsters. It's dangerous.'

Fire engines tore past, bells clanging, and almost shoved their car off the road. Everywhere was dangerous right now.

The coins brought home by Rob, Ned and Connie had meant that Christmas at the orphanage hadn't been as bleak as it could've been. It was just an ordinary day for the children, scrubbing the cold, tiled floors on their hands and knees, peeling potatoes and sprouts for the nuns' Christmas feast; a meal the children weren't allowed any part of. *'Do you think the Holy Family ate turkey in the stable on the first Christmas?'* Somehow that hadn't applied to the nuns. But with the money earned by their friends, there were treats and gifts. Nothing too much, nothing the nuns could find and take away. Nothing they could be punished for. Elsie had treasured her small wooden doll with the red smiling lips, made from a painted clothes peg. It was lost now, crushed beneath the ruins of the orphanage.

'All right, Princess,' Ned scowled. 'Maybe you can give us a job and an honest living and a nice soft bed? Yeah, I thought not.'

He shook his head, and gave an annoyed huff when Elsie elbowed him sharply in the ribs. Elsie didn't like that scowl, nor the way he had called Lisette *Princess*. Lisette hadn't behaved like a princess. She had dug away at the bricks just like Ned and Connie and Jack, and could've lost her life to save Elsie's. And even now they weren't safe. The air raid still screamed on. The car seemed tiny, like a toy in the city streets, thrown from one side of the road to the other as the bombs fell and shook the earth.

'Maybe you could try not acting like a brat for once, Ned!' Jack snapped. 'She's right. They're dangerous.'

'Yeah,' huffed Ned. 'And so are the bloody nuns. Least you know where you are with the crims. I'd rather deal with the Whitechapel gangs than the nuns any day of the week!'

In the front seat, Wyngate cleared his throat. He glanced in the rear-view mirror and Elsie met his gaze there. She saw that secret shared smile reflected in his eyes when he admitted, 'So would I.'

Lisette shook her head slowly. 'Maybe I *can* find you a bed, and keep you away from the gangsters.'

No one said a word as Wyngate piloted the car between two burning buildings, the flames rearing up like walls of fire. The air in the car was suddenly too warm, as if the flames had got inside.

'When we've got our house, maybe I'll buy a Rolls too,' Ned mused, as Wyngate took a corner on what felt like two wheels. 'You can be our driver if you like, Mr Wyngate. 'Cos I'm too short to reach the pedals just now and Jack's too well behaved to try until it's legal! Rob would've just about managed, but Rob ain't here no more.'

'You're very generous,' Wyngate replied. 'But how will you get the petrol coupons?'

Jack suddenly sat up straight, his eyes growing wide. 'That's where I saw you!' he exclaimed. 'You were at Rob's funeral this morning!'

Connie gasped. She hadn't gone; she'd stayed at the orphanage with Elsie because they both felt too sad. It had sounded like a wonderful send-off though; perhaps the stash had paid for it, because the nuns certainly hadn't.

'You was there at Rob's send-off?' Connie asked Wyngate. 'Was you his friend too?'

Elsie looked into the rear-view mirror but Wyngate's eyes were on the road as, with only inches to spare, he dodged the car past an enormous crater where a bomb had fallen. He'd known Rob. He'd said he was *Wyngate, Ministry*. What did that mean?

'I was paying my respects,' Wyngate replied as the looming hulk of the hospital appeared through the smoke. 'I saw you two lads there. Half of the East End too. That's what Mademoiselle Souchon meant when she said that the black market could be dangerous.'

'Leave it out!' Ned huffed, rolling his eyes theatrically. 'You tellin' me you got that suit on the up-and-up, mate? That ain't no bloody clothing coupon suit!'

Wyngate flicked his gaze to the mirror again. 'Someone's handing out money to East End runners. A *lot* of money,' he said. Ned shifted, setting his jaw and rolling his eyes again. 'And anybody who looks like they might be willing to talk about it has ended up face down in the Thames. The streets are changing; someone's moving in. Whoever it is sent Rob on the job that killed him.'

Ned shifted in his seat, no backchat for Mr Wyngate now. He and Rob had been good friends, Rob the general and Ned his lieutenant. But after Rob had died stealing petrol, Ned had appointed himself the man in charge. Or the nine-year-old in charge, anyway.

'There's good money in petrol,' he murmured eventually, as Wyngate pulled the Rolls-Royce up to the kerb.

The air crackled with the threat of the endless air raid; it wasn't safe here, not in the middle of the city. Wyngate could've walked off to a shelter and left them to get to St Bartholomew's Hospital alone. Instead, he had put his own safety aside and had driven straight into danger.

ELEVEN
ELSIE

Everyone piled out of the car, relieved to have made it to the hospital. The air smelt of smoke and was filled with the clanging of ambulance bells. Wyngate helped Lisette onto the pavement, and she rested her head on his shoulder, as if she could barely stand. Elsie watched, still wrapped in Wyngate's soft overcoat, and held Jack's hand tight. People were being helped out of the ambulances, some walking, others carried on stretchers, their heads lolling. There was shouting, crying. And blood was dotted along the path.

'Another one from Bank!' yelled a woman in a tin helmet. She was helping a man in a torn pinstriped suit down from an ambulance. Blood was running down the side of his face and his hands were shaking.

A nurse had appeared, her white cap knocked at an angle as if she hadn't had even a spare few seconds to right it. After a few, hurried words with Wyngate, she gestured over to a porter who came at a run. Lisette gazed at Wyngate for a moment, then turned to Elsie and her friends.

'Take care. Look after each other, please,' she said, and then the nurse and the porter spirited her away. To Elsie's surprise, though, Wyngate stayed with them, watchful and silent.

'We won't be seein' her in Whitechapel no more,' Connie said wisely, as they went towards the hospital entrance. 'They'll patch her up and she'll go back to her swanky club.'

Ned nodded. 'I reckon you're right, Con,' he murmured. Then he gave a cry of frustration. 'I should've found out what club she was singing at. I might've got some new customers for my nylons and what have yous! I've even got a nice bit of elastic squirrelled away!'

'I could've sung there, too!' Connie huffed in annoyance.

Jack knelt before Elsie and brushed her hair back behind her ear. He gave her a gentle smile and said, 'This is an adventure tonight, Elsie. We'll find somewhere safe to live, don't you worry. And I promise we'll find little Pippa; she's a survivor, that one.' He took Elsie's hand gently. 'We'll get by, you and me. We'll get by until Dad comes home.'

Elsie squeezed Jack's hand and nodded keenly. If only she could recall what had fallen out of her memory. It'd change everything.

Jack put his arms round her and hugged her tight as, at his shoulder, Ned and Connie appeared.

'What about him?' Ned whispered, jerking his head back to indicate Wyngate, who was scanning the bustling corridor with a hawk's gaze. 'He seems all right to me. He told me I could nick a car, so he must be!'

Jack shook his head. 'He told you we could requisition one,' he corrected patiently. 'He paid his respects to Rob and saved our Elsie and Lisette too.' He nodded firmly. 'He's decent.'

'He ain't run off yet,' Connie observed. 'Give him time, though. He's just lookin' for someone to palm us off to, I reckon.'

It didn't take long. A nurse with steel-grey hair spotted Wyngate, then glanced down at Elsie and her friends. Elsie shrank back from her.

'Are you with a patient?' the nurse asked Wyngate briskly.

'Here it comes,' whispered Ned. 'His chance to get shot of us.'

Elsie gripped the warm coat, not wanting to give it back. Because that would mean Wyngate would leave, and head off into the night without them.

'We're all together,' Wyngate replied, nodding to the children. *Together.* Elsie felt her heart leap. 'We're with Mademoiselle Souchon.' Then he added, 'The children need their hands looking at, they dug their friend out of a bombsite. I want someone to check Elsie over too; she was buried.'

'You're all walking, you'll have to wait,' the nurse said importantly.

Wyngate's eyes narrowed. Then he said in a voice that was more like a bark, 'These children have wounds that need to be cleaned and dressed, Nurse.' He looked down at his wristwatch. 'If that doesn't happen in the next ten minutes, I'll hold you personally responsible.' Then he flicked his gaze up to her. 'The clock is ticking.'

'Blimey,' whispered Ned, gawping up at Wyngate.

The nurse stared at him, before saying, 'Come this way.'

Mr Wyngate was an unusual sort of Pied Piper, followed by Elsie and her friends as the nurse led them down a corridor that reeked of disinfectant. People were lying on trolleys, or sitting on the floor. Then she turned a corner and led them into a ward, where she swished back a curtain, revealing a high bed behind it.

'Wait here,' she said. She gave Mr Wyngate a glance and he lifted his eyebrows. Perhaps that was what prompted her to add, 'Please.'

She sharply drew the curtain closed around them.

Connie climbed up onto the bed. 'This mattress is bloody hard!'

Elsie tried to climb up too, but it was so high. Then she felt a pair of strong hands round her waist. She glanced over her shoulder. It wasn't Jack helping her up, but Wyngate, and she smiled at him.

Soon, all four children were sitting in a row along the bed. A young doctor came in, with strawberry-blond hair and dark circles under his eyes. He checked them over, cleaned their hands and covered their cuts with bandages. He dabbed at the scar on Connie's face, but she brushed his hand away. It was too late for dressings and plasters.

He prodded and poked Elsie, asking her if this hurt or that. But aside from a few cuts and bruises she was all right, really. She'd been lucky that the door had landed on her, and she'd been lucky that Lisette had taken the impact when the wall had fallen onto them.

The doctor peered down Elsie's throat, as if he could see what was stopping her from speaking, but she knew he'd have to look further than that, right down into her heart.

Wyngate stepped forward and said, 'Elsie isn't ready to speak, Doctor.' Then he gave her a little nod, a nod that seemed to say he understood. 'Not yet.'

Jack took his sister's hand. 'She will one day,' he murmured.

'You've all been extremely fortunate,' the doctor finally said. He glanced at Wyngate as he carried on, 'You're really not safe here. You should be in the countryside.'

'We've been and come back, mate,' said Ned. 'And we ain't the only ones. There's a few kids like us, kids who'd rather be in London. The countryside ain't all milkmaids and rolling fields, you know!'

'You'd rather be blown to bits in an air raid?' the doctor replied. 'I don't want to have to patch you up again.' He looked at Wyngate, as if he was trying to work out if he was their father. 'You need to make sure these children are safe.'

And yet Wyngate had, he'd looked after them. He'd rescued them from the bombsite and brought them to the hospital.

'Thank you for seeing us,' Wyngate replied curtly. 'We'll wait for news on Mademoiselle Souchon.'

The doctor showed them out of the ward and pointed towards a waiting room down another corridor. It was empty apart from an old man asleep in a corner, his gnarled hands resting on his stick. The walls were covered with posters. *Take your gas mask everywhere*, one of them insisted, but Elsie hadn't a clue where hers had gone. Another said, *If you are bombed out and have no friends to go to, ask a policeman or a warden for your nearest rest centre.*

They could certainly do with that, but then they'd be bundled onto a train for the countryside.

Connie yawned and picked at the bandages on her hand, but Elsie was wide awake, and held tight to Jack's hand.

'Bet you could sell a few nylons to the nurses,' Connie said to Ned, with a defiant wink for Wyngate.

'I ain't got them with me, like a 'nana,' Ned tutted. He took off his army cap and ruffled his curly hair, then stretched his arms above his head and yawned. 'Maybe I'll grab a few winks. Work out a plan while I'm having a kip.' With that, Ned scrambled beneath the chairs and curled up on the hard floor. 'Sweet dreams, soldiers.'

'Try and sleep,' Jack whispered, arranging the coat over Elsie like a blanket. 'In the morning, we'll find the rest of the kids from the orphanage and get ourselves sorted out. You too, Connie, try and get some rest while you can.' With a smile for Connie, he looked at Wyngate. He was leaning with one shoulder on the wall, reading the government notices about gas masks and careless talk. 'Thanks, Mr Wyngate.'

Wyngate tipped his hat back a little and nodded. 'Don't mention it,' he replied. 'Get some sleep, all of you. If you wake up and I'm not here, I'll just be looking in on Mademoiselle Souchon.' He straightened his hat again, the shadow falling over his face once more. 'I won't leave you here.'

Before long, everyone was asleep.

Except Elsie. And Wyngate.

He took a seat on the end of the row, beside Elsie, and glanced down at her. She couldn't speak to him, but she wished she could. She shaped her lips so that she could say, *Thank you, Mr Wyngate.* No sound came out, so she affectionately patted his arm instead.

Wyngate smiled, then reached up and plucked down one of the posters from the noticeboard. He put his elegant hand into the jacket that had covered Lisette and took out a pencil. Then he rested the poster on his knee and wrote in neat handwriting on the back of the sheet, *Better not talk and wake them up. Not tired yet?*

He held out the pencil to Elsie. She took it and painstakingly wrote, *No, carn't sleep. Don't know why.*

Wyngate took back the pencil and wrote, *Same here. I don't say much either.*

Elsie stared at him, before writing, *Why not? I stopped after Mum died. I cried so much that I carn't.*

And his written reply astonished her. *My mum died when I was a boy. I was alone. I didn't have much to say for a long, long time. All I did was cry.* Elsie couldn't imagine him as a little boy, lost without his mum. Surely he was too strong to ever have been like that. Wyngate tapped the pencil against his chin, then added, *I'm sorry you lost your mum.*

Elsie wrote, *We didn't know. We come back from the farm and the house had gone. And Dad is missing in his plane. So we had to live with them nuns. I'm sorry your mum died too, Mr Winget.*

Wyngate smiled softly as he wrote, *I'm no fan of nuns either.* And he drew a little face, grimacing as though it had been sucking on a lemon, which made Elsie smile. Then he wrote, *Keep this safe. You can all call on me any time you need me*, before he moved the pencil down to the corner of the poster and wrote down an address in Spitalfields, followed by a telephone number.

She took it from him carefully, knowing, somehow, that this was an honour. He didn't seem the sort of man to give up his privacy easily. She reached out for the pencil.

Thank you, Mr Winget. We'll come and find you. Hope you won't get fed up of us! Haha.

Wyngate pulled a deliberately serious face that made Elsie chuckle, and shook his head from side to side. Then he took back the pencil and wrote, *Friends are for ever*.

Elsie smiled at him. She felt safe beside Mr Wyngate, the man who could bring people back from the dead. She leaned her head against his arm, and comfort washed over her; in moments, Elsie was asleep.

TWELVE
LISETTE

Everything was white. So white. The walls were white and so were the lights on the ceiling.

Where on earth was she?

Lisette's vision cleared as she blinked and finally, as a nurse went by pushing a squeaky trolley, and she smelt the sharp scent of antiseptic, she realised where she was. She'd been given a sleeping pill and her mind was still foggy, but bit by bit images and impressions, sounds and scents, came through.

The fire and smoke. Debris and rubble. The little girl. The wall. Mr Wyngate breathing life back into her. And now she was in bed, and her belongings were on the table beside it, the box containing her gas mask sitting on top.

'Welcome back.'

That was his voice. Lisette slowly turned her head. He was wearing his hat and his dark suit. Against the whiteness of the room, he seemed like a slash of night-time.

'You saved me,' she whispered hoarsely. It was only now she realised how thirsty she was, how dry and painful her throat felt. He crossed from the window towards the bed, moving with an elegant speed that was more like a prowl. Then he reached for the glass of water there and held it out to Lisette.

'Drink slowly,' her rescuer instructed. 'You'll choke otherwise.'

Lisette took the glass, her hand shaking. There was something she needed to ask him. She didn't want to take her eyes off him, in case he disappeared.

She lowered the glass. 'The children. Where are they? Are they safe?'

Wyngate nodded, sitting on the very edge of the chair as though he might need to spring to his feet again.

'They're fine.' He cocked his head to one side, regarding Lisette. 'You could've been killed.'

'And so could the children,' Lisette said. 'I had to go with them. I didn't want to leave the shelter, but I couldn't let them go out into the raid alone.'

'Children are resilient. More so than most adults.'

Lisette gave a shrug. 'I made my choice. And I am here. But you were out in the raid, too. And you stopped to rescue us.'

Perhaps it was Lisette's imagination, but he seemed to give the barest hint of a smile. Just a ghost of one at the thought of being remembered.

'You saved that little girl's life, you know.'

Lisette tried to smile in return, but the sudden realisation of what she had done – that she had gone out into the raid, despite her rushing heartbeat and her clammy hands, and had saved a life – overwhelmed her. She hadn't saved Tom, whose life had meant more to her than her own.

'I wish... I wish I could save them all,' she said, trying to swallow her tears.

'You were brave tonight.' Wyngate reached into his pocket and took out a pristine white handkerchief, neatly folded.

Lisette took the handkerchief, wishing he couldn't see her

tears. She dabbed her eyes, and as she looked up at him again she knew she'd seen him before the ruins.

Candlelight flickering against his face. He was holding a glass. He was surrounded by shadows.

He'd been to Jasper's club.

'You were brave, too,' she said, taking in the details of his face as the memory of him in the club became more and more solid. The dark eyes, the prominent nose, the square jaw. 'The debris could have fallen on you. But you rescued me. And the little girl.'

He shrugged one shoulder. 'How do you feel?'

How little he seemed to rate his own bravery.

'I feel sore.' She shook her head. 'I thought I was going to die...' She chuckled as she looked up at him, but it made her cough, and she held his handkerchief to her mouth.

And Wyngate did smile at that, shaking his head as he said, 'Not this time.' Then he asked, 'Would you like a nip of something?'

'Yes, please,' Lisette replied. 'If the nurses don't mind?'

'It isn't up to the nurses,' he deadpanned. He reached into the well-cut jacket again and withdrew a silver hipflask. As he unscrewed the cap, he kept his gaze on Lisette; it was a gaze that seemed to be full of secrets. 'You'll be back on stage before you know it.'

'You go to Jasper's,' she whispered. 'I knew your face.'

Wyngate held the flask out to her. 'I've been once or twice.'

But it was more than that; he was practically a regular. 'I like that I was saved by someone who knows me.'

As well as someone could know her when they'd only seen her on stage.

'I don't share the good Scotch with just anybody, you know.'

She smiled at him, and closed her shaking hand round the flask, but she couldn't quite lift it. 'I'll spill it, I can't take it. I'm sorry.' She couldn't waste his hard-to-come-by Scotch.

Wyngate rose to his feet and said, 'Lift your head a little bit; I'll help you drink.' He glanced over his shoulder towards the door. 'No nurses to see.'

Lisette smiled at his joke, then lifted her head. Her neck felt sore, but the prospect of a sip of Scotch was too good to refuse.

'I hope they don't. I don't want you to get into trouble,' she replied. Wyngate placed his other hand gently beneath her hair, cradling her head, as he brought the hipflask to her lips.

'They wouldn't dare.'

For a man who exuded so much strength, his touch was surprisingly gentle. Lisette felt safe, protected. The warming liquid burned a trail down her throat.

'Thank you,' she whispered, but she didn't want him to let her go. It'd been so long since she'd been so close to anyone.

'Thank you,' Wyngate replied. 'For the songs.'

Lisette smiled at him. It didn't matter that she felt sore, and tired and confused. Hearing that, from the man who had saved her, meant everything.

'I'll sing for you again soon, Mr Wyngate,' she promised him. 'What's your first name? You haven't told me.'

'It's just Mr Wyngate,' he said with that one-shouldered shrug. 'Hello.'

That was strange. Perhaps it went with working in the Ministry. Did he work in intelligence?

'You might just go by your surname, but I hardly ever use mine,' she explained. 'Maman always said singers never do.'

'She never met Vera Lynn, then?'

Lisette shook her head. 'No, she never has.' She bit her lip and looked away. 'No, you see, she's in France.'

He'd know what that meant. They were trapped. There were no letters, no postcards, no telephone calls; only silence.

Wyngate nodded. 'Then you'll have a lot to tell her when this is over.' He withdrew his hand from Lisette's hair and screwed the cap back onto the hipflask. 'You need to rest now.'

'Will I see her again?' Lisette laid her head back against the pillows. Without his closeness, she felt tired.

'I'm sure of it,' he said. 'And I'll see you again too, singing at the club. You did well tonight, Lisette; you've earned some rest.'

'And you too, Mr Wyngate,' she whispered. 'When I'm next at the club, I'll sing just for you.'

'Throw in a couple of French songs,' Wyngate requested. 'Just between us.'

'Of course,' Lisette whispered. 'Goodbye, Monsieur Wyngate...' She closed her eyes and started to drift off to sleep again, and she was only then aware that, the whole time, they had been speaking in French.

Just who *was* this man?

THIRTEEN
ELSIE

'You are wicked, wicked children to run away!' a voice spat. 'Wake up, you indolent brats!'

Elsie winced, rubbing her eyes. She felt so stiff after sleeping on the chair, but Mr Wyngate's coat had kept her warm. She looked up to see the dark shape of Sister Benedict looming over them in her black habit. A shudder went through her.

And Mr Wyngate wasn't there.

'Thank heavens for the kind gentleman who told me you were here,' said Sister Benedict. 'The Mother Abbess' – and here she rested her hand against her breast and cast her eyes to heaven – 'The Mother Abbess has ended her earthly journey and gone to God's right hand tonight. The doctors were unable to save her.'

Elsie couldn't imagine anything killing the Mother Abbess; she was a towering figure, a fierce, angry ogre. Her cane was used for every wrong, no matter how small, from an orphan waking screaming from a nightmare to a broken piece of crockery or a speck of dust somewhere in the nuns' quarters. All the orphans did was keep the nuns' quarters pristine or run their errands, making their food and fetching and carrying for them. The nuns didn't suffer under rationing either, because what they didn't have they took from the rations of the orphans. Elsie couldn't remember a time since she left home when she hadn't been hungry, and when she found the little stray dog and started feeding her, too, she was hungrier than ever.

Sister Benedict crossed herself as, from his hideaway beneath the chairs, Elsie heard Ned comment, 'Bet she's knocking on a hot door right now.' Then he chuckled and added, 'The devil's got his work cut out.'

Connie snorted with laughter, and Elsie's shoulders shook with silent mirth. The Mother Abbess was dead. And Ned was right, she would've gone straight to hell. On the first day they'd arrived she'd cut off Connie's plaits and thrown them in the fire, and snatched Elsie's ragdoll away from her. She'd made them kneel on the cold, stone floor of the chapel for three hours, saying their rosary to make them repent for the sin of saying they were hungry.

Sister Benedict raised her hand to slap Elsie, as she'd slapped her so many times before. She had learned early on not to do so when Jack was there, or he'd put himself between them and take the beating for her, but this time she had no care for his presence. Elsie flinched away, but the slap didn't land, because her brother had bolted from his chair and seized the woman's thin wrist in his own.

'Don't you ever touch her again!'

Elsie had never heard her brother shout like that. His face was just inches from Sister Benedict's. The nun, who had taken such delight in her sly pinches and fierce beatings, shrank back from him as though a thunderclap had sounded in her face.

'You're to come with me,' she said, but she didn't sound nearly so sure now. 'All of you are to come with me. The sisters and I will round up you runaways and we will find a new place of shelter.'

Elsie froze. They'd had a taste of freedom tonight, riding in the Rolls-Royce with Mr Wyngate and the kind lady. People who actually cared about them, not like the nuns, who seemed to hate them just for existing.

Jack was shaking his head. Elsie had never seen her brother so angry before.

'No,' he said. 'No. We don't need the likes of you, you nasty old cow. And if you hit any one of us or any of our friends again, we'll hit you harder than you ever did us!'

'The devil has you in his grip. We will thrash him out of y—'

But she didn't get any further, because Ned had seized her ankle, and she pitched backwards with a cry of alarm. As the nun reeled away, Jack released her wrist at last and, without him holding her up, she sprawled onto the floor.

'Let's get out of here!' Ned shouted. 'That bloody Wyngate sod gave us up after all! You can't trust nobody!'

'Told you, told you he'd leave us!' Connie yelled, already on her feet and bolting for the door.

Elsie was up and running too, gripping Mr Wyngate's overcoat, which he'd left behind him. The polished wooden floor was slippery, but she didn't lose her footing.

As the four of them hurtled along the corridor, she thought back to Mr Wyngate. He'd promised them he wasn't going to leave them, and he'd given her his address. He'd said he would check on Lisette. Maybe that was where he was, at that very moment. Surely he wasn't the man who'd told Sister Benedict where they were? Could they risk going to his address only to be betrayed again, and if not, where would they go?

FOURTEEN
ELSIE

June 1940

There wasn't anywhere in the village for Elsie and Jack to go, other than the farm. All the cottages they passed as they rode by in the trap were stuffed to the rafters with evacuees, Farmer Cook had said.

He didn't resemble the jolly farmers that Elsie had seen in books. He was a heavyset man, and he looked cross. Mum would've said that he smelt like a brewery.

'Sit still when you're on the trap, I don't want you falling off and cracking your head open,' he complained, even though Elsie and Jack were frozen in their seats. 'Children are seen and not heard, so there won't be any gabble from either of you. And I won't have any thieving – I know what you cockneys are like. Where's your ration books? You did bring them, didn't you?'

Elsie held tight to Jack's hand and didn't say a word.

'We did, sir,' said Jack politely. Mum and Dad would be so proud of him; he had shepherded them from the chaos of the station until he discovered where they were bound for and, all along the way, he'd kept hold of Elsie's hand. He'd read her stories and entertained her with a puppet show by her ragdoll, Ginger, spinning stories of the countryside that awaited them. But this didn't seem to be anything like the stories.

Farmer Cook nodded, and didn't say anything else to them for the rest of the journey. The village was very pretty with its stone cottages and thatched roofs, and there were flowers in the front gardens. The church was big and very old, with a clock on the tower, telling the wrong time. There were shops on the high street, and Elsie hoped she could buy a postcard to send back to Mum and tell her what Buckinghamshire was like. But the trap kept going, travelling along the country lanes. They got narrower and narrower, until thorny branches from the hedges brushed past their faces.

And finally they were at their new home.

Even though it was warm and sunny, the farmyard was so muddy it looked like a marsh. The farmhouse was made from grey stone, and the windows were small, peeping out like suspicious eyes. Elsie tried to hold on to the pictures from the books she'd read, of farmyards bustling with friendly animals and a farmhouse with bright gingham curtains in the window. But the images were fading fast.

Then a door opened in a wooden barn with a sagging roof, and two children appeared, each carrying buckets. The little boy had golden curls like a cherub, and the girl, who was a few years older, wore her hair in plaits. Their clothes were muddy and drab, their knees were scuffed, but as they looked up at the trap their faces were transformed with smiles.

'Maybe it won't be too bad,' Elsie whispered hopefully to Jack as they climbed down from the trap, the ragdoll clutched tightly in her hand.

'Don't clutter the door!' came a thunderous bellow, and from the barn followed a woman who looked like a twin of the farmer. Yet the thought that they might be brother and sister just like Elsie and Jack was shattered when the woman opened her mouth again, displaying a row of blackened teeth. They sat in her sallow face like tombstones. 'Husband, are these the second lot of brats?' She didn't wait for an acknowledgement, instead wiping her chapped hands down her filthy apron. 'Connie, Ned, show them where they'll sleep and get them working.' Then she stabbed her finger towards Jack and Elsie. 'I'm not having pampered city kids here. You work for your keep.' She held out her palm. 'Ration books.'

Jack stepped forward, putting himself between the woman and Elsie. 'My name's Jack and this is Elsie—' he began.

'I've no care who you are!' She cut him off snappily. 'Ration books, now, or it'll be the strap for you, little Lord La-Di-Da!'

The little boy who had come out of the barn looked at Elsie from behind the farmer's hulking wife. He gave her a smile and a thumbs-up, as though to promise that everything would be all right. As he did, another boy strolled round the edge of the barn; he only looked a little bit older than Elsie, but he was tall and rangy. He carried a bucket in each hand, his skinny arms stretched by his sides with the weight of his burden, and he gave Elsie a bright grin.

'Who's this?' asked the new arrival cheerfully. 'New evacuees?'

'Button your gob, Rob,' snarled Mrs Cook. Rob gave Elsie a wink that said, *adults, eh?* 'Book, now.'

'Here are our books, Mrs Cook,' said Jack, handing over the ration books. She looked down at them through narrow eyes, then nodded and stuffed them into her pocket. Mrs Cook didn't look as though she wanted for rations.

'Right,' said the farmer's wife. 'Get to work.' Then she turned and strode towards the house with a shout of, 'Husband, don't tarry!'

Farmer Cook glared at Elsie and Jack, and spat at the mud, before leading the horse and trap away. Elsie folded in on herself, hugging her ragdoll and sniffing back tears. She wanted to go home, to be with Mum and Dad.

Connie watched him go, then, once he and his wife were out of sight, she put down her buckets and ran across the yard towards Elsie and Jack. She had brown hair in long plaits and freckles on her nose, and a big smile. Elsie's tears retreated.

'I'm Connie, and this is Ned!' She beamed as she gestured to the little boy. 'And that's Rob. Nice to meet you.' Then she lowered her voice, her smile fading. 'Look, them two are a right pair of Tartars. But if you get your head down and do your work, it's not so bad. At least there ain't no Germans droppin' bombs on you out here!'

Elsie would have gladly swapped all the bombs that Hitler could send them for this horrible place. But what choice did they have? And maybe it'd be all right with Ned and his curls, Connie and her freckles, Rob and his cow's-lick fringe.

'And me and Ned'll look after you all,' said Rob. 'We've looked out for each other since we can remember, ain't we?'

'We have, back from our Whitechapel days. Rob's the boss and I'm the second in command,' said Ned. Elsie was surprised at his voice; he looked so cherubic, but he sounded like the lads she heard at the market with Mum, running errands for the stallholders. 'And I tell you this, Whitechapel wipes the floor with the countryside! There ain't nothing to do round here; no mischief, and the farmer's a right old bastard.'

Jack frowned and said, 'You're too young to swear.' Then he held out his hand to little Ned, who took it and shook as Jack's frown turned into a smile. 'I'm Jack and this is Elsie, my sister.'

'It's a pleasure to meet you, Jack and Elsie.' Rob put down the buckets and gave a low bow, like Robin Hood did at the pictures. He had a bright smile, a friendly smile. 'Ned and me decided to be brothers back in our orphanage when we were on the same ward. We've got a gang going on here, since the Blitz. Me and Ned and Connie!'

'Bloody right!' Ned grinned. 'Me and Rob got here and met Connie, so now she's our sister. Me and Rob ain't never had nobody but each other, but Connie's got a nan back home in London. We look out for each other.'

'And you're welcome here, Elsie and Jack.' Rob held out his hand to Elsie. 'And now, we'll look out for you and all.'

His hand was dirty from work on the farm, but that didn't stop her from taking it.

'We'll be friends, won't we?' Elsie said, smiling at the others. She liked the idea of being in a gang of kids. Trying to be as hopeful as she could, she added, 'And we'll have a lovely time! The kids who escaped the Blitz.' Then a thought occurred to her. 'We're the Blitz Kids!'

FIFTEEN
LISETTE

January 1941

Maman's embrace was so warm and loving. Lisette didn't want to leave her arms. But someone was shouting, and suddenly Lisette was awake.

She was still in the hospital bed, and everything hurt. As she blinked against the bright light, she realised that Wyngate was in the chair beside her, and that a doctor was standing at the foot of her bed, with a nun. Her wrinkled, oval face peered out sadly from the white surround of her coif and her veil.

'I've seen some strange things in this hospital,' the young, ginger-haired doctor said angrily. 'But this is madness. You helped a group of orphans run away, they assaulted this nun, and now they've disappeared!'

Lisette got the impression that Wyngate may have drifted off to sleep in the chair, but he rocketed to his feet at the sight of the new arrivals, his gaze fixed on the face of the elderly nun, who had begun to cry quiet tears.

'Those poor, poor children,' she sobbed, accepting a handkerchief from the doctor. 'All alone in this cruel city. The orphanage may have been hit by a Nazi bomb, but we will start again.'

There was Connie's scar, and how painfully thin the children looked. The nuns hadn't kept them safe, guiding them to a shelter, but had abandoned them when the sirens sounded. She could feel Wyngate's anger as he stood beside her, glaring at the woman.

Lisette pushed herself up against the pillows, shoving aside the grogginess of the sleeping pill. 'They *are* poor children,' she said, despite her painful throat. 'Hungry and uncared for!'

'Our Mother Abbess was brought here after the bomb fell; alas, she has gone to greener pastures,' sobbed the nun, her clawed hand squeezing the handkerchief. 'But as I grieved, this kind doctor told me of the children who had found their way here with you both. They are *our* orphans. God's children from our home for those lambs who have been lost.' She gave a smile and said to Lisette and Wyngate, 'Might you know where they have run away to? They were so afraid of the bombs, you see.'

Wyngate drew in a breath, then said calmly, 'You're a liar, Sister Benedict. I know your ways.'

There was something so cold in Wyngate's voice. He loathed the nun. And somehow, he knew her name.

'How dare you address a nun like that,' the doctor chided. 'An elderly, grieving woman.'

'You're cruel to helpless children,' Lisette said to Sister Benedict. It hurt to speak, but she couldn't hold back. 'Why didn't you take them to a shelter? You don't even feed them! They're so thin!'

The nun shook her head. 'We think only of them.'

'You think of your stomachs and your gin bottles,' Wyngate spat, taking a step towards the nun. 'And now you're sobbing because you've lost your slaves and their ration books. If anything happens to those children, you and your *sisters* will have their blood on your hands. Get out of this room.'

'Doctor,' Sister Benedict simpered, blinking at the physician. 'Will you allow this?'

The doctor shook his head. 'You'll have to leave, sir. And if you won't, I'll fetch the police.'

'I'm going to find those children. You won't get your hands on them again.' He strode towards the door, and paused as he reached it, 'And if you're right about what's waiting on the other side, I don't envy your Mother Abbess.' Then Wyngate looked towards Lisette and said in a tone that was almost gentle, 'I look forward to hearing those songs, mademoiselle. Good evening.'

'I'm sorry, Sister Benedict, I've done what I can,' the doctor said, wringing his hands. 'I'm sure you understand how busy we are tonight. We're overflowing with patients thanks to that direct hit on Bank Underground station.'

'That man saved my life,' Lisette told them as they headed for the door. 'Mr Wyngate will find those poor children. But they won't be going back to the nuns.'

SIXTEEN
ELSIE

Elsie had put on Mr Wyngate's coat, but it was too big for her and trailed along the floor as they ran through the hospital's endless corridors. He couldn't have betrayed or abandoned them, she refused to believe it. But when she tried to tell the others, no sound came out.

Each bandaged, dazed and bloodied person they passed made Elsie feel lucky that she had survived. Somewhere in this huge building was the kind lady who had saved her life. She wouldn't die, would she?

No one seemed to notice four children running through the hospital among the chaos. They made it to the front door without anyone stopping them. Not even Sister Benedict, who had sprawled on her back like a beetle when Ned and Jack had sent her flying.

'Bloody scab!' Ned spat angrily as they flung open the door and bolted out into the cold night. The air was still heavy with smoke, but dawn was brightening the horizon. Unless it was another fire, burning in the distance. 'Bloody arsehole, all done up in his black-market suit, telling that old bitch where to find us!'

'Watch your mouth, Ned,' Jack warned, pausing to catch his breath. Elsie gazed up at her big brother, sure that he would know what to do. 'Right. First thing, we stick together, agreed?'

Elsie nodded, while Connie replied with a strident, 'Yes! All four of us, together.' Then she lowered her voice: 'And if anyone says anything, the four of us are brothers and sisters. We're a family.'

'Blitz Kids!' Ned exclaimed, punching his fist into the air. 'We don't need nobody. *Nobody*. No social, no coppers, no bleedin' scabs neither!'

Connie cheered. 'We look after ourselves.'

Jack looked to Connie and asked, 'What do you think, Connie? If we hand ourselves in, d'you reckon they'll send us away again?'

She nodded. 'I bet they will. There's whole orphanages that they evacuated to the countryside, all the kids shoved together in one house. That's where they'd send us, and there'd be more bloody nuns. And who's to say they wouldn't make us work on another stinking farm?' She pouted, her eyes clouding with sadness. 'We'd have no say in where we go. And they'd split us up, too.'

Elsie shook her head. The prospect of being split up from Connie and Ned, her new family, was too horrible to even think about.

'And there's loads of places standin' empty,' said Ned with certainty. 'Nobody's going to notice if we move into one. Besides, once I've been back to Whitechapel and dug out my stash, we'll be in clover. We won't want for nothin'. And I got all my work with the wide boys, wheelin' and dealin'!'

Jack frowned. 'No, Ned, no more of that. I'll get a job.' His expression brightened and he gave Elsie a smile that looked like Dad's. 'How hard can it be to get a job in London, eh?'

As the hospital doors opened, Jack put his hand gently on Elsie's shoulder and shepherded her away from the building,

Mr Wyngate's coat trailing behind her like a wedding train. Connie and Ned followed, Ned muttering about betrayal.

The pavement was blotchy with white, and Elsie realised that it must've started to snow while they'd been in the hospital. The flakes were thin and light, tickling against her face.

'And when Dad comes home, he'll adopt you and Connie too, Ned,' Jack went on. 'We'll be a real family. But we need a place to shelter. Any ideas?'

Ned took off his cap and scratched his curly mop of hair. After a moment he said, 'When Sister Benny battered me that time for dropping them eggs, I slept the whole night in a bomb-site and it was nicer than the orphan ward. We'll find a place.' He rubbed his hands together and looked up into the softly falling snow. 'First thing, we go to Whitechapel and dig up my stash, all right? It's out under the bog block. Nuns never went out to that stinkin' hole!'

'Maybe we'll find a little house,' said Jack hopefully, taking Elsie's hand in his.

Elsie nodded again. There was Mr Wyngate's home, too, but the others didn't know about that. They didn't know that his address was in the pocket of his coat that Elsie now wore. She couldn't tell them that he was all right, really, that they'd had a conversation thanks to a pencil and the back of a government information poster. They'd take the address away and rip it up, because they didn't trust him.

'I say we do it,' Connie replied, wiping the gathering snowflakes from her sleeves. 'Our own little place, our own rules. No nuns about to spank us. We better find somewhere soon, though. I don't fancy turning into an icicle.'

'You pair was from Bethnal Green, weren't you?' Ned asked. At the name of the place where they had once been so happy, Elsie felt her eyes start to prickle. There was nothing where their little home had been now, just an empty hole in the ground, scattered with brick dust and broken glass. 'Why don't we go there? It's a bit nicer than Whitechapel.'

But Jack shook his head. 'No,' he said. He had grown tall since he turned fourteen, his limbs lanky like shoelaces, and he stooped to gather Elsie into his arms and hug her. 'I wouldn't do that to Elsie. Besides, people know us there and they might tell the authorities where we are. We don't want anyone reporting us.'

'Fair enough.' Ned nodded as he realised. 'And Pippa needs to know where to find Elsie, 'cos I know for sure she's coming back.'

Jack kissed his sister's cheek. 'She is,' he whispered. 'She is, Elsie. And she'll meet Dad when he gets home too.'

Elsie dragged the sleeve of Mr Wyngate's coat across her face, wiping away her tears and swallowing the new ones down.

'I know everybody who's got stuff worth buying. And we'll have good money.' Ned reached up and patted Elsie's elbow, then shone his smile on Connie. 'I'll look after you girls.'

'That's very nice of you, Ned, but I earn money from singin',' Connie said. 'And you just watch out what jobs you go on. We don't want to lose you, like Rob.'

Ned shook his head. 'No chance of that,' he assured her. 'Rob got a dose of bad luck is all. That don't happen twice.'

'All the same,' Jack told him, 'we're not criminals. We're going to live honestly.'

'And how're you getting a ration book, eh?' asked Ned. 'You put in for one of them and they'll have the lot of us shoved into another orphanage or packed off to one of them bastards in the countryside. We need ration books and I can lay hands on them. But first—'

Jack cut in. 'You've got to get your stash.' He nodded. 'Right. We'll go back to the orphanage. But carefully, we don't want anyone to grab us.'

'And then it'll be all the ration books you want!' Ned laughed.

Elsie's eyes were wide. Was that allowed? No one was supposed to take more than their fair share, and if you could buy yourself a new ration book, no questions asked, that didn't seem right. But the nuns had taken their ration books, and they were now somewhere beneath tons of rubble.

'I'm starvin'.' Connie held her hand against her flat stomach. None of them had eaten anything since their tea last night, which had consisted of grey bread and watery soup. 'We have to eat. I vote that Ned gets us them ration books, and I'll cook us something in our new home.'

Jack looked at Elsie, holding her gaze. 'Are you hungry, Elsie?' he asked gently.

Elsie looked up into her brother's kind eyes and nodded. She'd saved most of her bread to give to Pippa. It didn't seem like much of a feast for the little dog, and she wished she could've saved more.

'All right,' he said. 'But one each, Ned, no more; just what we're entitled to. And we'll need clean clothes. Can you help us from your stash? I'll get a job and I'll see you right, I promise.'

'You don't need to see me right, squire.' Ned beamed. 'I'll sort us a few bits and I'll get us a ration book each and a gas mask, too, since they've been flattened along with the Abbess. I know the shops to register with an' all, shops where nobody's asking no questions. But first things, we need a place to lay our heads!'

Elsie could've lived quite happily without a smelly, uncomfortable gas mask. But the posters said you needed to carry one everywhere, and four children wandering London without them would stick out.

Her gaze roamed around the streets that opened up from St Bartholomew's. Somewhere in this city, that had been so pummelled with bombs and where fires still burned, there was a place for the Blitz Kids to live.

SEVENTEEN
ELSIE

September 1940

It didn't seem to matter how hard they worked, or how good they were, Farmer Cook and his wife would always find something to complain about. Elsie was constantly hungry, but she didn't understand why, as she collected plenty of eggs from the chickens, and the Cooks had their ration books, too.

News was coming from London about the bombs, and Elsie cried because she was scared about Mum. Maybe she could come to the farm and live with them too?

When letters arrived from Mum, Jack read them to Elsie and they wrote back to her to tell her all about their happy life on the farm. None of it was true, but Jack and Elsie couldn't tell her about the cold or the hard work, the mattress on the floor of a bare room where wind whistled through the windows.

Elsie missed her school but every night after the long day's work was done, by the light of a candle, Jack and Connie held lessons for Rob, Ned and Elsie. The two young boys could read, an essential qualification for working as a messenger, they assured Jack, but their writing and arithmetic was a long way behind Elsie's. Jack stayed patient with them all though, helping them along with a gentleness that he had learned at his parents' knees. Elsie's big brother wasn't even fifteen, but he was keeping his promise to Dad. He was looking after his sister.

If they tried to write everything that happened on the farm in a letter to Mum, Farmer Cook and his wife might see and they'd find some new way to punish them. Elsie had tripped and spilled some feed, so she'd had to go without dinner. But Jack, as he often did, had kept back some of his meagre food and shared it with her at bedtime. Another time, Farmer Cook had raised his hand to hit her, but it was Jack who had come between them and taken the blow.

Connie had been hit by Mrs Cook for singing while hanging out the washing. And Jack, Rob and Ned seemed to come in for the worst of it; Farmer Cook often swung his belt at them for no reason.

Elsie and Jack had been sent to bed with no supper because they'd cried, the day that Mum's awful letter had arrived. The one that said Dad was missing. They had lain in the darkness of the bedroom, holding hands and telling each other that they had to keep cheerful for Mum, and that Dad would be found. He had to be.

In the letters that the Cooks insisted on checking before they went into the post, they told Mum about Connie, Rob and Ned. When the candle was extinguished or as they worked in the fields until night fell, Rob and Ned entertained them all with tales of their life and escapades in London. Elsie couldn't imagine a life without a mum or dad to care for her, but the two boys from Whitechapel had never known either of their parents. All they had known was the fearsome nuns of the orphanage from which they had come to the countryside, and their stories were of London streets that sounded like a different world from Bethnal Green. Not for them the neat gardens and white net curtains; instead, they mingled with the sort of characters who Elsie couldn't imagine existing outside of the pictures. There were gangsters and criminals and women who wore fox fur and always had a different soldier on their arm, and the boys longed to get back to the world where they had seen so much life.

One morning, after the children had milked the cows, they were called into the kitchen by Mrs Cook for breakfast. It was a cheerless room with a stove that didn't even have a friendly cat curled up in front of it. A pan of watery porridge sat on top of it, and Elsie knew it'd be cold and lumpy, as always.

'Someone's written to you,' Mrs Cook told Connie, but she didn't hand the letter over. She never did. Instead, she slit the envelope open with her yellowing thumbnail and took out the paper within. 'Oh, bloody hell,' she breathed with annoyance as her eyes moved back and forth. 'Don't tell me I'm bloody stuck with you. Your nan weren't worth much, was she? If she weren't, soon as the war's done, you're out.'

And with that, she threw the letter on the table in front of Connie.

The smile Connie had worn on seeing that a letter had come for her had vanished at Mrs Cook's words. She picked up the letter and started to read, but then her face puckered and she started to sob. Elsie wanted to get down from the table to give her a hug, but she knew she'd be told off.

'It's me nan,' Connie wept. She said something else through her tears, but Elsie couldn't make it out. Then she said it again and this time Elsie heard her. 'She's dead!'

Connie had been so kind when the letter had come about Dad that Elsie had to be kind in return now. She didn't care that she'd get in trouble. She got down from her chair, went over to Connie and hugged her tight. Her nan was dead, the only person Connie had had left in all the world.

'I'm so sorry,' Elsie whispered against Connie's hair as she cried hard, racking sobs that shook her thin body.

'Back to work!' said Mrs Cook, but the children ignored her. Instead they gathered around, hugging their friend tight. Jack picked up the letter in his pale hand and read it. As he did, Elsie saw the soil under his ragged fingernails, the same fingers that had once held his pen as he wrote in his exercise book, the same hands that had held toy trains as he played with his friends or gripped the handlebars of his bicycle before he went off with Dad to fish or fetch sweets for Elsie. 'Come on!' Mrs Cook insisted. 'It's a war; folks get killed. Best way to get over it is hard work.'

Rob scowled up at her and said, 'Where'd you leave your heart, missus?'

'Connie's lost her only family,' Jack said carefully. He put the letter back into its envelope and slipped it safely into his pocket, away from Mrs Cook's grasp. Then he swallowed and asked the farmer's wife, 'Why can't you show some kindness?'

Mrs Cook glared at him. 'You what?' she asked. 'Am I to call for my husband? Am I to fetch the strap?'

'Oh, give it a bloody rest, can't you?' Ned spat, furious. Then he stroked his small hand over Connie's hair. 'I'm sorry, Con. But we'll look out for you.'

'We'll be your family,' Elsie told her in a small voice. 'Me and Jack and Ned and Rob.'

Connie cried harder, and the other children clung to her even more tightly. There was so much pain in her weeping, a world of sadness and devastation that Elsie couldn't imagine. There was nothing they could do to take the pain away from her, but being forced to work surely wasn't going to help.

'We'll do Connie's jobs around the farm today, Mrs Cook, the four of us,' Elsie said. 'She can have a rest.'

'I should never've had the lot of you here!' Mrs Cook snarled. 'All you do is cry and eat and cost me bloody money. There's pigs to muck out and the bloody rain ain't stopping and I've had enough of the bloody bunch of you!'

She crossed the kitchen with a terrifying turn of speed for her size, and her hand darted out like a striking snake to seize Elsie by the back of her neck and pull her away from Connie. Then she grabbed Connie's arm in a fierce grip, hauling her from her seat.

'There's a war on!' Her face was inches from Connie's. 'You've got a bed here but you have to work to keep it. Now get on, girl, you can weep for your grandmother while you shovel that pig shit!'

Jack bristled. 'Don't you swear at her!' he warned Mrs Cook. 'And don't you manhandle them either. I'm going to tell my mother exactly what sort of people you are!'

'And we all know you and your husband are on the fiddle with the rations!' Ned bawled. 'You're all on the fiddle round here. A bit of mince, a few onions... we ain't seen our ration books since you and your no-good husband got hold of them.'

Rob nodded, bunching his little hands into fists. 'We're getting skinnier and you're getting fatter. At least with the nuns we could get a few bits down the docks, but this place is a bloody hellhole!'

Elsie nodded in agreement. She hated it here.

Connie was howling with grief, her face unrecognisable as tears coursed down it. It had turned so pale when she'd received her news, but now she was turning redder. She tried to shake herself free of Mrs Cook's grip.

'I hate you, you bloody cow!' Connie shouted.

Mrs Cook drew back her hand and slapped Connie as hard as she could. Everything seemed to stop as the blow sent her reeling.

Connie twisted round and fell hard against the range, the side of her face glancing against the scorching metal. It was always hot, filled with coal and wood, with pans bubbling on it, and water kept warm in a tank inside.

She curled up in a ball on the floor like a frightened animal. Elsie didn't know what to do.

'My face! I've burned my face!' she wailed in agony.

Jack dashed to the pail of water that sat on the table and grabbed it. He had pumped it from the well before dawn broke, his bare hands raw with cold as they worked at the rusty handle. Now, though, his hands were gentle as he tore a strip from his already tattered shirt and soaked it in the water. As Mrs Cook stormed from the kitchen, cursing in words that Elsie had never even heard before, Jack knelt at Connie's side. He wrung out the wet cloth and gently held it to her face.

'We're not staying here,' he told her. 'We're going back home to Mum. All of us together.'

Mum had told them not to come back, but they couldn't leave her all alone, and she'd look after Connie, Ned and Rob, Elsie knew.

They had to wait until Farmer Cook and his wife had gone to bed that night but, as soon as the sound of snoring reached through the rafters, it was time to go.

They crept out of the farmhouse with their bags packed and some bread and cheese in their pockets, stolen from the larder. Connie had a bandage tied round her face, but Mrs Cook hadn't let her go to the village to see the doctor.

Elsie held tight to Jack's hand, her ragdoll poking out of her carpet bag, which she held in her other hand. He'd planned it all.

'We'll be on the first train to London before the Cooks wake up,' Jack whispered as they crept down the long driveway. It was cold and damp, but they were going home. They'd be with Mum again soon. And the Cooks never woke up early; they expected the children to do that. It was their job to prepare breakfast for the couple before they ate their own thin porridge, but today nobody would wake the Cooks with breakfast, because they'd be gone. 'And Rob even managed to get hold of our ration books.' He looked at the young lad with a smile.

Rob gave a proud nod. 'And that ain't all,' he said. 'Show them, Neds!'

With a flourish like a magician producing a rabbit from a hat, Ned reached into his pocket and pulled out a handful of money. Elsie couldn't believe her eyes. 'When me and Rob run errands for Mr Mahoney and his people in London, we always saved our stash,' he explained. 'Them rotten old sods never found it when we got here.'

'So your train tickets are on me and Rob, courtesy of the dodgy geezers of London who we used to run messages for!' Rob beamed.

Ned nodded. Then he looked up at Connie and said gently, 'And when we get to London, I'm going to buy you and Elsie a pretty new frock, Con. And a big bunch of flowers to lay down in memory of your nan.'

Connie's eyes were still red from crying. She sniffed back tears, but she managed to smile. 'Thanks, Ned. You're the best brother I could have.' She patted him on the shoulder.

'Mum'll be so surprised when we turn up with you three,' Elsie said excitedly. She pictured her mum, opening the green front door with the number eight on it. 'But she won't mind at all.'

When they reached the lane that led down to the village, Elsie could already sense freedom. And once their mum knew all about how they'd been treated, Farmer Cook and his wife would be in trouble.

Jack's head was high as he walked, Elsie's hand in his. Connie had taken his arm and Ned and Rob strode on ahead, merrily counting their money as they went. Elsie watched her big brother in the moonlight and, as she did, she saw Dad once again. He'd be so proud of Jack, and, once he was found, he would welcome the boys and Connie as family too.

EIGHTEEN
LISETTE

January 1941

A nurse woke Lisette up to give her breakfast. She struggled to eat the thin porridge, as her throat was rasping from the smoke and dust. Then she remembered little Elsie, and suddenly it didn't matter.

She was leaning against the pillows, dozing, when she heard raised voices nearby. Someone was laughing, an aristocratic, carefree sort of laugh, as the nurses giggled.

Lisette watched as a man strolled into her room, ushered in by a nurse. The small room was suddenly filled with his expensive, spicy cologne.

She knew him. Everyone did.

Sir Rupert Cavendish, MP, was a member of the war cabinet, whose taste for dapper suits kept the tailors of Jermyn Street busy. He was dashing, his dark hair neatly swept back, and he wore a glittering diamond stick pin in his silk tie. She'd never met him before, but she'd seen him sometimes at Jasper's club. He made the most of Whitehall's closeness to the clubs and theatres of Soho.

He'd lost the sight in one eye during the Great War, but it didn't hold him back. He'd cut quite a dash in politics, and seemed to care about what ordinary people wanted. The camaraderie of the trenches, between the officers and their men, had clearly stayed with him.

'Bonjour, Mademoiselle Souchon,' said Rupert, bowing his head. When he spoke again, it was in fluent French. 'I hope you don't mind my popping in to see you. I'm such a fan.'

'I can hear you have spent a lot of time in Paris,' Lisette croakily replied in French. 'I'm very pleased to meet a fan. Forgive me, my voice is bad. The smoke and dust, you understand?'

Lisette had seen Rupert Cavendish in the papers, on his visits to people who had fallen victim to the Blitz. He'd helped find homes for those who had lost everything, toys for their children and clothes for their backs. He might not be able to fight for his country any more, but he did so much good. The likes of Sister Benedict could learn a lot from him.

'You must rest,' he told her, clearly as comfortable as a native in her language. 'London took an awful battering last night; I had to visit the hospital and see what help I could be.' Then he shook his head and sighed. 'Though what help a politician can be at a time like this, one wonders.'

'There is something you can do.' Lisette patted the edge of her bed. 'You *must* help the children. There was an orphanage in Whitechapel, run by nuns. It was hit by a bomb last night. Now it is just rubble. The children have nowhere to go, and the nuns are so cruel. The children are as thin as sticks! I'm very worried. They've got involved with black-market gangs – one of them was killed, trying to steal petrol. We must find somewhere safe for them. But I don't think they want to leave London.'

Rupert had settled on the edge of Lisette's bed, and he cocked his head to one side as she spoke, nodding thoughtfully.

'Evacuees have even come back from safety because they

don't want to leave their homes,' he told her. 'Coming back to their families is one thing; we can't have homeless orphans left on the streets.' He gave a nod. 'You're right. Something has to be done.' He reached over and rested his hand over Lisette's for a moment. 'Do you know where one might find them?'

Lisette shook her head. Her neck still hurt. 'I don't know. There was a nun here earlier. She said they had attacked her, which I don't believe! And now they've disappeared. Where could they have gone? Nowhere is safe.'

She thought of Ned and Toe Mahoney, how keen the little boy had been on the money the wide boys and low-league criminals were willing to dole out, no matter what danger it led him into. He'd said he was saving up for a house, and the thought struck Lisette as utterly heartbreaking. What if he got involved in something that ended as it had for his poor friend Rob?

'I'll do all I can to find them,' Rupert promised. 'I put my heart and soul into helping the war orphans, mademoiselle, and I won't ever stop.' He reached into his pocket with one manicured hand and took out a small silver case, monogrammed with the letters RC. When he flicked the catch with his thumbnail, Lisette saw that it contained visiting cards. 'If you need anything, even if it's simply a friend to listen, please do call on me.'

And Sir Rupert Cavendish held out one of the cards to her.

Lisette took the card from him. It was printed on thick, cream-coloured paper, the lettering elegant. 'Thank you, Sir Rupert, I will.'

She'd let Wyngate know that even Sir Rupert was on the case. But she didn't know where to find him. He'd left before she could ask for his address.

'If you do, please tell them I'm their friend,' Rupert said kindly. 'Now, mademoiselle, you must rest both your body and your voice. I'll look forward to hearing you sing at Jasper's again soon, but not until you're well enough.'

'I hope it won't be too long,' Lisette replied. 'It's hard to keep smiling in London at the moment, but I can keep people entertained by singing. But we must find the children.'

Rupert squeezed her hand again, then rose to his feet. 'I can be very tenacious,' he said. 'And I intend to find them.'

Lisette smiled up at him. 'Then they're very fortunate, to have a man like you looking out for them. It's so dangerous... I just hope we can find them before it's too late.'

NINETEEN
ELSIE

Elsie and her friends were picking their way out of the old City of London to Whitechapel. Smoke still lingered in the bombed streets, and snow fell on the piles of sandbags heaped up against the buildings.

'Look at us, squiring the prettiest girls in London,' said a beaming Ned. 'I'm going to buy us all some proper nice winter stuff.' Then he stuck his nose up into the air and said in a toffee-nosed drawl, 'And perhaps one will go skiing up on one's estate!'

Connie kept cupping her hands round her mouth and blowing against them. She wore fingerless gloves that were too small for her long fingers. 'I'll have a fur hat like a Cossack,' she said with a shiver.

'Look at you in that big coat,' said Jack gently. He let go of Elsie's hand, which he had been holding since they set off on their walk, and unbuckled the belt he wore round his narrow waist. Then he instructed, 'Arms up, little 'un!'

When Elsie raised her arms, the over-long sleeves tumbled back and she felt the sting of the cold, but she was cosy in Wyngate's heavy greatcoat. Jack put his belt round her waist and drew it tight, then lifted the hem of the coat and tucked it up and under the belt. Then he kissed her cheek and took her hand, then they were on their way again.

The streets were so damaged that there weren't many landmarks to steer by, but they found their way, the dome of St Paul's retreating behind them as they looked for Tower Bridge. As the snow went on falling, the landmarks looked beautiful, as if they were inside a snowglobe.

They had to avoid the main road that led to Bank Underground station, which was closed off with barriers and police. It must've got hit last night, just like the orphanage had.

As they went, Ned called out Pippa's name. He peered into every doorway and down every alley, calling for the little dog who was so dear to Elsie, but there was no sign of her wagging tail or shining eyes.

'She's still busy on war work,' Ned joked, as he hopped up onto a pile of sandbags that were stacked against a lamppost. He grabbed hold of the post in his wind-reddened hands and swung round it and, as he did. Elsie recalled the cinema again, the smiling dancers and swirling skirts and her mum's smiling face. Her heart blanched.

They were so alone. But they'd make the best of it. They'd find a house, and she'd write a letter to Mr Wyngate and ask him to come to tea. Maybe he could bring the nice lady with him.

'All that lovely money in my stash,' said Ned, beaming, as they crossed Leman Street. 'So close you can just about smell it. Shame it's under the crapper!' Then he nudged Elsie and said, 'I always said you couldn't trust a bank. But the crapper never let me down.'

They carried on through the falling snow, sliding on the pavement, before they rounded the corner of the street, where the hulking edifice of the orphanage used to stare down over Whitechapel.

It was even worse than Elsie remembered from last night.

Nothing was left, as if a bulldozer had smashed the place to bits. There were messy piles of bricks, wooden rafters torn from the floors and ceilings, and shattered doors; tiles from the roof had been thrown into the road. The nuns had hung onto their metal gates and fences, despite the effort to reuse railings to make planes, because they said they were needed to keep the children from straying. Now, the railings were nowhere to be seen.

The snow was falling thickly, covering the ruins, as if it was trying to hide the memory of the place. Elsie craned her neck, expecting to see Pippa appear from the ruins, and strained to hear her bark. But there was no sign of her. What would happen to the little dog, lost in the rubble and the snow?

'The old washhouse is... over there, I think.' Connie pointed to the place where Elsie had been rescued the night before. The door, which had saved Elsie's life, was covered by the bricks that had fallen as the perimeter wall had collapsed. She gestured towards another pile of bricks. 'So the toilets, and your stash, Ned, would be over there.'

Ned nodded, his mouth gaping as he stared at the pile of masonry and rubble that was now on top of his stash. Even if it had survived the bomb without being incinerated or blown to the winds, how could they even hope to dig their way down to find the money? He started forward, but Jack caught him by the sleeve.

'It's lost, Ned,' he said gently. Ned looked up at him fiercely, then wrenched his arm free and bolted into the bombsite, scrambling up and over the collapsed walls as nimbly as a cat.

Elsie stared at the ruins, wondering where in all that mess was her ragdoll, and the little dolly made from a wooden clothes peg. Her carpet bag and Jack's duffel bag that Mum had carefully packed with their clothes for their evacuation were under all of that rubble too.

All she had in the world was what she stood up in.

'What are you lot doing over there?' a voice called. Elsie

turned to see a policeman making his way over the rubble with little difficulty, no doubt from all the practice he'd had from months of the Blitz. 'This isn't a playground!'

'Our friend left something here before the bomb hit,' Jack said politely. Then he called, 'Ned, come on! Leave it!'

Ned glanced back, then looked down at the mound of bricks. Elsie saw the anger and misery mingled in his expression, the realisation that he had lost his stash. They had all lost everything, thanks to this war.

'You lived here, did you?' The policeman looked from Ned back to Elsie and her friends, then down at the rubble. 'You'll need to go back to the nuns. They'll have a nice convent in the countryside for you all to go to, I expect.'

Elsie held Jack's hand more tightly.

'We're not—' Connie said, then she suddenly changed her mind. 'Actually, we're going to see the nuns in a bit, so don't you worry about us.'

'Thank you, sir,' said Jack, tightening his hold on Elsie's hand. He jerked his head towards Ned, to summon him. 'You needn't worry yourself about us.'

'We can't have kids running around bombsites.' The policeman fixed them with a firm stare. 'You best come back to the station with me, so I can hand you over to the nuns.'

Fear ran up Elsie's spine. She glanced at Jack and Connie.

'Scarper!' Connie shouted, and suddenly she was off.

Ned was already leaping over the ruins with an athlete's speed, and he slammed into the back of the policeman with enough force to send him sprawling.

'Sorry, mate!' he called as he bolted onwards after Connie.

'Come back here!' the policeman shouted, trying to regain his balance.

Elsie and Jack hurried after them, the cold air rasping Elsie's throat and burning her lungs. Thank goodness Jack had looped up her coat or she would've tripped over.

The policeman's voice echoed behind them, but his words were lost under the thunder of their footsteps. They followed Connie down an alleyway between two warehouses. As they ran, Elsie couldn't help but look left and right for Pippa.

'Bloody hell!' exclaimed Ned, pulling up against the wall of the warehouse. 'We're buggered! We ain't got a penny between us!' He made a fist of his little hand and punched the wall, then sniffed deeply as though trying to hold back tears. Ned wouldn't cry, because he never did. Even when they heard that his best friend was dead, he tightened his jaw and said nothing.

All the plans they'd had, to find somewhere to live and for Ned's stash to cover everything they needed, were flying away like feathers in the breeze.

Connie came back a few steps and put her arms round him. 'You worked so hard for all that money, too.' She sniffed, trying not to cry as well. 'We're stuck now, ain't we? We can't go and ask for help from anyone, 'cos they'll send us back to the nuns or out to the countryside. But we ain't got any money. What'll we do?'

'We need to find some shelter out of the snow,' Jack said. He swallowed, then looked around. His eyes were filled with anxiety and Elsie saw him saying goodbye to their dad once again, promising to look after her and their mum. 'That's the first thing.'

Ned nodded. 'And I've got the money Toe gave me, so I can get a few bits for us. Then I can go and find some of my gang lads,' he said. 'Least they'll do is chuck me a few matches or whatever so we can build a fire. Then I'll get to work and I'll get another stash. Bigger than the last one!'

'Just be careful,' Connie warned him. 'But we need to get out of this snow. Maybe we could go down by them railway arches, the ones behind that bombed-out factory.'

Elsie was sure they wouldn't be found by coppers or nuns down there.

Jack looked down at Elsie and whispered, 'We'll be all right there,' then nodded. 'Just for now.'

Elsie knew he'd wanted to keep his promise to Dad and look after her, but none of this was his fault. Dad couldn't have known that Mum would be killed, or that they'd end up in an orphanage. And there was a shadow flitting in Elsie's mind that she just couldn't grasp. Something about Dad.

She reached up and stroked Jack's cheek to show him that she understood. He smiled and drew in a breath.

'Come on then,' he told the others. 'And Ned, you head off and get what we need for a fire. But nothing fancy, all right? And nothing pinched.'

Ned shot him a salute. 'Cross my heart.' He grinned.

After Ned ran off, Elsie and the others reached the walls of the burnt-out factory, darkened with soot. The roof had fallen in and the windows had all gone. The concrete yard surrounding it was full of broken glass and twisted metal. Elsie's foot met a bolt, which skittered across the cracked, snow-covered concrete, and the cold wind made a loose girder squeak as it swung back and forth.

Once they'd got round the back of the factory, the railway viaduct loomed above them. A bomb had hit the line a while ago, so no trains came this way any more. Each arch had been turned into storage rooms, with wooden frontages closing them off, but they'd been abandoned years ago. Some had lost their doors and their window glass, but others looked intact.

Piled up in front of them was a makeshift tip for locals trying to clear out their rubbish that the rag and bone men wouldn't touch, all their old tyres, cardboard boxes, greasy cloth, torn sacks, dirty mattresses and corrugated iron.

Connie ran ahead, and opened the door of one of the storage spaces, revealing a cracked floor and some tyres and boxes that someone had forgotten a long time ago.

She turned back to look at Jack and Elsie. 'What do you think?'

Jack looked around, the worry in his pale face all too visible. But this was the only option they had for now, until Elsie could somehow convince them that Mr Wyngate was their friend.

'It'll do,' he said. 'Just until we find somewhere better.'

Elsie nodded up at her brother. She wanted to tell him it was all right. Sleeping under the railway arches wasn't nice but it was better than going back to the countryside, or to the nuns.

Connie poked at the rubbish and looked up at her friends with a forced smile. 'My nan said to me, never judge a tramp. You don't know how they got there. And that's us now.'

Jack managed a smile too. 'And what a story to tell Dad when he gets home,' he said. 'He won't believe it!'

Elsie beamed at Jack. It was true; Dad would say, *You're pulling my leg!* And they'd all laugh, just like they used to in the old days.

They got to work, tidying their arch. The wind was blowing the other way, so at least the snow wasn't coming straight in as they helped each other roll aside the tyres and lift the old boxes. Connie found a blanket, which didn't look too dirty, even though it was ragged around the edges.

'You never know what treasures we might find,' she said optimistically.

Elsie brushed her hands off and looked out through the open door to the back of the factory. Someone was moving through the falling snow.

As the figure got closer, she recognised the army cap and the golden curls. It was Ned. She waved to him, hopping up and down to catch his attention. Ned lifted one hand to wave, then spun round to show that he was lugging a sack on his back.

'That's not a box of matches,' murmured Jack. 'What's he been up to?'

'It's Santa Ned!' called the little boy. He broke into a trot as he entered beneath the arch. 'I've got a ton of work to do in return for all this lovely gear, but I'm a working man, after all! I got brothers and sisters to provide for now, ain't I?'

Elsie bit her lip as she remembered Rob and his cow's-lick fringe. He should've been here with them, settling into the arch.

'Any time you want a job that ain't exactly honest, you talk to me,' Ned told Jack with a wink. He dropped to his knees beside Elsie and put the sack in front of him. 'I went straight down the docks and seen Mr Marsh. He's a man who knows a hard worker when he sees one. He's the bloke looks after Mr Mahoney's runners an' all.'

Jack drew in a breath and murmured, 'It's not safe, Ned.'

'But it's all we got just now, ain't it?' Ned emptied out the sack onto the ground. Then he reached into his pocket and took out a flask, which he put down next to Elsie. 'I've got work tomorrow and I've spent up what I made on the Underground last night. It's not much but it's a start.'

Elsie opened the green flask and a little trail of steam unspooled. She could smell cocoa. Warm cocoa on a snowy day, what a treat that had been when Mum had boiled it up on the hob. She grinned at Ned.

'Cocoa?' Connie chuckled as she rubbed her hands together. 'Cor, that's just the ticket on a day like today! What else is in your sack, Santa Ned?'

Elsie peered at each item. A box of matches, and some old newspaper to light a fire. Some paper bags of food – slices of bread, half a carrot cake – and some battered tins with their labels falling off. He produced a tin opener with a cracked handle, and fingerless gloves, which he gave to Jack. Next came some blankets, which had seen better days – they looked just as tatty as the one that Connie had found – but they were clean.

'And one last thing, because I miss hearing what my mate's got to say,' Ned said with a smile, reaching into his pocket. In his grubby hands, he brought out a handful of chits of paper, which she recognised as the betting slips he carried for a few pennies a time. These were blank though and with them was a little stubby pencil. 'I couldn't get you a proper book because of the paper rationing,' he explained. 'But it don't seem like the street bookies have a problem gettin' hold of betting slips.' He chuckled and gave a shrug, then held them out to Elsie. 'I thought maybe you could use the back of them until we get you a proper nice book and pencil.'

'Oh, Ned,' murmured Jack fondly. 'That's really kind.'

Elsie's eyes widened as she took them from Ned, and she held them tight. He'd given her a way to speak. She rested her head on Ned's shoulder to say thank you, and he tipped his head towards hers and whispered, 'Now you got your voice again.'

TWENTY
LISETTE

Maybe she shouldn't have left the hospital before she was entirely healed, but Lisette hated it there. From the moment that Wyngate had been forced out, she had felt lonely and fed up. She wanted to find the children, and she couldn't do that stuck in bed.

She'd slowly put her clothes back on, her body still bruised and sore. Red and grey powder covered the polished floor from brick dust falling from every seam. She'd managed to find a taxi, which took the long way back to Soho because the streets were filled with rubble. Would her home still be there?

She told the driver to take her to a different street among the maze of tottering, narrow old buildings that made up Soho, and headed straight for the hairdressers instead. The entire place was upholstered in various shades of pink, and was frequented by actresses and chorus girls, barmaids, and women who worked on the market stalls.

Ever-cheerful Eliza, a plump embodiment of the Blitz Spirit, tidied her up, eagerly telling her about a sailor she'd met at a dance. Lisette was grateful for her chatter because she didn't have to explain why she looked so untidy.

Once Lisette looked more herself, she went to Jasper's club. She had no intention of singing – her throat was still rasping – but at least she'd be among her friends.

Jasper's had a neon sign, which Jasper insisted on lighting for half an hour before blackout. As Lisette turned down the street, walking over inedible wrinkled cabbage leaves left from the market stalls, the red sign reflected in a puddle that had settled in the road's uneven surface.

A huge figure was standing by the door, wearing a Home Guard uniform. The red pinpoint of his cigarette was a flicker of colour against the khaki and beside his elbow, which was resting against the wall, was a broom handle.

'Tiny!' Lisette tried to call, her voice still croaky.

'All right, Lisette!' Tiny called. He flicked his cigarette away. Tiny was nothing like his name, as vast and terrifying to mouthy drunks and over-insistent servicemen as he was gentlemanly to the staff and *decent* patrons, as he termed those who knew how to behave. Childhood polio had left Tiny with a limp that kept him from the frontline, but he had rallied to the call of the Home Guard, often arriving at work straight from the night's patrol. As Lisette approached, he picked up the broom handle and said with a laugh, 'Got my rifle. Not sure where I'm supposed to stick the bullets though!'

Lisette chuckled. 'At least if the Germans invaded, you could poke them!'

Laughing about the looming threat of an invasion was the only way to deal with it. Everyone did. But when Lisette thought of it, for a second she saw overwhelming darkness, and wondered if her mother was safe.

'How are you, Tiny?' she asked. All the chaos of the hospital had been an unwelcome reminder that every day, every night, all of them were under threat; everyone they loved, and everyone they knew.

He shrugged one meaty shoulder and said, 'I'm all right, not bad.' Then he said, 'My platoon was helping them poor blighters at Bank last night, then I'm on the bus home this morning and we went right on past where that wall come down on them kids. I got home to my missus and I broke my heart, Lis.'

'No!' Lisette gasped. 'That's awful! The poor children.'

It was a different wall, other children. And yet, she saw the wall at the orphanage falling again as she shielded little Elsie.

She needed to find them, before anything else happened to them. She could hear it in Tiny's voice; the other children hadn't made it.

He nodded. 'Copper said they was looting houses after the all-clear went.' She saw his eyes cloud with tears again. 'And one come down on them. Four kids, gone like that.'

She remembered Jack standing on the heap of rubble, desperately trying to save his sister, and the moment Elsie emerged from under the door.

Lisette choked, covering her face with her hand as she felt tears rising.

Tiny ran his enormous hand over his eyes and sniffed back his sadness. 'I knew all of them,' he admitted. 'Always together, them lads. Right little gang, they was. They was all full of plans, how they was going to join up together in a couple of years and go and give Hitler a pasting. Sixteen years old and in the bloody grave. It's a bloody rotten thing.'

She rested her hand on Tiny's khaki sleeve. 'I'm so sorry you lost them.'

'You're a treasure,' he said, wiping his eyes again. 'Something's goin' on in this town, Lisette. They wasn't the sort to loot houses, someone must've put them up to it. Haven't you noticed, how things feel different?'

She nodded. Ned had talked so proudly about working with wide boys in that jarringly grown-up way. 'Someone is preying on children, the ones who have come back from the countryside. You have heard about the boy who died stealing petrol?'

'I heard he had a right nice funeral,' Tiny replied. 'But kiddies wouldn't be robbing petrol, it ain't their style. Somebody was paying him to do that. Whoever it is, he's got blood on his hands.' He looked up and down the street and exchanged a nod with a pair of women who strolled along the pavement in ragged fox furs, their heels clicking as they went. When he spoke again, Tiny had dropped his voice to a whisper. 'Word is, someone's tryin' to take over London. Question is, who's that likely to be?'

Was it Toe Mahoney?

But Lisette couldn't ask that out loud, especially not on a street where a pub nearby bubbled with the conversation of happy drinkers, and where two drunken airmen were trying to hold each other up as they staggered through the puddles.

And she didn't want Tiny to get drawn into it. He was a good, kind man.

'I am sure the police will find out,' Lisette said hopefully. 'Someone will know something. Especially now that so many children have died.'

'Coppers won't care,' Tiny said with a shrug of resignation. 'When have they ever cared about us lot? They didn't lift a finger when them toerags beat seven bells out of Jasper and Edgar last year, did they? We look after our own in this part of the world.'

Lisette shuddered as she remembered the cuts and the black eyes. Her two friends, set upon in the street on their way home from the club by a gang of louts bellowing, *Bloody fairies!* A gang of louts who Jasper and his boyfriend, Edgar, had never met before.

'We do, but we must be careful,' she said. 'Just one man can't bring down whoever it is who's doing this to the children.'

Tiny looked down at her, his brow furrowed, then widened his eyes in realisation.

'Oh, I ain't gettin' mixed up in this,' he said, and laughed as relief flooded through Lisette. 'We'll let the gang bosses fight it out between themselves. You know what, when I was growin' up down Southwark, I had mates used to flash gold watches, sharp suits, all that fancy stuff, 'cos they worked for the gangs. Not me. I went in the boxing ring – I might limp, but I can thump an' all – and when I got hitched, I went on the bins to earn an honest crust. And I'm happy. Heftin' the bins in the mornin', watchin' the doors at night.'

'You know, when I was in Paris, I knew thieves,' Lisette admitted. 'They had more money than everyone else, jewellery and fancy clothes. But they were always looking over their shoulders. And I couldn't live like that. You made the right choice, Tiny. And besides, you're part of the Jasper's family now!'

She glanced up at the neon sign, just as it fizzled out. The blackout had started.

'Time to go to work,' Tiny told Lisette with a smile. He reached out and opened the door to the club for her. 'Have a good 'un.'

She hoped the sirens wouldn't sound tonight. The children were out there in the city, somewhere, alone. She had to find them, but where could she even start?

TWENTY-ONE
LISETTE

The door opened onto a steep staircase that led down to the club in the basement, which rang with jaunty piano music. The walls were dark red, with framed photographs of the club's acts. Lisette was in several photographs, leaning close to her microphone like a sultry torch singer, and in another photograph she stood with her arms aloft, in a glittery gown. Her friends occupied the other frames, novelty acts in funny costumes, singers in fancy frocks.

Someone walking down these stairs might think that any of the women from the photographs might appear on stage that night. But Lisette knew it was impossible. Marianne, with her comedy songs and her cockney maid costume, was killed a week after Tom had died. But she still smiled cheekily from the picture frame, her eyes twinkling.

At the bottom of the stairs, she was immediately absorbed into the warm darkness of the club. It was unlit except for the stage and small candles flickering on the tables and along the bar. The stage was empty as Lucien sat at the piano. At each table were the dark shapes of the guests, who were chattering and laughing.

Jasper sat in his usual place at the end of the bar, immaculate in his pinstripe three-piece suit, his cigarette positioned in the ebony cigarette holder he was never without. At the sight of Lisette he gave a nod of welcome, lifting his cigarette holder to toast her arrival.

Lisette waved back. Jasper was a Soho institution, and seeing him made her glad that she hadn't gone home to rest.

She kissed him on both cheeks. 'How are you, Jasper? I got caught in the air raid last night. I can't sing.' As was obvious, as she croaked her words.

'You should have stayed at home,' he said kindly, then rapped on the bar. 'Lillian, a glass of my Scotch for Lisette, please. We need to keep that throat healthy.'

'No, no, I couldn't bear to go home,' Lisette told him. 'I wanted to come here, and be with my friends.'

She looked across at Lillian, who had worked in Soho all her long life. She always wore sequins and heels, with glittering earrings, and never seemed to be shocked by anything. Lillian reached up for a glass with her red-nailed hands, the fake diamonds round her wrist glittering. What tales she could tell, and often did.

'Lillian came through Bank five minutes before the bomb hit last night,' Jasper said quietly. 'She saw our lovely Mr and Mrs Fleet on the platform, waiting out the raid. They told her to stay there underground, where she'd be safe.' He took a drag on his cigarette, his eyes clouding. Only then did he add, 'Lills took her chance on the street; Mr and Mrs Fleet...'

'Nice couple,' said Lillian with a shake of her head. She put the glass of whisky down in front of Lisette. 'Drink that down in their memory; they always did like a glass of the good stuff.'

Lisette's hand trembled as she picked up the glass. She closed her eyes, remembering when the blast had hit, when anyone standing at Whitechapel had been thrown sprawling.

'I... I was sheltering at Whitechapel,' she told them. 'I heard it. We all felt the blast. Oh, the Fleets were a lovely couple. They were only trying to find somewhere safe. Like all of us do, every time.'

Lillian held up the glass in a toast. 'To the Fleets, and to everyone who died last night.'

Ruby, one of the other singers at the club, who wore her hair in a pile of ginger curls, sauntered up to the bar in a floor-length silk dress. She had been such a support when Tom had died, and the two of them had held each other up as they'd wept at Marianne's graveside.

She had caught the end of Lisette's toast, and said sadly, 'I can't believe they've gone.'

'Oh, Lord, a royal visit,' murmured Jasper, as four figures descended the stairs into the smoky bar. The two men at the back of the trio were so big, they made Tiny look slight. At their head were a stately couple, the woman in thick furs and the man at her side clearly not sharing everyone else's struggles to make their clothing rations stretch. They looked as though they'd stepped out of a fashion magazine.

It was Dupree, the man who ran Soho.

A ripple ran through the audience, as it did every time he appeared. Heads turned one by one, and even people who were new to the club and had never encountered Dupree before turned to look. Dotted around the tables were men who worked for him. Or least, Lisette thought they did. They certainly knew him, nodding towards him in a respectful greeting.

He wasn't like Toe Mahoney, though. While he did carry with him an air of threat, there was something gentlemanly about him. He spoke in a refined way, as if he'd been taught at the best schools. Lisette had no idea if he had or not. He paused for a moment to peel off his leather gloves, which he passed to one of the men behind him.

'Jasper, what *is* becoming of our city?' Dupree beamed, opening his arms wide in greeting. 'These Luftwaffe fellows have no sense of history.' He inclined his head to Lisette in a gesture of courtly politeness. 'And yet here one remains in London.' The gangster took Jasper's hand and shook it. 'One must set the example for the king and his family to follow. And one must keep an eye on business too.'

What on earth would happen to Dupree's businesses if he left for the countryside? Ned had talked so casually about the black market, and Wyngate had told them that people had ended up dead in the Thames. Something dangerous was going on, threatening the children; *her* children.

'I believe we have a viper in our breast,' Dupree told Jasper as he cast his serene gaze around the club. 'Now then, Jasper, you are a man of the world and you and I have always seen eye to eye, haven't we? Mrs Dupree and I enjoy the club and, because we do, you don't have any trouble within these walls.' He dropped his voice to whisper, 'Unlike those ruffians who took against you and your friend last year. Trouble found them, once word reached Mrs Dupree of your plight, did it not?'

And Dupree looked lovingly to his wife of more years than anyone cared to count.

She smiled proudly, her red lipstick gleaming in the candlelight. 'Anything for my dear friends.'

A prickle of fear ran up Lisette's spine, and she glanced at Ruby, who was examining her fingernails. Obviously, knowing that Jasper and Edgar's assailants had received a taste of justice was a good thing, but the way the Duprees could unleash violence just by giving the right people a nod was unnerving. Were Jasper and Edgar now in debt to the Duprees, or was it just a gesture of friendship?

'Thank you, Mr Dupree,' Jasper replied, neatly tapping a column of ash off his cigarette. 'You know how grateful I am, I'm sure. Besides, my ladies need their lipstick, and where else can they get it with this blasted war on?'

Dupree nodded that imperious nod of his. 'But there

appears to be a new operator in London,' he said. 'Someone's rounding up the small-timers and putting them to work. And there are a lot of small-timers in this city. A lot of money in nylons and petrol and ration books. I want to know, Jasper, what have you heard?'

'There's something in the wind,' Jasper said, lowering his voice. It was in his interests to help Dupree, Lisette knew. 'I couldn't help but notice that the bookies who come in here have changed their odds. I thought it was something to do with the war, but they don't seem to be rolling in money. And we've had more salesmen coming in, and they're rather... fresh-faced, if you see what I mean.'

Young. Ned was too young to come to Soho, but any boy who was a year or two away from being called up could put on a suit and comb his hair, and suddenly he'd be a black-marketeer.

Dupree thinned his lips and sniffed disapprovingly. 'London's got plenty of little ones hoping to earn a crust,' he replied. But I'll find out who's in charge. And when I do, the Blitz'll look like a kiddies' playtime.' Then he turned to Lisette and smiled, offering her a polite nod. 'Good evening, mademoiselle.' With that, Dupree offered his wife his arm. 'Mrs Dupree and I will have our usual, Lillian, and one for Jasper too.'

As he turned to go, a tall, thin man in a dark overcoat hurried down the stairs and passed the bar. He was going so fast that he almost collided with Dupree.

'Pardon me, guv'nor!' he exclaimed, touching the brim of his hat.

'Pardoned, Mr Marsh,' Dupree breezed. 'On this occasion.'

Marsh was a regular at the club, someone Lisette humoured but never got too close to. He was a fixer, and would find anything and anyone. For a price. Ruby had said that Marsh carried a gun in his pocket. He crossed the room and sat down at a table with a short, stocky man.

As Lillian poured the drinks, and the Duprees settled at

their favourite table – one that was always kept empty with a sign saying, *Reserved*, just in case they turned up – Ruby found a table in the corner for Lisette.

'You look like you've seen a ghost, mate.' Ruby stroked back Lisette's hair and saw the bandage on her temple. 'You got caught in the air raid! You should be at home.'

'I'm feeling better,' Lisette replied, 'seeing Jasper, and you, and hearing Lucien on the piano. I just wanted to be with my friends.'

'That's right, friends are the best medicine!' Ruby told her. 'I've got my set in a minute, but sit tight, and I'll send the other girls out to keep an eye on you when they're free. And fingers crossed we don't get interrupted by another air raid!'

Lisette sat at her table as familiar faces from among the audience came to say hello, sympathising with her injuries and hoping she'd be back on stage singing again soon. Her friends kept her company when they could, and their songs made it easier for her not to dwell on how worried she was about the children. Wyngate was out there somewhere, hunting for them, and as soon as she'd worked out a plan she would go searching too. But where could she begin, with the entire city spread before her? She could ask around, but someone in this city was using kids for their own criminal ends, and she didn't want to risk putting them in more danger by asking the wrong person.

The evening was wearing on, and there was no sign of the sirens. As she sat there alone at her table, Andrea, another of Jasper's singers, went through her music hall set in her sequinned corset, looking like an Edwardian showgirl. She patted her curly blonde hair and twirled a feather boa as she winked saucily at the audience.

Lisette saw someone from the corner of her eye and glanced round.

It was Wyngate.

He was leaning against the bar, the flickering candlelight casting shadows across his face. The smoke from his cigarette curled up from his fingers as he picked up his glass of whisky. He had come alone and was surrounded by shadows, as if he had brought the night in with him.

She gestured for him to come over. Wyngate glanced around, his gaze settling briefly on the Duprees and the handful of monied companions who had joined them. Then he took another sip from his glass and strolled across the club towards Lisette.

'Mr Wyngate,' Lisette said, rising from her chair to welcome him, even though she ached. 'I wondered when I'd see you again.'

'I went to see you at the hospital,' he replied, nodding his greeting. 'They said you'd left.'

Lisette smiled, and pointed to the empty chair beside her. 'Won't you sit down? Thank you for trying to see me at the hospital. I just felt so useless lying there, thinking of you going off to trace the children. I couldn't bear it. But I couldn't go home and sit by myself, so I came here, even though I can't sing.'

'You'll sing again.' Wyngate pulled out the chair and took a seat. He didn't look at the stage though; his attention was all focused on Lisette. 'Have you seen the children today?'

She shook her head. 'No, they didn't come back to the hospital. I suppose, after that awful nun came to claim them, they decided they wouldn't go back. You haven't heard from them either?'

Wyngate shook his head. 'No.' His jaw tightened. 'But I will find them.'

Lisette leaned close to him, dropping her voice to a whisper as Andrea sang 'A Little of What You Fancy Does You Good'. 'We must. I'm so worried. It's not just the bombs, it's the black market, especially after what happened to their friend Rob and'

– she sighed – 'four boys were killed last night, out burgling for a gang while the bombs fell. Someone is using children, no matter the risks.'

Wyngate nodded. 'Do you know how London works, Mademoiselle Souchon? How it's carved up by men like Dupree and Mahoney?'

'I do, a little,' Lisette replied. 'They call it their manor. Dupree is in charge in Soho. Mahoney runs his part of the East End. They know all the dealers, and they get a cut from everything.'

'Quite a business for the men at the top.' Wyngate dropped his cigarette into the ashtray. 'There's a lot of money sloshing about right now and the bosses have taken their eye off the small change, so someone's swooped in and started cleaning it up. Usually the bosses stick to their own patch, but whoever this new person is he's all over London, and using kids.'

'No wonder Mahoney and Dupree are so angry. But it's neither of them, is it? I suppose there is honour among thieves, and they would never dream of stepping on each other's toes.'

He raised an eyebrow and asked, 'You really believe men like that wouldn't tread on each other's turf?' He looked over at Dupree and, as he did, the gang boss looked back. For a moment each held the other's gaze. Everyone else pandered to Mr Dupree, but Wyngate was staring at him without a trace of humility or fear. 'They all would. Any one of them could be our man and every one of them will deny it. We might well end up with another war here, on the ground in London. And the children could be caught in the crossfire.'

Lisette instinctively reached across the table for Wyngate's hand. She looked into his dark gaze. 'I suppose the Ministry want to know, before this war breaks out. Or perhaps you are in the police?'

Wyngate gave a small laugh. 'I'm not police,' he said. 'And this isn't official. I don't care about the gangs or the bosses, and them using kids is nothing new. But putting them to work in the Blitz while the adults hide away?' His jaw tightened. 'They've crossed a line. The boy who was buried yesterday isn't the first casualty in this. He's just the one the papers picked up on.'

Lisette held his hand tighter. 'And you know about the boys who died last night?'

Wyngate nodded. 'And the two girls who were hit by the train at Westminster. They were stashing loot in a tunnel that'd been closed in a raid and must've missed the signs telling them it had reopened.'

The last moments of those two young lives were too horrible to contemplate. Hearing the rumble and screech of the approaching train, seeing the lights coming at them through the darkness.

'Those poor girls. And their poor parents. Unless...' She looked into Wyngate's magnetic gaze again. 'Were they orphans too?'

Wyngate nodded. 'We're failing them,' he murmured. 'They've got nobody, Lisette.'

This was clearly very personal for him. She held his hand very gently and whispered, 'Were you one of those children, Wyngate?'

'I don't have a past,' he said simply.

But he did. He'd spoken French to her fluently. And he knew all about the tyranny of the nuns.

Switching into French, Lisette said, 'You must have. But I'm intruding, I know. It must be painful. And yet it's driving you to do something for these children. I want to find them, too.'

'Is this the best place to reach you?' Wyngate asked, also in French. 'When one of us finds them?'

A shutter had come down, and the little boy who Wyngate once was had been safely packed away again.

'I'm here most evenings,' Lisette said. 'And sometimes in the afternoons for rehearsals. You can reach me on the telephone. Let me write down my address for you.'

'I'll remember,' he replied.

Lisette arched her eyebrow. She was impressed. 'Number thirty-three, Blake Street,' she replied. 'Flat D, right at the top.'

Wyngate nodded. He picked up his glass and drained it. 'I won't forget. Could I see you ho—'

'Bonsoir, Lisette!' A booming voice with a strong cockney accent interrupted. Doris, who worked backstage, primping the performers and looking after their wardrobe, arrived at the table in a dark blue satin dress.

'I'll be in touch.' The moment was gone. He rose to his feet and touched his hat towards Doris. 'Goodnight, mademoiselle.'

'Goodnight, Wyngate,' Lisette replied. 'Thank you for coming. Take care, won't you?'

'Always,' Wyngate assured her. Then he turned and disappeared through the smoky crowd, and was absorbed once more by the shadows.

A man who carried so many secrets in his heart, which he kept so safe Lisette wasn't sure she would ever see inside.

TWENTY-TWO
ELSIE

Now

The snow had stopped falling before it got dark, but it was still cold. The fire had warmed the arch up a bit, and they'd shared the food that Ned had managed to get for them, but it wasn't enough. They were still hungry as they'd fallen asleep on the hard floor, Ned and Elsie lying between Connie and Jack, who were trying to keep them warm.

Elsie had dreamed fitfully, of chasing Pippa through a snow-covered bombsite, the little dog always just too far ahead to catch her.

Light started to bleed through the narrow gaps of the planks that closed off their arch from outside. Morning had come. And it was time for Elsie and the others to find some work, so they could try to fill their empty stomachs.

The pavements were slippery under the snow, which was turning into slush under their feet. It was so cold that their breath came out as steam. At least Elsie had Mr Wyngate's warm coat, but Jack's winter clothes had patches and darns. He looked so thin and cold, and yet he refused to take turns with Wyngate's coat.

Elsie had helped Connie to tidy herself up, and their future star had gone off to find a pitch outside a pub. Meanwhile, Elsie held Jack's hand as they went from place to place, desperately trying to find some work. With every step, she glanced this way and that, trying to spot Pippa.

They tried a bakery, but they didn't have any work; they tried the newsagents, but they didn't need them either. They tried every shop they saw. Elsie tried to keep smiling for Jack, hoping it'd soothe his worried expression. But the more places they tried, and the more people said no, Elsie knew, the more their dire situation weighed on him.

They had all but given up when they arrived at a warehouse by the docks. A tall, thin man in a flat cap was loading boxes onto a trolley from a van.

'Morning, sir!' said Jack brightly. 'Help you unload? I'm looking out for a job, but odd jobs do just as well.'

The man looked at Jack and Elsie carefully before saying, 'All right, you can help me unload, and if you give me a hand with some other jobs, too, I'll give you a shilling.'

A shilling? They could buy a loaf of bread with that, and have a few pennies to spare. And maybe, once the man saw what a hard worker Jack was, he might ask him back.

'Any work you've got, I'm happy to do it!' Jack said to the man. Then he smiled at Elsie and whispered, 'A bob, Else! You wait inside the warehouse while I get on.'

While Jack set to work, Elsie went through the huge doors into the warehouse. It was like the big barn on the farm, only instead of straw bales and animals it was full of shelves laden with boxes and crates. She wondered where it had all come from, and where it was destined for. She wandered up and down the aisles, dusty with sawdust spilled from the packaging.

Eventually she found a corner that was out of the cold

breeze, and sat down on a pile of sacks with her stubby pencil and a betting slip. As Jack came by with the trolley, she drew a picture of him, his long legs and his fingerless gloves. She gave the drawing a big, broad smile, one she hadn't seen on Jack's face in a long time.

Next, Jack was sweeping up, then lugging sacks. Elsie decided to help. She strained with effort as she tried to pick up a sack, but Jack intervened, shaking his head.

Finally, after a few hours, the man in the flat cap paid Jack his shilling, but he shook his head and said he wouldn't be needed the day after. Elsie could see the disappointment in her brother's face as he tucked the coin into his thin coat, then held out his hand to his sister.

'I'll buy you a bag of chips for tea,' he said, and smiled. 'And tomorrow, we'll try the next streets. This is a good start, isn't it?'

Elsie nodded. At least Jack had been able to find *some* work. There were warehouses up and down the river where there had to be jobs for a boy like her brother. And a bag of chips to share would be a treat. Hot and steamy, with a shake of salt, and the sharp tang of vinegar.

Hand in hand, they went back into Whitechapel's streets, looking for Connie. She knew there wasn't much chance of them finding Ned; who knew where his jobs took him.

There was still no sign of Pippa.

They heard Connie before they saw her. Her voice was unmistakable, filling the street with 'Tea for Two', a song Elsie remembered her merrily singing on the farm as she poured swill into the pigs' troughs. People on the pavement looked up and smiled as they heard her. What a gift she had, making people happy.

Jack's face lit up and his step quickened as they rounded the corner.

She was standing by the door of a pub on the street corner, her bobble hat on the floor with coins glittering in it. She was dancing as she sang, twirling the end of her tatty scarf, beaming at her audience. An old man with white hair had poked his head out of the pub's door to listen, and on the other side of the crossroads a woman in an old fur coat swayed from side to side. A young man, wearing his fedora at an angle, walked briskly by and dropped a coin into Connie's hat. She broke off to call, 'Thank you kindly!', before going on singing.

'Oh, she's like an angel,' said a plump lady to her friend as she took out her purse. Then she whispered, 'Shame about her face, poor love.'

Elsie felt Jack tense, then he stepped forward and picked up Connie's hat. He rattled the coins inside it and said to the plump lady, 'Our Miss Connie, the voice of London! Give what you can, ma'am!'

Elsie was astonished. Jack was such a quiet brother; she had never imagined he would take up Ned's role, but Connie deserved a few pennies in return for her song, not out of charity because of her scar.

The lady smiled and dropped a coin into the hat as she said indulgently, 'You've got a very pretty girlfriend, young man, I didn't mean anything by it.'

And Jack blushed.

'Roll up, ladies and gents!' And through the people who were stopping to watch came the little figure of Ned, his cap set at an angle on his curls. He looked like he'd been hard at work all day; his face was grubby and his hands were raw with cold. But he had those blue eyes as wide as he could get them and was, even now, gazing up at the passers-by, getting ready to melt their hearts. 'Miss Connie, the Blitz Angel, singing live here in Whitechapel.'

Ned gave Connie a nod, as though he was her bandleader. Then he pushed open the door of the pub and, in a voice that sounded as woeful as it was innocent, he said to the drinkers within, 'I ain't got much in the world, but I got this young lady's voice. It keeps me goin', it does.' And he leaned against the now-open door, watching Connie with soulful eyes, then took off his cap and held it out. Elsie had the impression they might even make enough to have a little bit of fish with those chips tonight.

Connie started to sing 'Begin the Beguine'. The song was Jack's favourite. It had been a huge hit the year before, and the passers-by nodded with recognition. Elsie had realised that when Connie sang, she didn't sound like a cockney any more, but like one of the Andrews Sisters, even though she didn't have a fancy dress. An old couple, who'd been shuffling up the street, turned to each other and smiled, and a lady came out of the hairdressers opposite, some hair clips attached to her collar, and tapped her foot as she listened.

Elsie danced too. Just being with her friends stopped her thinking about being hungry.

When the song finished, there were shouts and cheers. Coins flashed past, landing in Connie's bobble hat and in Ned's cap.

Jack smiled down at Elsie, his affection warming her. 'You're a fine dancer,' he told his sister.

'Please, Miss Connie,' Ned said, his lip trembling. Elsie had known him long enough to know that he was as good an actor as she'd ever seen at the pictures. 'Please can we have "We'll Meet Again"?' He looked around the gathered faces, their brows knitted in sympathy at the sight of the cherubic little boy. He blinked, a single tear rolling down his pale cheek, as he declared, 'God bless London! God save Mr Churchill and His Majesty the king!'

Before Connie had even sung the first note, more coins had landed in Ned's cap.

It was impossible to go wrong with 'We'll Meet Again', especially with Connie's sweet voice, and Ned nearby, looking like a cherub. Elsie wondered whether she and Jack would meet Dad again. Mum had looked sad when the song played on the radio.

If only she could bring back the gap in her memory.

As the song ended, Ned was still collecting coins in his cap and Jack in Connie's woolly hat. The Londoners in wartime didn't have much, but Connie's song had touched their hearts and they were sharing something with the kids, even with rationing and bombs and the threat from Germany. Ned was pushing the coins into his pockets when Elsie saw him look over the heads of the audience. His eyes grew wide again, but not with play-acted sadness this time.

'Scarper!' he yelled and, without even knowing why, Elsie obeyed. Jack shoved the hat into his pocket and went along with her, towed by Elsie's hand. Connie was already flying after Ned, barely glancing back.

'Elsie!' a voice shouted. 'Jack! Wait!'

TWENTY-THREE

ELSIE

The pavement was uneven and slippery with slush, and Elsie had to take care not to fall. But she glanced back over her shoulder.

And there, behind them, was Mr Wyngate.

Her heart missed a beat. She didn't believe Mr Wyngate had betrayed them, even though the others thought he had, but she knew that, if she signalled to Jack to turn back, he would only want to run harder.

She was staring ahead, dodging past a woman with a pram, and an ARP warden painting a large white S on the wall that pointed towards a shelter. Elsie's heart was thudding, and she held tightly to Jack's hand.

But Ned had seen him. 'Come on!' he yelled. He was as fast as a whippet and knew the alleyways and streets better than anyone. He flew ahead, calling to the startled pedestrians, 'That bloke's spying for the social! He's after having us took off our ma and pa!'

A woman with salt-and-pepper hair, whose floral overall was poking out from under her heavy brown winter coat, gawped at Ned in shock. As they raced by Elsie chanced another look over her shoulder, and saw the woman was blocking Wyngate's path, grabbing his sleeve.

'Chasin' little kids! What are you playin' at?' she shouted.

A large man in an old suit, one sleeve pinned up as if he'd lost an arm in the last war or on the docks, joined in, and strode off to confront Wyngate. 'You should be ashamed!' he shouted.

Elsie barely had time to hear Wyngate's protests before they had rounded another corner and his voice was lost.

She dashed her free arm against her eyes to wipe away her tears. She had no idea where they were. The street was narrow and smelt of boiled cabbage; the gutters were clogged with old newspaper. On either side were tall, dark houses, so run-down that Elsie wasn't sure if the Blitz had caused their demise or if they'd looked like that before the war. Bombs had punched a hole through the middle of the street and smashed several houses to bits. The dark windows stared at them from behind torn curtains, grey with dirt and soot.

A rag and bone man had drawn his lopsided trolley up to the kerb and was carrying a broken headboard across the pavement. He shook his fist as they ran by.

'Bloody kids!' he shouted after them as his burden crashed to the ground.

On they ran, following Ned down a dark, narrow alleyway that cut between the windowless walls of two tall houses. It smelt of drains, and the snow had barely managed to fall here, as if its dirt repelled anything clean and white. There was no one there, and yet it felt as if they were being watched, as if something sharp and nasty was lurking in the shadows.

The alleyway opened out onto a street where the blackened remains of a bombed warehouse stood. The brick wall had collapsed on one side, the corrugated metal roof had fallen in, and what remained looked dangerously unstable. Elsie was sure she saw a face glance through a crack at them.

Ned pressed his back to the wall and held up one hand to

his friends to signal that they could catch their breath. As soon as he did, Jack dropped to his knees and hugged Elsie tight, whispering, 'It's all right' softly. But Elsie wasn't sure if he was telling her or trying to convince himself.

'That was bloody close,' Ned murmured. Then he took a few steps towards the warehouse. 'I'm just going to have a butchers and see if there's anything worth sellin' in here. Reckon my mates'll have cleaned it out already, but don't do no harm to look.'

And with that, he dashed off towards the collapsing structure.

Elsie shivered despite Jack's embrace and the warmth of her coat. Ned couldn't go in there, but she didn't know how to stop him.

'Ned!' Connie called, running after him. She stopped halfway as she eyed the unstable building, and cupped her hands round her mouth to shout, 'It ain't safe!'

'Bloody right it ain't!' Ned had come to a shuddering halt at the gaping maw of the warehouse's collapsed wall. 'There's only a Kraut bomb in there, sittin' pretty in a hole in the bloody floor!'

TWENTY-FOUR
ELSIE

She wanted to run, to get as far away as she could. An icy finger of fear crept up her spine and all she could do was cling more tightly to her brother.

A bomb. She'd lost so much to them. Her mother dead, vast areas of her city destroyed. And now they were standing only feet away from one.

And it could go off at any time.

'Oh, heck,' Connie gasped. 'We have to go and tell someone. We can't just leave the bloomin' thing there!'

'You stay here, Else. You too, Connie.' Jack kissed Elsie's cheek, then rose to his feet. He drew in a breath and squared his narrow shoulders. 'Show me, Ned?'

Ned turned and beckoned. 'Come on, then!'

Jack looked so much like Dad at that moment, and Elsie was so proud of him, but she didn't want him to go anywhere near a bomb. She shrank into herself, trying to make herself small, and opened her mouth, desperate to say something that would make him stop.

But no words came.

Connie put her shaking arm round Elsie, and they watched

as Jack strode over to join Ned and then together they disappeared into the shadows. Elsie trembled through her whole body.

What if the bomb went off, what if Jack and Ned were thrown through the air like ragdolls? She and Connie would be left all alone in the world. She couldn't lose her brave, loving brother. She couldn't lose her cheeky little friend Ned.

'Just you be careful, Jack Taylor!' Connie called tensely through the cold air. 'And that goes for you, Ned, and all.'

Elsie's eyes were blurred with tears, and she wrapped her arms round Connie, holding on to her as tightly as she could.

'He's right; it's an unexploded bomb!' Jack called as he emerged into the dull daylight. He looked determined. 'Connie, Elsie, you head back to the den. Ned can fetch help and I'll stand guard. It's not exactly busy here, but someone might wander through.'

Elsie shook her head. She didn't want to leave Jack here, alone, with the bomb. They had to face danger side by side.

'You're not stayin' here by yourself,' Connie declared. 'I'll stay here, too, and Elsie doesn't want to leave you on your tod neither. The three of us'll stand guard while Ned gets help.'

'No,' said Jack. 'I won't put you and Elsie at risk.'

'Well, I'm off to tell the coppers,' said Ned. 'Whichever one of you's stickin' around, there's one thing I've got to say about that bomb.' And he widened his eyes. 'Don't even fart on it. We don't want a nasty surprise!'

With a salute, Ned ran off along the alleyway, whistling merrily as he went.

'What's he like?' Connie giggled. 'Look, I'll stay with you, Jack. Elsie, are you sure you want to stay here? It's a bloomin' bomb, for heaven's sake.'

Elsie knew if someone came down the street and saw all three of them standing there, holding their arms out and keeping people back, they could save lives. So she nodded and caught her brother's gaze, hoping he could see the bravery and determination in her eyes.

'It'll be all right, Jack,' Connie assured him. 'It's better she's here with us, where we can keep an eye out, than her walkin' on her own back to the arch.'

Jack sighed, but nodded. After a moment he said, quite out of nowhere, 'Connie... how do we know Ned's right about Mr Wyngate? We just ran, but we never stopped to ask him if he'd done what Ned thinks.' He chewed his lip, then looked from Connie to Elsie. 'Ned only trusts his wide boy mates. He thinks everyone else is after something.'

Connie looked thoughtful. 'Because we know Mr Wyngate was in the hospital with us, then he disappeared, and Sister Benedict turned up like a bad penny.'

Hope blossomed in Elsie's heart at her brother's words, even if Connie still believed Ned. She'd held back from writing anything about Mr Wyngate, because everyone else had been so sure he was the enemy. But now that Jack was questioning Ned's unswerving belief, she had a chance to plead Mr Wyngate's case.

She took the pencil and the betting slip out of her pocket, and on the back of the picture she'd drawn of Jack she wrote

Mr Winget is our frend

Then she held it out to her brother.

Jack read the note and smiled. 'Elsie doesn't think he's too bad,' he said. 'Besides, if he was going to hand us over, why didn't he do it straight away? I don't know, Connie. Ned's not always right, is he?'

Connie chewed her lip, before replying, 'You know what he's like when he's made his mind up about something. He didn't like it when that Lisette was goin' on at him about the black-market geezers, and he thinks Wyngate agrees with her!'

Just then, Elsie spotted a young woman with a brightly coloured red scarf coming down the alleyway, pushing a pram.

She was with her friends, who were wearing winter coats with fashionably wide shoulders, their crisply styled hair topped with small felt hats. They were laughing and joking as they walked along the frosty pavement, heading straight towards them. And the bomb.

TWENTY-FIVE
ELSIE

'Excuse me, ma'am,' Jack called politely. 'I'm afraid the alleyway's out of bounds.'

Elsie and Connie stood beside him, their arms joined like a human barricade, trying to stop the women coming any further.

The women stopped, evidently surprised by the authority in Jack's young voice. The baby started to make fretful noises in the pram.

One of the women, with blonde hair and a turquoise hat, looked at him in surprise and said, 'You're a bit young to be a copper! What on earth's going on?'

'There's only a bomb over there,' Connie told her. 'It'll go off right in your face if you ain't careful!'

'A bomb?' The woman with the pram tightened her grip on the handle, and her baby grizzled. Her friends stood closer to her, their faces white with shock.

'Sorry, ladies,' said Jack apologetically. 'I hope it won't inconvenience you to go back along the alleyway.'

All Elsie could do was pull her most serious expression. This wasn't a game.

A group of young women appeared, looking like they were on their way home from work. An older man in a dark-coloured suit and a flat cap strode up the alleyway to Elsie and the others.

'What's all this?' he asked, his forehead furrowed with concern. 'Did I hear someone mention a bomb?'

Quite a crowd was gathering now. Some women with grey hair and shopping bags arrived, and a teenage boy walked over, his big yellow dog sniffing about and barking. News of the bomb passed quickly through the crowd, and despite the danger no one moved away.

Elsie, Jack and Connie stood their ground. They had to hold the crowd back, they couldn't let anyone near it and blow up the street and everyone on it.

Suddenly a young woman, wearing pinstriped trousers, a burgundy fedora on her dark hair, made her way to the front of the crowd. She was holding a notepad, a pencil poised above it, and Elsie wondered if she couldn't speak either.

But then the young woman asked, 'There's an unexploded bomb right here in the street? And you kids found it?'

Jack nodded. 'That's right,' he replied. 'Our friend's gone off to get help and we're trying to keep the area clear.'

'But you're only children,' she said, as she scribbled in her pad. 'Very brave children. I hope you don't mind me writing this down; I'm a reporter for the *Evening News*.'

Elsie smiled. Despite her fear, she felt very important. If she could've spoken, she would've told the reporter that they were doing their bit.

'We don't mind at all,' Connie replied with a grin.

As Connie was talking to the reporter, Jack was moving between the spectators, moving them along in his steady, polite way. Yet Elsie could hear his voice rising in volume as he went, calling out, 'Keep moving along please, folks, there's no throughway here!' And the more he commanded them to move, the more they did so. Elsie's heart swelled with pride. 'Pardon me,' he said to the reporter. 'Elsie, Connie, you go that end of the alley and I'll go the other. Don't let anyone come along here.'

And off he went again, clapping his hands to command attention. The crowd was clearing at last, heading to safety, all except the reporter.

'One penny a time to see the unexploded bomb!' a familiar voice suddenly called. 'And it ain't going to be here all day, the coppers are on their way. One penny a time to see what Adolf sent over!'

And there was Ned, the little ringmaster, heading back to his circus. At his heels were half a dozen people who looked to Elsie as though they had just finished work. Was there no opportunity Ned couldn't turn into cash?

But Jack had other ideas. 'No way through here!' he told them, giving Ned a fierce look. At his words, Ned's followers gave a grumble of disappointment. 'If you've already paid a penny, my friend will refund it.'

'They ain't paid nothin',' tutted Ned. Then he shrugged and told his hopeful audience, 'Sorry, lads, no bomb today!'

Ned's crowd of sightseers craned their necks and stared over Connie and Elsie's heads, evidently trying to get as good a look as they could from where they were standing, before turning back and walking away disappointed.

The reporter smiled at Ned. 'I don't suppose I could take a look?'

Ned narrowed his eyes, sizing her up and no doubt the size of her purse too. 'Who are you?' he asked. 'How come you ain't been chased off?'

'I'm a reporter for the *Evening News*,' she told Ned. 'What a story! *Brave children keep Whitechapel safe from unexploded bomb*. Do I need to pay you a penny to see this bomb?'

'A penny?' Ned scoffed. 'You pay me a penny and I'll go straight to the *Morning News* and tell them that the bloody *Evening News* exploits war orphans. A measly penny to see my unexploded bomb? I'll tell you this for nothing, I know you got expense accounts and all that gravy. You pay me a decent fist and I'll tell you a story'll make you hair curl. Rotten old nuns, an orphanage flattened and us, the kids of the Blitz, keepin' honest Londoners safe from a bomb!' He put his hands on his hips. 'What's your name, anyway? Who is it thinks they can give homeless orphans a penny when there's snow on the ground?'

Jack winced and warned, 'Ned!'

But Ned shook his head. 'No,' he said. 'A rotten old penny? I'll bet she'll make more than a penny when she puts *our* story in the paper. Ain't I right, miss?'

'My name is Esther Hammond.' She held out one manicured hand. 'Were you living at St Mary's Orphanage?'

Elsie wasn't sure they should admit to that. What if the nuns came and found them?

'We ain't naming names,' said Ned as he shook her hand. 'But a shilling'll do for now.' He turned his hand over to show a grubby palm as he waited for the money. 'Much obliged to you, Miss Esther Hammond of the *Evening News*. One shilling, if you please.'

Esther placed a coin on Ned's palm. He looked at it, then nodded his approval and slipped it into his pocket.

'Come on then,' he said. 'You three wait here and keep the alley. Coppers'll soon be here.'

And with that he led Esther away into the warehouse, where the bomb waited. Elsie could already hear him telling their story, starting with the farm where they'd become a family. Would Esther really write about what happened to them in the newspaper?

Elsie imagined Dad picking up the newspaper and reading about them. He'd come back to Whitechapel and find them, and he wouldn't be missing any more. The thought warmed her, even as she knew deep inside her that it couldn't happen. Wherever he was, he wouldn't be reading the *Evening News*.

'Down this way, lads!' a voice called, echoing in the alleyway. It was the police.

The tallest policeman stopped in front of them and gave them an unexpected smile. 'You kids've done well, raising the alarm and keeping everyone safe.' Elsie grinned proudly. 'We'll take over now, you can all run off home,' he went on. 'Who are you? I don't think I've seen you lot around here before.'

'Just doing our bit,' said Jack proudly. 'When you write it up, Officer, don't forget to mention us. We're the Blitz Kids and we're keeping London safe.'

It was getting dark as the children headed away from their post by the warehouse, leaving the police to take over. Elsie was relieved to go, and yet she felt a strange sense of responsibility for the bomb. But she knew they'd done all that they could.

Esther said she had to go off and *file her copy*, which sounded very important. She gave them another shilling as she left. 'And if you ever need anything, you know I'm at the *Evening News*.'

Elsie and her friends needed a lot, but how could they ask a newspaper to help them when a story could lead the nuns, or evacuation officers, straight to them?

Ned beamed, turning his face up to the darkening sky, as the little gang made their way along the alley. 'We've got the start of our very own stash!'

'I promised Elsie a bag of chips,' said Jack, squeezing his little sister's hand even as Ned shook his head, to Elsie's surprise. 'I think we should all have one; we need a treat. What do you think, Connie?'

'Chips? When did we last have chips?' she said with a grin, as her stomach rumbled loudly.

As the light faded, it got colder, and the promise of a warm bag of chips was even more appealing.

'Nah,' said Ned, to Elsie's surprise. She couldn't imagine why he wouldn't jump at a bag of golden chips, slathered in salt and vinegar. They didn't have their ration books any more and, until they'd made enough money for Ned to get them replacements, a few meagre mugs of soup and scraps from the shops who didn't ask questions were all they had. 'We've got to save what we make so's I can get the ration books. We can't chuck it away on chips. We'll go to the Jewish soup kitchen.'

Connie said, 'Are we allowed to go? We ain't Jewish. Me nan said her dad was, but I dunno if that means we can have their soup. You're definitely not Jewish, Ned.'

Ned winked. 'I am when they're doling out soup. Look, they ask anything thorny, just turn on the tears and they'll give you another cupful!'

'Ned!' Jack exclaimed, horrified. 'I promised Elsie chips and she's getting chips. As for the soup kitchen, you've been lying to good people, going there.'

'I've been lyin' 'cos I've been starving,' Ned huffed. He kicked a stone with the toe of his scuffed boot and, as he did, the sole flapped open. 'Why shouldn't I eat just 'cos I got stuck with the nuns?'

They headed down an icy, almost derelict street.

Connie said, 'It just don't seem right. But I s'pose we can use some of our stash to get your boot mended.'

Jack nodded. 'And we'll call by the soup kitchen, just to leave a penny or two. If Ned's been pretending to be Jewish to get what he can, we should leave a donation.'

The streetlamps were shielded for the blackout, giving out little light. Here and there, roof tiles on the houses were loose, letting in the snow, and some of the drainpipes hung half off the edges of the roofs. Bricks were missing from the walls, and somewhere a dustbin clanged over and a cat yowled furiously. Footsteps hurried away.

Pippa was here somewhere, she had to be, and yet, no matter how vigilant Elsie was, there was no sign of the little dog.

Maybe the street was completely innocent, but there was something about it that Elsie didn't like. She had that unnerving sensation again of being watched, even though the blackout curtains were drawn.

Elsie knew that people tried to go about their evenings as best they could, cooking their dinner, listening to the radio or reading the newspaper, hoping the sirens wouldn't go off. But if they did, they'd all be running to the shelters in their back gardens, or taking a chance and going to the nearest Underground station. Perhaps that was where the sensation of being watched came from; this was a whole country on the alert.

They followed Ned, his broken boot making a slapping sound against the snowy pavement as they went. His foot would be freezing and his thin sock soaked through with the snow leaking in.

They soon arrived at the soup kitchen, a brick building that looked at first like a pub. Snow had settled in the carving on the stone that ran above the door. *Soup Kitchen for the Jewish Poor*. The scent of vegetable soup drifted from inside, and Elsie's mouth watered.

'It don't say *Soup Kitchen for People What Ain't Jewish*,' Connie observed in a whisper.

An old man in a long winter coat and a fur hat that had seen better days was making his way along the pavement, leaning heavily on a stick. He looked over at Elsie and her friends.

He evidently recognised Ned, because he said to him with a chuckle, 'Ah, you've brought your friends! Come in, have some soup. It's a cold evening.'

'All right, Mr S!' Ned beamed. 'These here are my mates I

told you about from the farm, Connie, Jack and his little sister, Elsie. Elsie's the lass whose dog I've asked you all to keep an eye out for. This is Mr Solomons; you should hear some of his stories!'

Jack smiled and said, 'Pleased to meet you, sir.' He bowed his head and took a deep breath. 'I want to apologise for my friend, Ned. We're not Jewish, but it's so hard to find food without our ration books.'

Mr Solomons' face crinkled into a smile. 'Very pleased to meet all of you, too. And don't you worry, our food is for everyone. There's a war on.' He tipped his head to one side, and told Elsie, 'We've been hoping to see your little dog, but no sign of her yet. We'll keep looking, never you fear.'

He pushed open the door, which opened into a small, tiled hallway. Once they were all inside and the outer door was shut, to avoid leaking any light in the blackout, he opened a door at the far end.

The soup kitchen looked like a café, with tables and chairs laid out, and a hatch in the wall to the kitchen. Mr Solomons had gone up to the hatch and was talking to a woman, her hair in a bright scarf. There were the usual government information posters on the wall, but then there were others in a script that Elsie couldn't read but which she knew was Hebrew.

The place was noisy with conversation, and the sound of cutlery scraping against china. There were all sorts of people in the soup kitchen; some other old men like Mr Solomons, and old ladies too. There were younger adults, who looked pale and pinched with cold and hunger, and there were some children, a girl and a boy, sitting with their backs to the door.

'I'll just go and leave a donation to cover our soup,' whispered Jack.

The two children sitting at the table turned round, and Elsie was amazed. She pointed, bouncing on her toes. She couldn't believe it.

It was twelve-year-old Susan with her younger brother, Ben, who was the same age as Elsie and Ned. They'd all known each other from the orphanage. She hadn't seen them since the moment the siren had sounded on the night the orphanage was blown to bits.

'It's you lot!' Susan said, rushing to her feet. 'I wondered where everyone had got to!'

Ben had got up, too, and was smiling at them. 'I told Susan you'd be all right – Ned knows Whitechapel like the back of his hand!'

Elsie was stunned. They looked thinner than before, and their thin winter coats and scarves had blotches of dried mud on them. Susan's blonde plaits were in desperate need of a tidy, and Ben's light brown hair was standing on end as if he'd had a surprise. Where on earth had they been staying?

'No way!' Ned exclaimed, darting between the tables as he ran towards his friends. 'Where you been living?'

'We've been in a churchyard,' Ben replied. 'There's an old shed full of spades and the like. It ain't bad, but it's bloomin' cold, and the roof leaks.'

What a place to live in, Elsie thought, running for your life only to have to hide among the dead.

'We found this place, and asked if they could spare a little food,' Susan explained, 'and Mr Solomons said it didn't matter that we ain't Jewish, what with there being a war on.'

Ned frowned and dropped his voice to a whisper. 'We've got a place under the arches,' he replied. 'We've got some blankets and a fire, and look...' He took a handful of pennies from his pocket. 'We're havin' chips for tea. D'you fancy chips an' all?'

Ben's eyes widened in amazement. 'Course we fancy chips. Where'd all that money come from?'

'I was singin',' Connie replied, 'Jack got some work down a warehouse, and Ned, well, you know what he's like!'

Ned nodded proudly. 'And if you want, you can come

under the arches with us.' He shrugged. 'It ain't much of a place, but it's just until we've saved up for something better.'

Susan and Ben shared a glance, the sort of telepathic look that siblings shared.

'Yes, please!' Susan nodded, looking relieved. 'We'd love that. Don't worry, we'll help out and earn some money too if we can. If we're all together, there's nothing we can't do!'

TWENTY-SIX
ELSIE

London, September 1940

Elsie and Jack stood on the pavement in their old street in Bethnal Green, with Ned, Connie and Rob. They were carrying everything they'd brought from the farm, and they'd eaten their way through their bread and cheese.

The air was full of dust and smoke from the air raid the night before. As the smoke began to clear, Jack's lip trembled, and Elsie held his hand tight.

Right in the middle of the terrace, right where their home at number eight should've been, there was nothing but an enormous, rubble-strewn hole.

Elsie couldn't move, couldn't breathe. She held Jack's hand even tighter. He was frowning, his mouth puckered.

'If she got to the shelter in time, then—' Connie began, just as they heard footsteps.

Mr Woods from number twelve came up to them. His house was still standing, just. He looked pale, his hair uncombed.

'Haven't you heard the news? I hate to be the one to break it to you. Only...' His voice was suddenly choked. With effort, he said, 'I'm so sorry. Your mum didn't make it. She died in the raid.'

Elsie and Jack collapsed in on themselves, holding each other tight and sobbing until it seemed like all they'd ever do was cry. Then Connie, Ned, and Rob put their arms round them too. They sobbed in the blitzed street where the Taylors' home had once been.

It can't be true, Mum can't be dead.

Elsie broke out from the embrace of her brother and her friends, and scrambled down into the rubble, tears coursing down her face. But as she dug through the cracked bricks and soot-covered ruins, through the shards of broken furniture and torn scraps of curtains, she realised nothing had survived. Apart from...

She ignored the others as they called to her. It was a scorched scrap of paper. A letter. She recognised the spread wings of the bird on the RAF's badge. It was about Dad.

Elsie's throat felt tighter and tighter as she read it through her tears. She put the letter in her pocket. She couldn't show it to the others, because it'd make Jack sad, and losing Mum was bad enough, but she'd keep it safe and show it to him later.

She wanted to shout and scream, to call for Mum and Dad. But no matter how much she tried, she couldn't make a sound.

TWENTY-SEVEN
LISETTE

Now

Her home was hardly a palace, but at least it was her own, even if it was just one long room at the top of a rickety Victorian building. The dormer window had a view of the narrow Soho street below, and the skylight opened onto the roofs behind. Lisette had to share the bathroom on the floor below, but she had a small hob to make coffee, when she could find it, and heat up food. She had divided the room with a curtain, separating her bed, at the back, from the living room she'd made at the front. A pink scarf she'd draped over a lampshade gave the room a rosy glow, and the rag-rugs on the floor stopped the bare wooden floorboards from looking cold.

On the walls, she had tacked up posters from Jasper's club to hide the fading, peeling wallpaper. The only photograph she had of herself with Tom stood on the narrow mantelpiece. They had been standing in front of a mirror, grinning for their picture, Tom's dark hair neatly combed back, his patterned tie loose. Propped up on the table by her bed, and on the low bookcase in the living room, were photographs of Lisette with her mother.

Just as she was slipping her feet into her heeled shoes, ready to leave for Jasper's club, her doorbell rang.

'Maman, who could that be?' she asked the photograph of her mother, taken on a sunny day in the Jardin du Luxembourg years ago.

She turned off her lamp before lifting the blackout blind, then opened the window. She shivered as she spotted figures hurrying through the slush, women in their fanciest frocks and men in uniform. Down in the street, right by her front door, she saw the top of a fedora worn by a man in a dark-coloured greatcoat. He was reading a newspaper, and smoke coiled upwards from his cigarette.

Although she couldn't see the man's face, she knew who it was. *Wyngate.*

As though he sensed her gaze on him, he lifted his head and looked up at the window.

Lisette waved to him. A tremble went through her and she tried to tell herself it was from the cold, but it wasn't true. Wyngate had brought her back from the dead; there was a thread between them now. That was it, wasn't it? That was why he often appeared in her thoughts. But it wasn't a romance, because what would happen to Tom? Even though he was no longer here, he was still in her heart.

'Wyngate!' she called, her voice still a little sore and rasping. 'Just a moment.'

She closed the window and drew down the blackout curtain. She had to go carefully on the narrow, uneven staircase as she was still feeling bruised. She squeezed past the bicycle in the small hallway and turned off the bare lightbulb before opening the door.

'You found me, then.' Lisette smiled and gestured for him to come inside.

As Wyngate stepped into the hallway, he held up the paper so Lisette could see the front page. He tapped one gloved finger on a story towards the bottom of the page. Not the headline, which carried more news of the horror that had unfolded at Bank, but something rather more uplifting than that.

Lisette closed the door behind him and switched the light back on.

'*Whitechapel saved by brave children,*' she read. She looked up at Wyngate, but his expression wasn't giving anything away.

Early yesterday evening, four children found an unexploded bomb in the ruins of the old Cohen and Sons warehouse in Whitechapel. While one of them ran off to raise the alarm and summon help, the other three, ranging in age from eight to fourteen formed themselves into a human chain to prevent anyone from getting close. Doubtless, their quick thinking saved many lives, including those of a mother and her baby. These children, who did not wish to be named, call themselves the Blitz Kids. *They have had a difficult war; they were evacuated to a farm where they were ill-treated, and on returning to London were lodged at an appalling orphanage. Since it was bombed, they are now homeless. It is to their credit that these children, who have been let down by everyone, think nothing of risking their lives to help others. London ought to help them.*

What an amazing little gang of children they were. 'Yes, of course we must help them,' Lisette said. 'If we can find them.'

Wyngate took his cigarette from between his lips and held it out to her.

'It's a start,' he said. 'There must be somebody in Whitechapel who'll tell me something.'

'There must be, and I will help too,' Lisette replied, taking his cigarette. She took a grateful puff to steady herself, then passed it back to Wyngate. She was sure he was a busy man, but she said, 'I'm just going to Jasper's. Would you like to come along?'

He nodded. 'I might even stop for a drink,' he replied.

After Lisette had gone back upstairs to wrap up in her coat and scarf, and fetch her things, she and Wyngate headed off to Jasper's. It was only after she had linked her arm through his that she realised it'd happened without either of them thinking about it. She had been so used to walking arm in arm with Tom that it hadn't occurred to her not to. But it was nice walking like this with Wyngate.

She wished there wasn't a blackout, and that she could walk with Wyngate past the neon signs and the rectangles of light that used to shine through the windows of the pubs and clubs. But Soho still had its magic, even as Lisette lit their way with the feeble gleam of a blackout torch.

'I saw the four of them yesterday,' Wyngate said as they walked. 'Connie was singing for coins outside the Feathers in Whitechapel. She had quite a crowd.'

'You saw them?' Lisette gasped. 'But you weren't able to speak to them?'

Wyngate sighed. 'Ned got them all running before I had a chance,' he said. 'And as they went, he was shouting about me being a social services snoop, just to put people in my way. He's smart, that lad, Whitechapel doesn't like snoops chasing children.'

Lisette sighed. 'Why would they run away?'

'Because he probably thinks I told the nun they were in the hospital,' was Wyngate's bitter reply. 'But Whitechapel isn't such a big place. We'll find them.'

Although it was dark, Lisette spotted the door to Jasper's club, and the large figure of Tiny.

'Evening, Tiny. Do you know my friend, Wyngate?' Lisette asked him.

Tiny nodded. 'Not too well, which means he don't give me no trouble,' he said, eyes crinkling with a welcoming smile. 'Evening, sir.'

Wyngate acknowledged Tiny with a nod of his own as the other man opened the door and they entered the club together. Lisette felt proud to be on Wyngate's strong arm.

Lucien was playing 'I've Got You Under My Skin' as Ruby sang in a sequinned dress that glittered in the light. The club was starting to fill with customers – women in their best dresses, men in uniform and wide boys in their expensive suits – all watched by Jasper at the bar.

The siren might sound, but they'd be safe down here. There were even camp beds and blankets in the storeroom in case the raids went on so long that people couldn't get home.

Lisette gasped. She'd suddenly had an idea.

'I know how I can help the children!' she excitedly told Wyngate as they headed to the bar. 'They could stay here, in the club. It's safe, there's beds and blankets, and I could stay here with them.'

As soon as she'd said it, she realised how ridiculous her idea sounded. Children in a nightclub? How would that work?

Wyngate looked around, narrowing his eyes. Then he turned and put the newspaper on the bar in front of Jasper. 'Have you seen this?' He thundered his fingertip down onto the story he had shown to Lisette.

Jasper looked taken aback and dropped the ash from his cigarette. He glanced at Lisette with surprise, as if to say, *Is this your friend?* But he lowered his gaze and read, his lips moving silently, then looked up at Wyngate.

'They certainly sound like a brave bunch,' he said. 'I agree with this reporter, though, they should be helped. They shouldn't still be in London, for a start.'

'We met them the other night, when the orphanage was bombed,' Lisette explained. 'It was the night Bank station was hit. They're homeless, Jasper. They don't trust anyone. If they're sent to the countryside again, they'll come straight back. But we could help them – what if they stayed here, in the club?'

Wyngate was watching Jasper closely, his eyes unblinking. After a moment he said curtly, 'If it costs you money, I'll pay it.'

Jasper ran his hand over his oiled hair. 'It's not a question of money. This is a nightclub. Imagine kiddies running riot while you're in the middle of a song.'

Wyngate sighed, then nodded and turned to Lisette. 'I'll talk to some people I know. I'll find somewhere.'

'*Non*, they'll stay here.' Lisette put her hand on Jasper's arm, trapping him. 'Just until we can find somewhere permanent.'

Jasper puffed on his cigarette, returning to the newspaper. Then he sighed. 'At the risk that I might come to regret this – all right, they can stay here. But not for too long.'

Lisette beamed. 'I knew you'd say yes! You have a good heart, Jasper.'

But first they had to find the children. Where, in all the shadowy alleyways and derelict streets of London, could they possibly be?

TWENTY-EIGHT
ELSIE

Now

Where on earth was the letter she'd found in the ruins of their home? If only she could remember what it said, and where she'd hidden it, then she was certain they'd know where Dad was. But whenever she tried to think back to that day, no memory surfaced. It was lost to her, just like her voice.

Maybe, with time, it would come back to her. Elsie had been thrilled that Susan and Ben had moved in with them under the arch. She had missed them, and it gave her hope that they'd find the other children from the orphanage one day.

It was freezing cold in the arch, despite the small fire they lit in the evenings, and the floor was hard and uncomfortable. No one wanted to use the mattress they found after a rat had poked its head out of it. During the daytime, the boys went out to find jobs – Jack's legitimate work earned less than the jobs Ned was getting from the wide boys.

Elsie, with Susan and Ben, would stand with Connie while she sang, but the cold weather seemed to keep people at home; not many coins landed in their hats. It hadn't helped that

Connie had insisted on moving her pitch because Wyngate had seen them.

At least they'd had the promised chips, but it was only on that first night with Susan and Ben, a meal to welcome them to their little family. It was hard getting food without ration books. Even though cafés and restaurants weren't rationed, they suffered from shortages too, and the children couldn't afford to eat out three times a day.

Day by day, Elsie was getting thinner. She could see it in Jack's face, too, his eyes becoming more prominent as his face became more gaunt. He was fading away in front of her.

Thank goodness for the soup kitchen, which meant they each had one hot meal a day and could come inside from the freezing cold. Mr Solomons would get up from his chair to welcome them, and Miriam, who passed them their bowls of soup through the hatch, smiled when they came in. There was a small lavatory with a basin and soap, so they could wash.

Then, one morning as Elsie began to awake from a dream where she was walking endless streets, trying to find the letter, she felt someone tapping her arm.

She opened her eyes. The weak, early morning light came through the slats of wood, and the door was ajar, letting in the freezing air. Above her, in the semi-darkness, she saw a man.

He pressed one finger to his lips, then leaned close. Elsie could smell the drink and smoke and sweat on his skin as he whispered, 'Where'd they hide the money, love?'

He was tall and wiry, and even in the gloom she could make out his greasy, pockmarked face. The cuff of his overcoat was fraying and the brim of his fedora was bent. He wanted their money, their tiny stash of hard-earned coins.

She shook her head, cringing away from him. Her arm was under the blanket and she urgently prodded her finger against Jack's side.

'Come on!' the man growled, as Jack shifted and mumbled

in his sleep. 'I ain't got all day. I seen you kids singin' down on the corner. You made a pretty penny!'

That's our money! We earned it fair and square.

Her heart rushing in her chest, Elsie drummed her feet against the floor, trying to wake up the others.

Connie stirred, lifting her head as she asked blearily, 'What's goin' on?'

'Connie,' Jack murmured. Then his eyelids opened with a start and he shouted, 'Get away from her!'

Jack leapt from beneath the blankets as the man's hand lashed out. He went to seize Elsie, but Ned shoved her aside. The man's narrow fingers locked round Ned's wrist instead and he jerked the little boy towards him.

Dazed and trembling, Elsie rubbed her arm where she had landed against the floor.

Connie staggered to her feet, the blanket tangled round her legs. She slapped the man's arm, shrieking, 'Let go of him!'

Susan had jumped up and was trying to prise the man's fingers from round Ned's wrist, her face red as she yelled, 'Leave off!'

A flash of silver caught the hazy morning light and suddenly even Ned's flailing stopped. Because resting against his narrow, pale throat was a knife blade.

'Money,' said the man, throwing Susan aside with a jerk of his arm. 'Now.'

'Please don't hurt him,' said Jack, holding up his hands. 'We don't have anything but a few coins. And you want to take them? We're children. We're all on our own!'

Susan had hit the floor, and now crawled across to her brother. They hugged each other, staring up at the monster who had invaded their arch. Elsie huddled beside them. It seemed so unreal, like something from a film, but she could see the sharp blade, and smell the stink of stale sweat and booze.

Connie had stopped slapping the thief and had taken a step back.

'Look, mister,' she said carefully, her gaze fixed on the blade held to Ned's neck. 'We're starvin'. We ain't got much.' A sob rose up her throat, and she desperately cried out, 'Don't hurt my friend!'

'Then gimme the cash.' He pressed the blade harder against Ned's throat. Elsie saw Ned and Jack exchange a look and, in the younger boy's eyes, she saw unmistakable fear. This man was desperate. What if he lost his head and really hurt Ned?

Ned sniffed back a tear and whispered to Jack, 'It's in my cap, mate. Give it to him.'

And Elsie realised that even then, in the midst of his terror, Ned had thought not of himself, but of them. Because every night, he slept with their little stash under the flea-bitten old cushion that was his pillow. It made for an uncomfortable night, but it was the only way he trusted that the money would still be there in the morning. What was in his cap would be just a few coins, left there so he could sneak off early and get them what he could for breakfast.

Elsie looked up at her brother, his hair uncombed, his thin face pale and drawn.

Jack nodded. He backed away towards Ned's cap, where it rested beside the remains of their fire. As he went, he didn't take his eyes off Ned and the man, who was staring closely at him. Jack beckoned to the other children to approach him as he said, 'Let him go before I give you the money.'

Slowly, Elsie started to creep towards Jack, and Connie followed, helping Susan and Ben to their feet. Elsie heard a keening sound, and saw Susan, wiping her sleeve across her eyes, battling with herself not to cry.

The man shook his head. 'Money first.'

Jack picked up the cap, then approached the man as though he was a wild animal. Ned was completely unmoving in his grasp, his eyes wide. When he was an arm's length away, Jack emptied the coins out onto the floor.

'Now let Ned go,' he said. 'And you can pick up your money.'

The man narrowed his eyes, then flung Ned towards Jack. Ned landed heavily on his knees. He scrambled up onto his feet and darted past Jack towards the others. He grabbed Elsie's hand and held it tight as he whispered, 'I weren't scared of him.'

Elsie squeezed his hand in reply.

The man scrabbled on the floor for the coins. 'This all you got?' he sneered, cramming the coins into his pocket. 'What you bloody spent your take on?' He brandished the knife towards Jack. 'You had more!'

And suddenly Jack exploded. He bolted towards the man, his fists flailing as he yelled, 'Get out! Leave us alone!' The knife clattered to the floor and Jack snatched it up. Now it was he who brandished the blade, jabbing it at the robber. 'Go on! Before I do to you what you would've done to Ned!'

'Easy, easy, laddo.' The man raised his hands and chuckled, taking a step forward. 'Come on now, sonny, come—'

He gave a screech of pain as the blade swept across the palm of his hand. 'Get out!' Jack bellowed. 'Now!'

Elsie rushed her free hand to her mouth.

'That's told him!' Connie yelled. 'Go on, clear off!'

The man shook his bloodied hand.

'Bunch of little bastards,' he spat. 'I hope a bomb lands right on the lot of you.' Then he turned and ran, leaving the kids alone. Jack stood his ground as he watched him go, his breath coming in heavy, ragged bursts.

Elsie hurried up to Jack and flung her arms round him. She wanted to say thank you, but she still couldn't make a sound.

'You should be one of them commandos, Jack,' Connie said. 'I never thought I'd see you take on a mugger!'

Elsie could feel Jack shaking as he put his arms round her

and held her tight. He didn't say anything for a few seconds, as Ned came over and patted his back.

'You did all right, mate,' said Ned. 'We're all glad you're on our side. From tonight, we'll keep a watch out. Anyone comes near, they get chased right off!'

Jack drew back and kissed Elsie's cheek. 'Good idea, Ned,' he said firmly, but Elsie could hear the tremble in his voice.

Ben grinned up at Jack and said, 'You're our hero, Jack Taylor!'

'And I'm looking out for you all,' Jack said. 'We're *all* looking out for each other.' He drew Susan and Ben into a hug, then invited Connie to join them with a jerk of his head. 'Let's find some breakfast, then go to work and earn back what he just stole.'

But what if the man with the knife came back again?

TWENTY-NINE
LISETTE

Now

When she stepped down from the train at Whitechapel that afternoon, Lisette realised she was on the very platform where she'd met Ned and Connie. With a shudder, she remembered the racket from above ground as London was pummelled, and the dreadful moment when everyone was thrown sideways with the force of the bomb.

She steeled herself as she went up the escalator. She tried to distract her thoughts by reading the government information posters, advising people to wear white in the blackout, always carry their gas masks, count to fifteen before going into the dark.

She went out into the street, which was dirty with slush, and spotted Mr Wyngate standing near the exit. He stood out in his smart, dark blue coat, watching the street from under the brim of his fedora.

'Bonjour,' Lisette said with a smile, falling straight into French. She tried very hard to ignore the spicy scent of his cologne; Tom had worn nice cologne, too. 'I hope you haven't been waiting long?'

'We'll start at the pub, then retrace the path to the bombsite,' Wyngate replied in French, his gaze dropping to Lisette's feet; was he wondering if she could manage it in her heeled, fur-lined ankle boots? Then he held out the cigarette he was holding and said, as though it had only just occurred to him, 'Bonjour.'

They made their way down the street, over the cracked paving slabs. The shops they passed had little on display apart from war bonds adverts and home-made signs cheering the locals on. *Open as usual*, one shop declared. *Whitechapel stands against Jerry!*

'I've tried to speak to the journalist. She's never in,' he told her as they walked. 'I've told them it's War Office business. She'll suddenly remember how to use the telephone.'

'She must know more than she printed,' Lisette said. 'Would they have told her where they're staying too?'

Wyngate shrugged one shoulder. 'She'll tell me what she knows.'

They walked on, past a group of women. Lisette and Wyngate stopped to ask them about the children, but they insisted they hadn't seen a thing. They asked an old man selling newspapers and a woman stacking crates outside a greengrocer's; they both shook their heads.

'They haven't been back to the Feathers,' Wyngate said. 'That's my fault.'

'It isn't,' Lisette assured him, tightening her arm round his. 'So many adults have treated them badly. They can't trust anyone.'

Wyngate said, 'Then they're wiser than their years.'

For a moment, she thought a frightened child had peeped at her through his eyes.

'You know you can trust me,' she told him.

'I know the landlord at the Feathers. If he knew where they were living, he'd tell me.' Wyngate looked to Lisette again and gave the faintest hint of a smile, 'I think I probably can trust you, yes. Do you know Whitechapel?'

'A little,' Lisette told him. 'My friend Tilly lives here. She's a singer. That's why I was in Whitechapel the night that... I'd come to see her.'

'You trust her?' Wyngate asked.

'Yes, I do,' Lisette replied.

Wyngate nodded, then stopped mid-stride. He flicked his cigarette away and said, 'Then we'll start with her. Address?'

'Hooper Road,' Lisette replied.

Wyngate gave a curt nod and set off again, towing Lisette along through the filthy slush.

Soon they arrived on a short, narrow street of terraced houses. All the windows were criss-crossed with tape. There had once been railings outside the houses, and they looked undefended without them.

Lisette knocked on Tilly's front door. It didn't take long for it to open.

'Blimey!' Tilly said, pulling her fraying emerald silk robe around her. Her hair was under a matching scarf. 'I weren't expecting visitors, nor your new boyfriend! He's a handsome one, ain't he!'

Lisette blushed furiously. After Tom, she had decided she couldn't love anyone again. If Tom hadn't been coming to see her, he'd still be alive.

Wyngate was utterly unreadable.

'No, no, Wyngate is a friend,' Lisette insisted. 'We just need to ask you about something.'

'Come in,' Tilly said, and coughed behind her hand as she stood back.

They went into the sitting room, which smelt of eucalyptus oil and was packed tightly with Victorian furniture. Tilly gestured for them to sit on the overstuffed sofa.

'So you ain't inviting me to be the bridesmaid?' she chuckled as Lisette sat down.

She knew Tilly was teasing, but Lisette didn't want Wyngate to think she had a crush on him. She admired him, but her heart was like a shop with its shutters pulled down.

'Have you seen the children in the newspaper?' asked Wyngate, without any attempt at niceties. 'They raised the alarm about the unexploded bomb?'

'Yes!' Tilly dropped into her armchair. 'They call themselves the Blitz Kids.'

Wyngate nodded. 'They've been making money by singing on the corner outside the Royal Feathers,' he said. 'What do you know?'

Lisette tugged gently at Wyngate's sleeve. She gently teased, 'You can sit down beside me, Wyngate. You don't need to stand like a policeman.'

Wyngate looked from Lisette to Tilly, then finally sat beside Lisette.

'I saw a girl singing outside the Feathers,' Tilly replied. 'Such a sweet voice. I didn't realise she was one of them Blitz Kids.'

'That might be Connie; she's fourteen or fifteen. She has a scar on her face.' Wyngate touched his gloved fingertips to his cheek. 'Was it her?' He kept his gaze on Tilly's face.

Tilly's eyes widened. 'Yeah! I've seen her around with some other kids too – a little girl bundled up in a huge coat, a girl with blonde plaits and a little lad with dark hair.'

Lisette's heart leapt. Wyngate's eyes had widened just a little and the air between them had filled with a fizzing energy.

'Where?' he asked.

Tilly rubbed her chin. 'I was on Cable Street, and they was comin' the other way. It was late afternoon, so maybe they were goin' back to wherever they've found to sleep. If I'd known, I would've helped them.'

Cable Street had become infamous when Oswald Mosley's fascists had tried to march through Whitechapel. They had been outnumbered by thousands of ordinary people, who had fought them back. It had become known as the Battle of Cable Street.

'Cable Street,' Wyngate murmured. And Lisette was sure she saw that flicker in his expression again. 'Towards Pinchin arches?'

'That's it.' Tilly sighed. 'You don't think them poor kiddies are sleepin' under the railway arches?'

Wyngate sprang from his seat, leaving Lisette with no choice but to join him, her hand still holding his. He gave Tilly a nod, then he was heading for the door, not even pausing.

They were out in the street again. All of London felt so tired, and Lisette saw the exhaustion even more clearly in Whitechapel. The people they passed in the freezing, slushy streets looked like they wanted nothing more than a good night's sleep. But even if there wasn't an air raid, it was impossible to sleep deeply; everyone kept an ear out, just in case the siren started to wail.

The area had never been wealthy anyway, and the war was leaving its mark. Houses damaged by time and neglect stood no chance of being patched up. They had to change their route twice to avoid streets that were fenced off, where rubble had cascaded over the roads and unsafe houses leaned at drunken angles.

Lisette slipped a few times on the slush, so held tightly to Wyngate's arm. They picked their way past the rickety shell of the factory. An image of Tom flashed before her eyes, the blanket being pulled back so that she could see his face. The once lively, loving Tom, lying there grey and frozen. Gone.

Lisette fought herself to push the image away. She wouldn't be any use to the children if she gave way to her grief.

Behind the factory, they saw a row of arches under the

viaduct, most of them sealed off with wooden panels. The paint was peeling, and holes were smashed through the panels. The doors were hanging off their hinges. Rubbish was piled up; old rags, torn mattresses, threadbare tyres.

Wyngate paused and drew in a deep breath of the frigid air. Then he whispered, 'Children shouldn't live here.' He reached out and placed the flat of his gloved hand on the dripping bricks of one of the arch supports, where the thaw had run rivulets in the soot.

There was something in his voice, as if he was trying to hold something in. A memory, something painful; she could hear the echo of it.

Then at the sound of a scraping footstep echoing through the arches, Wyngate darted up his hand and pressed his finger to his lips. He took a few stealthy steps forward, edging along the road in the shadow of the brickwork. Lisette couldn't imagine staying here for even five minutes, let alone children living here alone. It was freezing and filthy, the only sound now a scurrying that might have been rats. If the children stayed here, she had the feeling that something dreadful would happen soon.

Broken glass crunched underfoot. There were definitely rats here; one ran across their path a few feet ahead of them. There was a stench of drains, and the air was musty and dank.

The door to one of the arches was half open, and Lisette heard the footstep again. Her stomach clenched.

There weren't any voices. Children were always making a noise, chattering, laughing, joking. But a couple of footsteps scraping against the concrete?

As she tightened her hold round Wyngate's arm, she glanced up at him again, trying to read his tense expression.

'Stay here,' Wyngate mouthed, but Lisette had no intention of doing anything of the sort. Instead she renewed her grip as they crept silently towards the sound of footsteps, which were punctuated by a heavy, phlegmy cough.

As she and Wyngate peered round the edge of the opened door, she knew they must have found the children's makeshift home. There were darned blankets, patchy cushions, a chair with a broken back, some dented tins of food lined up in a row.

A man in a fraying overcoat was poking through the blankets, a man who stank of stale booze and cigarette smoke.

Wyngate closed his hand over Lisette's and lifted it gently from his arm. Then he moved with a surprising turn of speed beneath the doorway, leaving the interloper with no time to so much as move before his arm was twisted up his back.

THIRTY
LISETTE

Now

'Chalky!' Wyngate said with cold cheer as the man wriggled and swore in his vice of a grip. 'What on earth are you up to so far from home?'

He knows him. But this wasn't a friend. And he was no friend to the children either. The man's sallow, unshaven face looked unhealthy in the half-light. He'd obviously fallen to the bottom of the bottle and couldn't get out again.

Lisette didn't feel any pity for him. There was something sneering in his expression, something taut and threatening even though he was immobile in Wyngate's strong grasp.

'Get off, you bastard!' Chalky bellowed, but there didn't seem to be much fight in him. Instead he coughed again, then spat a thick wad of yellow phlegm onto the floor and held up his hand. A filthy, bloodied rag was wrapped round his palm. 'Look what them little sods did to me! I only come asking if they had a couple of pennies for a starving veteran of the trenches.'

Wyngate gave a mirthless laugh. 'You've never been near a

battlefield,' he told Chalky. 'What did you do to get that wound?'

Could the children really have drawn blood? Lisette shook her head. Not unless they were frightened.

'How dare you come for money from children who are living like this!' she snapped, stepping through the door into the damp, cold space. 'And now you're back! What sort of a man are you?'

He turned his gaze on her and gave a lascivious smile.

'A pretty lass like you wants to be careful round these parts; pretty girls and kiddies ain't so tough as the folks who call Pinchin Street home.' Chalky glanced over his shoulder, then slid that gaze back to her. 'They found a lassie like you down here when my old nan was a girl, God bless her soul. No head, she had. No legs neither. Just the bits that matter left, eh?'

Chalky's laugh was something between liquid and rusty metal and Wyngate twisted his arm even tighter.

'Still hawking that old story?' He sighed. 'I'm too old to be scared of Jack the Ripper these days, Chalky. Now tell me what you've done.'

'Yeah…' Chalky sounded rather wistful. 'Yeah, you grew up, didn't you? I remember when you was just a little mute Frog. Still a motherless son of a whore, no matter what you call yourself.'

Lisette's hands clenched with anger. So he remembered Wyngate back when he was a little boy, and he'd lived here too. This repulsive man, who preyed on children who had nothing, had done the same to Wyngate back then.

'Don't you dare say those ugly things!' Lisette's hoarse voice echoed around the arch. She'd been called a Frog when she'd first come to England. And when she was a child, some of the kids on the street had called her mother a whore. 'Wyngate is worth a million of you – even more!'

Wyngate smiled that cold smile again. 'Oh, Chalky doesn't

mean it,' he said with surprising lightness. 'I hear you still owe Mr Dupree for that window you put through in Soho,' he told Chalky, whose unctuous smirk evaporated at the gangster's name. When Wyngate spoke again, his tone was as cold as the air. 'I hope nobody tells him where to find you.'

'I was only havin' you on!' Chalky laughed, but Lisette had seen the fear in his expression at Wyngate's threat. 'I come down this mornin', didn't I, just playin' a trick on the kiddies. I didn't mean to frighten them, poor little lambs, but the lanky lad slashed me with my own bloody blade! How about this? I'll just take my leave and I won't show my face round these parts again, eh? Maybe I'll have a wander down the Spike, see what's up?'

'That's a good idea.' Wyngate released Chalky's arm and the skinny, ragged man darted away, quick as a rat down a drain. He turned as Wyngate peeled off his immaculate leather gloves and, to Lisette's surprise, held them out to him. 'Don't let me hear your name around here again, Chalky. And wear these, don't sell them. Keep that hand warm.'

Chalky reached out and snatched the gloves away. Then he gave a nod of thanks and, with one last smirk for Lisette, skulked away.

As she watched him go, she whispered to Wyngate, 'How can you be so kind to him? I don't know what the Spike is, but I hope it pokes him!'

'Camberwell. It's a shelter for homeless men. Miserable, but it's a roof over his head on a freezing night.' Wyngate looked up and around the humble arch. 'They can't stay here tonight, Lisette. They'll freeze to death when the snow comes.'

Lisette bent down to pick up one of the blankets that Chalky had disordered and folded it. 'They can't stay here another moment. But what do we do? Do we wait here until they come back?' She laid the blanket down on the broken chair, so it wouldn't be on the hard, cold floor. As she picked up another blanket, her gaze was suddenly hazy with tears. 'It's awful. This is no childhood. And you'll think I'm ridiculous, but what makes it worse – as if it could be any worse – is that there's no toys. I had a doll when I was little. My mother saved and saved so that she could afford to buy it for me. I loved it. I still have it, I brought it with me when I came to England. But look around you, there's no toys here at all.'

And she wondered about Wyngate too, so closed off, so full of secrets. The immaculately dressed, handsome man from the Ministry who spoke French like a native. Who knew the nuns and the arches, who had been terrorised by Chalky as a mute child years earlier. Had he had any toys when he was a boy?

'We could wait for them, but if they see us here they might run before we can reassure them. We'll leave money and a note,' Wyngate decided. As he spoke, he was already reaching into his coat for a small notebook and silver pen. 'We tell them to come to Jasper's. That they're not in trouble and not in danger. What do you think? If they don't, we'll try again tomorrow. I hope we can make them listen.'

'Good idea,' Lisette said. 'Could I write the note?'

Wyngate gave his little smile, and held out the pad and pen. 'Don't you trust me?'

Lisette took them from him with a chuckle. 'I think if you wrote it, it might sound like an order,' she replied. 'And Ned thinks you're trying to send them back to the nuns.'

She flipped the leather cover open and started to write.

Dear Blitz Kids, my name is Lisette, the French lady. We were all rescued by Wyngate. Please trust me. I sing in a nightclub in Soho called Jasper's, on Preston Street. There's camp beds and blankets, food and water. It's warm, and it's in a basement so it's safe. You'll be looked after, and there are definitely no nuns! Will you please come as soon as you find this note? We read your story in the newspaper – we are so proud of you. Much love, Lisette xxx

'No nuns in a nightclub?' deadpanned Wyngate. 'Can you be sure of that?' He gave her an almost mischievous look, then took out his wallet and withdrew a note. 'We'll leave this too. If I do have to come back tonight, I'll bring all the blankets I can carry.'

'I might be a nun in disguise!' Lisette teased as she drew a note from her pocket and laid it down on the blanket that she'd folded on the chair.

With a shudder, she glanced out of the door at the dark clouds gathering over Whitechapel. 'We've done what we can. I only hope they'll come before it's too late. There's a snowstorm coming.'

THIRTY-ONE
LISETTE

As they walked back through the cold, slushy streets of Whitechapel, Lisette wished she'd stayed to wait for the children. But it was dark now, and blackout would follow in about an hour. There was time to go to a pie and mash shop for dinner, but they couldn't linger.

She felt like she was abandoning the children, just as she'd abandoned her mother to the Nazi invasion of France. And Tom, poor Tom.

Guilt clung heavily to her, weighing her down.

'I should apologise for grabbing your arm,' Lisette told Wyngate. She'd done it again, without thinking.

Wyngate glanced down pointedly at her feet again. 'Is it a choice between grabbing me and wearing wellies?'

Lisette chuckled. She was glad he was teasing. 'I don't own wellington boots. I'm not designed for the countryside, you know.' She glanced down at their joined arms. 'I hope you don't mind me telling you this, because we haven't known each other long. Only, you see, there was a man once, and... we always walked along like this. I didn't think – I just took your arm. It's silly, I know.'

'I don't mind,' he replied, brisk again in the face of her revelation. Then he asked, perhaps with just a whisper more gentleness, 'Is he fighting?'

Lisette shook her head, unable to reply at once, as her throat felt tight. If only he was. She'd be worrying about him every day, but at least he'd still be alive. 'He wasn't in the forces. I thought he'd be safe, he made government information films, you see. But... but he died. Last year, when the Blitz began.'

'I'm sorry.' Wyngate was silent for a moment as they walked on, but she got the impression that there was something else he wanted to say. As they turned a corner, he asked, 'Why did you come to England, Lisette?'

'There's plenty of women singing French songs in Paris,' Lisette replied, thinking back to the day she'd packed her suitcase and gone with her mother to the Gare du Nord. She hadn't realised that, only a few years later, darkness would fall across Europe. 'But not many singing them in London. And because... well, I am a little bit English, and just wanted to see what it was like. And you came here when you were very small, didn't you?'

He shrugged one shoulder. 'How long have you been here?'

He was a closed book, but bit by bit she was piecing together parts of his life. A little French boy who didn't have any English, who came to London and was left to the mercy of the nuns, before ending up under the arches.

'Since 1936,' she replied. 'I got a job at Jasper's, and I decided to stay. It's not as if I can go back to France.'

'You will,' Wyngate assured her. 'You said you were a little bit English. Grandparent?'

Lisette bit her lip. She didn't usually tell anyone.

'My father,' she whispered. The pie and mash shop was just ahead, the windows too steamed up to see inside. The blackout curtains would drop soon. 'He was an English soldier. He met Maman in Paris during the war, and they had a romance. Then he was off, and she never heard from him again.'

Wyngate nodded. He reached out for the doorhandle with his bare hand and Lisette saw that his skin was red raw with the cold since he had handed his gloves to Chalky. She hoped the children would come to Jasper's.

'After you.' Wyngate stood back and held the door for Lisette. As she passed, he looked up at the sky, where barrage balloons hung beneath snow clouds. His eyes were narrowed as he murmured, 'It's a bomber's moon. There'll be trouble tonight, and not just the snow.'

'The children.' Lisette shivered. She wished she could bring them here, sit them at one of the tables and buy them all dinner. 'I cannot—'

The siren suddenly blared.

Lisette quickly turned back to Wyngate and grabbed his arm, as around her the café filled with the sound of grumbling customers and chairs scraping back.

'Everyone out!' a woman in an apron shouted from behind the till.

Lisette and Wyngate were back on the street. Figures were hurrying around them, and as she tried to still her panic and focus she realised they were heading towards the station. It wasn't far, but how safe was it? After what'd happened at Bank station, after all those deaths, were they much safer down on the platform than in the middle of the street?

Her arm was tight round Wyngate's again, as they were buffeted by the hurrying people. There was a low hum of voices, a mixture of complaints about yet another raid.

On and on the siren wailed, echoing along the street. The red, blue and white circle of the Underground sign glowed just up ahead.

'I'll come by Jasper's after the all-clear; if the kids don't come, I'll go to the arch and try not to spook them,' Wyngate said, drawing Lisette to one side as they reached the station. 'Stay in the shelter, Lisette. No risks.'

'Where are you going?' she asked him, gripping the lapel of his coat as if it was enough to stop him. She saw Tom's face again, grey and still. He couldn't go into an air raid.

'They need all the help they can get,' he replied, meeting her gaze. 'Nothing's going to happen. I promise.'

'Don't do anything dangerous,' she pleaded, her words coming out in a sob. 'I'll look for the children in the station, they'll come here to shelter, won't they?'

There was a vibration under her feet. The hum of engines. The planes were overhead. Without thinking, she rose up on her tiptoes and pressed a kiss to Wyngate's cheek.

'Now get to the shelter.' His voice was gentle. 'And I'll see you when it's over.'

She reached up to brush her fingertip over the place she had kissed him, just to make sure the kiss would stay. A kiss that would keep him safe.

'Goodbye, Wyngate,' she whispered. 'Take care.'

With a wrench, she turned away from him. She pressed her back against the wall to stop herself from being absorbed into the crowd that rushed through the station's entrance.

The ticket hall was at street level and wasn't safe, but she would wait here for the children, then take them down to the platform. It wasn't without its dangers, but it was safer than where Wyngate was going, out into the streets where bombs fell from the sky.

THIRTY-TWO
ELSIE

Someone had been in the arch. They had folded their blankets and put them on the old chair that Ned had brought home. And they'd left money, and a note. The place felt different, as if their kindness had left a different sort of air behind them. Not musty and smelly, but something clean and nice.

Jack picked up the note and, as Ned busied himself lighting the little fire that was their only warmth, knelt beside the humble flames that the little boy conjured to life. He held the paper close to his face, the only way to read its contents in the dim light. After a few seconds, he lifted his eyes to the others.

'I'll read this to you all,' he said. 'Then we'll take a vote.' And he cleared his throat like a teacher addressing the class, then began to read.

The note was from the French lady who had saved Elsie. And Elsie knew that when she said, *We are so proud of you*, she meant Mr Wyngate too. She promised them food, and somewhere to stay that wasn't a cold, dirty arch. Elsie bounced on her toes with excitement. Jasper's place sounded like heaven, compared to where they were now.

Connie's eyes were dancing with joy. 'A blinkin' nightclub in Soho? That's a bit fancy, ain't it? I say we go.'

Susan looked wary, and protectively put her arm round her brother's shoulder. 'Sounds a bit odd to me. No one'd want kids in a nightclub.'

'Yeah, that's where grown-ups go,' Ben agreed.

'I know Jasper's,' said Ned. 'It's run by a couple of fruits! Proper la-di-da for Soho; a lot of my black-market blokes'd give their right arms to get in there. Mr Marsh boozes down that way. I heard that that dandy king who ran off with the Yank bird used to drink the place dry!'

The king who gave up his throne? Elsie remembered Dad grumbling about him abandoning his responsibilities *for a bit of skirt*. Maybe the nightclub was too posh for them, but Lisette wouldn't have invited them if she thought that.

'Lisette don't like your black-market pals, though, do she?' Connie reminded Ned. 'If we go to this place, you ain't bringin' them along!' Then she nudged Jack, grinning at him. 'What do you think?'

He looked down at the note and chewed his lip.

'I don't know,' he admitted. 'I don't like to think of Elsie and you and Ben and Susan in a Soho nightclub.'

Ned furrowed his brow, but after a second his frown turned to laughter. 'Yeah, you know better than to fret about me. I'll own a joint like that in a year or two anyway... full of gorgeous girls!'

Jack chuckled too, Ned's humour having seemingly lightened his mood.

'But,' he went on, looking at Connie, 'it's freezing and getting colder and after that character came round this morning... look, I don't think they'll call the social or the nuns. They've no reason to do that. They already know where we are, they could just send them here without leaving notes or money.'

Ned wiped the back of his hand across his nose and said,

'Vote on it! All them who's in favour of going to Soho, stick up yer hand!'

Elsie shot her hand up like a rocket, and Connie followed suit. Susan and Ben looked unsure but, tentatively, Susan raised her hand. Ben, glancing around the arch as if reminding himself that it wasn't much of a place to live, raised his hand too.

'Well, that's decided it,' Connie said, her arm still in the air. She waved it back and forth and whooped. 'Put on your gladrags, we're goin' to Soho!'

'A proper democratic decision,' said Jack with a smile, reaching to take Elsie's hand. 'And Ned, if we see Mr Wyngate, we're going to hear him out. No running, all right?'

Ned tutted, but murmured, 'Yeah, all right. Maybe he ain't a scab, I dunno.' He looked towards Elsie and said, 'You look right happy, Else. Your face is all lit up.'

Elsie grinned. She'd see Mr Wyngate again. If only Rob was still here, though, to go with them.

Jack beamed as he nodded his agreement. 'We've finally got a reason to smile,' he admitted. 'And we'll be in a warm place when the snow comes down tonight.' Then he drew his sister into a hug.

Just as he did, the sirens started to wail. Elsie sighed. She'd wanted to set off to Soho right that second, and now the Nazis and their planes were coming over. There wasn't time.

'Let's get to shelter!' Jack commanded the little group. 'Grab your blankets and stay together!'

They each put a blanket round their shoulders, and Connie handed out the tins of food for them to jam into their pockets. They were off into the freezing winter evening, as a large moon tried to penetrate the snow clouds that hung overhead. No one spoke as they worked their way past the wreckage of the bombed factory. Once they were on the street, the sound of hundreds of hurrying feet filled the cold air.

Everyone was flowing in the same direction, towards the

station. Elsie wondered if Pippa would hear the siren and follow the stream of people to the shelter, and then Elsie could take her to Soho with them.

There were people carrying suitcases, others with their possessions crammed into old prams. A baby was crying somewhere, and a young man rushed by on his creaking bicycle, ringing his bell and shouting, 'This way to the shelter!'

Elsie was so little that her legs already felt tired as she kept up with everyone. She held tight to Jack's hand, but she hated the fact that she was slowing him down. The thud-thud-thud of aeroplane engines had joined the racket of the sirens, along with the rat-a-tat of the anti-aircraft guns.

The ground shook. A loud boom filled Elsie's ears. She screwed her eyes tightly shut as the agonised sound of screams wrenched the air.

Jack plucked her up into his arms and drew back against the wall. As he did, he shouted, 'Everybody get back, are we all here?'

'Yes!' Susan replied.

Elsie opened her eyes and saw Connie running up to them. They were a small group, huddling against the wall, as the screams went on. She peered round Connie and her stomach clenched. On the other side of the road, where some shops had once been, there was nothing. Two buildings or more had gone, leaving snapped-off rafters and a collapsed floor, a bedroom door that opened onto a void.

In the street in front was a heap of bricks. Elsie's hands were clammy; she remembered the orphanage, the bomb dropping, the darkness, the ruins. People had been running to the shelter. And now they were buried under bricks, just like she had been.

'There's people under there!' Connie gasped, looking back. 'We have to dig them out!'

Jack nodded, then swallowed hard. 'I want you all to go to

the shelter,' he told them as the panicking crowd surged forward. 'Then I'm going to help those people.'

'I'm helpin' too,' Connie insisted, but Susan was crying, and Ben had buried his face against her arm.

The bomb had split the crowd. Most people went on hurrying for the station, even faster now that the bomb had shown them what to be afraid of. But there were others who were sacrificing the chance to get to safety in order to hurry to the pile of rubble. The lad on the bike jumped off and threw it aside, rolling up his sleeves. And there was a man in an overcoat and fedora, picking up the bricks and throwing them aside as if they weighed nothing. He—

It was Mr Wyngate.

Elsie pointed, jabbing her finger towards him. Her friend had come back and he was trying to save the people trapped under the collapsed building.

As Elsie gestured, Wyngate looked up, straight into her gaze. This time Ned didn't run, but Mr Wyngate did, dashing across the rubble towards them as he shouted, 'You should all be in the shelter!' He barely paused before he swept Ben off his feet and seized Susan's hand. 'Come on!'

And then they were all running towards the Underground.

'Lisette's looking for you inside,' Wyngate told them urgently as they reached the crowd that was pushing for the entrance. 'When the all-clear sounds, go to Jasper's in Soho. No arguments, no running away. Just for once, do as you're told.'

'Wyngate!' a voice called from inside the ticket hall. 'You've found them!'

Elsie craned her neck and saw Lisette waving, a dark red hat on her blonde hair. One of the station staff was trying to make her go down the escalator, but she shook her head. She started to come towards them, fighting the tide of people.

'Let me through!' Lisette shouted.

'Go with Lisette, all of you,' Jack told the children. 'There're people trapped under there. I've got to help get them out.'

Ned nodded. 'Me an' all,' he said.

'And me too,' Connie said. The three of them suddenly looked so grown up. Elsie wanted to help but she knew Jack would bring her back to the station, and put himself at even more risk.

'I wish you wouldn't— oof!' Lisette gasped as she was shoved against them by the crowd.

Mr Wyngate squeezed Elsie's hand, then said, 'I promise to look after them, Elsie, even if I wish they would go with you.'

Jack kissed Elsie's cheek and whispered, 'I love you, little treasure.' He handed Elsie into Lisette's embrace. 'Stay with Lisette, all of you, and we'll come to the station when we're done. If we don't get there before the all-clear, we'll come to Jasper's.'

Elsie saw pride in Mr Wyngate's face when he rested his hand on Jack's shoulder. 'I'll make sure of it.' He jerked his head back. 'Come on, they need our help.'

The crowd closed behind them as they went into the station. Elsie chanced one last look over her shoulder as they crossed the packed ticket hall towards the escalators, and saw Jack and Wyngate, Ned and Connie. They were heading out into the night, where the sirens shrieked and the bombs fell. And yet, how Elsie wished she was with them.

THIRTY-THREE
LISETTE

Lisette took the three children to one of the busy canteens that had opened in the tunnels. They were run by Lyons' Cornerhouses, and the tube train that travelled from station to station, keeping them stocked, was affectionately known as the Meat Pie Train.

She wished she could buy everything the canteen had so that she could feed them. She'd never seen children look so gaunt and thin, or dirty. She was aware of people staring, and she knew what they were thinking; that she'd looked after herself and neglected them.

She bought them a pie and a mug of cocoa each, and three more pies to give to the other children later. Although Lisette had missed out on her dinner, she wasn't hungry any more; all she could think about was the children.

They found a place to sit on one of the platforms, and Lisette made a nest for them with the blankets; although they were dirty and stained, it was better than the children being cold.

They seemed to have been kept awake by nerves alone, and

now that they were eating and drinking they were relaxing and starting to get sleepy.

Susan had introduced herself and her brother, Ben, and Lisette had told them a little about herself. Then she let Elsie rest her head on her lap, as Susan and Ben curled up around each other like commas. Lisette gently stroked Elsie's greasy hair as she fell asleep.

Around her, the other people sheltering were settling down too. Snoring already ricocheted off the tiled walls. An argument raged at the other end of the platform, and two old men were playing cards and smoking. A few feet from Lisette, a couple were snuggled under a blanket, having a kiss. He was evidently a sailor, as his girlfriend was wearing his naval cap. She glanced at them for a moment, remembering sheltering with Tom, leaning her head on his shoulder as they waited for the raid to pass.

I hope he stays safe. I hope he sees peacetime.

The trains were still running, and passengers knew not to stand on anyone's blankets, just as the people sheltering avoided bedding down in the area set aside for travellers. Even with the hum and squeak of the trains, Whitechapel's locals were getting their rest.

But Lisette couldn't sleep. Wyngate and the other children were out there, where the bombs were crashing down, where buildings were on fire, where walls were collapsing.

It was barely evening, but something about being down here as the battle raged in the skies above seemed to transform time. It might've been the middle of the morning or the dead of night, but hidden in the earth, huddled on the platforms and tracks, people were beginning to settle. The minutes ticked by and the crying babies grew content, a buzz of conversation filling the space where usually trains rattled, and still the couple just along the platform kept on canoodling.

She looked up and saw an older woman with copper-coloured dyed hair striding along the platform. She was dressed as if she was planning a night out on the town; a fox-fur stole, with shiny jet eyes, was draped round her neck, and she glittered with diamond earrings and a matching necklace. Her lips were ringed in red and her eyelashes were so thickly mascaraed, Lisette was surprised she could see. Her heels were so high that her confident stride seemed like a feat of acrobatics. And she was a big woman, too, as fat as a pie, which was quite an achievement with rationing.

There was something about her that looked familiar; perhaps she sometimes came into Jasper's. As she reached the sailor and his girl, who were wrapped tight in each other's arms, the woman gave a tut. Then she drew back her foot and kicked them. It wasn't a hard kick, but it was deliberate.

'Not in front of the kiddies,' she warned in an accent that was pure East End. 'There's a couple down there halfway to being at it and I won't have it. Not when there's kiddies around!'

The couple stared at the woman, and hurriedly sat up, the sailor reaching for his hat, his girlfriend tidying her hair.

'Blimey, Ma Mahoney!' the girl exclaimed. Lisette suddenly realised why the elaborately dressed member of the moral police had looked familiar. She was Toe Mahoney's mother. 'We're sorry. Len was just comfortin' me. We was only havin' a kiss.'

Ma Mahoney's rouged mouth fell open and she gasped, 'Mrs Windsor's girl!' She shook her head and pointed a red-nailed finger at the young woman in warning. 'I won't say nothing to your mother this time, young lady, but you keep your head. And keep one hand on your ha'penny. Sailors can be a rum lot.' Then she shifted her finger to point at the sailor. 'And me and my ladies'll be up and down this platform all night if we have to be. Any of that sort of thing, you'll get another bruise on the other leg!'

The sailor nodded dumbly at Ma Mahoney, clearly terrified. Lisette was astonished. A young man, who might end up escorting the merchant navy across the Atlantic where Nazi submarines lurked, must have nerves of steel. But he had crumbled in the face of Ma Mahoney.

'All right, Ma Mahoney, we'll behave,' the sailor said. 'By the way, me and my family was very sorry to hear about your boy.'

Ma Mahoney gave a nod of appreciation and replied with more gentleness, 'Well, that's very decent of you, young man. He was on the *Glorious*, you know.' She gave a long sigh. 'You'll know this, son, but the Krauts rammed her. Went right through her. And when they saw our lads in the water, they turned round and sailed off. Left them there to drown.'

As much as Lisette wasn't a fan of Ma Mahoney or her gang leader son, it was impossible not to feel sympathy for the family.

'It's dangerous out there,' the sailor replied, 'and we ain't fightin' gentleman. All we can do is hope that we'll come home. I'm sorry your son didn't.'

'I do miss my Wally. He was a brave lad. Handsome an' all, oh he was a heartbreaker all right!' Ma Mahoney said wistfully. Then she seemed to draw herself up a little taller. 'But I've got my Toe to look after and he's a good boy, is Toe. He's only got one hand you know. He lost the other saving a kiddie who'd gone under a train, so he's here at home with me. My Toe breaks his back for them who hasn't got a lot; dawn to dusk, charity, charity, charity. The East End's lucky to have him, he's a saint, that boy of mine.'

If Toe Mahoney was the charitable angel his mother believed, then why hadn't he helped the children? He would've known they had nowhere to live after the orphanage was bombed. As for saving a child who'd fallen under a train, Lisette didn't believe that for a second.

Ma Mahoney turned to look at Lisette and her face lit with dawning recognition. Lisette remembered Toe's words, that his mother was a fan, but the older woman's joy at seeing her seemed to darken as she looked at the ragged children who were cuddled around her, sleeping with full bellies.

'*Well*,' she said in a disapproving whisper. 'You're not as good a mother as you are singer, I can certainly see *that*!'

Lisette knew that getting on Ma Mahoney's bad side wasn't a good idea, but she bristled.

'I am not their mother,' she replied, trying to keep anger out of her voice. 'But they have no one else. As soon as this raid ends, I'm going to put a roof over their heads, and care for them.'

Ma Mahoney's mascara-heavy eyes grew wide. 'Are these the kiddies Toe saw singing down here on the night the orphanage was flattened?' She took her patent leather handbag from where it hung from her forearm and clicked open the gold clasp. 'Where's little Ned? He's a hard worker, that boy, always round at Toe's office, doing his odd jobs.'

'These are their friends,' Lisette explained. At least Ma's heart was in the right place. 'Ned, and the girl Toe saw singing, and Jack' – she gestured to Elsie, her head in Lisette's lap – 'this little one's brother, wouldn't come to the shelter. They're out in the air raid, trying to help.'

Ma Mahoney took out her purse and shook her head in sympathy as she said, 'There's always work with Toe. And the lads should get along to his boxing gym, that'll put some meat on them skinny bones of theirs.' She took out a note, then leaned down to hold it out to Lisette. 'Get them some decent shoes; they'll catch their death in them. Go along to Fieldgate Street and see Mr Sharp.' She glanced around and whispered, 'He won't ask for coupons if you say Ma sent you.'

Lisette nodded as she took Ma Mahoney's money. She didn't want to buy on the black market, but the children didn't have ration books. 'Thank you, Ma Mahoney.'

Ma smiled and nodded. 'Now I'd better get along on my patrol; me and my ladies are all that stands between this station and moral ruin!' She returned the purse to her handbag and snapped the clasp shut. 'I'll come along and watch you sing again, miss. You knock that smug Vera Lynn right off her perch!'

Lisette watched Ma Mahoney stride off to spoil another couple's evening.

She tried to doze, and she must've fallen asleep, as the next thing she knew Connie was shaking her shoulder.

'Mamzelle Lisette!' she said. 'We're back.'

Lisette blinked up at her and saw Connie, Ned and Jack. Their faces were darkened with soot, to the point that Connie's scar was no longer visible under the grit. Their clothes were even dirtier than she remembered. Where was Wyngate?

THIRTY-FOUR
LISETTE

Lisette hadn't wanted to leave Whitechapel without Wyngate, but she needed to get the children to Jasper's. And he knew that, if he couldn't find them at the station, they'd be at the club. She paid for the children's tickets to get to Piccadilly Circus, and was relieved when they only just managed to catch the last train. She had to hope the train wouldn't be another victim of the raids.

Trying not to panic, she kept an eye on the children instead. The youngest tiredly swung their feet, while Connie combed her dirty hair with her fingers.

When Lisette's reflection caught in the carriage window, her face floating like a pale ghost's, it was no longer herself she saw but Wyngate, his eyes closed like Tom's had been when they'd drawn back the sheet.

She shook her head, trying to cast the memory aside.

'You did see Wyngate just before you came back to the station?' she asked. Jack, Connie and Ned had already told her, but she needed to hear them say it again.

Ned nodded. 'You should've seen him, an' all!' He looked

from Connie to Jack, wide-eyed. 'He's digging through them bricks like a man possessed, bare-handed, pullin' folk out!'

Jack took up the story, telling them, 'It was enough to convince even Ned that Mr Wyngate can't be *all* bad.'

'He's such a kind man,' Lisette said. 'Was everyone all right? Were they all rescued?'

'Yeah, everyone come out.' Connie nodded. 'Only they had to be taken away in the ambulance and some of them looked like they was in a bad way. Remember that old lady, Jack, the one you helped with the broken arm?'

Lisette saw Jack's face light up, despite the tiredness in his eyes and the soot and brick dust that covered him.

'Agnes,' he said. 'Her husband was beside himself, but they got off to hospital all right.'

'Agnes and Ern!' Ned laughed. 'I liked them. They said I could come down their way and do their garden work for them if I needed a bit of money. Not like it'll pay as well as my gangsters, but you've gotta put a bit back in, ain't you?' Then he bounced on his seat. 'Oi, wait 'til that Esther type hears what we been up to. She's got herself a right scoop here.' He skimmed his hand across the air. 'Blitz Kids to the rescue again!'

Connie laughed. 'That's right, we were! I'll have to get a nice hairdo so Esther can take our photo!'

But Lisette noticed that Elsie was suddenly downcast, fiddling with a button on the coat that Wyngate had given her. She must've been so worried about her brother.

Once the train arrived at Piccadilly station, Lisette shepherded the children up the escalators and onto the darkened street. The famous statue of Eros had been removed, and the fountain he used to stand on was banked with sandbags. Other than the feeble glow of the muted streetlamps, the lights of the West End were out. Lisette led them through Soho's dark, narrow roads.

'Soho,' Ned sang, holding Elsie's hand protectively as they

walked. 'Full of saucy girls, but I don't know nothin' about any of that palaver.'

'And you shouldn't talk about that palaver either,' Jack warned good-naturedly. He gave Connie a warm smile. 'Not with ladies present.'

Connie grinned at Jack. 'Thanks, mate! I dunno, though, I'm pretty saucy!'

'The only saucy ladies you'll meet are the singers,' Lisette said. Tiny was on the door, and nodded hello. 'Tiny, meet the Blitz Kids. They're staying here for a while.'

Tiny gave the children a respectful nod.

'I read about you in the papers,' he said. 'You're moving in, are you?'

Ned nodded and replied, 'And you need anything, mate, you ask me. I've done of my trade in Whitechapel lately, but I'm expanding my operations into Soho.' Tiny nodded again, then gave Lisette an amused look. 'Ciggies, nylons, chocolate... even a bit of something for the petrol tank. Ned can lay hands on it!'

'No, you can't, Ned,' Lisette told him. 'You're here to keep safe.'

Lisette put her hand on Ned's shoulder and guided him towards the door. She wondered what would happen if Ned bumped into Dupree here, but they couldn't go on living under a railway arch.

They headed down the stairs, to the soundtrack of Ruby's voice and Lucien's piano.

Heads turned as Lisette ushered the children through the club. She just hoped that none of Ned's wide boys were in tonight. At the tables, women wore fashionable little hats and dresses made from silk or velvet. Men wore evening dress or their best suits. The children, their faces filthy with soot, their clothes fraying and torn, were a world away from the finery worn by Jasper's clientele, who stared at them in astonishment.

She noticed Ned wave to a man in a checked jacket with a

little moustache, and he gave a thumbs-up to a man in evening dress. Her heart sank. But at least she could keep an eye on him here, and maybe try to peel him away from the wide boys.

'We'll go backstage,' she said, with a nod for Jasper at his spot at the bar.

He froze, his cigarette halfway to his mouth, as he looked at the troop of ragged children, who gazed about his club with wonderment. 'Just let me know what you need.'

Lisette pushed open the black-painted door that divided backstage from front of house. She opened a door into an empty dressing room. There were posters on the walls advertising shows and films, which caught the children's attention. And most importantly of all, there were camp beds and blankets.

The children helped Lisette to set up the beds, and soon they were tucked up asleep, Ruby's voice and Lucien's piano an unusual lullaby in the background.

Lisette slumped in an armchair, but sleep wouldn't come. She saw Wyngate's face, hovering just out of reach. His hands would be red with cold, cut by the debris he had hurled aside to save strangers caught by the bomb. Even once the raid had ended, the unstable buildings could collapse. Nowhere was safe.

Please come back safe, Wyngate. The children need you. And so do I.

THIRTY-FIVE
LISETTE

It must've been the early hours of the morning when Lisette finally found out what had become of Wyngate.

He arrived at the club, his tired eyes looking out from a mask of soot, his smart overcoat grey with dust, spattered with mud and goodness knew what else.

Wyngate shook his head, the gesture barely perceptible. Then he murmured, 'Everyone's all right?'

'Yes, they're all right.' Lisette assured him. 'They're all asleep. They told me you saved people, digging with your bare hands.'

She glanced down and saw cuts across the backs of his hands. Would he let her help him?

'Nothing else to dig with,' was his simple reply. 'I went back to the arch to pick up their things.' He swallowed. 'It wasn't there any more.'

Lisette was suddenly cold in every limb. The bleak place the children had tried to turn into a home had been obliterated.

'They're here now, they're safe, and so are you,' she said. 'Come to the dressing room, I can help you get tidied up, and pour you a little whisky.'

Wyngate nodded. 'Which one's the dressing room?'

'The children are sleeping in this one; let's go to the one next door.' She opened the door and let him go inside.

The mirrors were crowded with photographs and good luck cards, and the dressing tables were covered with make-up palettes, powder puffs and perfume spritzers. Cotton wool dotted with make-up filled the bin, and a shoe with a broken heel lay under the sink.

'Being glamorous is a messy job,' Lisette told him.

Wyngate didn't say anything as he stepped over the threshold into the dressing room. Instead he stripped off his coat and threw it over a chair, then paused and tipped back his head, letting out a long breath of relief. What he'd seen tonight, Lisette couldn't guess, but she could imagine.

She wanted to rub his sore shoulders, but that would be too familiar. Instead, she went over to the sink and turned on the tap.

'You are a very brave man,' she told him. 'You went out into danger and saved lives.'

Wyngate went over to the sink and stood there, holding on to either side of the basin as he looked at his reflection in the mirror. He was silent for a long moment, then said, 'I could do with that whisky.'

Lisette went into the main room to the bar and poured Wyngate a double measure of Jasper's best whisky. When she returned, he was still standing exactly as he had been.

'Here's your drink,' she said gently, holding the glass out to him. Their reflections were cast back at them from the mirror; Lisette was rumpled from her doze, while Wyngate looked exhausted.

'There are a lot of people in this city that nobody cares about,' Wyngate said as he took the glass from her. 'They're thieving for someone, syphoning petrol, keeping the black market running. And it's like a business, Lisette. He has stores and he has employees. People who don't matter. People nobody really notices.'

Wyngate took a drink of whisky, knocking it back as though it was water.

'People who aren't going to run for shelters,' he went on. 'Because they need the few pennies they'll make for keeping his operation going.'

'I can't imagine what it's like to be so desperate for a few pence that they'd risk not going to a shelter,' Lisette replied. 'And tonight, these people that nobody cares about, were they caught up in the raid?'

Wyngate nodded. He put the glass down and began to unbutton his shirt.

'An illegal petrol store ignited,' he said. 'It's probably still burning. There must've been a dozen people inside; street people.'

In her mind, Lisette saw a wall of flames. She thought of Rob, the little boy who'd died stealing petrol because whoever had told him to do it hadn't cared a scrap for him.

'What an awful way to die,' she said. She watched Wyngate's fingers on his buttons and saw just how badly cut they were. 'I'm so sorry you had to see that.'

Wyngate took off his shirt and balled it in his fists. His knuckles beneath the blood and dirt were white as porcelain, his jaw tightening. 'The silly old fool should've gone to the bloody Spike.'

Chalky. She'd been so angry with him for preying on the children, and yet she hadn't wanted him to die.

'And nobody's going to care. Just like nobody cared about Rob.' He threw his shirt aside and turned back to the mirror. 'And whoever's running this show knows that.'

'But you cared about Chalky,' Lisette said. 'And the children, they cared about Rob. That has to mean something.'

She knew, though, that in the grand scheme of things it

didn't. Men like Chalky, thieving to feed their addiction, and children like Rob, left to the harsh mercy of the nuns, fell through the cracks, especially in a war.

They didn't speak as Lisette helped Wyngate to tidy up. As he washed, she found him a comb and a brush, and laid out a towel for him. She glanced at his bare torso. He was toned, but that didn't surprise her; she knew how strong he was. She shook the dust out of his clothes. Then, when he'd dried off, she opened the first aid kit. She dabbed his cuts with iodine, and put plasters over the worst of them.

'Will you stay?' Lisette had a feeling he wanted to bolt. 'There's a couple of armchairs in the room next door. They'll be so pleased if you're there when they wake up.'

His gaze darted to the door, then settled on Lisette, and he nodded. 'If you'd like me to.'

'I would.' She nodded. As she did, she wondered if Wyngate was the sort of person who liked to be alone after they'd been faced with horror. And yet there was something lonely about him that seemed to suggest that he didn't want to be on his own.

Once Wyngate had put the filthy shirt back on, she led him into the other dressing room, which was filled with the sound of gentle breathing and contented sleep. As she gestured to one of the armchairs, she heard someone stirring.

Elsie was rubbing her eyes. A broad smile illuminated her face as she pushed back her blanket to sit up. She got off the bed and came straight over to Wyngate, hugging his legs as if she wouldn't let go.

Wyngate dropped to his knees and took Elsie's hands in his.

'All right?' he asked the little girl in a gentle whisper.

Elsie nodded keenly. She looked so tiny next to him.

'I've got something for you. My mum didn't have much money. We didn't have anything, really.' As he was speaking, Wyngate released one of Elsie's hands. 'But I had one toy. And I think he's probably brought me a fair bit of luck.' He reached into his pocket. 'And now he can bring you and the Blitz Kids the same.'

In Wyngate's hand, Lisette saw a wooden doll, made from a clothes peg and painted to look like a pilot in a leather jacket with a flight helmet and goggles on top of his head. Elsie and Jack's father had been in the RAF; the little toy was a tiny version of their missing father. It was such a simple but beautiful little toy, slightly worn but undamaged.

Elsie took it carefully. She was evidently aware of how special it was to Wyngate, and she gazed at the toy with wide eyes. Then she smiled at Wyngate and her lips moved. She slipped her other hand from Wyngate's and brought out a pencil stub and some grimy betting slips.

She took her time writing something down, then handed it to Wyngate. *Thank you, Mr Winget! I'll treasure him! He looks like Dad. Haha. Ned and Rob got me a peg doll for Christmas but I lost her 'cos I left her in the orphanidge. He could of had a girlfriend!*

'He'd probably like one. It's been a while.' Wyngate smiled. And was it Lisette's imagination, or did his gaze dart up to meet hers? 'I'll bet you could make a real stunner for him.'

'We'll make one for him,' Lisette promised her, with a smile for Wyngate. The warmth of his smile remained. 'Would you like that?'

Elsie nodded.

'Tomorrow. Which is today.' Wyngate smiled again. 'Come on, back to bed. We'll still be here in the morning.'

Elsie grinned, then she got back under her blanket, holding the peg man tight.

Lisette and Wyngate settled in the armchairs. She reached across the gap between them and squeezed his hand.

THIRTY-SIX
LISETTE

After living under a freezing railway arch, the children's new home must've seemed like paradise. They wanted to know everything: who came to see the shows, what the performers were like, and where the magic came from that transformed a woman who was one minute powdering her nose to a performer on stage the next.

On their first morning, Wyngate went out to get some breakfast for the children, and dropped it off before heading to work. Lisette had found a waitress's pad behind the bar for Elsie and, as the other children were eagerly digging into their meal, Elsie had written a note: *Will Mr Winget be back soon?*

'I hope so,' Lisette had replied.

Lisette made sure they washed, and tried her best to hide her dismay at how filthy the water was. After she'd washed their hair, Connie explained that her uneven, shoulder-length hair was the result of the nuns cutting off her plaits, so Lisette did her best to tidy it up with nail scissors.

She tried to find pieces of clothing to replace their dirty, tattered clothes. There were long-abandoned coats in the storeroom; they needed taking up, and Elsie refused to wear anything but the coat that Wyngate had given her. She'd have to take Ma Mahoney's tip and take the children to visit Mr Sharp for new shoes.

Lisette rummaged through a box of discarded costumes. Connie wanted to wear the sequinned 1920s flapper dress. Lisette found some serviceable khaki shirts that would do for the boys. She told Ned they'd match his hat. For Susan and Elsie, there were pink dresses from a Shirley Temple routine, with matching ribbons.

'Shouldn't you be at school?' Lisette asked, as they stood in a group on the stage. 'I'm not much of a teacher, I'm afraid.'

'Connie and me were giving the young ones lessons at the orphanage,' said Jack. 'We started when we were on the farm.' He looked at Connie and smiled. 'We'd be happy to start again, wouldn't we, Con?'

Ned scowled and murmured, 'Stinkin' lessons.'

Ben pouted sullenly in agreement. 'I hate school.'

'But it's not exactly school!' Connie told them. 'And our lessons are the best. My nan always told me to do my best at school, so I know lots of stuff, and Jack's basically a genius.'

Lisette listened to the children in amazement. 'That's perfect. And I can teach you French.'

That seemed to catch Ned's attention and he said, 'Yeah... yeah, that'd be all right. Lots of cash washin' around with them Free Frenchies. I wouldn't mind a bit of the old Frog lingo!'

'Ned!' Jack warned, as Ned rolled his eyes. 'Don't be disrespectful.' Then he told Lisette, 'You'll have to excuse Ned; he doesn't think he needs an education because he has all his petty criminal friends.'

'I can see me chatting a bit of the old French,' Ned said. 'Might impress the birds an' all!'

Lisette chuckled. He was rather young to think about ladies, and yet it suited his swaggering, miniature wide-boy personality. Ned looked thoughtful, then pushed back the cap he always wore and said in his thick cockney accent, 'Tray bon, madame. I'll do it.'

Lisette sat them down on the stage and tried to teach them some French. Then she fetched paper and pencils for Jack and Connie to give their lessons. She perched on the edge of the stage, listening to them as they taught the younger children. They were naturals.

By early afternoon, the nightclub staff started to arrive. Lillian gave Jack a job as her cellar and glass man. Ned insisted on heading off to do some work for the wide boys. Brenda, who worked backstage, looking after the performers, was showing Elsie and Susan how to mend a torn hem. Even Jasper smiled as he came in and saw Jack lugging a crate of beer bottles while Connie, glittering in sequins, sang along to Lucien on the piano.

Jasper had brought a copy of the *Evening News* with him. He proudly laid it out on a table and read aloud.

Blitz Kids are Whitechapel heroes again!

Last night, London suffered at the hands of the Nazis in an early raid. In Whitechapel, a bomb hit a row of shops, and locals running for shelter were trapped under the rubble. The plucky Blitz Kids – who recently stood guard around an unexploded bomb – were immediately on the scene. With bare hands, they stood side by side with adults, clearing the rubble away and pulling victims to safety. When will the city thank these children, who have so little, but deserve so much?

'The *plucky Blitz Kids*, here in my club,' Jasper said, as Connie gave a twirl of delight.

'And it was Elsie who came up with it!' said Jack, beaming proudly, stooping to hug his sister. 'My clever-clogs little 'un!'

'One thing I wonder,' mused Ned, knitting his brow. 'Why ain't we chargin' for our services?'

Jack tutted and gave his friend an indulgent smile. 'Because,' he said, 'It's the right thing to do. Because me and Elsie know what it's like to lose your home. Hitler's trying to do for London and we're not going to let him, isn't that right?'

Ned shrugged and gave a wink. 'Well, when you put it like that... I'll kick Hitler in the bum for free all right!'

The children laughed, and Elsie grinned, but there was something in her expression that struck Lisette. She didn't seem as pleased about the article as the others did. Her large eyes kept returning to the newspaper.

Lisette took the children to get something for dinner from a nearby café, and on the way she dropped a letter in the post to Sir Rupert Cavendish, to let him know that the children were safe.

Lisette bought the children pies and steaming vegetables, fruit cake and custard. As Ned had disappeared, she took a pie back to the club for him to eat later.

Once evening arrived, Lisette let the children watch from the wings of the stage. Candles flickered on each table in the darkened room, casting light and shade across the faces of the audience as Lucien played the piano. His back was to them and, without missing a note, he'd look up and pull silly faces at the children, reducing them to giggles. Smoke curled up from cigarettes, glasses clinked, and low conversation buzzed around the room.

'Can I have a quick word?' Jack asked in a whisper. 'Just to say thank you really. Since we lost Mum—' He choked on his words, bringing up his fist to stifle the threatened sob. He glanced across to Elsie on the opposite side of the stage, her eyes wide as she watched the scene. In her hand, so clean and warm at last, she clutched the little peg doll that Wyngate had given her. 'Sorry.'

Lisette put her arm round Jack. His shoulders were so thin. 'It's all right, you can cry if you need to. I cry about my maman,' she said gently.

Jack shook his head and whispered, 'Elsie shouldn't see me getting upset.' He turned away a little. 'She used to talk, you know, before Mum. We were on a farm and they beat us and worked us to the bone. We ran away to come home and the house was gone, flattened by a bomb.' Another sob threated and Jack drew in a deep breath before the words came tumbling out. 'Elsie never talked again after that. She found this little stray dog around the orphanage and called her Pippa; but she lost her too on the night we met you. I'd give anything to find that little stray, Lisette, 'cos I think she might talk again then. She needs to know there's something good left in the world. We've lost everything except each other.'

And Jack buried his face against Lisette's shoulder, crying silently in the shadows.

Lisette couldn't reply at once as she held him. Her throat was too tight.

She swallowed. 'You're so brave, looking after your little sister, and all the others too. I listened to your lesson earlier, you were very good. There are things you could teach me. We'll do our best for Elsie, so she'll talk again. I wonder how we can find Pippa?'

'I look out when we go into the air raids to help,' he said. 'But I haven't seen any sign. And we have to keep going out, so other kids don't end up orphans like us.' He dashed his hand across his eyes. 'Do you think Mr Wyngate might be able to help track Dad down? Find out what happened to him?' He rubbed his eyes again, sniffing back the tears. 'We asked the neighbours in Bethnal Green if they'd heard about Dad – but they didn't know anything.' Jack swallowed again, gathering himself before he said, 'And we need to know where Mum's buried. I want to put flowers on my mum's grave, Lisette.'

'That would be a lovely thing to do,' Lisette replied, blinking back her tears. 'I'm sure Mr Wyngate can help find out where your mother's been laid to rest. And find out what happened to your father. You know, Mr Wyngate is the sort of man who can do *anything*. But you must be careful. Elsie needs you, Jacques.'

And he deserved his life, too. A future where he wasn't always looking out for everyone else. A future where someone would care for him.

THIRTY-SEVEN
ELSIE

Elsie was in the dressing room with Ben and Susan, listening to Jack and Connie read Enid Blyton stories. She'd been making a peg doll girl for her peg doll pilot, sticking alternating pieces of lace and ribbon round it, when Ned returned.

He swaggered into the dressing room and following in his wake was Lisette, and a man in full black tie and dinner dress. Esther Hammond, the reporter, was on his arm; Elsie remembered her from the day they'd found the unexploded bomb in the warehouse.

'Ladies and gents, meet Sir Rupert Cavendish!' announced Ned brightly. 'He's the bloke who's telling all the politicians that us kids need more help!'

Elsie hadn't met a *sir* before, and couldn't take her eyes off him. He looked out of place in the dressing room. He was so tall that Elsie felt tiny as she sat on her bed, staring up at him.

Sir Rupert's fine overcoat and the suit he wore underneath it, with the diamond tie pin, reminded her of Dad's stories from when he'd gone to the races at Ascot and seen the lords and ladies in their finery.

With Sir Rupert Cavendish in the room, Enid Blyton was

forgotten. Susan and Ben, sitting side by side, hadn't met Esther before and they looked from one to the other in astonished silence. Rupert greeted them all with a bright smile and, from inside his warm overcoat, produced bags of sweets so full that Elsie wasn't sure she'd ever seen so many treats in one place.

'I'm not used to being in the presence of such famous folk,' said a beaming Rupert. 'And I have lots to tell you, but first things first.' He dipped into his coat again and produced a handful of blue ration books, just like those the nuns had snatched away. 'A miracle! Ration books for all the Blitz Kids, personally approved by Winston Churchill himself. You shall go hungry no more and mademoiselle, I will repay any costs you have incurred.'

Elsie wondered what Sir Rupert would produce from his overcoat next.

Lisette gasped. 'You have made all the difference, Sir Rupert. But really, you don't have to give me a penny.'

He waved one hand to dismiss her concerns, then asked the children, 'Would you mind awfully letting Miss Hammond take your photograph with me? The people of London want to see their heroes!'

Ned nodded enthusiastically and said, 'Yeah, definitely we'll pose for a snap.' He beckoned to his friends. 'C'mon, pals, gather round old angel Rupert here! Everyone grab a ration book and make sure you hold them where the camera can see them.' He jerked his thumb against his chest. 'I know what makes a picture a picture!'

As the children got to their feet, Connie self-consciously rubbed at the scar on her cheek. Jack touched her arm gently and put his lips close to her ear, but Elsie heard him whisper, 'You look lovely.'

Connie blushed. 'And you don't look half bad yourself.'

Esther posed Elsie and the other children around Sir Rupert, proudly clutching their ration books. Elsie glanced up at Sir Rupert's huge smile, and it reminded her of the time Mum had taken her and Jack to Selfridges to meet Father Christmas.

The dressing room door was half open and Elsie heard footsteps in the passage outside. Her heart skipped – she recognised those steps; and then she saw him.

Mr Wyngate, carrying a large cardboard box, safely tied with string.

Elsie waved to him. He greeted her with a nod and the little smile he saved for her, but stayed out in the corridor as Esther snapped her photographs.

'Now, since you appeared in the newspaper, Londoners have sent gifts to Miss Hammond's office,' Rupert said happily. 'Gifts to say thank you to all of you. I'll have them conveyed to the club tomorrow. Safe to say, children, London loves you!'

Jack stepped forward and held out his hand. Rupert took it and they shook and Elsie was reminded again of Dad. The smile, the polite gestures, even the focus on lessons and education. How proud he would be.

'Thank you, sir, and Miss Hammond,' said Jack. 'We're very grateful for all you've done for us.'

Rupert nodded, then clapped his hand to Jack's shoulder. 'It's the very least I can do,' he said. 'Someone is using the most vulnerable people dreadfully. I won't allow that, Jack.'

'If the children were looked after in the first place, they wouldn't need to work with criminals,' Lisette said, as Esther's camera clicked.

Elsie thought of Rob, trying to steal petrol and vanishing into the flames. Ned glanced at Elsie and gave her a smile, then raised his hand towards Mr Wyngate and waved a little warily, prompting Rupert to follow his gaze.

'You have another visitor!' Rupert chuckled. 'I shall leave you to receive your guests. Mademoiselle, would you mind awfully walking out with Miss Hammond and me? So we can make arrangements to have the gifts sent over.'

'Of course.' Lisette guided them through the door. Elsie noticed that, when Lisette smiled at Wyngate, it was like the way Connie smiled at Jack. 'I cannot thank you enough for helping the children.'

Wyngate gave a curt nod as they passed. 'Gas masks,' he said. He stepped into the dressing room and put the cardboard box down on the ground. 'One each.'

'You what?' Ned exclaimed, as he followed Rupert, Esther and Lisette out of the dressing room. 'Sir Rupert brought sweets and ration books. You'll have to do better than gas masks, mate.' And with a shake of his head, the little boy trotted away.

Wyngate looked at the children, then at the bags of sweets. He settled on the edge of Elsie's bed and asked, 'Can I have a sweet?'

Elsie, who was sitting on the bed again, holding her half-made peg doll, smiled at Wyngate, taking in the angle of his hat and the darkness of his eyes. Thank goodness he'd come back.

Susan had dipped into the aniseed twists, and Ben was already working hard at a gobstopper. He tried to say something in reply to Wyngate, but gave up and nodded instead. Jack, however, shook his head.

'*Thank you* for our gas masks, Mr Wyngate,' Jack said, emphasising the first words. Wyngate frowned, then looked at Elsie as though to say, *what?*, before he took out a packet of cigarettes, then immediately put them back in his pocket.

Connie held out the bag of rhubarb-and-custard sweets to Wyngate. 'What Jack's too polite to put into words is that you didn't say please! But we're all sayin' thank you for the gas masks. Well, all of us except Ned.'

Wyngate fixed Jack with a steely glare, but Elsie could see the humour flickering in his eyes and, from her brother's shrug, she knew that he could too. After a moment, Wyngate took a sweet and said, '*Thank you.*' He popped the sweet into his mouth, then asked Jack, 'How was that?'

'It's a start.' Jack smiled. He settled onto his own bed as Wyngate picked up the little peg Elsie had been working on.

'She's going to be a stunner,' Wyngate whispered to Elsie. 'Just the thing for a bachelor like our pilot friend.' For a moment he was silent, before adding, 'I'm sorry I haven't been around. War got in the way.'

Elsie wrote Wyngate a note. *I'm making the doll look like Lizet. I know you can't help being away. Like our dad can't help it. But you're hear now Mr Winget!* Then she put her arm round him.

'I'm here now,' he assured her gently. For a long moment they sat in contented silence, before Wyngate closed his hand round the peg and whispered, 'He's going to be a lucky fellow, with a girl like her.'

I'm making her dress. And she needs her face drawing on. Will you help? Elsie wrote. With a hopeful smile, she held out the length of bright pink ribbon to him.

Wyngate opened his fist and looked down at the peg. Then he nodded.

'I'd love to,' he said.

The evening passed in happy business, as Elsie and Wyngate worked on the peg doll. In the background, Elsie heard the muffled sound of Lucien's piano, and Lisette singing, and, although she could never understand the words, she could understand the feelings. Lisette sounded happy.

Jack and Connie took turns reading aloud to Susan and Ben, and their voices drifted in and out of Elsie's mind as she and Wyngate finished the doll's dress and glued a little snip of yellow silk to the peg doll's head.

She watched as Wyngate carefully drew tiny eyes and red lips, with two little dots for her nose. And then she was finished. Elsie had been keeping the peg doll pilot in her pocket so that his girlfriend would be a surprise for him, and now she pulled him out. The pilot looked a bit like Mr Wyngate, she decided.

'A happy ending for Mr and Mrs Peg,' said Wyngate softly. 'He's waited a long time for that.'

The dressing room door opened and Lisette appeared in her red, white and blue gown, which she said looked like a French flag. Her blonde hair was decorated with ribbons in the same colours and she'd put glitter on her cheekbones.

'You've all been busy,' she said, glancing down at Wyngate and Elsie. Ned followed her through the door, stifling a yawn as he threw his cap onto his camp bed. 'It's bedtime now. Wyngate, if you don't need to hurry off, would you help me get them to bed?'

'We don't want blinkin' nightmares,' teased Ned. He punched Wyngate in the arm as he strolled past. 'Havin' you on, mate. Seein' if I can crack that face of yours into a smile.'

Wyngate exchanged a look with Elsie and it made her chuckle silently. Then he said, 'Only when I have something to smile about.' But then, to Elsie's surprise, Wyngate did smile.

It was Ned's turn to look suspicious now. 'What you grinning about?' he asked.

'It's your bedtime, little Ned,' Wyngate replied, giving Elsie a mischievous nudge. 'But for me, it's time to have a glass of Scotch and watch Lisette sing. So I have the winning hand tonight.'

Once they were all tucked up in bed, a small light glowed in the corner of the room. Elsie lay back against her pillow, clutching her peg dolls, as she listened to Lisette. She pictured her in her costume, and she imagined Mr Wyngate sitting at a table right in front of her, sipping his glass of Scotch.

As she started to drift off to sleep, she pictured her peg dolls, and slowly, slowly, they began to grow and become real. And they looked just like Wyngate and Lisette.

THIRTY-EIGHT
ELSIE

Even in the dressing room, Elsie could hear the sirens. And so could the other children. Jack and Connie had been reading to them, but now they put down Enid Blyton and got to their feet. Ned did too. If the sirens were sounding, there were people to save; the Blitz Kids had to go.

And Elsie had to stay behind.

'We'll be back before you miss us.' Jack hugged Elsie close. 'Love you, little sis.'

Elsie pouted, her arms folded, as she watched them put on their new coats and scarves and head off into the night.

Susan picked up one of the books and told Elsie, 'It's better if you stay here with me and Ben. We'll all be safe down here. And we've got this box of presents, too.'

Elsie looked over at the box, which had arrived earlier. It was overflowing with gifts from well-wishers. There were toy planes and battleships, comics, storybooks, small dolls and jigsaw puzzles. There were clothes: handknitted scarves and mittens, shirts and blouses. Elsie was humbled how much they had been given by people who didn't have a lot in wartime.

Some of the gifts looked quite expensive, but then the bombs could fall on anyone, rich or poor.

'And we get to find out what happens next in the book,' Ben told her, his eyes shining with excitement. 'Books can't kill you, Elsie, we'll be fine!'

Elsie wanted to be with her brother, and help, because she was a Blitz Kid, too. And she'd even come up with the name. But she was always left behind.

Jasper's nightclub didn't need to close when the sirens went off. The audience would stay in the basement, sheltering while Lisette and the others performed.

After a round of applause, Elsie heard Lisette singing another of her French songs. Although Elsie didn't understand it, it was so upbeat and even brave that it got her mind whirring.

She pictured the searchlights strafing the sky, and the ground shaking as the bombs fell, the darkness illuminated by the orange glow of the fires. She shivered as she imagined what was going on outside; she saw the silhouette of her brother, tall and thin against the flames.

Elsie wrote a note and handed it to Susan. *I'm going to watch Lizet!*

'You have fun.' Susan grinned. 'See you later!'

The fact that Elsie was wearing Wyngate's coat didn't tip Susan off, because Elsie wore it most of the time. It'd become a comfort blanket for her. There was no reason for Susan to suspect what Elsie was actually planning to do.

The audience were so absorbed in Lisette's song that Elsie could creep through the darkened room without being noticed. Jasper was at his usual perch by the bar, and she waited until he was whispering to Lillian before she risked edging past him. In only a few more steps, she was at the bottom of the stairs.

The siren had stopped for now, and she could hear the thud of the planes coming over and the rattle of gunfire trying to take them down. Her heart in her mouth, she tiptoed up the stairs, trying to make as little noise as possible, then peered round the door.

Tiny was a few feet away. Elsie could just about see the tin hat worn by the man he was talking to. They were both staring at the sky. She edged round the door, as stealthily as she had at the orphanage, when disturbing the nuns would have earned her the cane. Keeping to the edge of the street and hoping she'd be absorbed by the shadows, she walked in the opposite direction to Tiny. Her heart was beating so loudly, she thought that at any moment he would hear it. But she managed to reach the end of the street without him calling her back.

As she ran along the pavement, the distant boom of a bomb filling her ears, she realised she had no idea where the others were. How did they decide where to go?

East. They'd go east, wouldn't they? Where home used to be, and where most of the bombs seemed to fall.

She found her way to Piccadilly Underground station and merged with the crowd that was still flowing down the steps. Then she went straight to the spot reserved for passengers while other Londoners tried to get comfortable on the platform.

She got on the first eastbound train and stood behind some soldiers who were divvying up a precious packet of cigarettes. In the seconds before the doors slid shut, she could've run back onto the platform. Part of her longed to return to Jasper's, where she could be safe. But there was no turning back.

A few stops later, Elsie changed trains, and still no one noticed her, and finally she arrived in Whitechapel. The stench of smoke hung heavy, and grew stronger as she went up the stationary escalator, carefully climbing over the people who were sitting on the steps. The lights were off in the ticket hall, and she could see the thin glow from a blackout torch as an ARP warden in dark blue, with *W* painted on his white helmet, tried to read the paper in the gloom.

She got to the doors, and realised the metal grille hadn't

been pushed all the way across, perhaps to admit any dawdlers. Elsie saw her chance, and squeezed through the gap. She ran along the street with her hands clapped over her ears, trying to block out the scream of the planes' engines cutting through the sky and the clang from the fire engine bumping over the hoses laid across the road.

Elsie ran down a side street she recognised, and saw the fierce orange of flames up ahead. Her hands were clammy and she swallowed hard. She couldn't run away. Someone might need her.

When she reached the top of the road, she saw a row of terraced houses. Several of them were already ablaze, angry flames shattering the glass and bursting through the windows.

Elsie glanced this way and that. There was no fire engine in sight; the one she saw hadn't been coming here. Her friends were nowhere to be found. Had she made a terrible mistake?

She was about to turn and run back to the station when she heard a scream.

Elsie looked up at the last house in the row and saw the face of a woman at the window. She had flung up the sash and was calling for help as thick smoke billowed from the burning house next door and flames tore through the roof tiles.

'Help!' the woman screamed. She coughed, then shouted again, 'Someone, please, help me!'

THIRTY-NINE

ELSIE

There wasn't time to think. What if Mum had shouted from the window too, and no one had been there to rescue her?

With the woman's screams echoing in her ears, Elsie ran to the tiny front garden. Remembering where Mum used to leave the door key, she found one under a plant pot by the door. She scrabbled to unlock it and, once she was inside, saw flames beginning to take hold on the stairs, a fringe of orange trickling along the steps.

Elsie ran up the stairs, wincing as she squeezed past the dancing flames, and hurried into the front bedroom. The woman was wearing a dressing gown over her nightdress and her hair was covered by a scarf. She turned away from the window and stared at Elsie, and for a moment Elsie thought she was looking at her mum.

Through the open sash window, she could hear the clang of the fire engine's bell. They were almost here.

But they couldn't wait. Elsie yanked the eiderdown off the bed and beckoned the woman to follow her. Smoke was filling the landing, and Elsie headed for the stairs, trying to keep low, then flung the eiderdown over the flames.

It was enough to choke them out, but Elsie wasn't sure how long they had. She gestured to the woman to follow.

'Who are you?' she asked, before coughing violently. Elsie took her hand and guided her down the stairs and out into the fresh air. Just as they reached the pavement, the fire engine pulled up and the firemen jumped down.

'A woman and her little girl!' one of the firemen shouted.

'She's not my girl, she ran into the house and saved me!' the lady said, looking down at Elsie in surprise, then let go of her hand and coughed again.

The fireman looked amazed. 'You need to get to safety, both of you. Go down to the station – we'll handle this!'

But Elsie needed to find the other Blitz Kids, and there were more people to help. As the woman went on coughing, Elsie glanced down the street, wondering which direction to go in. And just as she did, over the sound of the planes and the shouts of the firemen, and the crackle and roar of the flames, she heard another sound.

Pippa's bark.

Elsie's heart was filled with a rush of love. There she was, a few yards up ahead, grey and black and so small, even as the flames cast an enormous shadow behind her.

'Pippa!' Elsie called. She froze where she stood, surprised by her own voice that she hadn't heard for so long. It was strained and scratchy, and barely audible, but it was the first time she'd been able to speak aloud in months.

But she couldn't lose Pippa now she'd found her. She ran towards the little dog, and tried her voice again. 'Pippa, it's me!'

The little dog turned and ran on, and Elsie saw now that she had a limp. Elsie thought Pippa was running away and her stomach gave a lurch of dismay, but the dog kept stopping and turning back, barking and wagging her tail.

Her little friend who had given Elsie back her voice.

Elsie caught up with her, and Pippa limped on, through a

side street, down an alley, the houses unlit, some left in ruins, the streets empty apart from fire engines and ambulances rushing by.

Eventually they came to a street where a whole row of houses had been flattened, and were collapsed sideways like dominoes. Pippa paused by the house at the end and sniffed at a sheet of corrugated metal that partly covered what had once been the front of the house.

'Is this where you've been living?' Elsie asked her. It was so strange to have her voice back.

Pippa headed through a gap between the metal and the side of the house, and Elsie followed, crawling after her. She needed to get help for Pippa, but she didn't dare carry her. What if she jumped out of Elsie's arms and was lost again?

Inside the flattened house, Elsie found Pippa sitting in a bed made from a velvet curtain. The little dog was proudly dragging her paw against something. A tiny figure.

And then Elsie saw what Pippa had brought to her nest. It was Ginger, Elsie's ragdoll, that Mum had made for her when she was a baby. She thought she'd lost it for ever in the wreckage of the orphanage.

Ginger looked back at Elsie with her button eyes, as if she was trying to tell Elsie something.

FORTY
LISETTE

It was late when Jack, Connie and Ned returned from the air raid. They were tired and dirty, and Lisette went with them to their makeshift bedroom to get them ready for bed. Ben and Susan were already asleep.

And Elsie was—

'Where's Elsie?' Lisette glanced around. She hadn't meant to wake the others, but Susan blinked blearily up at her.

'She was going to sit in the wings and listen to you sing,' Susan replied. 'But that was ages ago.'

'I didn't see her. And she's not here.' Lisette's heart was pounding faster now. She asked the others, 'Have you seen her? Did she go outside?'

Jack's face was white beneath the soot and grime from the air raid as he said, 'She can't be gone. Where would she go?"

Connie gripped Jack's arm, her eyes wide. 'You know she gets into a grump when we're out being Blitz Kids – maybe she went off to help?'

Ned nodded. 'She was mad as anythin' that she had to stop here while we went out. She's gone it alone.' He looked up at Jack. 'We'll find her, mate, I promise.'

'We have to!' Jack exclaimed. 'Anything could've happened to her on her own.'

All Lisette could picture was a little figure, silently moving through the streets while bombs fell and the ground shook.

'Would she have gone to Whitechapel?' Lisette looked around. She could hear Wyngate's footsteps.

'Mr Wyngate!' Jack said as Wyngate stepped through the door. His words were a confused garble, filled with panic and fear. 'Elsie's gone. We think she went out into the air raid alone and—' He choked. 'And she hasn't come back.'

Wyngate's jaw tightened, then he nodded. 'Right,' he said, matter-of-factly, but Lisette saw a flicker of worry pass over his eyes. 'Then we'll find her.'

Wyngate's reassuring presence was enough for them to see through their panic and come up with a plan.

They'd go to Whitechapel and split into groups, and comb street after street. They'd tell everyone they met to look for her, too: a small, silent girl, out on her own in the devastated city.

They'd find her. They had to.

FORTY-ONE
ELSIE

Elsie wasn't sure what woke her up first; the watery morning light creeping into Pippa's nest, or the sound of a voice calling her name.

As she sat up, trying not to bang her head against the low, sloping ceiling, she clutched her ragdoll. Was she dreaming? Was someone really calling for her? Perhaps she'd wake up and find herself back in the nightclub without Pippa.

But as Elsie blinked away the last remnants of her sleep, she knew she wasn't dreaming. Holding tight to Ginger, she crawled forward, Pippa beside her. Her paw was obviously still bothering her, and the little dog kept licking it. Where could Elsie find a vet?

She nudged aside the fallen sheet of corrugated metal and peered out at the street.

It was shrouded in mist, glowing pink from the sunrise. A crisp, white frost had covered the ruins. A familiar figure was emerging from the mist, and Elsie stared, wondering if she was only imagining it.

'Elsie!' Mr Wyngate called. 'Elsie, where are you? If you can hear me, make a sound!'

Elsie coughed away the dust. She'd never said her friend's name out loud before. But she was determined to try. And maybe he could help Pippa.

'Mr Wyngate...' she said with effort. Her voice sounded like sheets of rusted metal scraping over each other. She tried again, and this time it came out louder. 'Mr Wyngate! I'm over here!'

Mr Wyngate paused. He lifted his head just a little more, as though he couldn't quite be sure he'd heard what he thought he had. Then he turned in the direction of her voice and came running towards her with a cry of, 'Elsie!'

'Mr Wyngate, I can talk!' Elsie called, waving to him from inside the collapsed house. She couldn't bring herself to leave it. It was Pippa's little home, which she had claimed all for herself and invited Elsie into. Pippa thrust her head out of the space beneath Elsie's arm and gave a bark, but it sounded more like a welcome than a warning. She lifted her head and licked Elsie's face.

'I've never been so happy to hear a voice!' Wyngate admitted as he picked his way over the desolate rubble towards them. 'Everyone's out searching for you. Oh, Elsie, we've been so worried.' He dropped to one knee in front of them. 'And I assume this is the famous Miss Pippa?'

'Yeah, meet Pippa,' Elsie said slowly, the words feeling odd in her mouth. She held Pippa's good paw and waved it at Wyngate. Then she bit her lip as she thought over his words. People had been worried, out searching for her. 'Am I in trouble? Only, I found Pippa and she's hurt her paw.'

Wyngate dropped to one knee amid the rubble and passed the palm of his hand gently over Pippa's woolly head. 'The lady you saved – she wouldn't have got out without you. The firemen are all talking about the little girl who came out of nowhere.' He reached for Elsie's hand, and murmured, 'You're freezing.'

'It don't matter. I saved the lady.' Her voice still sounded harsh to her, as if her lungs were full of dust and cobwebs from all the months when she couldn't speak. 'See, I *am* a Blitz Kid, too. Jack'll be cross, but Pippa's hurt. Can you help her, Mr Wyngate?'

'I'll see what I can do. Which paw's giving her trouble?' As soon as he asked the question, though, Pippa answered on Elsie's behalf; she started licking her paw again and gave a little sigh of discomfort. As Elsie stroked Pippa soothingly, Wyngate lifted the little dog's paw and gently drew the tips of his fingers between the pads, his brow furrowed in concentration. After a moment, he gave a twist of his fingers and Pippa let out a yelp, then immediately lifted her head and licked Elsie's face. 'She had a little stone caught. All mended now.'

And Wyngate flicked the stone away into the rubble.

'You're my hero, Mr Wyngate!' Elsie smiled. 'Are my mates angry?'

Wyngate shook his head, then nodded. 'Maybe a little bit cross. But very proud. And very relieved.' He stroked one hand over Pippa's head. 'Can I take you both home?'

'Home?' The crater in Bethnal Green rushed back into Elsie's mind. 'But they bombed it, Mr Wyngate. The Nazis left a big hole.'

'Jasper's,' Wyngate said gently. He studied Elsie's gaze. 'You were very brave, Elsie. You did exactly what I would've done last night.'

'I wanted to help and they wouldn't let me.' Elsie coughed as her throat tightened. She forced herself to keep talking. 'But I hate Jack going out into them bombs without me. I know he wants me to be safe, but I want to help, and look out for him.'

She glanced down at Ginger, one button eye hanging loose, a tuft of her ginger hair torn off. She remembered her mum, sitting by the fire as she carefully fixed Ginger each time a seam wore through and stuffing poked out. An image returned to her of coming home, only to find a bombsite, and she hugged Ginger tighter still.

'I dunno...' she whispered. She felt ungrateful, after Lisette and everyone had given them somewhere to stay at the club. 'I like Lisette, and the music, and the dresses. But it just ain't home, Mr Wyngate.'

Wyngate nodded. 'Where's home?' he asked softly.

'Here,' Elsie replied. She looked around the tiny space Pippa had found in the crushed building. 'Well, not here exactly. But it ain't Soho. It's Whitechapel, or Spitalfields... somewhere in the East End. Because that's where me and Jack lived with Mum and Dad. But not Bethnal Green... I don't want to see the gap where our house was.'

She knew that Wyngate would understand.

'That's all right,' he assured her. Then he nodded towards Ginger and asked, 'Is this the doll you lost?'

Elsie nodded. 'Yeah, she's Ginger. Pippa made a bed from some curtains, and Ginger was right there in the middle. She must've got her out of the orphanage, what was left of it.'

'Good job, Pippa,' Mr Wyngate said, stroking Pippa's woolly back as her tail wagged. 'Very good job indeed.'

'See why I missed her so much?' Elsie smiled. 'She's the best dog in all the world, Mr Wyngate. So if it's all the same to you, I'll stay here with Pippa in her house.'

Wyngate glanced at Pippa. 'It's going to get very cold when night falls. How about we make a deal? Come back to the nightclub; Pippa and Ginger too,' he said. 'We'll bring Pippa's bed, and once we're back at Jasper's we'll have a think about what happens next. I've been where you are, Elsie, but I didn't have what you have. I didn't have friends or a brother who cared about me. I didn't have a roof over my head or a bed to sleep in. But you've got so much.'

Her brother was worrying himself to shreds. And her friends, too. Ned would have put aside his money-making schemes to find her, Connie and Susan and Ben had been calling her name. She shivered as a cold breeze trembled the corrugated metal, and dust scattered as a piece of brick fell from the ruins, landing only a couple of feet from Wyngate.

The East End was Elsie's home. But the house she'd lived in with Jack and Mum and Dad hadn't been like this. They hadn't lived in a bombsite.

'All right, we'll come back with you,' she replied.

'We'll get a taxi, travel in style,' said Mr Wyngate kindly. 'Do you want to carry Pippa or shall I?'

'I'll carry her,' Elsie told him confidently. 'But you'll have to carry Ginger.'

And without a word of complaint, Mr Wyngate took Ginger carefully and put her in the pocket of his overcoat, so she could look out at the world. Once Elsie was safely out, he stooped to gather up the curtains. They were dusty and ragged, but Mr Wyngate didn't seem to notice or care as he carried them against his immaculate overcoat with the same care he might afford a mink.

'Let's find a taxi,' he told Pippa and Elsie. 'Mr Churchill can pay for this trip.'

No taxi was going to stop in this street; half the houses had disappeared, and the ones that were still standing were condemned. Elsie and Wyngate walked beneath a bitter winter sun to the top of the road, to a street where there was more life. On either side were rows of small terraced houses with immaculate front steps.

The door of a house that didn't bear one of the warning posters opened and an elderly man peered out, stooped and small. Over his shoulder peered a lady of similar years, but tall and slender.

Elsie wondered what had caught their attention. 'Mornin'!' she greeted them, pleased to use her voice again.

'Morning!' called the man cheerily. 'Is that your little dog? We've been worried about her. We've fed her and watered her, but she always wanted to go roaming; Agnes said, *she's looking for someone, she is.*'

Wyngate nodded his sharp nod. 'They've found each other now.'

'You was lookin' after her?' Elsie gasped. 'Yes, she's my dog. I lost her after the orphanage got bombed. I looked everywhere. And she was here all along!'

'She was.' The old man smiled. 'You just wait here a second, young miss. Agnes went and bought her a collar and lead in case we could get her to stay. You can have it if you like?'

Without waiting for a reply, he turned and disappeared.

His wife was still by the door, in a thick cardigan and tweed skirt. Her arm was in a sling.

'Wait a minute, haven't I seen you in the papers?' She glanced over her shoulder and called, 'Ern, don't be long, we've got a celebrity out here!' Then she looked back at Elsie. 'We've got a Blitz Kid standing right here on our doorstep! I have to thank you, because if it wasn't for your friend – the tall lad – I wouldn't be here now!'

'That's my brother, Jack.' Elsie puffed her chest up with pride. She fussed Pippa as she said, 'He's the best brother in the world. And yes, I am a Blitz Kid.'

'I knew you was! There you were in the paper.' The old lady grinned. 'You're never out of it. This morning, there's another story, another lady who wouldn't be alive if it weren't for you.'

From behind the lady Elsie heard her husband's voice, and when he returned he was holding up the newspaper, reading from the front page.

I owe my life to that little girl, said Mrs Knowles. She looked like a little angel with her blonde curls. I thought I'd already reached the pearly gates when I saw her in the flames.

He lowered the paper and said, 'That's you, ain't it? We saw you with Sir Rupert!'

Mr Wyngate nodded. 'This is Miss Taylor,' he told the couple as the man laid his newspaper down on a table just inside the door. As he approached, holding out a collar and lead, Mr Wyngate added, 'And Pippa.'

'Mr Wyngate, why don't you tell them your name?' Elsie looked up at him, wondering why he was quiet and kept himself to himself so much. Why didn't he ever put himself forwards?

Her glance returned to the collar and lead, made from dark red leather, and she hopped from foot to foot with excitement. 'Pippa'll look proper smart in that. I can take her for walks now. Maybe go down Hyde Park!'

'Hello, Elsie and Pippa, and Mr Wyngate too. I'm Ern Hall and that's my Agnes.' As Ern spoke, he fastened the collar gently round Pippa's neck. 'If you ever want a cup of tea and a slice of war cake, you're welcome here.'

'Ever so welcome,' Agnes said. 'And what's all this about you and your pals living in a Soho nightclub?'

Elsie swallowed, coiling Pippa's new lead round her hand. 'It ain't so bad. Before that, we was living under the railway arches, and then a bomb blew them up!'

Agnes patted her chest, gasping with alarm. 'You poor lambs!'

Ern laughed and said, 'Well, you ever fancy Whitechapel, there's a right nice little row down the way. The council condemned it after a bomb dropped, but I said to Agnes, I wouldn't mind moving into one of them myself!' He laughed.

'I don't think there's anything wrong with them at all. They're still standing!' Agnes grinned.

Elsie glanced down the street. It reminded her a bit of Bethnal Green. Could they live here instead of the nightclub, in their own house?

Holding the bundle of curtains under one arm, Wyngate

held out a note to Ern. 'For the collar and lead. And for looking after Pippa.'

As Ern took the money he murmured, 'This is too much, Mr Wyngate, far too much.'

In reply, Wyngate gave the Halls a nod that seemed to signify the conversation was at an end. Once his wallet was safely in his pocket again he tapped his bicep and said to Agnes, 'Sorry about the arm.'

It was odd for Elsie to witness how uncomfortable Wyngate was with small talk, especially when he talked so naturally to her. But he was trying.

'Just a little scratch, nothing to worry about.' Agnes smiled at Wyngate. 'I was all dazed that night, and little wonder, but the funny thing is, I think I saw you there, too. Digging with your bare hands. Folk like you are the guardian angels of this city.'

Wyngate lowered his head a little, as though to escape the praise, though Elsie couldn't understand it. She had loved it when Agnes and Ern had recognised her as one of the Blitz Kids and had just about burst with pride when they'd talked about Jack with such admiration. Yet Mr Wyngate seemed to want to disappear, even as he said, 'There's a war on, after all.' Then he gave another of his nods. 'Right. Taxi.'

'Thanks for lookin' after my Pippa, Mr and Mrs Hall.' Elsie beamed. 'I hope we'll see you again soon!'

As Elsie and Wyngate walked along the pavement, she felt taller somehow. She had her voice back, and she had her friend Pippa trotting along on her smart new lead. And she and Mr Wyngate, and the rest of the Blitz Kids, were famous. The next time the sky darkened with Nazi bombers, they'd save even more lives, and this time Elsie would be with them.

FORTY-TWO
ELSIE

Elsie rode all the way in the taxi snuggled up against Wyngate, Pippa and Ginger in her arms. She wondered if he was teasing when he'd said that Churchill was paying, but then he worked for the Ministry. Perhaps he really would take the receipt to Churchill.

The taxi took them through the bomb-ravaged city, detouring around roads that were closed, and driving slowly past the shells of what had once been shops or homes. Elsie chattered to Wyngate about Pippa's adventures in Whitechapel; she was getting used to the sound of her voice. She was so busy talking that she didn't give much attention to the streets going by.

'I work for a man who knows a lot of things,' Wyngate told Elsie once she had paused for breath. 'And I've told him all about your mum and dad. We're going to find out where your mum was laid to rest, Elsie, and, if we can, what happened to your dad. I wish I could make you promises, but I can't.'

Elsie looked up at him. 'If you could tell us anything, anything at all, then me and Jack want to know. Even if the news is really sad. We know our mum's not comin' back and that even *you* can't bring her back from the dead.' She fussed Pippa, stroking her woolly fur. 'And we could tell ourselves Dad's still alive and go on thinking it for years and years. But it's better to know the truth, even if it's the worst news.'

Wyngate nodded. 'I think so,' he admitted. 'I'll let you know what Mr Gray finds out.'

'Mr Gray,' Elsie repeated, trying out his name with her new-found voice. 'Whatever he finds out, me and Jack'll thank him, even if we can't find a box of chocolates for him. Thank you, Mr Wyngate. I've never had a friend like you before.'

Wyngate rested his hand on Pippa's back and said, 'I hope I'm doing all right?'

Elsie nodded keenly. 'Yes, you're great!'

The taxi pulled up outside Jasper's and Elsie felt a stab of guilt.

'You're sure they won't be angry?' she asked.

Wyngate held his thumb and forefinger an inch or so apart. 'Only this much.'

'Back to base, troops!' came a booming, plummy voice along the street as a thunder of footsteps filled the air. 'We'll regroup, look at the maps and widen our search area. Operation Find Elsie isn't over yet!'

Sir Rupert was at the head of a search party, his overcoat flowing behind him, while Esther skipped along sideways beside him, snapping her camera. Following Rupert was Jack, and then the other Blitz Kids. Lisette was ushering them along from the back, along with Ruby and Lucien and Brenda.

They looked tired and drawn, their eyes circled with shadows that darkened their pale faces. They were worried, and it was Elsie's fault.

Her stomach turned somersaults as she wondered what their reaction would be. The driver leaned back and opened the door, and Elsie stepped out onto the pavement, holding Pippa in her arms.

'It's all right, I'm back!' she called, surprising herself at the sound of her voice echoing in the street. 'And Pippa too!'

They seemed to stop as one, or rather, everyone stopped except Jack. He alone picked up pace into a run, dashing towards his sister with his arms flung wide even as he called out, 'Oh Elsie, I've missed that voice! I thought I'd lost you.'

Elsie closed her eyes. She felt the strength and love of her Jack's embrace. She was all he had left in the world, and then, in a finger-snap, she'd disappeared.

'I'm so sorry, Jack,' she whispered. She glanced around and saw the astonished looks on her friends' faces at her voice. 'I won't run off again!'

'You want to watch out.' Ned chuckled. 'You ain't the only one with a voice like honey, Con! And Pip's bound to bring in some fresh customers!'

Ben and Susan giggled, and Connie beamed.

'There it is, there's that voice!' she said gleefully. 'You'll be singin' for ha'pennies with me soon! Put a ribbon on Pip's collar and we'll be a trio!'

Lisette blinked in surprise. 'I hope to hear lots from you now, little Elsie! We want to hear more from you!'

'All's well that ends well,' Elsie heard Rupert say merrily. 'And Mr... Wyngate, is it? Mr Wyngate saves the day again! Think of that in the headlines, Miss Hammond, the handsome hero bringing home our Blitz angel after she spends the night saving lives!'

'The camera would love you, Mr Wyngate,' Esther replied. 'With your matinee idol looks! Can I get a photo of you, standing with Elsie and Jack?'

Wyngate shook his head and took a step back. 'No,' was all he said. His next words were directed at Elsie, who was still tight in Jack's embrace. 'I'd better get to the Ministry. I'll come and see you—'

'There they are!' cried a shrill, angry voice. 'They're the scoundrels who have kidnapped our orphans! Arrest them, Officer, and return those children to my care!'

FORTY-THREE
ELSIE

Elsie tensed in every limb and clung on to Jack, Pippa pressed between them. She knew that voice; it haunted her nightmares.

Sister Benedict had found them.

She was furious, and her black robe seemed to swallow the light. Three women in dull-coloured skirt suits, one carrying a clipboard, strode along importantly in the nun's wake. A tall policeman was scanning the scene of Elsie hugging her brother, while the Blitz Kids hurried to surround them. Ben was crying, and Susan was trying to comfort him, while Connie put her arm protectively round Ned's shoulders. Lisette, still with red, white and blue ribbons in her hair and glitter on her cheeks, stood in front of the kids, her arms spread to block the nun's way.

Esther started to take photographs of them too, and the policeman intervened.

'You stop that right now, madam,' he ordered. 'This is a serious police matter.'

'Sir Rupert Cavendish!' Sister Benedict exclaimed, fluttering one hand to her chest. 'Sir, these children fled when St Mary's Orphanage fell to a German bomb. The Lord saved the lives of our orphans and these good ladies have done all they can to ensure those that we have found have been given a safe place to lay their heads.'

Her eyes filled with tears, her expression softer than Elsie had ever seen it. *No.* No, that wasn't quite true. This was the innocent, gentle mask that Sister Benedict donned whenever she hoped to convince someone that she was a harmless, kind nun. The nun pointed a trembling finger at Lisette. 'This woman is no better than she should be and her friend here is a vile character known to me of old. They have taken the children and filled their heads with nonsense.'

Wyngate folded his arms and cocked his head to one side, his dark gaze fixed coolly on the nun and her companions. Sir Rupert, meanwhile, was nodding sympathetically as he listened.

'Sir Rupert, I know that you are doing all you can for the displaced children caught here in London,' Sister Benedict went on. 'Please, sir, these ladies are from the social services. I'm sure you will do all you can to ensure the children are placed in my care today.'

Elsie stared at Wyngate. He knew Sister Benedict? He must've been in the orphanage, too, back when he was a little boy who couldn't speak. The uncarpeted corridors of the orphanage, the musty smell of the room where Sister Benedict kept her cane, the thin cabbage soup that smelt of drains, the gnawing hunger and the endless chill of that place came back to her.

'You must, Sir Rupert,' the woman with the clipboard insisted. She pursed her lips as she ran her gaze over Lisette and her colleagues, then glared at the neon sign. 'It is an utter disgrace that vulnerable children are living in a pit of immorality in Soho.'

'I will tell you what is disgraceful!' Lisette rose up like an angry queen, the ribbons in her hair fluttering. 'Nuns who dirty their holy vows! They are cruel to the children they should protect!'

'Now, now, madam, none of that!' the policeman warned her.

Wyngate unfolded his arms and jabbed one finger towards Sister Benedict. 'She beat these children,' he said, his voice strong and clear. 'They all did in that place. They stole their food and used them as slaves.' He looked towards the policeman. 'Don't hang your reputation on dealing with the likes of her, Constable.'

Sister Benedict gave a gasp of horror and appealed to Sir Rupert again, her voice trembling with emotion, 'Please, sir, please do what is right.'

'We don't want to go back,' Jack announced. He squared his narrow shoulders and put his arm protectively round Elsie. 'We were battered by her and the nuns and we were beaten by the family we went to as evacuees. If you try to split us up or send us away, I'll make sure every newspaper hears that the so-called authorities are out to get the Blitz Kids.'

Ned nodded, setting his hands on his hips. 'Spot on, Jack! Imagine that, eh, ladies? Bein' the ones from the social who stick their oar in and ruin London's favourite Blitz story?' He tutted and shook his head. 'That'll pour a bucket of cold fish all over wartime morale, won't it?'

'Quite right, boys.' Esther lifted her camera again, smiling as she aimed it at Sister Benedict. The policeman gave her a warning look, but didn't intervene.

'Well now,' Rupert said, 'I think we should do what we do in the good old House of Commons and take a vote, don't you?' He turned to the children, beaming. 'All those in favour of politely declining the invitation to go into the care of social services, say nay! All those who would like to go with these nice ladies, say aye!'

'What about all them as don't want to be so polite about it?'

asked Ned mischievously, much to Sir Rupert's obvious delight. "Cos I'm tellin' them right now, they can get knotted!'

'Yes, they can,' Lisette chimed in. 'You have let these children down. You're not taking them. They're our children. We care for them. Tell them what you think, children! You don't have to go with them.'

Elsie opened her mouth to say nay, but her throat was tight again. She couldn't get the sound out. All she could do was shake her head.

'Nay! We ain't goin' anywhere with you!' Connie roared, stamping her feet, and, when she yelled again, Susan and Ben joined in too. 'Nay!'

The woman with the clipboard glared at them. 'Such dreadful behaviour!' she snapped.

'Nevertheless, this is a democratic vote, albeit a most irregular one,' said Sir Rupert. 'I think that we should adjourn for now, don't you.' And he turned to Lisette. 'Would you mind unlocking the club so we can go inside, mademoiselle?'

But Sister Benedict lunged forward, jabbing her fingertip hard against Wyngate's breast as she spat, '*You!* Don't think I don't remember you. You were always a deceitful creature. It doesn't surprise me one little bit to see that you're here in London, skulking away while others are doing their bit.'

Elsie trembled with fury. She put Pippa down on the pavement, then shoved Sister Benedict's arm.

'You leave – you leave him alone!' she rasped with effort. 'He's my friend! Get off him!'

'If I see you again,' said Wyngate calmly, taking hold of Sister Benedict's finger and lifting it from his lapel, 'I'll give Miss Hammond an exclusive all about you and your so-called sisters. Do you really want that?'

The other kids stepped forward too, standing shoulder to shoulder with Elsie and their friend as Jack said, 'We all will. We haven't named names up to now, but we'd happily do it.'

For a long moment Sister Benedict and Wyngate were toe to toe, their gazes locked onto one another. Elsie had never seen the nun look afraid but now, deep in her rheumy eyes, she saw a flicker of fear. This fearsome woman, who had wielded so much terror, was afraid of him.

'Very well,' she said. She stepped back. 'But children cannot live alone for ever. The social services will deal with you eventually.' Then she pointed that withered finger again. 'And one day, so will the Lord.'

'That's all right by me. I'll offer him some nylons for his missus.' Ned laughed. 'C'mon, Lis, let's get inside, shall we? It's been a long night.'

FORTY-FOUR
ELSIE

Before leaving with Esther, Sir Rupert treated everyone to breakfast pastries. The children sat round the tables in front of the stage and tucked in. Even if the pastries weren't as light and buttery as the ones Elsie remembered from before the war, it was still a welcome treat. He'd even bought a sausage for Pippa, which she was tucking into from a saucer by Elsie's seat. Connie was looking after Ginger, repairing her loose hair.

Lisette had made coffee for herself and Wyngate, and they were drinking it out of bowls and dipping their pastries into it. Elsie frowned. Why weren't they using cups?

'Elsie, it is wonderful to have you back, and to hear your voice,' Lisette told her, and stroked Elsie's hair.

Elsie blushed. 'It just sort of come out when I saw Pip and I called her name.'

'I don't think we can stay at Jasper's much longer,' Jack told them all, giving Elsie a fond glance. 'We can't put the club at risk, it wouldn't be fair. I don't know what rules we're breaking being here.'

Connie tugged on her needle and pulled the thread through. 'It's been the best livin' here, but you'll want your spare dressin' room back one day. And what if that copper and the social workers come back, never mind Sister Ben and her penguins? They'll drag us off to the countryside.'

'And they'll split us up.' Susan patted her brother's arm affectionately. 'We've only got each other.'

Lisette looked thoughtful and glanced at Wyngate. 'I know it isn't ideal living here, but where would you like to go?'

Wyngate looked to Elsie and said, 'Elsie would like to stay in the East End. It's the area she and Jack know best, Ned and Connie too, I expect.' He looked to Ben and Susan and asked gently, 'What do you two think about that? If we can find somewhere that isn't a railway arch and has a bolt on the door?'

Susan smiled. 'Back to the East End? I'd love that. We lived in Wapping. Our dad worked down the wharfs there.'

'I want to live back East and all,' Ben replied. 'It was our home, right up until we had to go to the orphanage.'

Elsie lifted Pippa onto her knee and fussed her. 'On the way back, me and Mr Wyngate met this old couple, Ern and Agnes. And Jack, you'll never guess – she's the lady you rescued!' She smiled at her brother before carrying on. 'They was looking after Pippa, and said there's empty houses in the street what the council said ain't safe. But he reckons they are. We could live in one of them. Our own house!'

She glanced from face to face around the table. Connie was nodding eagerly, and Ben and Susan too. Lisette smiled but her eyes looked sad.

'I know you're worried. When they find a place, I'll give it the once-over, just to be sure it's safe,' Wyngate said, watching Lisette. 'But I did it myself, Lisette. I didn't have a family like this one either. It was just me.'

Ned nodded. 'And he turned out sort of all right, didn't he?' He took off his cap and scrubbed at his curly hair. 'Way I see it, we've got something here. We're in the papers, the city loves us and there's got to be other kids out there who need help. If they know where the Blitz Kids HQ is, they can come and find us.' He held up a hand towards Lisette. 'Before you say it, yeah, all sorts of toerags can come and find us an' all. Except if we hole up in Whitechapel, there ain't many toerags is going to risk making a stink in Toe Mahoney's manor. And I'm Toe Mahoney's best runner.'

Wyngate shifted his gaze to Ned. 'What does he think about you working for the new man in town?' he asked.

Ned narrowed his eyes. 'He knows we've got to make money where we can,' he replied. 'And Toe's beef ain't with us kids, it's with the blokes who worked for him and run off to take the new coin. Blokes like Mr Marsh, who've followed the money, they're the ones Toe'd like to do damage to.' Then he gave a laugh of realisation. 'That why you're so keen to help us lot, is it? So you can try and find a grass?'

Elsie slapped Ned's arm. 'What a thing to say to Mr Wyngate. He's our mate, that's why he's helpin' us!'

Wyngate responded with a hollow laugh of his own. 'We've a lot more in common than you think,' was his reply to Ned's accusation. Then he told the group, 'If you do this – go it alone – we need to agree some rules.'

Connie sighed.

'Rules are important,' Lisette said. 'Like here at the nightclub we can't go on stage and say and do whatever we like, or brew our own beer in the dressing room. Rules keep everyone safe.'

Jack nodded. 'I agree,' he said. 'First rule I'd like to suggest is that lessons continue.' Ned gave a groan of complaint. 'Even for you, Ned.'

Wyngate took a sip from his bowl. 'Second, Jack and Ben, you keep your jobs here. It's good to have a wage,' he said. 'And most important, you check in with Lisette or me every single day. If we don't hear from you, we'll come looking.'

'Can Connie still go out singing?' asked Ned, earning another nod from Wyngate.

'If you do, stick to the Feathers,' Wyngate requested. 'The landlord's a good man and it's a safe pitch.' He gave a mirthless smile. 'Toe Mahoney's made sure of that.'

'Brilliant, I love singin'!' Connie grinned.

'Yes, you need to check in with us so that we know you're all right,' Lisette told them. 'And you can tell us anything, anything at all. Even if you think it's tiny. And in the evenings, you can come here. One day, Connie, I'd love for you to sing here. There's no rules saying we can't have a young performer on our stage.'

Wyngate nodded. 'That's a good idea,' he said. 'Come here in the evenings so you're safe under the surface if the sirens go. Jack'll be working here anyway and, if nothing happens, you can go back to your own beds at night. And don't worry about bus fares, I'll make sure you're all seen right.' He looked across the assembled faces, his expression grave. 'Don't be under any illusions – even for the famous Blitz Kids, life's going to be hard. But you're not facing it alone.'

Elsie thought of the lady she'd rescued the night before, her pale, terrified face at the window.

'There's another rule,' she said, as she stroked Pippa's woolly ears. 'You can't leave me behind when them sirens go off no more. I'm a Blitz Kid, too.'

'No—' Jack began, shaking his head. But then he caught himself and reached for his sister's hand. He held it tight, as protective now as he had always been. He was her anchor, the one who kept her smiling. 'But you'll just run out on your own and do it anyway, won't you?' Without waiting for a reply, he nodded. 'But you stick by my side, agreed?'

Elsie smiled as she held Jack's hand. 'Of course I'll stay by your side, through thick and thin. You look out for me, just as I'll look out for you.'

FORTY-FIVE
ELSIE

The winter afternoon sun shone on Whitechapel as Elsie and her friends picked their way through the ruined streets. Pippa trotted ahead on her lead, sniffing here and there. The streets were eerily quiet without the wail of the sirens or the drone of the planes. Wallpaper trembled forlornly in the breeze on the exposed walls that were left standing. A sink hung haphazardly, half ripped from a wall, a mirror still hanging above it.

Elsie shuddered. What if someone had been in that house when the bomb hit, just like their mum?

Jack squeezed her hand. Then he told them, 'We need somewhere that's been empty a couple of weeks. We don't want anyone coming back once we're settled.'

'Down near the docks,' Ned murmured thoughtfully. 'What about St Joseph's Terrace? There might be somewhere down there, you know. It ain't all come down.'

Elsie nodded. 'The place Ern was telling me about was down that way. It'll be nice to have them as neighbours. And it's where Pippa's been living.'

The children made their way through the battered streets.

Even the terraces that were still standing had suffered broken windows, or had scorch marks on their walls. All the iron railings had been removed, leaving stone and concrete walls with rusting, stubby remains. Ben climbed onto one of the walls, his arms spread like a tightrope-walker at the circus.

As they got closer to the docks they could hear shouting, the chug of engines and the tugboats hooting. Elsie wondered if Ned was thinking about all the riches he could find down here with his black-market friends.

'We'll have a home,' Jack told his sister gently as they walked. 'Just like we used to with Mum and Dad. No more nuns to bully us.' Then he smiled. 'And we'll find the others from the orphanage or just kids like us, kids who don't want to leave London. If they want, they can join our family too. Does that sound all right?'

'The more the merrier, like Dad used to say,' Elsie replied with a grin.

She glanced at Susan and Ben, who were walking along hand in hand. There were still other children from the orphanage somewhere, and Elsie wondered where they'd got to. Had they already been rounded up by the social workers and sent to the countryside?

They walked down a narrow path behind a warehouse. One end of it had been hit, the roof caved in, and the corrugated metal had melted in the heat. But the other end was still standing, and was still in use. No matter how many bombs Hitler sent, London carried on.

At the end of the path, there was a terrace of houses that were all in one piece. Elsie saw Agnes at her window, waving with her good arm. A pram stood outside their neighbour's house, and a radio played a dance tune inside another. Connie skipped along in time, twirling her scarf as she sang along. They went through a windowless alleyway at the far end, between two empty shops on a ruined street, then Elsie saw a road sign attached to the front of a house with the windows all gone and the roof full of holes.

St Joseph's Terrace

'We're here!' Connie said, still skipping.

Half of the terrace had gone, reduced to broken bricks and smashed tiles. The other half had been abandoned, roofs had disappeared and broken rafters poked up at the sky. The chimney stacks were leaning, but Elsie wondered if they were like that before Hitler sent over his bombs. The windows were smashed, but they could be easily filled with rags. And they had front doors that were only a bit damaged, the door numbers dangling and the letter boxes dented. A sign painted on the wall pointed to a nearby shelter.

It wasn't too bad at all. As she looked up and down the row of remaining houses, Elsie decided that Rob would've liked it here, too.

'It's like where we lived in Wapping,' Susan told them, and Ben nodded. There was something wistful in their expressions, and Elsie understood. The houses they had lived in with their parents had vanished into the unreachable past. But here was the chance to start again.

'It looks all right,' agreed Jack. 'Quiet and with a shelter close by.' Then he looked to Connie and winked. 'Somewhere the girls'll be safe while we blokes go out and earn a crust!'

'Stay at home?' Connie planted her hands on her hips. 'Is that so, Mr Jack Taylor? I've got my singin'! If you think I'm goin' to be polishin' the front step while you and Ned are off having your adventures, you've got another think comin'!'

Elsie laughed. 'Exactly, us girls aren't just staying at home! We've got people to rescue, for one thing.'

'We'll all do our bit,' said Jack. 'We might be too young for the Home Guard, but we don't need a uniform to help our neighbours and the more we do for them the more they'll look out for us.' He looked to Elsie and smiled. 'Mum always said you couldn't do better than good neighbours, so that's what we'll be. The best neighbours anyone could ask for.'

At the mention of their mum, Elsie felt tears rising, but she pushed them back. Mum would be proud of them.

Even though each house had a sign nailed to the front door saying *DO NOT ENTER! UNSAFE!* Jack stepped up to one of the doors and read the sign, his eyes skimming across the small print beneath the warning.

'We'll be trespassing,' he said. For a moment Elsie was worried that he was about to declare a change of plan, but instead he turned to look at his friends and nodded. She knew that nod, the nod that her brother gave when he had reached a decision. 'But there's a war on and we Blitz Kids need a place to live, don't we?'

Ned looked to Elsie and asked, 'What's your favourite number, mate? We can see if it's still standing.'

'We lived at number eight,' Elsie told him. 'And it's my favourite number, because I *am* eight!'

'Number eight!' Ned smiled. 'Loud and clear.' He held his hand out to Elsie. 'If I may, my lady, I'll escort you to your new abode!'

Elsie took Ned's hand and they walked towards their new home, Pippa just ahead.

'How you gonna get the door open?' Connie asked, jumping down from the steps. 'We ain't got any keys!'

Ned rolled his eyes. 'You don't need to worry your pretty head about that, Miss Connie,' he assured her. 'I know how to unlock a door.'

In front of them was a brass number eight on a green front

door, just like there used to be at their home in Bethnal Green. The window in the front room was cracked, and the curtain was torn. Roof tiles lay broken on the path, and the gutter was hanging off.

Yet the house was still standing. And it was home.

FORTY-SIX
ELSIE

Everything inside the house was covered by a thick layer of dust, but it all seemed to be intact. The hallway's multicoloured tiles would look cheerful after a mopping, and a print of the Tower of London hung on the wall.

The front room – Connie grandly called it *the parlour* – had a pair of china dogs on the mantelpiece, which Elsie was sure Pippa liked, and comfy armchairs and a sofa. On the sideboard, there were gaps where family photographs must've stood. The bookshelf wasn't very exciting; it just had books about ships and old London. There was a kitchen at the back, with an old coal-fired range. In the cupboards they found mouldy bread, which they chucked out, tins of Spam and peaches, and a sack of potatoes under the sink.

Upstairs, they found two bedrooms. The double room at the front was claimed by Elsie, Susan and Connie, because the wallpaper was sprigged with pink flowers, and there were two single beds at the back for Jack, Ben and Ned. They could get some camp beds and make sure everyone had a bed each.

The boys' room had a view over the small, weed-filled garden to the alleyway at the back, the sort of place where Toe

Mahoney's black-market men would make deals. Ned even got a little nostalgic as he remembered meeting his employers here before the war, men in sharp suits with oiled hair and pencil moustaches, who gave him messages and packages to deliver when he wasn't going around the pubs and streets selling whatever he could get his hands on. He ran off down the steps with a fresh spring in his step, bound for Soho to deliver their new address to the friends who had been so kind.

But it wouldn't be long before their own small collection of clothes would fill the empty wardrobes and drawers. Elsie would be able to put Ginger on the chest of drawers, and there was plenty of space for Pippa to have a bed.

Jack had kept a photograph of the family, taken on a sunny day at Southend, with the pier stretching off behind them. He put it on the mantelpiece, creased from his pocket.

Connie found a floral apron and a scarf behind the kitchen door and took on the job of cleaning the house. She shouted, 'Get out of my kitchen, I've just mopped the floor!' and it made Elsie smile at Jack, because it was just like Mum used to say.

Elsie and Susan helped anyway, wiping the shelves so that once they started using their new ration books they could proudly store their food.

Jack and Ben had their jobs now, and there would be a roof over their heads for their daily lessons. The money they made might be less than Ned could bring in, but it was honest, and they would bring every penny back to the little family in their new home. Then at night they would wait in the club or go out into the streets, helping the people who needed them. They were the Blitz Kids, after all.

Although the house didn't have electricity or gas, there was running water, and candles under the sink. They found coal in a lean-to shed in the little backyard.

Jack was standing in the little sitting room, his gaze on the photograph of their parents, when Elsie wandered in with

Pippa. He turned to look at his sister and asked, 'What do you think, Else?' Then he smiled and shook his head. 'I'm going to ask you loads of questions, you know, just so I can keep hearing that voice of yours.'

'It's smashing,' Elsie replied, linking her arm through Jack's. She looked at the photograph too and for a moment it was as if their family was together again, with Pippa their newest member. 'Only now I've started talking, I might not shut up!'

'Don't ever shut up,' Jack requested. 'I think we might be all right here, Elsie. With Mr Wyngate and Lisette on our side and Sir Rupert too. We owe him a lot, don't we?'

Elsie nodded. 'I thought politicians were just all talk, but he actually *does* stuff. And it's going to be great living here! A proper house of our own, just like the old days, when—.'

Pippa barked and sprinted to the front window, leapt onto the sill and barked even louder.

'Pippa, what's all that racket for?' Elsie asked, but her answer came as she heard someone knock at the door. She grinned at Jack. 'It's our first visitors!'

She ran to the front door and pulled it open to reveal Ern and Agnes.

'I told Ern I'd seen you all walking down this way, so we came to see which house you'd picked,' Agnes explained. 'As soon as we heard Pippa barking, we knew exactly which one it was.'

Ern nodded. In his hands he was holding a biscuit tin, decorated with a painting of Buckingham Palace, and he held it out to Elsie.

'Welcome to Whitechapel.' He grinned. 'We've brought you a little bit of something for a housewarming. It ain't much, mind, just a bit of war cake.'

'I'm Jack.' Jack took the tin in one hand, then shook Ern's hand. What a welcome that was from their new neighbours; Elsie could already taste the dark brown, spicy fruit cake even as it sat in its tin. 'Elsie's brother. We won't be any trouble, sir. We'll be the best neighbours you could wish for.'

'I know who you are.' Agnes smiled warmly. 'You're the lad who saved my life. I can't think of anyone else we'd want living near us. Anything you need, you just ask.'

'If you want, we'll come round and help you,' Elsie said, 'what with your broken arm.'

Ern nodded. 'And we can write to Mr and Mrs Fellowes up in Yorkshire with their lad and tell them that their house is being properly cared for,' he said with a smile. 'That'll be a weight off for them.'

Elsie smiled back. She was so glad they'd found a home in Whitechapel. And if maybe, one day, Dad came to find them, he wouldn't have to look too far.

FORTY-SEVEN
ELSIE

As soon as they saw the car appear on their street, Elsie banged open the door and her friends ran outside with her. They cheered with excitement to see Wyngate and Lisette. Elsie was carrying Pippa, Jack staying close to her, while Connie waved enthusiastically. Ben went straight up to the car and knocked his knuckles on the bonnet, with a cheeky, gap-toothed grin through the windscreen at Wyngate.

Lisette got out of the car and smiled warmly at the children. 'We've brought your things from the club.'

Elsie went round to Wyngate's door and waved Pippa's paw at him. 'Pippa says come and see the house!'

Wyngate waved his hand in reply and opened the door. 'Your palace at last,' he said with a smile. Then he stroked the top of Pippa's head and asked, 'Nice neighbours?'

'The best!' Elsie told him. 'Ern and Agnes came round with cake!'

'First things first,' Wyngate told Elsie as he opened the boot of the car and took out a metal toolbox. 'It'll be getting dark soon, so let's get the electricity turned on, shall we?'

Jack shook his head quickly and said, 'We won't have the

money for that, Mr Wyngate. We'll make do though, it's all right.'

This time, Wyngate's smile was for Jack. He slapped his gloved hand to the lamppost beside the car and glanced down at the metal service hatch. 'It's not only your little Ned who knows how to work the system,' he said. 'Show me the way to the fuse box, Elsie.'

Everyone crowded back into the house, and Elsie opened the door to the understairs cupboard where the fuse box awaited them.

'Where did you learn to be an electrician?' Elsie asked him as he worked.

'Nobody asked how I got into Jasper's either,' he replied, working by the flame of a candle that Elsie was holding up in the dying afternoon light. 'I have hidden talents.'

'You definitely do,' Elsie said, impressed.

The others were crammed into the hallway, watching too.

'This house'll be better than Buckingham Palace once the lights are working,' Connie announced confidently. Even Ned, who had come home and promptly made himself useful gathering lengths of wire and handfuls of screws and anything else Wyngate might need from the bombed-out houses further along the street, was standing on the bottom step.

'Bet you can't do it,' Ned declared. 'Bet you throw the switch and we get a fizzle and a pop!'

Wyngate looked over his shoulder at Ned, then told him, 'That cable we've got running under the door out to the lamppost, tuck it away under the carpet. Job done.' With that, he blew out the candle Elsie was holding. 'And we'll see what happens.'

Connie helped Ned tidy the cable underneath the narrow red carpet that ran the length of the hallway, then shouted, 'I bet you can do it, Mr Wyngate!'

'Mademoiselle Souchon,' Wyngate said. 'Flick the switch.'

'Please,' added Jack, looking pointedly at Wyngate.

'Please, Monsieur Wyngate?' Lisette grinned. She stood with her hand on the switch. 'This is more of an honour than launching a ship!'

She flicked the switch and suddenly the bulb hanging above the hallway in a cobwebbed shade fizzed for a second, then cast a yellow glow over them.

The children cheered as Elsie put her arm round Wyngate. 'You did it, Mr Wyngate! I knew you could!'

'And I'll get you some keys cut too,' he promised. 'But I want you all to remember, you don't have to go it alone now. If you need help, you come to me or Lisette. Agreed?'

Jack nodded. 'We promise,' he said. Then, as if the fates had been waiting for the lights to go on despite it being an hour before blackout, the sirens wailed overhead and Jack flicked the light off without a moment's hesitation. There was a grim inevitability to it, but somehow Elsie wasn't afraid even though she would be heading out into the Blitz with her new family. Afterwards, they'd come home to St Joseph's Terrace. 'Here we go again!'

Elsie clipped on Pippa's lead, and they put on their winter coats, hats, and scarves. If only there'd been time to show their visitors around the house; but that could wait for another time.

'We'll make sure you get to a shelter,' Connie told Lisette. 'But we'll be busy, see, so we won't be waitin' out the raid with you.'

The aeroplanes droned overhead and made the whole street vibrate. A distant boom heralded a bomb plummeting to earth, and shouts echoed in the street.

'Ben, Susan, you go and knock for Agnes and Ern,' said Jack as Wyngate moved along the hallway and into the street after Lisette. He seemed content to simply observe, watching the children organise themselves. 'Go to the shelter with them and let the locals know they've got a couple of Blitz Kids with them;

tell them if they need any help after the raid to come and find us. That's your job and it's just as important as being outside tonight. Come straight home on the all-clear, all right?'

Susan nodded. 'All right, Jack!'

'And take Pippa with you,' Elsie said, a tremble in her voice. She handed the lead to Susan, and her friend closed her hand firmly round it.

'Don't worry, we'll look after her,' Susan promised. She looped her other arm round Ben's shoulders, and they ran off together up the road, Pippa bounding ahead.

'Go with them,' Wyngate whispered to Lisette. Elsie saw his hand move just a little, just enough to touch his fingers briefly against Lisette's before he drew them away again.

Lisette swallowed. Her hands were trembling, and she turned as if she was going. But she stopped and shook her head. 'Ben and Susan will be safe with Ern and Agnes. But I'm not going with them,' she said. 'I can't stop you from staying out, I know I can't, but I'll stay with you.'

'We just go where we're needed,' Jack explained as they set off into the night. 'Sometimes we find the air-raid wardens or the Home Guard, others we just follow the noise and the flames.' He looked over the houses, where flames flickered on the near horizon. 'Tonight, it's pretty obvious where we're needed.'

Scraps of cloud moved across the ice-haloed moon. As they hurried along the street, Elsie gasped as she saw the silhouette of plane after plane crossing before it. The beams of the searchlights rocked back and forth across the sky until they caught a plane and followed it, with lines of bullets chasing after. The planes needed to be brought down before they could drop their bombs, but what if they smashed into people's homes?

At the top of the road, they saw a stream of people desperately hurrying for shelter, pushing prams, carrying suitcases. Elsie thought back to the moment when they'd seen that building collapse on top of all those people who'd only wanted to get to somewhere safe.

But tonight, the Blitz Kids, Wyngate and Lisette were heading for fires that were already raging. If Elsie needed to go into another burning building to save a life, she would.

FORTY-EIGHT
ELSIE

Elsie told herself not to be scared at every boom she heard, even though some were very close. The freezing winter streets were dark, apart from the orange glow of the fires and the silvering of the moon when it emerged from the clouds. The racket of the air raid echoed along the streets, the relentless drone of the planes and the rattle of gunfire.

Elsie glanced up at her brother's face. He was serious, reminding her so much of Dad again. His promise to look after her, she realised, extended to the entire city they called home.

She coughed. The air was full of smoke. 'I suppose you get used to the smoke, don't you?'

Jack nodded, rapping his knuckles against his gas-mask box. 'And you never come out without this,' he said. 'You stay close.'

Elsie tapped her gas-mask box, too, and looked over her shoulder at Wyngate, who had brought the masks for them when Rupert had brought sweets.

They turned the corner onto a wide road, just as a double-decker bus was driving past. It had posters on its sides advertising war bonds. Even in an air raid, Londoners were on the move, but they had to sit in darkness, just silhouettes. They needed to get—

A piercing whine filled the street. It was a bomb. And it was coming straight for them.

'Everybody get down!' Wyngate bellowed, throwing his arm round Lisette as Jack reached for Elsie and Connie. Ned, who had run on ahead, threw himself to the ground in the seconds before the bomb thundered into the earth, his hands sheltering his head as he went.

The deafening explosion seemed to tear a hole in the air, as if Elsie would never hear anything again apart from that noise, like a sound from the end of the world.

They lay still on the pavement for what seemed like a long time, but could only have been seconds. Elsie shivered against Jack, clinging on to him. She didn't dare to look. What about Ned? Was he safe?

'Is everyone all right?' Lisette asked, her trembling voice cutting through the noise of the raid.

'I-I think so,' Connie said. 'Jack, Else, you in one piece? Ned, mate, you all right?'

'Fine and dandy!' Ned called back as the scream of brakes filled the air. Elsie heard it dull against the thudding in her ears, but there was no mistaking what it was. As she did she felt Jack's arm tighten round her, holding her safe.

She tried to lift her head. The bus. All those people on the bus, they just wanted to go home. And now—

She peered over Jack's shoulder, and froze.

In the moonlight, she saw a huge crater in the middle of the road, gouged out by the bomb. The bus was hanging head first over the edge. The back wheels were turning helplessly, like a beetle on its back, and the silhouetted passengers were beating against the windows.

'The bus!' Elsie gasped. 'It's falling down the bomb crater!'

Wyngate was on his feet already and sprinting towards the

stricken bus as he called out, 'Everybody to the back of the bus! Now!'

Ned went hurtling after him, calling to those people who had dropped to the ground when the bomb hit, 'Come on, we need your help!'

Elsie scraped her knee in her haste to get to her feet, but she didn't stop. She and Jack, Connie and Lisette, were running towards the bus. Other people were running too.

Elsie stared up at the enormous dark hulk, the cables and axles underneath the bus revealed as the wheels kept turning. Faces appeared at every window, and some gingerly peered round the edge of the bus's open back door, reaching for help.

With a metallic groan, the bus tipped forward even more. The air was filled with piercing screams. Then the engine cut out, and the screams fell silent. Despite the racket of the air raid, there was an eerie quiet.

'What are we going to do?' Elsie whispered to her brother. The road beneath her feet suddenly felt as if it could cave in if anyone so much as coughed.

'Everybody get on the bus!' Wyngate shouted. 'We need as much weight as we can on the back. If people start trying to get off, it's going to tip over the edge before it's empty.' He clapped his hands together and turned to the shocked bystanders. 'Come on, get on the bloody bus or half these people are going to die!' The driver, who was halfway along the aisle, turned back to his cabin, his face white with fear in the moonlight. 'Stay where you are,' Wyngate told him. 'I'll see to it.'

Elsie was rigid with terror at the prospect of getting onto the stricken bus. But Wyngate was right – what else could they do but force its back wheels back to earth?

Connie reached up for the platform and nimbly pulled herself up, then got to her knees and grabbed the pole. The bus rocked slightly as she stretched over the side. 'Come on, I'll give you all a hand up!' she shouted to them.

One by one, the bystanders climbed up through the back door. It was painfully slow, but any fast movements would've sent the bus plunging down to who knew where.

Once on the bus, Elsie carefully got to her feet. The passengers were packed together shoulder to shoulder, a mass of terrified humanity. Their knuckles were white where they gripped the backs of the seats. Elsie heard the scrape of footsteps on the top deck, and the unseen passengers calling for help.

'We're going to die,' a young woman gasped, her hat knocked askew, her gloved hand tight round one of the straps dangling from the ceiling. 'We're all going to die.'

'No, you aren't,' Elsie said, sounding braver than she felt. 'Mr Wyngate will save you. He saves everyone.'

It was then that her gaze met that of someone she recognised. As pale and as terrified as everyone else. Ma Mahoney. Even though her son ran Whitechapel, she was trapped, teetering on the brink, just like everyone else.

Suddenly there was a flurry of movement as a middle-aged couple began to push their way through the crowded passengers towards the back of the bus. Their eyes were wild with fear and as they surged forward, and that fear seemed to be contagious.

'Get off!' the man told the other passengers. 'We have to get off! There's nothing but the sewers under here. If it goes in, we're all dead!'

The young woman let go of the strap and pushed against the crowd too, edging her way forward. 'I'm not hangin' around here to die!'

The bus creaked, the back lowering an inch or two under the sudden, displaced weight, before lurching up again and slipping further forward into the crater.

Elsie grabbed the man's arm and desperately clung on. 'Stop it!' she yelled.

'You stay where you are!' Ma Mahoney instructed furiously. 'Unless you want a visit from my boy Toe!'

A mumble ran through the passengers at the mention of Toe. Trapped in a bus that was heading into the sewers, and faced with the threat of Toe if they climbed off, no one moved.

A man in a flat cap with a newspaper tucked under his arm shook his head. 'Now, now, Ma Mahoney,' he said, clearly trying to sound confident, although Elsie could hear a tremble in his voice. 'No one on this bus is going anywhere.'

Heads nodded, but only slightly, as if they were too scared to move any more than that.

'So get to the back of the bus and stay there,' said Ma Mahoney. 'And my Toe will stand you all a pint in the Feathers.' She pointed to the panicking woman. 'You too, miss! Don't try me!'

Connie spread her arms wide. 'You listen to Ma! No one's goin' anywhere!'

'You get off this bus and I'll arrest the pair of you for manslaughter,' Wyngate spat from where he stood on the shattered pavement. 'And that goes for anyone else!'

The young woman froze. She lowered her head and Elsie heard a sob. Letting go of the man's sleeve, Elsie patted the woman's arm.

'Don't be scared, we'll be all right,' she told her.

Lisette climbed onto the platform and reached for Ned and Jack to pull them up. The others clambered up beside her, clinging on to each other for dear life, but, even as they did, Elsie felt the bus lowering back down to the ground. Its wheels made contact with the earth once more, yet she knew that this was just the start. It was like the seesaws in the park; if anyone got off now, those who were still stuck on the vehicle would fall when it seesawed forward into the bomb crater.

'I'll try and reverse her up,' said the driver. But as he took a few steps back towards his seat, the bus teetered and creaked once more.

Wyngate immediately shook his head. 'Stay up this end,' he instructed. 'I'll do the driving.'

But how was he going to reach the driver's cab at the front? The bus was rammed with people – the passengers who had already filled it, as well as the Blitz Kids and passers-by who had followed Wyngate's order to climb on. If any of them moved to make space for him to pass along the narrow aisle, it could overbalance the bus on the edge of the precipice.

Lisette called to Wyngate in French, then pressed her fingertips to her lips and blew him a kiss.

Wyngate acknowledged her with a sharp nod and a final warning of, '*Nobody* gets off this bus until I say so. If anyone tries, knock them out.' Then he nodded towards Ma Mahoney. 'And believe me, her boy will do a lot worse than that if anyone risks this bus falling.'

Ned nodded. 'He'll nail your feet to the floor,' he said cheerily.

Elsie offered her hand to the young woman. 'It's all right,' she went on whispering, as she watched Wyngate flex his gloved hands before hauling himself up to the side of the bus.

Her heart was in her throat. He was edging along the outside of the bus, clinging to the edges of the windows. It was like watching a Buster Keaton film at the Saturday matinee, when he inched his way along a narrow sill a hundred storeys up in New York.

Far below the tarmac that the Nazi bomb had splintered like matchwood, the sewers and underground of London yawned like the mouth of hell. By some miracle the device hadn't detonated, but that would be no comfort if the bus followed it into the chasm.

Connie put her arm round Lisette's shoulders, and Elsie held the young woman's hand even tighter as Wyngate carried on, his face a mask of silent determination. He held the lives of everyone on that bus in his hands; hands that were gripping the tiny handholds afforded by the windows as he got closer and closer to the front.

It wasn't worth thinking about what would happen if he slipped. Not only would he plunge to his death, but the bus would tip up and send everyone else plummeting beneath the London street.

As he painstakingly made his way to the driver's cab, no one on the bus said a word. Some looked away, others watched through their fingers. Elsie heard the moan of the planes' engines overhead. What if another bomb fell close by and shook the ground and sent the bus falling? He was so close now. Elsie saw him grab the driver's door and—

A metallic shriek filled the air and the bus suddenly lurched, angling downwards. Passengers were screaming, and Elsie nearly lost her footing; suddenly the mass of passengers were bearing down on her, pushing their way to the door to escape.

'Stop!' Elsie shouted. It sounded reedy to her ears, and she tried again, using her voice that had been silent for so long. Heads turned towards her. 'Everyone stop! Didn't you hear what Mr Wyngate said? Or Ma Mahoney? You can't get off the bus!'

'They need help!' came a Welsh voice from somewhere in the night and suddenly, in the glare of the searchlights, Elsie saw half a dozen men in the khaki uniform of the Home Guard hastening across the road towards them, followed by a trio of tin-hatted ARP wardens. As they approached, the middle-aged Welshman at their head called, 'What do you need us to do?'

Elsie's thoughts returned to the seesaws at the park. She remembered all her friends piling onto one of them, almost catapulting each other off the other end.

'The bumper!' she called from the bus. 'Push down on the bumper so's the wheels are on the road!'

The men were quick to obey. They clambered onto the bus

any which way they could, stepping up onto the running board and leaning their weight on the bumper and window frames, as Wyngate wrapped his fingers round the window in the driver's door. Now that the Home Guard and ARP had provided that vital extra stability he was able to force it down in just a few seconds and, nimble as a cat, he hauled himself inside.

'Come on,' Ma Mahoney urged quietly as the engine started with a throaty rumble, sending a tremor the length of the vehicle. Then she addressed the woman who had made a panicked bid for freedom earlier. 'Won't be long now, lovey.'

Elsie heard the heavy gear clunk into place. A second later, painfully slowly, the bus began to edge backwards, the wheels that still clung to the earth dragging the weight of the bus along the shattered tarmac. It sounded like great metallic nails screeching down a blackboard, but they were moving. They would soon be safe.

'A bit more,' called the Welsh Home Guardsman. 'Nearly there, son, nearly there!'

Elsie heard sighs of relief from the passengers as moment by moment they inched closer to safety. With a lurch that would've sent people falling if the bus hadn't been so full, it came to a groaning halt. The front wheels must've caught against the rough, torn edge of the crater. Even Mr Wyngate couldn't reverse the bus back any further.

But it was enough.

'Ding ding!' shouted Ned. 'Everybody off!'

'See, I told you Mr Wyngate would save you!' Elsie called, and suddenly everyone on the bus was cheering and clapping.

One by one they climbed off, the Home Guard and the ARP wardens helping everyone down. Elsie held tight to Jack's hand.

She might not have climbed along the side of the bus as if it was a cliff face, like Wyngate had, but, even so, she'd helped to save the lives of these ordinary Whitechapel folk who'd nearly died just getting the bus home.

FORTY-NINE
LISETTE

If she'd gone to the shelter, then Lisette would never have seen Wyngate's extraordinary act of bravery. It had been one of the longest few minutes of her life. She hadn't known whether to watch. If he'd slipped, then she would've seen the moment that he—

Lisette forced the image out of her head. Wyngate had survived, and not only that, he'd saved the lives of dozens of people. She linked her arm through his, anchoring him to her.

As they walked away from the crater, and the bus that the Home Guard would winch free, Connie skipped down the street, and Elsie was beaming, even though aeroplanes still thrummed overhead. Risking their own lives to save others was as normal to them as a Sunday stroll.

They carried on to the fires. Streets burned, warehouses were in flames, and hapless cars and vans were silhouettes caught in the inferno. Lisette had rarely seen such chaos; the fire engines drawn up in the road, the mass of hoses, the shouting, people in blankets with sooty faces, exhausted firemen who wouldn't give up.

They carried the heavy hoses to the firemen and unrolled

them. Lisette hadn't realised how tiring it was – her arms ached – but the children threw themselves into it, never once complaining. Lisette's ears rang with the noise; the orders shouted from one fireman to another, a call for a stretcher, the roar of flames tearing through the buildings. The heat and the thick smoke were almost unbearable.

Then the ladder turntable on one of the fire engines jammed. Lisette watched Wyngate go, without a second's hesitation, and haul himself up onto the engine. He put his shoulder to it, pushing and pushing until the turntable was freed. And when he came back to them, there was no suggestion that he believed he had done anything remarkable.

Eventually, the all-clear sounded. No more planes had come over for a while, but it still wasn't time to go home. The fires were still burning, although less fiercely now. As people began to make their way home from the shelters, the four children stood in a line at the entrance to a road where a building was still on fire, while the police set up their wooden diversion barricades.

On another street, the children spotted an elderly man who was struggling to get back to his house; the force of a nearby bomb had knocked a lamppost sideways, blocking his front door. The children were there in seconds, all four of them dragging the crumpled lamppost aside.

It was two o'clock in the morning when they made their way back to St Joseph's Terrace, via a stop at Ern and Agnes' house. They were sitting before the fire with Susan and Ben, each eating a slice of bread and dripping, and Pippa was eating a corner of the crust.

It was only once they were through their own front door that Lisette realised how tired she was, and how dirty they all were from the smoke and soot.

'Would you mind if I stayed the night?' she asked the children. They stood by the kitchen sink, washing the soot off their faces with a bar of Imperial Leather soap, a fancy gift from one of their well-wishers.

The younger children looked as one to Jack and Connie. Jack nodded and replied, 'You're always welcome.' Then he smiled and added, 'Our first house guest.'

'What about the bus driver?' Ned asked, looking up at Wyngate. He hadn't joined them in the kitchen, but was lingering in the darkened hallway, watching the group at the sink. 'You stopping an' all? You can have the sofa for a tanner.'

'Ned!' admonished Jack. 'We wouldn't charge our friends for staying at the house.'

Elsie went over to the hallway and tugged Wyngate's sleeve. 'You're our hero! You can stay too.'

'It'll be safer if you drive home in daylight,' Lisette said. She wanted him to stay, even if a house of six children might seem noisy and chaotic to a man who kept himself to himself.

'I'll take the sofa,' Wyngate decided. 'And I'll pay the tanner.'

Elsie grinned, as she towed him towards the sink. 'Ain't this fun, everyone together?'

'He's usin' our soap an' all?' asked Ned archly. 'That's another tanner.' He winked and told Wyngate, 'I'll have a leccy bill to pay, after all!'

FIFTY
LISETTE

Once Lisette got the children into their beds, they were asleep within moments. Lisette had taken off her dress and her stockings, and her slip was doubling as a nightdress.

She lay on the edge of the double bed with the girls. Pippa lay across the foot of the bed. They were breathing softly, and the room was calm. But even though Lisette was worn out, she couldn't fall asleep. Her mind kept replaying the night's events and, whenever it returned to Wyngate scaling the bus, her mind made the crater bigger and bigger, until it seemed as if he was dangling over the side of a cliff.

After a while, she gave up, and decided to go to the kitchen for a glass of water. She put her coat over her slip and softly went downstairs in bare feet.

She paused at the foot of the stairs; she had heard a noise in the front room, where Wyngate was sleeping. The door was open a crack and she glanced round it, wondering if he was still awake. The remains of the small fire glowing in the grate illuminated the room just enough for her to see him, half-sitting, half-lying on the sofa under the blankets, watching the dancing flames.

She tapped on the door and whispered in French, 'I can't sleep either. Is there space for me on the sofa?'

Wyngate looked up at her. He didn't reply, but instead lifted the edge of the blankets in an unspoken invitation.

Wordlessly, she came in and sat down beside him, not sitting too close, although the sofa wasn't enormous. Her knee brushed against his, but she didn't move away, even when she realised his legs were bare because he'd undressed for bed.

'Thank you,' she whispered. Now she could see him better, she realised he was wearing the T-shirt that would usually be hidden under his suit. He'd carefully draped the suit over an armchair, and his hat was placed neatly on the seat. 'I keep thinking – but you must be thinking the same thing. What you did tonight—'

'If I can't be here, will you keep an eye on them?' Wyngate asked. The flames were reflected in his gaze as he spoke, and his voice was a hushed murmur. 'Somebody needs to.'

Lisette nodded. She tried to smile, even though she wondered if he was planning on going away. Or was he shoring up the kids' safety if, risking his life again, he didn't make it home?

'I will, please don't worry,' she replied. 'I know you're busy at the Ministry, but not many people would make time for the children like you do.'

'I do what I can,' Wyngate said. Then he shifted his gaze to Lisette. 'But if you need anything and I'm not here— Mr Gray at the War Office. You can trust him.'

Lisette covered his hand with her own on top of the blanket.

'But you will be careful? Please, Wyngate.'

'Charmed life,' he said with the ghost of a smile.

'Please.' She was still holding his hand. 'After Tom died, I... it comes back to me. It sounds silly, because you're not Tom, but I worry that... but losing my sweetheart like that – I couldn't bear to lose you as well.'

Wyngate swallowed. For a moment he didn't move at all, then he turned his hand over beneath Lisette's and curled his fingers round hers. When he spoke again, his voice was hushed.

'I'm sorry you lost him.' He held her hand tighter. 'Do you have anyone else in England?'

'I have my friends, but...' She closed her eyes, trying to hold back the pain that had suddenly filled her chest. 'My family are in France. Maman, she's... I tried to get her to come. I pleaded and pleaded, and she kept saying, *Lisette, I just need to put my affairs in order, I can't run away from Paris.* I told her it didn't matter, that she just needed to leave. And then... then it was too late.' She looked up at Wyngate through tears. 'I don't know what's happened to her. I don't even know if she's still alive. I just tell myself she's not suffering. If I thought for a moment about just how bad things are— I couldn't bear it.'

But what could he do about it? Despite his secrets, his friends in the War Office, the man from the Ministry was powerless when it came to this. And now he seemed to be warning her that she might lose him too.

'Give me her name and address,' Wyngate whispered, studying Lisette's gaze. 'Nothing in writing.'

Lisette blinked at him. The bales of barbed wire she had pictured, running all the way along the French coast, keeping Maman's fate hidden behind them, began to disintegrate.

'But surely it's dangerous,' she whispered, as if someone might overhear. 'If you could find out anything, anything at all, it would mean the world to me. Her name is Madame Antoinette Souchon – she always goes by Madame, even though she never married – and she lived at number forty, Rue Lamarck, in Montmartre. I hope she is still there...'

'She is.'

Two words. Two unremarkable, simple words, carrying with them a wealth of hope.

'How do you know?' Lisette breathed. Surely he couldn't

say, but his so-quiet confidence made her wonder what he did at the War Office. Was he a spy? Did he travel into occupied France to help the resistance?

But if he did, how could he know Maman, unless...?

'*That's* why she wouldn't leave.' A shiver ran through her as all the cards fell into place. 'She'd joined the resistance.'

Wyngate lifted his finger to his lips and whispered, 'Careless talk.'

Lisette nodded. Her brave mother was alive, and she was doing what she could to fight the Nazis. 'Careless talk. Not a word. Not one. But— oh, Wyngate, you cannot imagine!'

Without thinking, she flung her arms round him and held him tight, this man who had lifted away the dark veil that had hidden Maman's fate.

'If you have a message for her,' Wyngate whispered. 'No promises, but I can try.'

Lisette loosened her embrace but her arms were still looped round Wyngate's neck, the tip of her nose only an inch away from his. 'Tell her I love her,' she said. 'And I'm so proud of her. And that one day, we'll meet again and tell each other about our adventures.'

He nodded, then gave the hint of a smile and replied, 'I'll tell her.'

'Thank you,' she said, and kissed his cheek. She gazed at him, this man who had once been a motherless boy living under the railway arches. His eyes were so dark that she felt as if she was falling into him. She felt a pull, and she wondered if he did, too. She touched her fingertip to his soft lips, and immediately wondered if she should have done. But he didn't retreat. Instead he lifted his hand and tenderly cupped her cheek, then put his lips to hers in a gentle kiss.

Lisette felt as if she was melting into him. It was such a tender kiss, so soft. And yet she felt a promise in it; a prelude to heat, and longing. As she gently kissed him back, she stroked his nape, where his neatly trimmed hair met his neck, that intimate, vulnerable space. Even Wyngate, so brave and so much an island, could sometimes allow his defences to fall.

When they broke from their kiss, there was nothing awkward in the air between them. Just a shared closeness. Lisette rested her head on Wyngate's shoulder and took his hand again. Without any need to say a word, they sat together under the blanket, watching the remains of the fire smoulder in the grate, two people awake in the night.

FIFTY-ONE
ELSIE

Among the gifts for the Blitz Kids, Elsie had found a bright blue ball decorated with red stars.

The fire was alight in the front room, and she sat in front of it, bouncing the ball towards Pippa. The little dog watched it approach before plunging after it, reducing Elsie to fits of giggles. The other kids were ranged along the sofa; Ben was making a paper aeroplane, Connie was plaiting Susan's hair, and Jack was reading one of the books that the house's former residents had left behind. Ned had gone off on his rounds for the wide boys, even though Lisette, who was laying the table for breakfast, had told him it was too cold to go outside. Elsie knew that wasn't the real reason, only Ned wouldn't listen anyway.

Mr Wyngate had gone out to find some food. His return was heralded by Pippa, who abandoned Elsie's game and leapt up at the front window to bark.

'Mr Wyngate's back!' Elsie got to her feet and rushed to the front door before he had time to knock. She opened it and smiled brightly up at him. 'Did you find something tasty for us?'

He pressed his finger to his lips and nodded, then stepped over the threshold. Only once the door was closed did he tap on the parcel that was tucked beneath his arm, along with a bundle of newspapers.

'Courtesy of the very grateful Ma Mahoney and family,' he said. 'It's sausages. Don't tell the ration book.' Then he handed the newspapers to Elsie and added, 'You're on every front page; expect more presents.'

Elsie's short arms were overflowing with the newspapers and she juggled them as she stared at the front pages.

Blitz Kids in bus crater rescue!

Bus saved by Blitz Kids – grateful passengers applaud bravery!

'Well, I never!' Elsie chuckled, then she looked up from the newspapers at Wyngate. 'I hope they wrote about you and all. You're the bravest person I've ever met!'

'You go and show the others,' Wyngate smiled. 'I need to talk to Mademoiselle Souchon.'

Lisette's voice drifted into the hallway from the half-open kitchen door. She sounded very happy, and kept singing a song that mainly consisted of one word: *amour*.

'All right, I'll show them,' Elsie replied. 'And just wait until Pippa hears we've got sausages for breakfast!'

She gave Wyngate a wink, then hurried into the front room. The other children crowded around the newspapers as she laid them out on the floor. Together they read the stories of their escapades the night before and of the mysterious unnamed bystander who had taken control of the bus to reverse it back from the brink. Wyngate had preferred to remain anonymous and fade into the night, but the Blitz Kids were as famous as the film stars Elsie so loved. Jack had started cutting out each story about them and saving it in a biscuit tin they'd found under the sink. It was to show Dad, he explained.

They were so absorbed, Elsie didn't notice at first that Lisette was standing in the doorway. She wasn't singing any more.

'Jacques, Elsie, could you come through to the kitchen for a moment?' she said. Her voice was very soft. Then she glanced at Pippa, who was chasing a discarded sheet of newspaper across the hearthrug. 'You can bring Pippa.'

Elsie glanced at her brother, wondering what this meant. She picked Pippa up and followed Jack through to the kitchen. Wyngate was sitting at the little table. He had taken off his hat and it hung from the back of his chair. His expression was grave but soft as he watched them approach.

'Thank you for the papers,' said Jack. 'And the sausages. Ma Mahoney seems to be able to get hold of anything. I expect that's because of her lad, eh? Ned looks up to him, you know. I wish he didn't.'

Wyngate nodded. 'You're doing it the right way. Ned might realise that in time,' he replied. 'Sit down, it's all right.'

They sat down at the table, Pippa resting her chin against it, her black button nose twitching. Elsie hugged her little dog, and asked, 'What's wrong, Mr Wyngate?'

'I spoke to my friend, Mr Gray, this morning,' Wyngate said gently. 'He let me know that your mum was laid to rest at Bow Cemetery.'

Elsie didn't reply at first. She didn't have the words. She reached for Jack, pressing her cheek to his arm, hoping she wouldn't cry. But she couldn't hold back, and she shook as she sobbed. It wasn't until that moment she realised that there had been a tiny space in her heart where a grain of hope had remained – that perhaps their mum wasn't really dead after all.

She knew where Bow Cemetery was, in the East End near Mile End station. But to think that Mum was there, in a wooden box, under the earth, cold, and still. Even so, Elsie wondered if she still smelt of blackberries, and if her fingers were still stained by their dark juice.

'Th-thank you, Mr Wyngate,' she murmured. Jack put his arm round her and drew her close, whispering her name as he embraced her tight. They would look after each other, she told herself, and somewhere Dad was waiting to come home, to be part of the family that had come together here in a little house in Whitechapel. Mum would know it too, because she was looking down on them, guiding them together and bringing them Lisette and Mr Wyngate.

'I'd like to pay for her stone,' said Wyngate in a soft voice. It was only then that Elsie felt a sob rack through Jack as he stammered his thanks. 'We'll mark her grave for you.'

Lisette came to stand behind them, resting one hand on Jack's shoulder, and the other on Elsie's hair. 'We can go and visit whenever you want to,' she said gently. 'We'll take some flowers. What was her favourite colour?'

'She liked pink,' Elsie said. She glanced up at the ceiling as if she could see through it, up into the sky, and further, into heaven.

'And blackberries,' Jack added as he kissed Elsie's hair.

Wyngate nodded. 'Then we'll take pink flowers,' he promised. 'And one day, we'll grow blackberries for her.' Then he reached out and stroked his hand over Pippa's head as the little dog turned and licked Elsie's face softly, cleaning away her tears. 'I know how this feels. I lost my mother and my sister. You have one another and you have all of us. You're not alone.'

FIFTY-TWO
ELSIE

Elsie and Jack stayed in the kitchen with Wyngate, while Lisette went into the front room to tell the others. Connie, Susan and Ben had come back with Lisette, bringing one of the newspapers with them, and, while Wyngate cooked the sausages, their special treat, Elsie and Jack were surrounded by their friends. They looked over the newspaper article together, but there was gentleness in their pride and bravado. Behind it all was Elsie and Jack's mother, and it was as if she was an unseen visitor in the room, glancing over the article too.

Suddenly the front door banged open, and Elsie's heart leapt with alarm.

It was Ned, returning early from his work.

'Get your gladrags on, Blitz Kids!' he bellowed merrily. 'This afternoon, we've got a party to go to!' He swaggered into the kitchen, and stopped in his tracks. He looked from Wyngate at the stove to the little gathering at the table, then dashed over to Elsie and asked her, 'What's happened?'

'Mr Wyngate's found our mum's grave,' Jack replied. Ned didn't say anything in reply to that at first, but flung his arms round Jack, Elsie and Pippa as one, hugging them close.

'I'm sorry,' he said against Elsie's shoulder. 'This rotten bloody war...'

'It's all right,' Elsie murmured, although she knew it wasn't really. 'We know where she is now. It was horrible not knowin'.'

Ned drew back and settled his gaze on her. 'We'll give her the best gravestone ever,' he promised. 'You want a massive marble angel tooting on a trumpet, you've got one. I'll save up all my pay!'

Wyngate turned from the stove and said, 'All you need to do is be the friend you are.' Then he rattled the frying pan. 'And eat black-market sausages.'

'Thanks, Ned, you're the best,' Elsie told him. He never kept his earnings to himself. 'Ma Mahoney gave us the sausages, and we're all over the papers. And what's this about a party?'

'I ain't been to a party in ages,' Ben said in awe. He smoothed out the newspaper on the table, as if he still couldn't believe what his friends had done last night.

Ned scrambled up onto a chair as he told Ben, 'This afternoon, Toe Mahoney's chucking us a proper knees-up at Jasper's! He's going to fetch us there and all that, so you and Jack have both got a day off work.' He beamed and spread his fingers in the air like a conjurer about to perform a trick. 'On account that we saved Ma Mahoney's life from Hitler! Mind you, I wouldn't fancy Adolf's chances if he took Ma on. She'd give him a right pasting and no mistake.'

'Will you come too, Mr Wyngate?' asked Jack.

To Elsie's disappointment, Wyngate shook his head. 'I can't,' he said apologetically. 'I have to go into the Ministry. But I'll come by later to hear all about it.'

Ned suddenly made a fist of his small hand and rapped on the table. 'I clean forgot! Mr Marsh says he wants to see you later down Hallows' Wharf at the agreed time. He ain't lookin' too well, that one. Reckon there's some malarky that's got him scared.' He shrugged his shoulders and Elsie shivered. There was something about the lurking Mr Marsh that she wasn't keen on. 'He said I should tell you, 'cos he couldn't find you. I mean, obviously he couldn't find you 'cos you're in our kitchen, frying bangers!'

Elsie looked up at Mr Wyngate. Most people wouldn't have noticed a change in him, but she did. It was as if the air around him had tightened, and his eyes looked darker than before.

She wondered if Lisette had noticed, as she had gone to stand next to Mr Wyngate at the stove.

Was Mr Wyngate afraid? But it was impossible for a man who had dangled over a crater to be scared of anything. And yet, something had changed in him. It was as if he was on high alert, like a fire-watcher scanning the sky for the enemy.

He gave Ned a curt nod, which earned him a whispered and mischievous admonishment of, 'Thanks Ned,' from Jack. Wyngate turned to Lisette and said something to her in French, then stepped back from the stove.

'I'd better go to work,' he said as he picked up his hat. 'Enjoy the party; you've more than earned it.'

'I wish you could come,' Elsie said. 'We'll tell you all about it later!'

'It might end up being a long meeting,' Wyngate replied. 'But tomorrow morning, I'll make breakfast again.'

'Promise?' Elsie insisted. 'If there's cake, I'll bring some back for you.'

He smiled and nodded. 'I promise. Though I might not be able to conjure up sausages twice.'

Elsie chuckled. Lisette picked up the spatula, and held it so tightly that her knuckles turned white.

'Come and put the bolt on after me, Jack,' said Wyngate as he passed, and Jack trotted after him.

After breakfast everyone ran upstairs, to decide what to wear to the party. There were new clothes to choose from, courtesy of their well-wishers, and Connie's sequinned flapper dress had ended up coming to St Joseph's Terrace, along with the Shirley Temple dresses.

Ginger sat on the chest of drawers, watching as Lisette helped Elsie and Susan. She combed their hair and tied ribbons, when Pippa wasn't playing with them. Connie was all sparkly in her sequins, and Lisette made her hair look grown up with curls and rolls.

Elsie tied a ribbon onto Pippa's collar that matched the Shirley Temple dresses. Lisette had some make-up in her handbag, and they all tried it out, with a smudge of blue eyeshadow, dots of rouge on their cheeks and a touch of crimson on their lips. She'd put on one of her gowns when she got to Jasper's. The girls spruced her up, brushing her hair and styling it for her, using a clothes brush from the wardrobe to clean away the last grains of soot from last night.

Meanwhile, Jack was helping the boys get ready, and Elsie heard whoops of excitement from them. After everything they'd been through, an unexpected party was even more special to Elsie, and she knew it was the same for her friends too.

When the girls walked into the living room, they found their friends waiting, Jack and Ben smart in their best shirts and Ned wearing a cosy blue sweater that had arrived in Rupert's box of gifts from the people who had come to cherish them. Round her brother's neck, Elsie recognised the dark red tie that Mr Wyngate had been wearing last night and when he had left the kitchen with Jack following on. That must have been why he asked Jack to join him, Elsie realised, so he could make him a gift of the tie.

Each of the boys wore shoes that had been polished to a mirror and Ned was packing away the little boot kit that they had found in the kitchen, chewing his lip as he concentrated on fitting each item back into the sponge bag that held them. When he lifted his head to greet the girls, he gave a wolf whistle and announced, 'Gorgeous gals incoming!'

Elsie giggled and Susan blushed. There was a buzz in the air, like Christmas, as if something marvellous was about to happen. Connie did a twirl, her arms aloft.

'Ain't we got some handsome men to take us to the party!' She smiled cheekily, then said, 'And don't you look smart, Jack Taylor!'

'And you look ever so pretty,' Jack replied, but Elsie noticed that his cheeks had blushed red. 'Like Deanna Durbin!'

Jack adored Deanna Durbin, the pretty, sprightly child actress who was becoming a grown-up film star. He must really like Connie.

And Connie was blushing too. 'And that's coming from Cary Grant!'

Elsie looked at her brother, not quite able to see the suave and handsome, well-dressed star, but Connie did, and that was all that mattered.

'And me and Ben get the pleasure of two very lovely lasses on our arms,' said Ned cheekily. Then he gave a courtly bow to Lisette as a knock sounded at the door. 'Make that troys, as the French would say for three!'

Jack went to answer the door, his cheeks still beet red, but before he could slide back the bolt Ned was at the window. His eyes were big as saucers and he gasped, 'Bloody hell...'

Elsie ran over to look as well, Pippa at her side. There was Toe Mahoney's Rolls-Royce. It was the same car that Ned had stolen the night they had been rescued by Lisette and Wyngate. They'd left it outside the hospital, but evidently someone had recognised it and, knowing who the owner was, had dutifully returned it.

Pulled up behind it was another Rolls-Royce, this one in white. It looked so sleek and clean in the run-down street.

'Whose car is that?' Elsie gasped.

'Mr Dupree. He's the man what runs Soho. And my mate, Toe!' replied Ned, awestruck. 'Look at them motors. Mind you... I reckon I'd suit a nice sporty number like our Mr W.' He turned to Elsie. 'Don't you? You and me, out for a motor in our drop-top!'

Elsie remembered hearing Dupree's name being mentioned while they were living at Jasper's. He'd been spoken of in awe. And now his car was outside their house.

But even though the Rolls-Royces looked like something from another world, she preferred the idea of Ned's sports car. 'We'll drive down to Brighton for a day trip, and go for a paddle!'

Jack ushered Ma Mahoney into the room in a cloud of floral perfume. As she bustled through the door, she was already cooing, 'What a gorgeous little house!' Then she threw her arms wide. 'Here's all our angels, two-legged and four! Come on, lovelies, your carriages await!'

At least Elsie's second ever journey in a Rolls-Royce was more glamorous than her first. People trudging along the pavements stopped to look up and point as the two fancy cars sped past.

They waved from the windows like the king and queen, all the way from Whitechapel to Soho.

When they arrived at Jasper's, there were streamers round the door, with Tiny proudly standing guard in his best suit. They headed downstairs, where Lucien was at the piano, playing a medley of toe-tapping songs. There were balloons, and a handmade banner across the back of the stage declared, *LONDON LOVES THE BLITZ KIDS!*

There were so many people crammed into the club. People Elsie recognised, like Jasper and Ruby, Lilian and Brenda, Rupert and Esther. Ern and Agnes were here as well, grinning with joy. But there were lots of other people who Elsie had never seen before. Men and women of all ages, some in suits or dresses, others in uniform.

A huge cheer went up, so loud that Elsie was surprised the

room didn't shake, and Susan clamped her hands over her ears. When she did, Jack stooped to whisper in her ear and Elsie knew that he would be telling her not to be worried. Then there was applause and a resounding chorus of, 'For they are jolly good fellows!'

Susan dropped her hands and at the end of the song all six of them took a bow, as Pippa merrily barked.

'It ain't often I come into Soho and Mr Dupree comes into Whitechapel. Least, not without some business to discuss and a car full of big lads following on behind,' said Toe, earning a nod from Dupree, who stood at his side. 'But that ain't what matters these days. We're all Londoners, whether you knock about up west or in my East End. Kids, you're the best of London; the sort of stuff this city was made of!'

As a roar went up, Mr Dupree added, 'And on behalf of all Londoners, I thank you. And if Adolf hears about this, I hope it'll really boil his blood. Thank you to our wonderful lucky mascots, for keeping all of us smiling as the bombs fall. Three cheers for the Blitz Kids!'

Mr Dupree led the guests in their cheers and Elsie looked around, her heart swelling at the smiles on her friends' faces and the pride in Lisette's eyes. She wished that Mr Wyngate could be there with them. And Mum too, but she would be looking down on her children. She would be so proud of all that they had done.

All of these people had gathered together just for them. So many boxes of gifts had been sent, and there was the growing pile of newspaper clippings, the thanks and smiles of the people in the streets... they were helping. Even men like Sir Rupert, who was cheering more loudly than anyone, men who had everything, were roaring their thanks to the Blitz Kids.

'Now, nobody can chatter like a politician,' said Sir Rupert, laughing. 'But today, I shall be brief. Thanks to you all, Parliament is taking a very close interest in the welfare of the children who have fled back to London, and not before time. So many people have so little, yet still the people not just of London, but of our wonderful country, are sending gifts for you.' He reached into his pinstriped suit and withdrew an envelope. 'This is a letter of thanks from the prime minister himself. Mr Churchill has asked me to pass it on with his thanks and his assurance that, one day, he would be honoured to enjoy a personal audience with the Blitz Kids!'

Elsie was rooted to the spot with amazement. Churchill himself wanted to meet them?

Connie, sparkling in her sequinned dress, stepped forward to take the envelope. 'Cor, we'll give him an audience any time he likes!'

And with that, the party started. Lucien started to play 'Maybe It's Because I'm a Londoner' and the crowd stepped back to reveal a table full of treats. Of course, it wasn't laden as high as it would've been without the war, but it was a thrill to see the party food laid out on fancy plates with gold trim. There were sausage rolls, which Elsie knew would be padded out with vegetables, slender cheese straws, squares of carrot fudge and carrot cake in several different guises. There was a jug of orange squash, and bottles of ginger beer, which would be watered down, but it didn't matter.

There was dancing, and Connie looked like a star when she got up on stage to sing 'Happy Days Are Here Again'. Elsie noticed that she kept looking at Jack while she sang, and that it made her brother smile. And Elsie beamed when Jasper presented her with the curtains Pippa had made into her makeshift nest in the ruins, now laundered and stuffed and stitched into a comfy bed.

It almost felt as if there wasn't a war on – as long as Elsie managed to ignore the gas masks that hung over everyone's shoulders, and the number of uniforms in the crowd. Or the reason they were here at all, that the Blitz Kids had taken to the streets and saved lives as bombs rained down on the city they loved.

As Elsie danced with Ned, she smiled at the other dancers spinning by.

London loved them too.

FIFTY-THREE
ELSIE

Wyngate didn't come to the party. Elsie had brought the two peg dolls with her, though, and kept them safely in her pocket, so that he'd be there in spirit. Although Lisette was smiling, Elsie noticed that she'd kept glancing at the door.

Elsie had hoped she might see Wyngate waiting by their front door when they got back home, but there was no one there. The sirens didn't sound tonight, as if the Nazis had decided to give them a night off.

When Elsie got up the next morning, she hoped that she'd find Wyngate asleep on the sofa, or in the kitchen preparing breakfast. But he wasn't there, and, as the Blitz Kids sat round the table with steaming bowls of porridge, she kept glancing at the front door. Pippa sat beside her on the floor, her head tipped to one side as she followed Elsie's distracted gaze.

'Mr Wyngate won't be long,' Susan assured her. 'He did promise he'd be here for breakfast.'

Elsie prodded her untouched porridge. Her stomach was in knots and she couldn't eat. 'But there weren't a raid last night for him to get caught up in. Mr Wyngate isn't the sort of bloke to break a promise. I think something's up.'

'Come to the club with us when we go to set up. We can ask if anyone's seen him,' Jack suggested. The job he and Ben had been given had just become part of the routine now. They would go off to Soho after breakfast to help clean and restock or do anything else that was required of them, while Connie and Elsie went out to sing. Then they would all return just in time to meet Ned as he reached home for lunch and the lessons, which Connie and Jack held every afternoon, despite Ned's grumbles. 'Ned'll probably have news even if nobody else does. Not much passes him and his dodgy friends by.' Then he gave Elsie a smile. 'Now come on, eat up.'

Elsie forced herself to eat, even though it tasted like cardboard.

They all headed off to Jasper's, except Ned, who had business in Whitechapel. Brenda was surprised to see the girls arrive with Pippa, so she found some jobs for Elsie and Susan in the dressing room, while Connie looked through music scores with Lucien. Pippa kept busy, sniffing around.

But as the hours went by, there was no sign of Wyngate, not even a message.

'All right, Bren!' Elsie lifted her head at the sound of Ned's voice. He wasn't usually back from work so early and, even if he was, she couldn't imagine why he would come to Jasper's instead of going straight home. Yet she could hear him in the corridor even now. 'I'm lookin' all over town for that toerag Marsh. You see him last night?'

Brenda opened the dressing door for Ned. 'Nah, I didn't see him last night. Must've been busy selling nylons, I expect!'

Elsie's needle froze. 'Ned, didn't you tell Mr Wyngate yesterday that Marsh wanted to meet him?'

'Yeah, down Hallow's Wharf,' Ned said, saluting. 'I went down there and hollered for him but there weren't nobody.' His eyes lit up. 'You should see that place. Like a bloody Aladdin's Cave. Whoever's payin' the big money, they're using the old warehouse down there to store the stock. Everythin' you'd want from nylons to petrol coupons. I'd go back with a bloody suitcase and fill it if I didn't know what I know.'

And he widened his eyes as though to say, *ask me what I know.*

Brenda went out into the corridor and closed the door behind her.

'What do you know?' Susan asked him. She had pink and blue powder on her hands from tidying Ruby's make-up. 'The fact that if anyone touches that stuff they end up in the river?'

Elsie swallowed. The room was too stuffy; she couldn't breathe.

Ned looked disappointed, his *I know something you don't know* expression crumpling.

'Well... yeah,' he said with a shrug, stooping to fuss Pippa. 'And Mr W works for the Ministry, don't he? So what was Marsh wanting to talk to him about down the wharf? You know what I reckon?' Ned looked around, as though they might be observed, then dropped his voice to a whisper. 'I reckon Marsh was ready to grass.' Then he raised his voice again to add furiously, ''Cept he went and grassed and legged it before he paid me what he bloody owes me this week!'

'Maybe he did,' Elsie said, her voice trembling. She put her sewing aside. 'But that doesn't explain what's happened to Mr Wyngate, does it? You can't find Marsh, Mr Wyngate ain't here even though he promised. Something's wrong.'

Ned furrowed his brow. He looked up at Elsie and asked, 'You really think so?' He didn't even wait for her reply before he went on, 'It might be, you know. Because it ain't like either of them.'

The door opened and Jack and Ben wandered in, greeting their friend with a smile.

'Ready for home?' asked Jack.

'We can't go home,' said Elsie. 'Not yet. We have to find

Mr Wyngate. He never turned up, and Marsh has disappeared and all. We're going to Hallow's Wharf.'

And if he wasn't there, they'd go to Spitalfields and the address that he had given her on the night he brought Lisette back to life. Or to the War Office, or anywhere else they had to go to make sure he was safe.

'I don't even know where Hallow's Wharf is,' Jack admitted. 'Ned?'

Of course Ned knew. 'It's all the way out in Limehouse,' he said. Elsie had heard of Limehouse, but never seen the place. She pictured a place that glowered, dark and forbidding, a place that could swallow a man.

'Let's go there first,' Elsie said, trying not to shudder. 'We're the Blitz Kids. If we can't find Mr Wyngate, then who can?'

FIFTY-FOUR
ELSIE

After leaving a message with Brenda to tell Lisette, Elsie and the other Blitz Kids hurried out of the club with Pippa and caught a bus. They didn't have long to wait for one, but the already full bus seemed to groan at the seams as the six children and Pippa piled on. The conductress recognised them immediately and refused to take any money.

'You saved a bus and everyone on it.' She chuckled. 'We should be paying *you* for a ride, not the other way round!' She announced to the other passengers, who were looking wearily out of the windows at the tired city, 'Look who we've got – the Blitz Kids!'

The mood changed at once. The passengers cheered, and people stood up to offer them their seats. The children declined. Ned held the passengers rapt as they journeyed through the city, sharing stories of their escapades. A couple of times he took off his cap as though to collect donations but, whenever he did, a swift nudge from Jack soon saw the cap back on Ned's curls. When people reached for their purses or ventured to ask if they could help, Jack and Connie thanked them but said no. There were plenty of other causes they could donate to, they explained politely, and Sir Rupert Cavendish was doing all he could to publicise those causes too.

They only had to look out of the windows as the bus travelled through the streets to see how many people in the city needed help. On every road, at least one building had been lost; sometimes even most of the buildings had gone, either smashed by a bomb, or incinerated. The bus took diversion after diversion, as policemen stood by wooden barriers, the roads beyond them a mass of rubble. Sometimes it was hard to work out where the route of the street had gone, as there was nothing but ruins.

Barrage balloons floated above the city, looking drunk when one of their awning ropes had snapped. Every advertising hoarding mentioned the war somehow; either a company that sold soap or shoe polish assuring customers that their goods were still available but looking less fancy due to the war, or posters put up by the government to keep the population aware and motivated. A jolly pig lifted a dustbin lid, keen to eat food scraps, while other posters warned that LOOSE LIPS SINK SHIPS

Somewhere in this warren of bombed-out buildings and soot-stained walls, they would find Wyngate, Elsie hoped.

After winding through Whitechapel and Shadwell, the bus finally arrived in Limehouse. They piled off and Ned said, 'Take a good look at Limehouse, pals... 'cos it makes Whitechapel look like bloody Mayfair!'

'Watch the language, Ned,' admonished Jack gently. He looked along the street and shivered, then took Elsie's hand. 'Right, Ned knows where he's going, so we all stay close and follow him.'

It was strange that this place was so near Whitechapel. It was colder here, the wind more penetrating as it blew across the huge Limehouse Basin. It had come in for it badly, with so many buildings reduced to ruins, and there weren't many people around. It didn't seem right that a warehouse stuffed with riches could be in a place that was so deprived.

Connie guided Susan and Ben along as they followed Ned, and Elsie clutched Jack's hand even tighter. A short woman with a piece of rope tied round her waist for a belt was making her way along the shrapnel-pocked pavement.

'Hey, ain't you the Blitz Kids? What are you doin' down our way?' she asked, through a mouth that only had three teeth.

'Lookin' for a bloke called Marsh.' Ned didn't seem at all fazed by the woman, addressing her with the same casual cheer with which he greeted men from the Ministry and knights of the realm. 'Looks like a starved rat suckin' on a lemon. You seen him?'

The woman screwed up her face in thought. 'You know what, I have seen a bloke like that. Hangin' around Hallow's Wharf, he was. But you best keep your distance from fellas like that!'

'You seen a lot of coming an' going down by the wharf?' asked Ned.

The woman scratched her chin with a grubby, threadbare glove. Elsie could smell stale cigarettes and damp.

'Why would you want to know? I thought you was all about rescuin' people from the bombs, not fighting the black-market lads!' Then she nodded. 'All right, I have. People comin' and goin'. I was off to the shelter one night, and they was busy even durin' a raid. I reckon that's 'cos they think no one'll be watchin'. I wouldn't mind havin' a good look in that warehouse myself, but I know what folk like that are about, and I ain't gettin' involved. And you'd do yourself a favour not to either.'

'It's kids like us, ain't it?' Ned looked to his friends as he asked. 'Kids and folks who ain't got nowhere else, like them who got burned the other night?'

The woman nodded. 'Yeah, that's it. Hungry-lookin' kids with their shoes half-hangin' off, their clothes too thin for winter. And down-and-outs, the drinkers, and the mad, who've just been forgotten about by everyone. I might not have much meself, but I know what happens. I don't want any part of that. And neither will you if you've got any sense. It ain't worth it.'

'It ain't, you're right. You've been a treasure.' To Elsie's surprise, Ned reached into his pocket and took out a few coins. He held them out to the woman and said, 'You see any kids who look like they need a family, send them to St Joseph's Terrace in Whitechapel and tell them they've got a place with the Blitz Kids.'

'I can't take coins off of a kid.' The woman hesitated. Then she took only half of them from Ned, even though it was obvious that she could do with more. 'I'll tell them, if I see any. I bet they'd be proud to join you. And thank you, you're good kids. But be safe, won't you?'

Ned nodded. 'You an' all,' he said. 'Come on then, let's go and find ourselves a Wyngate!'

With that, the children hurried along the road after Ned, Elsie's heart pounding as she held Pippa tight.

They ran from one warehouse to another, the towering sides of them blocking out the daylight. Some were just relics, blackened with soot and twisted from the heat of flames, but others were still in business, with vans loading up beside them. There was something rotten about Limehouse; Elsie couldn't get the stink of it out of her nose, like gone-off eggs and old cabbage, blocked drains and rancid meat. At the water's edge, the river looked brown and dirty, and old wooden posts and pram wheels poked out of the mud.

But eventually, teetering on the edge of the basin, and tucked away just enough that anyone who shouldn't be there wouldn't be noticed, they found Hallow's Wharf. It looked just like any other warehouse from the outside, with a few windows that were boarded up. *HALLOW'S WHARF* had been painted along the wall in large white letters, but someone had pasted a poster over the O advertising cheap cigarettes. The cold wind whistled past and stirred sheets of old newspaper, making them dance with the dust.

Now that they were here, Elsie wished they hadn't come. But they had to, just in case Mr Wyngate was there. Ned pressed his finger to his lips and cocked his head, but there were no sounds from within.

'Nobody here earlier,' he reminded them.

Pippa was fidgeting in Elsie's arms, and she put her down on the ground. The little dog started sniffing, her sensitive nose brushing over the concrete. Then she lifted her head and twitched her nose. She gave a sharp bark and lunged forward, dragging Elsie after her on the lead, heading towards a large, dilapidated wooden shed that ran alongside the warehouse. There were gaps in the roof, and the edges of the wooden panels were green and rotten.

The door of the shed was half open and Pippa poked her head round it, then went inside, Elsie following. It was so dark and gloomy inside that she couldn't make out very much at first, but Pippa suddenly barked.

Elsie had never heard such an urgent tone from the little dog before. And as her eyes adjusted to the light, she suddenly saw a figure sprawled on the dirty floor. At first she thought she was looking at a guy left over from Fireworks Night.

Then she realised that the torn and dusty overcoat and the cut and bleeding face belonged to Mr Wyngate.

And he wasn't moving.

FIFTY-FIVE
ELSIE

'I've found him!' Elsie desperately called to the others as Pippa went on barking. She sank to her knees beside Mr Wyngate. He couldn't be dead, not this hero who could do anything.

She had no idea what to do, so carefully took him by the shoulder and gently shook him. 'Mr Wyngate, it's me, your friend Elsie. We've come to help you.'

'Bloody hell...' Ned murmured. He dropped to his knees and peered down at Wyngate. His gaze travelled along the dusty floor to Wyngate's outstretched hand and his leather glove, darkened with blood. Beneath his palm Elsie could see something else, shining silver and stained with red. 'Jesus bloody hell, he's only stabbed somebody!'

'No!' Elsie snapped, but Ned wasn't lying: there was a bloodstained knife under Wyngate's hand. She battled with hot tears as she tried to understand what could've happened. He wasn't a murderer, he couldn't be. 'No, he'd never stab nobody! And look at the state of him!'

The other children had come in and were staring down at Wyngate. Connie drew back, trying to take Ben and Susan with her, but they were rooted to the spot.

'Someone's beaten him up!' Susan gasped.

Jack had blanched white and was staring at the stricken man, his eyes wide. For a moment he looked utterly lost, then he swallowed and knelt beside Elsie, reaching his hand out to Wyngate's neck to search for a pulse. As he did, Ned scrambled to his feet and dashed across the warehouse into the shadows.

'If it's Marsh he's nobbled, he's got to be in here somewhere!' he shouted as he clambered over a pile of rotting crates. 'I don't like the look of this at—'

Elsie knew at once what Ned had found. She could see it in the way he was standing, frozen and tense, and the way that his voice, which never usually seemed to stop, had fallen so abruptly silent.

'Oh, heck, Ned...' Connie whispered. 'It's Marsh, isn't it? He's dead.'

Elsie couldn't leave Wyngate's side. He wasn't a murderer! 'You didn't do it, did you, Mr Wyngate?' she murmured to the unmoving man. Pippa had stopped barking and was instead pawing at Wyngate's sleeve as if she was trying to wake him up. His body suddenly convulsed and he began coughing a laboured, rasping cough. He clutched his fingers into a fist, then straightened them again, sending the bloodied knife skittering away across the filthy floor.

'He's alive!' Elsie tried to wipe the blood away from his face, relieved that he was still in the land of the living. But what on earth could they do? 'Mr Wyngate, it's all right, we're here. We'll get you to hospital and you'll be fine!'

'Elsie, don't be daft, we need to get the coppers!' Connie warned her, but Elsie shook her head. They couldn't go and get the coppers, because what about the knife? But Wyngate hadn't killed Marsh. He couldn't have.

Jack looked over to where Ned had disappeared, then back down at Wyngate.

'It's Jack and the kids,' he said urgently. 'Can you hear me?'

'Mr Wyngate, please!' Elsie begged him, rubbing her thumb across his cheek as she tried to clean his face. Ignoring the blood, she took his hand. 'You have to wake up, Mr Wyngate! You have to tell everyone you're not a murderer!'

Wyngate's eyelids flickered open but Elsie thought that it looked like it was taking an effort to do even that. He coughed again, then let his eyelids fall with a groan of pain.

'What are we going to do?' Elsie whispered urgently to her brother. 'Could we ring Lisette? She'd know what to do.' Then she leaned close to Mr Wyngate. Speaking slowly and clearly, she asked him, 'Do you want us to get Lisette?'

'Someone attacked me...' he gasped. 'Didn't see who.'

'We'll get you back to our house.' Jack swallowed again as he told Wyngate their plans. 'And we need to talk to the police.'

Wyngate's eyes opened again and he murmured, 'No police. Someone— Marsh.'

'Yeah,' called Ned. 'You only stuck him!'

'No, he never!' Elsie shouted. 'Mr Wyngate wouldn't. Isn't that right, you wouldn't, you—' But he didn't want the police. Was he guilty after all? But Elsie couldn't believe that. And clearly neither did Pippa, who was nuzzling Wyngate's cheek.

'And if we take him to hospital, the coppers will turn up,' Connie said, coming nearer now with Susan and Ben.

'But we've got to get him to a doctor or something,' Ben said. 'When our mum was ill, we got a nurse to come.'

Jack nodded. 'He needs help.'

Wyngate suddenly moved, pushing himself up to his knees on the concrete. His head hung low, his eyes closed as he breathed that rasping, painful breath. Then he forced his eyelids open again and said, 'I didn't kill him. Whoever did... they nearly did for me.'

Ned darted back across the warehouse, but not to Wyngate. Instead he stood close to Ben and Susan, resting his hand on Ben's shoulder as he whispered, 'You all right, mate?'

'All that blood...' Ben murmured. 'It's like... it's like when Mum...'

'It's all right,' Susan said gently. She had taken her handkerchief out of her pocket and was twisting it round her fingers. 'We couldn't save her, but Mr Wyngate's still alive. He's got a chance. We just need to get him help.'

Susan and Ben never spoke about their mother's death. They'd both been quite young when it'd happened. Elsie wasn't sure what was worse; seeing someone you love fall dangerously ill in front of you, or only finding out later that they'd died.

'Look, I've got an idea, and you can tell me it's stupid if you like, but hear me out,' Connie said. 'We can't take him to hospital, and I dunno what'd happen if we took him back to ours, seein' as Toe Mahoney's keepin' an eye on us. I don't reckon he'd want trouble, do you? And we've got a dead geezer in a warehouse, and a bloke what's only half-alive. What about we take him to Jasper's?'

Wyngate shook his head. 'I'm fine,' he gasped, his jaw tight. He didn't sound or look fine though, he looked like a man who needed his friends.

'No, you're not,' Elsie told him. 'Connie's right, we'll take you to Jasper's. We'll— oh, blimey, how are we going to do that? He can't get the bus!'

Wyngate turned his head and looked at Elsie. She knew then, without any doubt, any question, that he was innocent. There was no other option.

For a long moment they looked at each other, then he said, 'Ned, commandeer a car.'

Ned broke into a smile, but the expression froze on his face when from somewhere outside there came a call of, 'This better not be a wild goose chase, Harry. Two toerags killing each other down the wharf? I don't believe it for a moment!'

'Mark my words, this *anonymous well-wisher* will be a couple of kids with nothing better to do,' came the reply as heavy footsteps approached the shed. 'Laughing at the Met wasting its time chasing phantoms.'

'Coppers!' Ned exclaimed. 'Get him on his feet and out the back. I'll find a motor.'

Connie rushed over and helped Jack get Wyngate to his feet. Elsie wished she was bigger, so that she could've helped, but they needed to be fast. She picked up Pippa and held her finger to her muzzle, hoping the little dog would realise that she needed to be silent, rather than try to make friends with the policemen. Pippa seemed to understand, and licked Elsie's finger.

She heard Ned outside, doing his best impression of an innocent little angel as he said, 'Pardon me, constables, but you might want to look in the warehouse there. I think it belongs to one of the gangs, but I dunno really.'

'All right, sonny,' said the voice of the first policeman. 'We'll give it a once-over.'

Connie and Jack had Wyngate between them as they dragged him to the door at the back of the shed. What they would do if it opened onto a closed yard, Elsie didn't know. But they couldn't go out through the front. In seconds, they were all outside, in a narrow alleyway that stank of drains and ammonia. Water dripped monotonously from a broken gutter on the side of a warehouse high above them, splashing on their heads as they hurried by.

At the end of the alleyway, there was a van. It was dented, and the bumper was wonky, but it looked like it'd go.

Wyngate paused and lifted his head, blinking up into the winter sunshine. Then he glanced back over his shoulder at the shed as the sound of a child's footsteps thundered along unseen. Ned was on his way.

'I'm holding you all up.' Wyngate sounded exhausted and in the daylight Elsie could see that he'd been badly beaten, from the bloom of bruises and blood on his face to the sheer effort every step seemed to take. But until he gave a racking gasp and pressed his hand to his side, she hadn't noticed the blood there too. And there was so much of it.

'He's been stabbed,' Jack said urgently. Then he hauled Wyngate higher onto his shoulder and they set off again at pace, the older man's feet dragging on the ground as consciousness deserted him.

Elsie blinked back her tears. They had to get Wyngate help. How long had he lain there on the filthy floor of that old warehouse, bleeding into the dirt?

'The van,' Elsie whispered.

Susan tried the handle on the back and it opened right away. There was no driver, and no merchandise in the back, just some sacking laid across the floor.

'Climb in, everyone,' Connie whispered, and she and Jack lifted Wyngate in and laid him down carefully in the back. Elsie, Ben and Susan followed, Elsie clutching Pippa as she settled beside Wyngate.

'I'm sorry it ain't a Rolls-Royce, Mr Wyngate,' she whispered. He gave her a weak smile, then reached out and took her hand before closing his eyes again. As Elsie clung to Wyngate, Ned climbed up into the driver's seat. He fidgeted on the seat, then gave a huff of annoyance.

'I need all your coats,' he called into the back. 'So's I can get high enough to see over the dashboard!'

They took off their coats and passed them over to Ned, and then, after he had fiddled with the wires, they were off, bumping over the uneven road. Elsie didn't dare look back – she didn't want to see the police appear, or whoever owned the van turning up as well. How many crimes were they committing? But she didn't care, because they had to get Wyngate to Lisette.

It said a lot about Ned's chosen profession that he knew where he was going even when he was piloting them down a nondescript backstreet somewhere in the East End. But with every turn he was taking them closer and closer to Jasper's. Elsie stroked Mr Wyngate's cheek and whispered to him all the way there. Jack had wadded up the sacking from the floor of the van and was holding it to the slash in Wyngate's shirt.

'Don't worry, Mr Wyngate, we know you're not a murderer,' Elsie told him.

'I'm sorry about everything,' he murmured. Elsie had never seen anyone so pale, someone who looked as though they were dying, until today. And it was the man who had come to mean so much to her. He shifted his tired gaze to Jack, then back to Elsie. 'Brothers and sisters... you'll always have a friend.'

'Jack's the best,' Elsie told him. 'You can be my big brother, too, if you want a little sister?'

Wyngate closed his eyes again and whispered, 'My sister died. Tiny little thing.'

'Oh, Mr Wyngate...' Elsie sighed. He seemed to go through life like an ironclad ship, never revealing much about himself, but the knife in his side had cut through his defences. 'I'm so sorry you lost her. You must've been very sad.'

He acknowledged her with a very faint nod, then murmured, 'So long ago...'

Elsie gently stroked his cheek again. 'I bet she loved being your sister, though, even if it weren't for very long.'

'Jasper's!' Ned announced. 'I'll pull in the alleyway round the back... beats bloody lessons!'

There were better ways to avoid lessons than this, Elsie thought. The police who'd been poking around the warehouses wouldn't think to look in Soho. But as Ned drew up behind the club, something occurred to her.

They'd left the knife behind.

FIFTY-SIX
LISETTE

Lisette cursed herself for arriving at the club too late. She would've gone with the children if she'd been in time, but, once Brenda had told them they'd left to look for Wyngate, she knew there was no point in trying to follow. At least if she waited at the club, she'd be here in case they rang.

She kept an eye on the telephone behind the bar as she stood by Lucien's piano, practising. She tried to keep her worries at bay, but she knew Lucien could hear it in her voice. It wasn't like Wyngate to vanish and break a promise. Something must've happened to him, and she couldn't do anything but wait.

Then she heard an engine in the yard behind the club, and a clatter, and the thud of footsteps. She abandoned her rehearsal and ran to the back door.

She ran up the slope behind the club to help Jack and Connie edge Wyngate out of the van. It barely even looked like the smart man who bristled with energy and vigour. Instead, he was a crumpled, bloodied figure, pale and bruised.

'Where on earth did you find him?' Lisette gasped.

'Limehouse,' Ned said, clambering down from the van.

'With Mr Marsh's dead body. Looks like a scrap turned really nasty.'

Lisette dreaded to think what had happened. She'd always known that the criminals who hovered around the club were no good, and she wished that Ned had listened and realised just how dangerous it was.

Wyngate's head was lolling, as though it was too heavy for his neck, but at Ned's words he jerked awake. 'I didn't do it,' he gasped. 'Ned, please—'

And Ned gave a sharp nod before he admitted, 'I believe you. I don't reckon you're the sort.'

'Oh, Wyngate, my poor man,' Lisette said to him in French, before switching back into English. 'Get him to the dressing room and I'll patch him up. Quickly.'

They took Wyngate through the club. Lucien leapt up from his piano and opened the door to the backstage for them. Elsie hurried ahead and pushed open the door to the dressing room, where she and the other Blitz Kids had once found sanctuary. Now it would be Wyngate's place of safety.

Lisette directed Connie and Jack to lower him onto one of the camp beds that she hadn't had the heart to pack away, then she hurriedly gave the children orders.

'He needs a whisky, and someone get the first aid kit, and could one of you fetch warm water and towels?'

The children didn't argue. They rushed out of the room, each with a task to perform. Lisette perched on the camp bed beside Wyngate and took in the extent of his injuries; his battered, bruised face, the blood at his side and the pain in his dark eyes.

'I'll need to take off your jacket and shirt,' she told him, already trying to ease him out of his coat without hurting him any further. He sat forward, helping her as best he could. Lisette couldn't imagine such resilience even now, even as he pushed through the pain.

'I was stabbed,' he said in between sharp breaths. Lisette couldn't help a gasp of shock when she saw more clearly what they were dealing with. What looked like an expensive shirt – handmade, probably – was wet with fresh blood. It shone in the electric light, slick and dark.

'Missed anything important. Can you sew?'

'Yes,' Lisette replied, as she threw Wyngate's coat aside and began to remove him from his jacket. She breathed as evenly as she could, trying to hold back her panic. 'But I've never had to sew a person before.'

He really needed to be in a hospital, but she knew there had to be a very good reason why the children had brought him here. If Marsh was dead, and Wyngate had been stabbed, then it would look bad for Wyngate.

'Disinfect the wound,' he instructed as Ned dashed in and handed him a glass of Scotch, which he knocked back in one before handing the glass back and sending Ned running for a second with a nod. 'Needle into the boiling water. Stitch.'

Susan appeared with the first aid box, followed by Connie and Elsie bringing towels, and Jack carrying a bowl of hot water and soap to clean Wyngate up. They laid them down on the empty dressing table, and Lisette sent them off to get boiling water as quickly as they could, to sterilise the needle. When Ned returned with a second glass of Scotch, Wyngate held it tight.

She peeled Wyngate out of his torn, bloodied shirt. His taut muscles were stained red with his own blood, and Lisette reached for cotton wool and iodine from the first aid kit. She bathed the wound, wincing on Wyngate's behalf at the soreness of the iodine in his open wound.

'I'm sorry it hurts...' she whispered.

'Don't let the children see it,' he told her.

'I'll try my best,' Lisette replied. 'But you mustn't worry about that. We just want to patch you up, mon cher.'

There was a sewing kit on the dressing table, and Lisette took out a packet of needles. They ranged from tiny and thin to broad darning needles for wool.

'I don't know which size you need,' she said, hoping that she didn't sound helpless.

Wyngate tapped one finger against the cardboard packet and replied, 'That one.'

Lisette looked down at the metal sliver in the packet, trying not to think too much about what she was about to do. She took a reel of thread from the sewing box, just as she heard someone in the corridor.

'I've got the boiling water.' Elsie came through the door, holding a striped blue and white jug. She flinched, quickly turning her head away, but it was too late. She'd seen Wyngate's wound.

'Thanks, Elsie,' Lisette said, and the little girl came over with it.

She looked at Wyngate again, and this time she lifted her gaze, and kept it on Wyngate's face.

'I'll stay and help,' she said to Lisette.

'No,' Wyngate whispered. 'Elsie—'

'I'm *staying*,' Elsie insisted. 'Lisette might need some help. And I'll hold your hand, Mr Wyngate.'

Lisette threaded the needle as Elsie sat down on the other side of Wyngate. She carefully dunked as much of the needle and thread as she could into the boiling water without scalding her fingers, then she was ready.

'Turn aside a little so I can get to your back,' Lisette directed, trying to sound matter-of-fact. 'And if I sound like I know what I'm doing, I can assure you I don't.'

Wyngate shifted and turned, just as she had instructed. He looked tense, but it wasn't the tension of a man anticipating pain, it was something that seemed as natural to him as breathing. He was like a coiled spring even through his exhaustion, always ready to move.

'Ready?' she asked him with a tremble in her voice, the needle poised an inch above his skin. Wyngate gave a very firm nod and took a quick drink from the glass.

'Ready.'

She tried to pinch together the two sides of the wound. His skin slipped out of her fingers, fresh blood beginning to pool. She heard Elsie draw in a sharp breath. Lisette swallowed, grasped the sides of the wound again and pressed the needle through his skin. She couldn't go too deep, she realised and pierce the muscle. She fed the needle through and the thread followed, then she drew it through the skin opposite and pulled on the thread. There it was, a stitch. She couldn't believe what she'd just done.

'That's the first one done,' she told him. 'Do you need a breather?'

'No, just get it done,' Wyngate instructed. He reached out and took Elsie's hand in his. 'The quicker the better.'

Lisette carried on. It didn't get any easier. She could see the muscles tensing in his back, then relaxing. Trying to take her mind off her gruesome task, she pictured Wyngate standing on a beach in crisp, white shorts, staring out to sea, his hair tousled by the breeze and his back tanned by the sun. And under his shoulder blade, there was the white ghost of a scar. As Lisette drew the thread through again, she noticed other marks on his body, and she didn't know how long those scars had been there. Perhaps some dated to the beginning of the war, but others might have been older, the results of adults terrorising the little boy.

She started to hum a tune, but broke off to say, 'I'm so sorry, I'm better at singing than... than...sewing people up.'

Wyngate looked over his shoulder, regarding Lisette, for a long moment. His eyes were dark, but the bloodshot, dazed expression she'd seen when she'd helped him out of the van was gone now. Instead, he was looking at her with a clear, watchful gaze.

'Why would you say that?'

'Because I'm just a singer,' Lisette replied. 'I could've done more for the war than sing. Look, you need a nurse or a doctor, and I... I've told myself I'm keeping up morale, but...'

'You don't think that's valuable?' Wyngate asked, still watching her. 'Why?'

'Everyone likes singing,' Elsie said. 'Think of all them people who smile when they hear Connie outside the pub.'

'Someone wagged their finger at me once and said, *no one needs singers*,' Lisette told them. 'I said *of course people do!* But deep down, I think... perhaps I was too scared to do anything else. I just sewed tricolor ribbons onto a dress. I hope I made the English remember the French, and I know the Québécois love my songs, and de Gaulle's people too, but is that enough? Is it really? I know I helped last night during the air raid, but...'

'It's enough.' He nodded, then took a deep breath as though he was about to say something monumental. *A confession?* 'When' – he swallowed and drew in another breath – 'When I can't come to hear you sing, I miss the music.'

'You do?' Lisette grinned. 'It means so much to hear that. I don't know what to say. Other than... I'm sorry, I hope this doesn't hurt too much. But it's the last one. It's nearly over.' She carefully pulled the last stitch through. Wyngate turned his head away and she heard him catch his breath, the only sign of discomfort he'd shown throughout.

'Don't ever stop singing,' he murmured. 'We *do* need it.'

She tied a knot in the thread, then snipped it. The puckered line of the wound looked better than it had when she'd first seen it. At least it wasn't gaping open any more. Her needlework wasn't brilliant, but it would have to do. 'You're all sewn up, mon cher. I'll make up the camp bed for you, you'll be cosy. And I'll find you some aspirin.'

Wyngate nodded. He glanced at Elsie, who seemed to be silently urging him to say something, though he couldn't guess what. But Wyngate gave another little nod and added, 'Thank you.'

'Don't mention it,' Lisette replied as she wiped his firm chest with one of the towels, trying to wipe away any trace of blood. After cleaning up his face as well, she got to her feet and Elsie helped her to make up the bed next to Wyngate, using the neatly folded sheets and blankets that the Blitz Kids had once slept on. She didn't have any spare clothes for him, but Elsie helped Lisette to settle him under the blankets, and he looked as cosy as he could for a man who'd been left to bleed to death.

Once he was settled, Elsie went off, leaving Lisette alone with Wyngate. She sat down beside him, stroking his hair, and only now did she allow herself to accept her fear.

FIFTY-SEVEN
LISETTE

Lisette stayed by Wyngate's side until he fell asleep, then she turned off the light and gently closed the door. Jasper had arrived and Lisette found him surrounded by the children as they told him what had happened.

Jasper was stunned, his eyes wide in astonishment. He kept glancing towards the door that led backstage. He clearly wasn't comfortable about his club being used as a makeshift hospital for a man who the police were after, but equally he knew all about Wyngate's bravery in saving a bus full of passengers from a bomb crater.

'If we can't show our thanks by letting him sleep it off here, then I don't know what we can do,' Jasper said.

A few hours went by. The children were restless and Lisette tried to find things for them to do, but they were worrying about Wyngate, and so was Lisette. When the club opened the girls went to the other dressing room to help the performers get dressed, while the boys stayed in the wings, watching the audience.

Lisette went to check on Wyngate, taking a jug of water and a glass. She opened the door softly, and peered round it. He was sleeping soundly beneath the blankets. He deserved this rest, she knew; she had the distinct impression that rest was probably something he didn't allow himself too often.

She watched his chest rise and fall and her heart was suddenly so full of love that she trembled. It was as if something had always connected them, but it was just waiting for the moment to bring them together.

He'd saved her life, breathing for her when she couldn't. And now she'd helped to save his, stitching him up and giving him shelter.

She put the jug and the glass down by the bed, and gently stroked the hair away from Wyngate's forehead. She was fussing, but she couldn't help it.

'This feels strange, you know,' Wyngate murmured sleepily. 'All this... caring.'

Lisette smiled at him. It wasn't right that he hadn't been looked after. 'I hope you don't mind, because I intend to care for you.' She perched on the camp bed next to his, and asked, 'How do you feel? Do you need anything?'

Wyngate shook his head. He blinked up at her from the pillow and said, 'I feel like a train went through me.' Then he asked, 'How're the kids? Was Elsie all right after she saw... you know what she saw.'

'They're all a little shaken.' Lisette gazed into his dark eyes. It was typical of him to worry about the children rather than himself. 'Ned especially, although you wouldn't know it. Elsie's fine, she wanted to come and help. I think she would have felt more upset if she hadn't been able to see that you've been stitched up. She knows you'll be all right, mon cher. They decided to stay at the club rather than go back to Whitechapel. They're your team.'

'Are you on my team?'

'Of course,' Lisette assured him. She stroked his cheek with her fingertips. 'Don't worry about anything. You're safe here.'

Music floated through the wall, and Ruby began to sing. There was laughter coming from somewhere in the club, courtesy of a guest who had no idea what drama had unfolded earlier that day.

'I didn't do it, Lisette.' He coughed, and winced. The stitches in his side must have pulled with the motion. 'Someone set us up; killed Marsh and tried to do the same to me. They wanted me framed for it. Whoever Marsh was going to hand over must have found out.'

'I know you wouldn't kill in cold blood,' Lisette said. He was caught up in something dark and tangled, but there was nothing she could do, other than look after him. She poured him some water, then put her arm round his shoulders and helped him up. 'So they knew Marsh was going to inform on them. And decided to sort all their problems out in one go. Get rid of the person who was going to hand them over, *and* the person who's been investigating them.'

Wyngate drank down the water as though he'd been stuck in the desert for a week. 'Marsh was dead when I got there; I'd barely seen him when someone attacked me. I didn't get a good look before they stuck the knife in.' Lisette couldn't bear to even think of it, to let herself acknowledge how close they'd come to losing him. 'There was a bunch of drunks out in the street... they must've scared off the killer. And he phoned it in as an anonymous tip-off, hoping the coppers would find two bodies waiting for them.'

Lisette shivered. What must go through someone's mind to plan an attack like that, to take two lives in a city where death was round every corner and came out of the sky?

'We must be careful,' she whispered. 'They mustn't know you're here. I don't think they can, unless they know that you've been here with the Blitz Kids.'

She recalled the banner across the stage at the party –

LONDON LOVES THE BLITZ KIDS! Would anyone be stupid enough to touch them?

But could they make it look like an accident? She wouldn't let them, though. No one was going to hurt Wyngate or the children any more.

'I need to go,' Wyngate said, trying to sit up. 'I can't bring the police here and I don't want whoever attacked me near you and the children.'

He was in no fit state to go anywhere yet, especially not alone. Lisette put her hand on his bare shoulder, trying to gently push him back. 'You need to recover, and it's safe here. Jasper won't say anything. He told me it's the least he can do. You just need to rest and get better.'

He let her ease him down onto the mattress again, still murmuring, 'I can't stay here...'

'Where else would you go?' Lisette whispered to him. 'I won't let anyone hurt you again, you must believe me.'

Wyngate blinked, then settled his gaze on hers in the low light, 'I'm not used to being cared for, Lisette.' He drew in a breath. 'It's been for ever.'

She thought of the scars on his back, and the look in his eyes when Sister Benedict had burst in.

'When you told me that my mother is still alive, I felt so happy,' Lisette told him. 'But then, when I saw the children the next morning, I was filled with guilt. They are so young, and they don't have mothers any more. And you, too... you must've been so little when your mother passed away. I'm so sorry that you lost her and were left alone in the world.'

'Four, maybe five? I don't know how old I was,' Wyngate replied quietly. 'So I don't know how old I am. No birthdays, not really.'

'Do you remember coming to England on a boat?' she whispered. 'That must've been so exciting, but so scary for a little boy. Wyngate... what happened to your mother? After coming all the way to England with her son, it's so sad she passed away.'

Wyngate closed his eyes and swallowed and for a long moment Lisette thought that he wouldn't tell her, that he would draw down the shutters again. But, just as the silence stretched, his eyelids flickered open again and his gaze settled on her once more.

'I don't remember much, I was so young,' he murmured. 'I have scraps of memories of Paris, but... just me and her. And we had nothing. Then I suppose my father came back and he must've been English, because we left France to come with him. But in London, we had even less than we had in Paris. We couldn't even speak the language.'

'Oh, that's so sad,' Lisette said. She had wished, when she was small, that her father would come and sweep her up in his arms, and take her back to England with Maman. And yet it hadn't occurred to her, until then, just how bad it could've been. Wyngate's life had begun to fall apart the moment he'd arrived in England. She had a vague recollection of the influenza pandemic, the masks everyone wore, the empty streets, the church bells tolling as people died. 'But after your father brought you to England, what happened? Did he pass away?'

Wyngate shook his head. 'He just... vanished. Bored, I suppose. And my mother had to make money.' He held Lisette's gaze and murmured with meaning, 'I was born in Pigalle.'

Lisette knew exactly what he meant. Pigalle bordered Montmartre, where she had grown up with Maman. Overlooked by the elaborate wedding cake of the Sacré-Cœur church, down the hill was Pigalle. Women in tight skirts plied the most ancient of trades, for the night, or just for an hour or two.

'It's nothing to be ashamed of,' she assured him. 'Your mother did what she had to, to keep a roof over your heads.'

'She fell pregnant and life was even harder then. And one

night, I had a baby sister. Elise.' He took a deep breath, steeling himself. 'By the next morning, I had nobody.'

Lisette didn't say a word. She stroked his hair, as if he was still that little boy who had woken up alone in the world. Losing his mother, and his baby sister in mere hours, before being flung into an orphanage, was a fate too cruel to contemplate. And yet, it had happened to Wyngate.

'Elise? That is almost the same as Elsie,' she said softly. When Wyngate saw Elsie with Jack, he pictured himself with the sister he had lost. It wasn't just the fact that Elsie hadn't been able to speak that had drawn him to her; finally he had found a little sister to love. 'I'm so sorry there was no one there for you. But now you have me, you have the Blitz Kids... we love you, Wyngate. But... I can't keep calling you Wyngate. What did your mother call you?'

'Careless talk,' he warned with an affectionate smile. Then he said, 'She called me Adam.'

'Adam...' Lisette repeated his name, and decided she liked it. 'Can I call you Ad—'

An eruption of sound silenced her. There were yells, crashes, screams. A loud voice bellowed, 'This is a raid!'

Lisette leapt up from the bed, her heart pounding so fast that she was breathless. There were footsteps in the corridor and Elsie and Ned suddenly appeared in the doorway, their faces pale, their eyes wide with terror. Pippa, held tight in Elsie's arms, barked sharply in warning.

'It's the police!' Elsie gasped. 'They've come for you, Mr Wyngate!'

FIFTY-EIGHT
LISETTE

'Keep them busy!' Wyngate threw back the blankets and pushed himself up off the camp bed, wincing as the stitches pulled against his skin. 'I'm no use to the country and these kids if I'm in a prison cell.'

'Stay in bed!' Lisette ordered him. 'I'll get rid of them!'

She ran into the corridor, just as the backstage door burst open. Policemen in uniforms shoved their way in, wielding truncheons, followed by men in smart overcoats and fedoras, their eyes narrowed and steely. Were they detectives or secret service? All Lisette could do was scream, her arms outstretched to block their way.

But they pushed straight past her and the children, shoving her aside so hard that she bashed her shoulder against the wall.

'Here he is, lads!' a bull of a man in an overcoat bellowed as he marched into the room where, not long ago, Wyngate had been peacefully sleeping. He was on his feet now, dressed once more in the bloodied shirt.

'This man is a hero!' The voice belonged to Rupert Cavendish, who was following the men in, no doubt having been enjoying a peaceful night in Jasper's bar when they arrived. There was no trace of the good-natured friend of the unfortunate now though, as he stood in the doorway beside Lisette like a furious avenging angel in full evening dress, the children clustering around him and Pippa barking in their midst. 'How dare you apprehend him?'

A huge detective roughly grabbed Wyngate by the arm, and shouted to Rupert, 'Because he stuck a knife in someone in Limehouse!'

'No he never!' Elsie shouted, tears streaming down her face, but her small voice was lost in the crowd of people.

'He's injured, don't hurt him!' Lisette pleaded desperately, putting her arm round the crying girl's shoulders. But they weren't listening to her.

She peered through the forest of men, her stomach twisting as she watched them yank Wyngate about, before she heard the click of handcuffs.

'You're under arrest,' the man snapped, and read Wyngate his rights so fast that the words merged into a drone. Wyngate said nothing, his jaw set as he stared ahead with those dark eyes, glittering now with anger. He looked from Rupert to the children, before shifting his gaze to Lisette, and she saw the anger fade into sadness.

'Bloody bastards!' Ned bellowed, pushing his way past them and bursting into the room. 'You'd get right on with Adolf, you lot! Don't you even think about carting our mate off!' He flew towards the policeman who had handcuffed Wyngate. 'You'll be sorry, you will. All of you will!'

Wyngate spoke then, addressing Ned alone as he said, 'I'll get out of this, Ned. Look after everyone for me until I do.'

Connie and Jack shoved their way in. Connie's face was red with fury. Lisette tried to catch her shoulder as she passed her, but she slipped away and went straight up to the policeman who looked like a bull. She furiously grabbed his arm.

'Connie, no!' Lisette called.

'You leave off, you bunch of old bastards!' Connie screamed in his face, spittle flying. 'Ain't you got anything better to do, you ugly old bully?'

The man raised his huge hand and slapped her hard across her cheek, right across her scar, and she screamed as she let go of his arm. Jack lunged forward and punched the man so hard in his jaw that he reeled backwards. Then Jack, usually so mild-mannered and polite, was upon him, fists flying as he yelled things that Lisette could scarcely follow, sobs punctuating the words as he swung.

'Don't you hit her!' he was screaming when Rupert reached out and put his hand on Jack's shoulder, gently easing him backwards. 'Nobody's hitting us again!'

Elsie's face was pale as she clutched Pippa to her. 'Jack, don't!'

'Jack, stop it!' Susan pleaded, huddling against the wall beside Ben.

'Take these two in,' one of the men in fedoras said coldly, nodding towards Jack and Connie. Yet the policemen seemed to hesitate at the unthinkable suggestion that they drag in not only children, but two of the Blitz Kids. 'I said take them in!' He seized Wyngate's shoulder and pushed him roughly towards the door, then turned to address the policemen once more. 'And give this place a thorough going-over. You never know what sort of people are hiding in the darkest corners of a dump like this.'

'I'll go with them,' said Rupert, then he looked down at the children and added gently, 'We'll soon get this straightened out, never you worry.'

Tears rained down Connie's red face as she struggled against the policeman who was reluctantly cuffing her. Beside her, Jack was being cuffed too, and Elsie cried even harder, trying to pull the policeman away from her brother.

'You can't take them away!' she wept, as Pippa growled.

Lisette caught her elbow, trying to make her stand back.

'Elsie, there's nothing you can do,' she said softly. Jack looked beaten as he cast his eyes down, but he tried to give Elsie a brave smile.

'We're all coming back.' Wyngate's defiant words were directed at all of them, but Lisette knew that they were really for Elsie. 'Don't worry about us.' As the man in the fedora shoved him hard through the door, Wyngate shifted to catch his shoulder on the frame. It made a sickening thud, but it was enough to hold him there, despite his captor's efforts to force him over the threshold. He put his lips to Lisette's ear and whispered in French, 'My key wasn't in my coat when I got here; someone's stitching me up.' The man gave him a warning jab, aiming right for the place that Lisette had stitched. Wyngate barely flinched, but Lisette heard the gasp of pain he almost caught. 'Find Mr Gray.'

Hope flared within Lisette, a bright light displacing the darkness of her fear. She nodded eagerly. 'I'll find him,' she replied in French. 'I won't let them do this to you, mon cher.'

Wyngate pressed his lips to Lisette's in a fierce kiss, then turned to instruct Ned, 'Ned, tell the whole damn world that the Met arrested the Blitz Kids. Burn the bloody thing down.'

Lisette's lips tingled and she touched her fingertips to them, as if she could hold on to his kiss for ever.

Connie started to sing 'If You Want to Know the Time Ask a Policeman'. But she sang the jaunty song with rasping fury. Suddenly, all of the children joined in, even Elsie, through her tears, as Pippa licked her cheeks. Their high-pitched voices echoed around the corridor, and Lisette saw the police lower their heads as if ashamed. As he followed them out, Rupert joined them in their song, his voice booming and defiant.

Lisette watched them go, and slipped her arms round the children who were left. It was an effort not to give in to the exhaustion that washed through her.

'We'll clear their names, somehow,' she told them. 'And whoever framed Wyngate will regret the day he was born.'

FIFTY-NINE
LISETTE

There was no time to lose. Lisette and the four children, with Pippa, took the Underground to Spitalfields. She'd had no idea where Wyngate lived but, once the police and the secret service had left the club, Elsie had produced a worn piece of paper from her pocket, with an address written on it. Wyngate had given it to her weeks ago at the hospital. It was as if she'd kept hold of it like a lucky talisman.

The police would head for Wyngate's flat too, but, if Lisette and the children got there first, they could make sure that whoever had stolen Wyngate's key couldn't lay a false trail that would result in him being slammed behind bars.

Or worse. The punishment for murder was execution.

They found Wyngate's address opposite Spitalfields Market, where vans and lorries were coming and going, bringing food from the countryside to the tired, bomb-riddled city. Even though it was nine o'clock at night, with the looming threat of an air raid, the city had to be fed. There was no fancy West End apartment for Wyngate, the man who dressed with such care. Instead he lived in the thick of it, keeping to the East End, where he'd made his home as a little boy.

Lisette stood on the pavement, looking up at the dark windows of Wyngate's flat. 'We don't have a key,' she said, shaking her head.

'You're dead right that you ain't got a key,' said Ned casually, reaching into his pocket. "Cos you've got every key in London.' And when he withdrew his hand, he was clutching a long piece of thin metal, bent into a hook at the end. He slid it into the keyhole, then pressed his ear to the door just above, listening intently as he turned the hooked metal this way and that.

'You're a very handy boy to know,' Lisette told him.

She glanced up and down the street, crossing her fingers that Ned would be quick. How would it look if the police and the secret service turned up?

'Bank of England next,' Ned told Ben and Susan with a smile that Lisette knew was intended to settle their nerves. He withdrew the metal and turned the handle, opening the door with ease.

'You've got to teach me how to do that!' Ben said, clearly impressed.

'Happy to, mate!' Ned beamed. 'I wouldn't have expected a Lord living in these parts. Mr W maybe, he's a closed book, that one. But a bloke like Rupert? Must have a bird here!'

'What do you mean?' Lisette asked him. 'Have you seen Sir Rupert here?'

'Yeah, this morning,' said Ned. 'When I was looking for Mr Marsh to get my money, 'cos he hangs around the market sometimes, chatting up the lasses. I saw Rupert coming out this same door. Maybe he knows Mr W from the secret service or something?'

'Perhaps he does,' Lisette replied.

But why would he be looking for Wyngate at home instead of the War Office?

'I'll run up and get the next door open,' Ned told her.

'All right, Ned, you do that,' Lisette said. 'Elsie, I want you to come up with me, but Ben and Susan, you need to stay down here on the street. You're the lookout. As soon as you see the police coming, I want you to make a noise. And don't talk to strangers!'

The two children nodded. Lisette hated leaving them on their own in the blackout, with only the thin light of a shielded lamppost nearby, but she wouldn't be far away.

'You can look after Pippa,' Elsie told them, handing Pippa's lead to Susan. 'She might be little, but she's a guard dog at heart!'

Susan took the lead carefully, then told Lisette, 'If we see the police, we'll sing "If You Want to Know the Time Ask a Policeman"!'

Lisette smiled as she patted her shoulder. 'That's perfect! We'll see you very soon.'

She ran up the steep stairs with Elsie, their footsteps echoing against the tiled walls. She felt as if she was running in a dream, as if she couldn't move fast enough. The stairs were old and rickety, and once they reached the top there was a small landing with a lamp on the wall, with a shade shaped like a shell. Ned was busy working on the lock.

'He don't muck about with his locks, our Mr W,' Ned said, glancing over his shoulder. He was working in darkness, his ear pressed hard to the door as he worked. 'This bloke don't want nobody getting in.' Then he gave a satisfied nod and opened the door. 'But he reckoned without us Blitz Kids.'

'Ned, you are brilliant,' Lisette told him.

They crept into the flat. It was so dark, but in the gloom Lisette made out the shape of a blackout torch on a small table by the door. She turned it on. In the weak light, she saw a colourful rug on the wooden floor, and the walls painted in a sober blue. Hanging on the wall was a print of a village on the side of a hill. *Bramble Heath*, it said underneath it.

It was strange going into his flat for the first time, creeping like a burglar. Even though he wasn't there, she could feel his presence, as if he was just out of reach.

They had to be quick. If the police arrived, they'd be too late to save Wyngate.

SIXTY
ELSIE

Elsie was so tense that she had to force herself to put one foot in front of the other. She listened out for sounds in the street, taking in everything that Lisette caught in the torchlight as well. The engines of the vans and lorries coming and going from the market opposite throbbed in her ears like the sound of Nazi planes.

'There's only one flat up here,' Ned said quietly. 'So Sir Rupert must've been— yeah, he and Mr W must work together. That'll be what it is.'

A prickle of heat ran across Elsie's skin as she opened a door, and, in Lisette's torchlight, she saw a sitting room. The blackout blinds were drawn, but during the day it must look over the street and the market. She took it all in, the shelves of books, the colourful tapestry cushions on the armchair and the sofa, the rug with the swirly pattern. A radio with a sunrise cut-out stood under the window. On the mantelpiece, a clock in a dark wood frame ticked away the minutes. A smiling ceramic pig, with floppy ears, sat on one side of it.

On the other side was a portrait photograph of a lady in a wide hat, with beads on the bodice of her dress. She was young, with a gentle smile and dark hair. There was something about her that seemed familiar, and in a flash Elsie knew that the lady in the photograph had to be Wyngate's mum.

'That Sir Rupert seems like a nice bloke,' Elsie said carefully, wondering how to put her concerns into words. She had to say something. Lisette went on running the torchlight around the room. 'Only, doesn't it—'

'What's this? A wallet?' Lisette interrupted, shining the torch onto a square of worn, dirty leather sitting on the arm of the sofa. It couldn't have been Wyngate's. With a look of distaste, she picked it up with her gloved hand and held it out to Ned. 'Ned, could that be Marsh's?'

Ned nodded. 'Yeah,' he said. 'Could be; it'll have a ticket for the Hammers' Christmas Day match inside if it is.' He shrugged. 'Mr Marsh won big that day, had a bet on and cleaned up. That ticket was like his lucky whatsit.' Then he added with a shrug, 'Oh yeah, it'll have his identity card in it an' all. But you never know with Marshy, might not even have his own name on it!'

Lisette handed the torch to Elsie and she held it for her, aiming the light at the wallet. Lisette flipped the wallet open and, inside the pocket at the back, she found the dog-eared ticket for the West Ham football match. There was something sad about the limp piece of paper, which had belonged to a man who had been so heartlessly killed. His lucky charm hadn't been so lucky after all.

'West Ham,' Lisette read from the ticket. She carefully put it back, and looked through the rest of the wallet. 'An ID card—no, wait, there's three of them.'

She laid them out on the arm of the sofa. They didn't have photographs on them, so they were easy to fake. There was a Joseph Ward and a John Waller, a Thomas Sharp. But no Mr Marsh.

'Give it here,' said Ned. He pulled on a pair of woolly

gloves, and only then did he peel back the lining of the wallet and take out another identity card. 'Edwin Marsh. Just like him to hide the real one, so's the coppers didn't get hold of his real name if they pulled him in.'

Lisette sighed. 'We'll keep this. Now what else could they have planted here? The knife?'

Elsie remembered it lying under Wyngate's hand. 'No, it was in the warehouse. The police would've found it.'

Ned furrowed his brow, then gave an exclamation. 'The wallet puts Marsh here, don't it? In Mr W's flat. Like they came up here for a drink and then headed off to Limehouse together.'

Then he picked up a thick book that was lying on the coffee table and opened it. 'Look at this... it's a ledger for the bloody warehouse!' He nodded to Lisette to shine her torch on the page, then said, 'Else, you got that bit of paper he wrote his address on?'

'Yeah!' Elsie drew it from the pocket of what had once been Wyngate's coat. She held it out to Ned as Lisette's torch scanned along the page. 'The writing in this book ain't Wyngate's. And look what it's saying! *Twenty crates of whisky. Two hundred pairs of nylons.* Barrels of petrol, too, and how much chocolate is that? This is everything in Hallow's Wharf, ain't—'

The strains of 'If You Want to Know the Time Ask a Policeman' suddenly rose from the street below, as Susan and Ben sent up their warning. Elsie's heart rushed in her chest and she clenched her hands in her gloves.

'Ned, hold on to the ledger,' Lisette told him. She gathered up the ID cards and wallet, and put them in her bag. 'We're going to the War Office.'

SIXTY-ONE
ELSIE

Elsie held Pippa's lead tight as they all ran from the Underground station to the War Office. They had only left Wyngate's flat in the nick of time, and Elsie's heart hadn't slowed since.

The Nazis were quiet tonight. There was still no sign of a raid, and yet the possibility of it hung heavily in the air. As they hurried down Whitehall, Elsie saw government buildings banked up with sandbags, the windows criss-crossed with tape. The white stone, glowing in the moonlight, was scarred and pitted from the remorseless raids.

As they passed the entrance to Downing Street, Ben cheekily shouted, 'Evenin', Mr Churchill!' They all laughed, even though they had little to laugh about.

'There, that's the War Office,' Lisette told them. It almost looked like Buckingham Palace, with columns and turrets. Piles of sandbags had been heaped up against the walls, and there were guards in uniform, rifles at their sides, standing outside.

They reached the foot of the steps that led up to the front door, just as the street was torn apart by the sudden, piercing yell of an air-raid siren.

'We can't stop now,' Elsie insisted, and they hurried up the steps as a guard in uniform called to them.

'Where do you think you're going with that dog?' he shouted after them. 'That's not the way to the public shelter!'

'Cheers, mate!' called Ned. He threw the door open and Lisette found herself in the grand foyer of the War Office. It bustled like a rush-hour station but Ned looked confident as he approached the vast reception. It was polished to a high shine and, somewhere in the unseen office behind it, Lisette could hear the incessant ring of telephones. 'Look at this, Pippa. We're runnin' the country now.'

Women in uniforms, with perfectly styled hair and make-up, were sitting behind the reception desk. They were from the army, the air force and the navy, all brisk and efficient. Elsie hoped she'd look like them when she was older. They were still working, ignoring the siren's racket.

One of them, in a dark blue Wrens uniform with gold brocade round her cuffs, got to her feet. 'I'm sorry, we can't let civilians – or dogs – use our shelter, you need to go to the public one down the street.'

'We need to see Mr Gray,' Lisette told her briskly. Pippa gave a sharp bark. 'It's a matter of life or death. We must see him, at once!'

'Mr Gray?' The Wren's mouth was set in an unsmiling line. 'You can't walk in off the street and demand to speak to Mr Gray.'

Elsie swallowed. The sound of the siren was now joined by the thrum of aeroplane engines. But they couldn't run and hide, not when their friends were sitting in police cells.

Ned rapped his knuckles on the polished counter and said, 'Tell him it's Mademoiselle Souchon, the chanteuse of Jasper's, Soho, accompanied by little Pippa, Elsie, Ben, Susan and Ned of the Blitz Kids.' Then he gave her a wink. 'Or do I turn on the waterworks and start simpering about how rotten you lot are to my mates on Fleet Street?'

'Don't think he's bluffing, he will, you know,' Elsie added.

The Wren drummed her perfectly manicured fingers against the desk. 'He's a *very* busy man.'

Ned's eyes grew wide as saucers, his lower lip trembling as he prepared to launch his act.

'Into the shelters, if you please! No paperwork is worth a life!'

The plummy voice boomed through the reception area, ricocheting off the old marble walls. It even seemed to silence the siren and the planes for a moment. It was the sort of posh, commanding voice that Elsie had only previously heard in films at the cinema, from characters who lived in big houses and drove fancy cars.

Then she saw the owner of the voice, a towering man in a vivid blue tartan suit and a shimmering blue bow-tie. A neatly trimmed moustache balanced on his upper lip, beneath a large nose. He advanced into the reception on long legs as the milling staff parted before him.

'Who's that?' Elsie whispered. He strode across the floor towards the little party and for a moment Elsie thought he might surge straight through them. At the last moment he stopped and peered down his long nose.

'I've seen you on the front pages!' the man announced. 'And you must all go down to the shelter. Dogs, children, ladies alike!'

The women behind the desk were gathering their things, but the children didn't move.

'These are the Blitz Kids. And we're not going anywhere until we've seen Mr Gray,' Lisette told him defiantly.

'I am he.' Mr Gray pressed one elegant hand to his breast, his gold signet ring catching a flare of light. He was like a rock in the middle of a fast-flowing stream, standing unmoving as the foyer bustled around him. 'And I have a pressing matter to attend to tonight, I'm so sorry.'

'So do we,' Elsie said. 'You've got to help Mr Wyngate and my brother, Jack, and my friend Connie!'

'Please, Mr Gray,' Lisette said, her words clipped with tension. 'You are one of the few people Wyngate trusts!'

'He's been stitched up,' Susan told him, her hands clenched inside her mittens.

Ben nodded. 'And they left him for dead!'

'Somebody planted evidence in his flat,' Ned told him. 'But we've got it safe.'

Mr Gray chewed his lip, then said, 'Go to the shelter and keep it safe. Mr Wyngate has been taken to hospital for that stab wound someone gave him.' He dropped his voice to a whisper. 'I believe you.'

Elsie's mouth went dry with fear. Hospital?

'Then you'll help.' Lisette almost sounded relieved, but she was following Mr Gray as he began to move again. And Elsie and the other children went with her, Pippa's claws clicking along the polished floor. 'We must speak now. We have something to show you. Please, Mr Gray!'

'I can't,' he said apologetically, striding on again. His legs were so long that all of them had to run to keep up. 'I have to see Mr Wyngate and then I'm battling with some damned rascal at social services who is hell-bent on sending two of your own number back to the countryside on the first train they can find. I intend to rain down hell on whoever ordered that children be handcuffed and taken to Scotland Yard!' Mr Gray finally paused. 'I simply cannot spare a minute.'

That was when Elsie's hand shot up and took Mr Gray's. With a bright smile, she said, 'We'll come along for the ride!'

SIXTY-TWO
ELSIE

In moments, they were in Mr Gray's fancy car, which smelt of polish and leather. The four children sat across the back seat with Pippa, while Lisette sat in front. Elsie watched the city go by, the buildings that were only still standing by chance among the ruins. Fires raged in the distance, the sky glowing orange from the flames.

As Mr Gray drove, Elsie and the others told him everything they knew. They started with Rob's death, then the inferno that had killed the street people, and what Wyngate had said about a shadowy new boss who was trying to take over the whole city. They told him about Marsh, and the warehouse, and what they'd found in Wyngate's flat. And Ned told him that earlier that day he'd seen Rupert leaving the flat.

Elsie felt the atmosphere change, as if a freezing breeze was blowing in. Sir Rupert Cavendish, friend of the most vulnerable people in London?

And Mr Gray listened. Even as he navigated the dark streets and the bombers roared overhead, he was listening intently to everything they were telling him. He already knew about Wyngate's efforts to get to the bottom of the new black-market boss who had taken over London's forgotten people and, most importantly of all, he believed that his man couldn't possibly have committed murder.

'Is he going to be all right, Mr Gray?' Elsie asked him.

But this time, Mr Gray afforded them a very small smile that filled Elsie with hope even before he said, 'He's very clever. A man might still escape from a hospital; if he's taken to a cell, it makes escape a darn sight harder.' He glanced in the rear-view mirror. 'I've spoken to Rupert and he was on his way to Scotland Yard to make a case for the children. He isn't at the hospital with Mr Wyngate.'

Elsie relaxed a little. And although Mr Gray hadn't put it into words, perhaps Mr Wyngate had pretended to be more unwell than he was, because he knew he could escape.

They arrived at St Bartholomew's, and Elsie tensed, remembering the last time they'd visited and Sister Benedict had appeared like a bad dream. Ambulances were pulling up, and people with bloodied faces were being carried into the hospital on stretchers. Once they'd climbed out of the car and were heading for the front door, a man with torn and bloody clothes, who was being helped along by a nurse, called out, 'It's our lucky day, it's the Blitz Kids!'

The children cheered in reply, but they couldn't hang about. Mr Gray was striding along the hectic corridors, and they had to run to keep up. Lisette's heels were tapping along the floor and Elsie had to carry Pippa. There were patients staggering on crutches, and people trying to hold each other up as they cried. A woman was calling for a doctor, while someone screamed in pain.

A nurse with a crisp, white hat and immaculate apron tried to stop them as they hurried by, shouting, 'No dogs in the hospital!' But Mr Gray didn't stop, so Elsie didn't either.

They reached a set of double doors, before which stood a

uniformed soldier. At the sight of Mr Gray he stood up dead straight, bolting to attention.

'Unlock, please.' Before Mr Gray had issued the command, the soldier had already put a key in the lock and turned it. Mr Gray pushed open the door and led the way over the threshold, and then Elsie heard the key turn again, locking them inside.

It was quieter here. Just ahead of them, Elsie saw two policemen standing side by side in front of a door. She was sure Mr Wyngate was behind them.

An office stood opposite the room that the policemen were guarding, and Elsie caught sight of a man in a fedora, who looked like one of the men who'd raided the club. She disliked him right away. He was sitting at a desk, flipping through a file, a cup of tea steaming beside him.

As Mr Gray sailed past the policemen, he issued a polite command of, 'Find my companions a place to sit and a cup of tea.' Then he turned to the little band that had followed him all the way from the War Office and said, 'I shall be yelling appallingly at this gentleman for the next few minutes. Please do excuse me.'

With that, he walked into the office and slammed the door.

The policemen looked at one another and shrugged. Mr Gray had spoken.

'I'll go and get you some nice cocoa,' one of them said, an older man with white hair. 'Take a pew. I'll be back in a tick.'

Before they sat down on the wooden benches lined up against the wall, Elsie tugged his sleeve. 'How's Mr Wyngate?'

'He's been patched up, and he's tucked up in bed with something to help him sleep,' he replied. 'I'm sure he'll be back on his feet soon.'

Elsie sat with Pippa on her lap, and she swung her feet because they didn't reach the floor. Lisette was tense, perched on the edge of the bench, her gaze fixed on the door of Wyngate's room.

Just as they were settling, Elsie jumped as Mr Gray's voice erupted from behind the closed door.

'He'll get Jack and Connie out and no mistake,' Ned said proudly. 'Listen to him shout!' He slipped down from the bench and wandered along the corridor to stand at the door behind which Wyngate lay. ''Scuse me, Officer, can we go in and see our pal?'

The policeman shook his head. 'Sorry, young 'un,' he replied. 'No visitors allowed. You know he's on a murder charge.'

'I know it's bloody twaddle,' Ned shot back. 'Why can't I go and see my mate?'

This time the officer sighed, obviously resigning himself to being Ned's straight man for a little while yet.

'Because he's been sedated,' he replied. No doubt anticipating another question, he added, 'And he's not on his own either way. Sir Rupert Cavendish is sitting in with him, just to make sure he's all right through the night.'

Elsie froze. Mr Gray had said that Sir Rupert was on his way to Scotland Yard. What was he doing in Wyngate's room?

SIXTY-THREE
LISETTE

Awash with panic, Lisette was on her feet at once, and rushed towards Wyngate's room.

'No, you can't leave Rupert alone with him!' she shouted. She shoved the policeman aside, and flung open the door. In moments, she took in the room; the lone bed with the red blanket and Wyngate's hair dark against the snowy white pillow.

And standing over him, a pillow held to Wyngate's face, was Sir Rupert Cavendish.

'Get away from him!' Lisette yelled, fury rushing through her every limb. She made a grab for Rupert's arm, gripping tight. He jerked his arm violently and sent Lisette sprawling back against the wall. The force of the blow knocked the breath out of her. But Lisette wasn't alone and the kids threw themselves at Rupert, surrounding him and dragging him back from the bed where Wyngate lay helpless. The murderous peer let out a cry of agony as Pippa sank her teeth into his shin.

Lisette hauled herself up and ran to the bed. She stroked Wyngate's hair. 'Please stay with us, Wyngate, please,' she urged him, wishing like mad that he would breathe, but he looked so pale and still.

She was aware of other people in the room now. The policeman had appeared, along with the man in the fedora and Mr Gray, all summoned by Lisette's shouts and Rupert's wail of pain.

'Arrest him, for God's sake!' Lisette called out. 'Wyngate's no murderer – but that vile man is!'

Rupert suddenly moved like a striking cobra, his hand darting out and seizing Elsie. She gave a scream as he dragged her closer and pressed a penknife to her pale throat.

'Nobody move,' he snarled as Pippa began to bark, the noise filling the room. 'I will kill her if I have to.'

'No, no, not Elsie!' Lisette wailed. But she didn't dare move. The little girl swallowed, her large eyes imploring someone to help her.

'Come on, old man,' said Gray carefully. 'You don't want to hurt a little lass like that.'

But Rupert gave a cruel smile. 'I don't care,' he declared. 'There are thousands just like her. She wouldn't be miss—'

The word was cut off in a strangled splutter as Wyngate, so unmoving until now, lunged from the bed and wrapped his arm tight round his throat. Lisette saw the muscles grow taut beneath the skin, throttling Rupert until the hand that was tight round Elsie's wrist grew limp and she was able to dart away. The knife hit the floor with a clatter and Rupert's real eye bulged in its socket, before he crumpled to the ground in a dead faint.

'Arrest him,' Wyngate told the policeman, looking down at the stricken man who would have killed him given the chance. 'And cuff the right person this time.'

Even though Wyngate was only wearing underwear and a bandage, he commanded the room.

The policeman nodded and cuffed Rupert, even though the

peer was out cold. Lisette put her arms round Elsie, holding the shivering little girl tight.

'It's all right, you don't have to worry about me,' Elsie assured her. She wriggled free and turned to hug Wyngate. 'Mr Wyngate saved me. He saves everyone.'

Lisette smiled at him over Elsie's shoulder. Yes, he did.

But even a hero like Wyngate needed friends who could save him.

SIXTY-FOUR

ELSIE

Elsie, Ned, Susan and Ben marched arm in arm, Pippa trotting alongside them. Lisette and Jasper, Brenda and Lillian, Ruby and Andrea, Tiny and Lucien walked just behind them, holding aloft the banner that declared, LONDON LOVES THE BLITZ KIDS. Esther darted just ahead, then to the side, everywhere at once, snapping photographs of them as they filled the frosty, wintry street with their protest chant.

'Free the Blitz Kids!' they shouted.

Elsie might be small, but she felt like a warrior. She had her voice and she was using it. And now Wyngate was a free man, although he needed to stay in hospital to recover from the two attempts on his life by Sir Rupert Cavendish.

But Jack and Connie were still locked up at Scotland Yard.

Elsie and the others had slept at the hospital that night, and in the morning Mr Gray had them driven back to Whitechapel in style, Lisette with them. As they went through London, Ned came up with an idea: they should go to Scotland Yard and demand Jack and Connie's release. Before long, his idea had snowballed into a protest march.

Lisette had made telephone calls from the Feathers pub.

Elsie had cheered when Esther had appeared at St Joseph's Terrace with her camera. Ned had gone through the streets of Whitechapel and drummed up Ern and Agnes and even Ma and Toe Mahoney. And where Toe Mahoney went, those who looked up to him gathered too, joining the march in droves.

As they headed towards Scotland Yard, the Blitz Kids picked up new marchers. Dupree and his wife, who had been driving down the road when they had spotted their protest parade, hurried to join in. People passing in the street, who Elsie didn't know but who evidently knew the Blitz Kids, joined in too. Their chant grew louder and louder, as if it would shake the windows of every building they passed.

'Free the Blitz Kids!' they shouted. Elsie wanted to scream down the street.

She saw men and women in uniform, who did all sorts of brave things to fight the Nazis, and ordinary Londoners, who did their bit too. She recognised regulars from the club, who'd come to their party in happier times. She spotted people who had been on the bus they'd saved from plunging into a crater, and she saw a woman with a pram, along with her friends, who Elsie and the Blitz Kids had kept safe from the unexploded bomb. There were firemen who remembered them fighting fires alongside them, and ambulance drivers too.

They weren't alone in the city any more. The Blitz Kids wouldn't be forgotten. But they had to save Jack and Connie. If Jack went back to the countryside, Elsie would lose her brother. And there was that foggy memory that she couldn't bring back to the surface. If he was sent away before she remembered it, would she ever be able to tell him?

They weren't far from Scotland Yard when Elsie turned at the sound of an engine. There beside them, driving along the street, was a flatbed lorry, with a camera man standing on the back. It said *Pathé* on the side of his camera, a name Elsie recognised from the newsreels at the cinema.

And then she smiled, because she saw who else was on the back of the lorry: Mr Wyngate.

He didn't look like a man who'd been left for dead, then nearly smothered in hospital, but was his usual immaculate self in his overcoat and fedora. The truck was moving at a slow pace, filming the march, and Wyngate waited until it drew level with his friends before he hopped nimbly down onto the pavement to the cheers of the kids and Lisette. He reached down to take Elsie's hand, joining the end of the chain that the kids had made, then looked back over his shoulder towards Lisette, raising an eyebrow. Lisette smiled warmly at him and took his arm, and now they were a chain of seven, marching proudly up to the wrought-iron gates in front of Scotland Yard.

Somewhere in the maze of corridors inside the hulking police headquarters, Jack and Connie were waiting to find out their fate.

'Free the Blitz Kids!' Elsie shouted at the top of her lungs.

SIXTY-FIVE
ELSIE

Two policemen were guarding the gates, but the many windows of Scotland Yard that looked down onto the road meant their arrival was seen by many. Pippa growled a warning.

'You'll have to turn round and go home,' one of the policemen at the gates told them. He was tall with a narrow face, his eyes like beads. 'We don't have marchers here!'

'My brother's in there!' Elsie shouted. 'You've got to let him go! And my mate Connie, too!'

'We're not marching any more, because we've arrived,' Wyngate told the policeman, coming to a halt in front of him. 'And we're staying here until Jack and Connie are released.'

Ned nodded, then turned towards the newsreel camera and the photographers who had clustered alongside the march, snapping images for the front page of what looked like every newspaper in England. His eyes were huge, his face a forlorn portrait of a child in need.

'Write our story,' he implored the journalists, who scribbled in their notepads. 'Write that a copper slapped my friend Connie in her face and took her and Jack away. We're lost without them, we ain't got no street smarts.'

Ned had more street smarts than anyone else, but those golden curls of his always made him look like an angel, no matter what he was getting up to.

'You have to go through the proper channels,' the policeman said. He ran his gaze over the restless crowd. 'I can't just open this gate for anyone. Not even for the prime minister.'

'They're children,' Lisette implored him. 'They shouldn't be in a cell!'

Wyngate set his jaw and fixed his gaze on the policeman as he said briskly, 'The prime minister can be arranged, but he's rather busy winning the war.'

Just then, the sound of a purring car engine interrupted the restless chatter of the marchers. Elsie turned to look, and saw a sleek, black car draw up. It looked very important.

'Stand aside, please,' the policeman shouted. 'Stand aside.'

But the car didn't move any further. Elsie peered through the windscreen and saw an impassive man wearing a bowler hat, sitting behind the wheel. His passengers were sitting behind. The driver's window was slightly open and pungent blue smoke curled out.

The driver climbed out, took a pipe from his pocket and clamped it between his teeth. He opened the passenger door of the car, and Elsie stared in surprise when she saw Mr Gray emerge. He must've wanted to join the march.

'Morning, troops!' Mr Gray beamed at them. He was wearing tartan again, a vibrant green this time, and he greeted the marchers with a polite nod. The people who had joined the protest gave him a cheer and Elsie got the distinct impression that he must be something of a celebrity. She decided she would ask Mr Wyngate or Jack, as they seemed the people most likely to know. Mr Gray strode round the car on his long legs and opened the door to allow his other passenger to disembark. Unlike Wyngate's boss, however, the emerging figure moved at a stately pace.

He was a short man, but he seemed huge in his homburg hat and dark overcoat. He was busy puffing on a cigar, and for half a second Elsie had the strangest feeling. Was he a friend, or someone she'd met before but couldn't place? Then it hit her.

It was Winston Churchill, the prime minister.

Elsie squealed with excitement, and around her their friends and the other protestors were cheering too, apart from Wyngate, who smiled at Churchill and gave him a small wave. Pippa barked, because even she recognised him; Mr Gray had brought the most famous man in Britain to the protest.

The chant started again. 'Free the Blitz Kids! Free the Blitz Kids!' Elsie joined in at the top of her voice. Did cells have windows? Could Jack and Connie see what was unfolding outside? It would give them hope that everything would be all right and that they wouldn't be sent back to the countryside.

'Do you want to tell him you won't open the gate?' Wyngate asked the policeman placidly. 'Or shall I?'

Churchill walked to the front of the protest and raised his hat to the kids and Lisette. At his side, Mr Gray knitted his hands behind his back, standing so straight that he reminded Elsie of the soldiers who stood outside Buckingham Palace, unmoving and unsmiling. Except Mr Gray was smiling. He was smiling very broadly.

'We have an appointment with Commissioner Game regarding a most worrying matter,' said the prime minister. 'Please open the gate, Constable.'

Wyngate put his lips close to Lisette's ear and Elsie heard him tell her, 'Game's the man at the top of the police.' There seemed to be nothing and nobody that he didn't know.

'Good morning, sir, of course, I'll open the gate right away,' the policeman said, with obliging humbleness.

He unlocked the gate, while his colleague stood in front of the protest, arms spread. 'Stand back, everyone!'

Elsie felt the pressure of people behind her. She wanted to

surge forward through the gates as well, and bring Jack and Connie safely home.

Churchill turned to look at the marchers and raise his hat again before he walked through the open gates. Mr Gray executed a flamboyant spin on one immaculate heel, walking backwards after the prime minister as he told the crowd, 'Keep singing. Let's get right up these coppers' noses, eh?' And with that, he spun back to follow Winston Churchill and decide Connie and Jack's fate.

Someone at the back started to sing 'Land of Hope and Glory', and Elsie sang with gusto, as all the other protestors joined in.

'Pipe down!' the policeman shouted, but his voice was lost as the singing voices swelled. Elsie glanced around, watching everyone sing. A jeep loaded with men in army uniforms drove by, and all the soldiers cheered and waved.

Elsie looked back through the gate, and saw a door open. There was Churchill and Mr Gray, and between them—

She bounced on her toes, and shouted, 'It's Jack and Connie, they're free!'

They stared in amazement at the sight of the protest, then waved to the crowd. There were whistles and cheers. Elsie tried to push forward, desperate to hug her brother, but Jack and Connie were running across the yard, and the next thing Elsie knew was that her brother's arms were tight round her and Pippa.

'Oh, Jack, I thought I'd lost you!' Elsie said, and then there were other arms round them, too. Connie and Ned, Ben and Susan, Lisette. They were all together again.

'Wyngate, join in!' Lisette told him.

Elsie looked up from her brother's shoulder and grabbed Mr Wyngate's arm, just as Lisette tugged his other one. He couldn't refuse now. Instead he was pulled into the hug, just as he should be. He was a part of this little family, after all.

The singing died down and the protestors started to cheer instead; for the Blitz Kids, and for Churchill. Tears ran down Elsie's face, and Pippa licked them away.

Slowly, they emerged from their hug, to even more cheering. And then Elsie saw Churchill standing next to Mr Gray, as if he was patiently waiting for them to calm down. He stooped to fuss Pippa with obvious affection and Mr Gray looked down at Elsie from his great height and confided with a fond look, 'The prime minister is a great fan of dogs. And heroes like the Blitz Kids.'

'Pippa's the best dog there is. She found Wyngate,' Elsie smiled broadly as she told Churchill. 'And she found me, too.' And while Pippa had found Elsie, Elsie had found her voice.

'You are all a lesson to everyone in this country,' Churchill told the children. 'And everybody who is facing an uncertain future in these dark times. Let this be a lesson to the tyrants who would subdue our spirit, that we will not be ground down, no matter what hardships may be thrown in our path.' He took his cigar from between his teeth and went on. 'On behalf of everybody in this land, it's truly an honour to thank the Blitz Kids in person for all that they have done for our morale. We all owe you a debt.'

Mr Gray gave a decisive nod and announced, 'Three cheers for the Blitz Kids! Hip hip!'

'Hooray!' the crowd cheered. 'Hip hip, hooray!'

Elsie hugged Jack again as the cheers rang out. She hoped Mum was looking down on them at that moment; she would've been so proud.

She lifted her gaze to the wintry sky, which was fluffy with lamb's-tails clouds criss-crossed by vapour trails from aeroplanes. And Dad?

SIXTY-SIX
ELSIE

Life at St Joseph's Terrace wasn't too bad. There was no more cable connecting their power to the streetlamp, now that Churchill had directed that their electricity be switched on. Elsie thought of him every time she flicked on a light.

There was a good, firm lock on the door, which Churchill had arranged for them too, a formidable sort of lock that Elsie thought they must have on Downing Street as well. They each had a key, which they wore on a ribbon round their necks. The one thing the house didn't have was a doorbell, because Pippa shot to the window, barking, before their visitors could even knock on the front door.

More gifts arrived for the Blitz Kids. Elsie and her friends would stand around the boxes, deciding what to keep and what they would send to other children who had even less than them.

Elsie wondered what had become of the other children from the orphanage. Perhaps they were rounded up by social services just after the orphanage was bombed, and had been evacuated straight to the countryside. But at least Elsie and her brother had a home here in Whitechapel with their friends, and, if any other children needed somewhere to live, then Elsie and the Blitz Kids would welcome them to St Joseph's Terrace with open arms. She just wished that Rob had been spared to come and live with them too.

One morning, Elsie joined Pippa at the front window and saw Wyngate and Lisette outside. She rushed to the door and flung it open to greet them.

'Mornin'!' she said. 'We wasn't expectin' you!'

There was something about them, Elsie realised, a shared secret. Lisette could barely keep the smile from her face and Wyngate's eyes were twinkling with good humour as he said, 'I've received a very important letter for Mr Jack and Miss Elsie Taylor.'

'You have?' Elsie blinked at him in surprise. She looked around, calling to her brother. 'Jack! It's Mr Wyngate and Lisette! They've got a letter for us!'

Jack came to the door and said brightly, 'Then they'd better come in!'

Elsie brought them into the front room, where Jack had been reading a book about Churchill and Ben was building a tower out of wooden bricks. Ned was tending the fire, prodding it with the poker, while Susan was dressing a doll who had been sent to them by well-wishers. Connie welcomed their guests in and gestured to them to sit on the sofa.

'Welcome to our parlour,' she said proudly.

'Wyngate has something very important to tell Jack and Elsie,' Lisette explained, as she and Mr Wyngate sat down side by side. Pippa jumped onto the sofa and settled next to Mr Wyngate, her head against his thigh. He rested his hand on the dog's back, stroking softly as he addressed the siblings.

'I saw Mr Gray this morning,' he said carefully. 'We have news of your dad. He's being held as a prisoner of war in Germany. The Red Cross have confirmed that he's safe and well.' He looked from Jack to Elsie, his eyes glittering in the firelight.

Elsie knew that, for the rest of her life, she would remember this moment. The heat from the fire against her legs, Wyngate's hand moving gently across Pippa's back. Ben's wobbling tower, and the lace trim on the doll's dress. The poker in Ned's hand. The way Lisette was smiling. The look of joy on her brother's face.

She and Jack had hoped so much that Dad had survived, but all they had was silence. And now they knew the truth. He'd been spared.

'He's alive! Dad's alive!' she said, so excited she thought she might burst. 'I knew he was! I knew—'

There it was. The memory that had been hidden from her.

She'd known because it was on the letter she'd found in the ruins of their home. Their mother's death had robbed her of the memory, just as it had taken her voice. But where on earth was the letter?

Then she glanced over at Ginger, who was leaning against the bookcase, staring back with her button eyes. Elsie remembered, then, exactly where she'd hidden it for safe keeping. She'd slipped it between Ginger's seams. The doll that Pippa had rescued contained the news that their father was captured. The news that Elsie had forgotten for so long, and which Mr Wyngate had found out for them.

'Wait, wait!' Elsie ferreted her finger between the seams of Ginger's arm. There in the stuffing, she felt it. The letter she'd found in the ruins of their lost home. 'I forgot I had it! Oh, Jack, I'm sorry I forgot. My mind went blank. We'd just found out about Mum and...' Elsie pulled out the scorched, creased letter and handed it to Jack. He unfolded it and started to read. It was from the RAF, telling them that their father was a prisoner of war. They hadn't been orphans after all.

Elsie watched as Jack paused, before reading on, a lump in his throat.

We are delighted to hear that he is uninjured, along with the rest of his crew. I trust this news will give you hope that your family will be reunited soon. I am sure he will be missing you all, just as much as you are missing him.

She looked up at her brother through happy tears and he hugged her tight.

SIXTY-SEVEN
LISETTE

Lisette went up the escalator of Embankment station, wondering why she had been summoned to the War Office. Mr Gray's secretary had sounded very friendly over the telephone, but had left her with no idea of why she needed to attend.

As she walked past the ticket booths, she spotted a group of men in Free French uniforms, and her thoughts turned to Maman. Was it news from Paris?

She clenched her hands, trying to push the awful idea away.

She was meeting Wyngate at the War Office; he'd promised to come with her to see Mr Gray. But when she stepped out of the Underground station, she saw him, a solitary figure in his dark blue overcoat and grey fedora, smoking a cigarette. Snow had started to fall and was dusting his shoulders with white flakes, but he didn't seem to notice.

'Wyngate!' Lisette called, waving to him. 'You came to meet me.'

Wyngate flicked the cigarette away and strode towards her as he replied in French, 'Of course.'

Lisette greeted him, kissing him on both cheeks. They were

dating now; they'd met for a drink in Soho. He seemed preoccupied, and yet she knew he was lonely, and she wondered how to breach the gap and reach him without him feeling that she was invading. But he'd come to meet her from the station. It had to mean something.

'Thank you,' she replied, and looped her arm through his. Did he know why Mr Gray had asked her to come in? She tried to read Wyngate's face, but, as usual, he wasn't giving much away.

A boy was selling newspapers by the station from a stand. 'Read all about it!' he shouted into the freezing air. 'Children's champion dead!'

Lisette read the headline written large on the stand:

SIR RUPERT DEAD! Children's Champion Killed in Shooting Accident.

She shivered, but it wasn't from the snow. 'Sir Rupert's dead. I had no idea.'

Perhaps the world would be better without him in it, the man who tried to murder Wyngate and had pretended to protect the very people he was exploiting. But how could he be dead from a shooting accident when he was being held at Scotland Yard?

Wyngate gave a sharp nod. 'Cleaning his gun. It went off.' He dropped his voice and murmured, 'Different rules for officers and knights.'

'He'll never get his day in court,' Lisette said gloomily as they carried on towards the War Office. 'That was no accident.'

And the fact that the newspaper headlines were still calling him the *children's champion* told Lisette that Sir Rupert's crimes were being buried, along with his corpse.

'We'll talk behind closed doors.' And he glanced around, as though they might be being observed.

Lisette held tighter to Wyngate's arm. She pictured Sir Rupert's hands, bent like claws as he pressed the pillow over Wyngate's face. It was a secret she would have to keep.

They arrived at the War Office. Men in uniform were standing outside, guarding it, while men and women hurried up and down the steps. Surely the building never slept; it didn't even seem to stop for an air raid. They went through the doors and into the foyer, but there was no waiting at the reception desk for Lisette today. As the telephones jangled, Wyngate kept going, leading her into the frenetic building.

More people than Lisette could count filled the grand, marbled corridors. Wyngate seemed as assured here as he did everywhere he went. They swept up a wide staircase and through a set of double doors, beyond which was a corridor as wide as Lisette's flat. It was carpeted in a deep red, and oil paintings of battles from centuries past lined the walls. Above them were glittering chandeliers.

They walked past a painting of a rather downcast Napoleon, and Lisette caught Wyngate's eye. 'Oh, dear, let's not mention him!'

Wyngate offered her a smile. He was about to reply when the doors at the end of the corridor opened and two uniformed men came through. They greeted Wyngate and Lisette with a polite nod as they passed, striding away along the hall. Wyngate glanced over his shoulder, then quickened his pace.

The second set of doors carried them along another landing, then they were in another of those grand hallways, and Lisette wondered how Wyngate ever found his way around. She wondered too who all these officials were who occasionally flitted between offices, some in uniform, some in civilian clothes.

'He's a deckchair today,' Wyngate whispered as they paused before a door. 'But he's a good man.'

Lisette wondered what he could mean.

With a glance along the empty corridor, Wyngate knocked once, then opened the door and walked into the office.

Lisette hadn't been expecting anything plain and workaday, but she certainly hadn't expected the Versailles splendour that met her gaze. The ceiling was double-height, and the walls were covered in mouldings of dancing cherubs. There was gold detailing everywhere. The sofa in front of the enormous marble fireplace had a velvet-draped canopy like a four-poster bed. A vast family portrait hung on the wall, the father in a tricorn hat and the mother in a huge, powdered wig, with children in silk gambolling at their feet.

A huge walnut desk stood by the window, and behind it was Mr Gray. He had swapped his blue tartan suit for one in wide blue and white stripes. Lisette wondered if it really had been made from a deckchair.

'How lovely to meet you again,' Lisette said. 'What a beautiful office!'

'Mademoiselle Souchon, Mr Wyngate!' Mr Gray rocketed from his enormous seat and bounded across the office towards them. As he did, he was saying in fluent French, 'I must apologise for the atrocious errors of my colleagues and the Metropolitan Police. I hope' – he paused and kissed Lisette on either cheek, then bowed his head to Wyngate – 'that you can forgive them.'

Lisette smiled at his warm, French greeting, and kissed Mr Gray on his cheeks too.

'Mr Gray, I would like to be able to forgive them, but I don't understand what's happened to Sir Rupert Cavendish,' she said. 'He didn't really die in a shooting accident, did he? Will the public ever know what he really did?'

'Please, sit.' Mr Gray gestured to two throne-like seats opposite the desk. On the blotter stood a tray holding a silver coffee set and three bowls. Lisette had never seen anything like it in England, but perhaps Mr Gray was French too. 'Coffee?'

'I'd love some, please,' Lisette replied in French, and sat down in the chair, which felt like a museum piece.

Wyngate sat beside her, watching Mr Gray as he poured coffee into the bowls. He took one for himself, then turned the tray in an unspoken invitation to Lisette and Wyngate to add their milk and sugar as he returned to his own seat.

'Mademoiselle Souchon, I shall have to ask you to sign an agreement regarding the sorry affair with Cavendish,' he said. 'I hope you have no objections.'

'It's a polite gag,' Wyngate told her. 'Usually, I'd be the man asking you.'

Lisette had never had to sign a document that would silence her. But she wanted to know what had happened, and she knew that there was no point running down the streets shouting about what she knew.

'All right, I'll sign,' she said, as she took a bowl of coffee. A moment later there was a sheaf of paper on the desk in front of her, with a silver pen resting atop it. Clearly there was to be no explanation before she had given Mr Gray her autograph. Lisette flipped through the pages, which told her in several dozen different ways that she was not allowed to divulge any official secrets, and signed.

'Cavendish was haemorrhaging money. Gambling, drinking, women, every way a chap might burn through the family inheritance.' Mr Gray was giving Lisette her explanation before she had even laid the pen down. 'So he turned his mind to making money. And he was soon on his way to a black-market empire, using the most unfortunate Londoners as his slaves. People he believed that most people would ever miss.' Mr Gray turned his gaze on Wyngate. 'But Mr Wyngate has never been most people.'

Wyngate nodded. 'Somehow Marsh found out who was behind it all and was ready to talk. Cavendish got to him first and tried to frame me for his murder. If not for those drunks out in Limehouse, I would've been dead too.'

'It made no sense,' Lisette replied. 'I thought he was wealthy. Even when little Ned announced that he'd seen Rupert leave your flat, Wyngate, I tried to tell myself that there had to be an innocent reason for him to have been there.'

'He was planting evidence,' said Mr Gray. 'If it had been up to me, Cavendish would have stood trial.' He sighed and took a sip of coffee. 'But it was not up to me. Rupert Cavendish was a war hero in the trenches; highly decorated for gallantry. The people who make such decisions offered the once-gallant officer the officer's way out.' He put his bowl down on the blotter. 'And Cavendish took it.'

Lisette tensed. It was as if she could hear the echo of the gunshot that had gone through Rupert's skull. Despite what he had done, a tiny part of her pitied him. A hero who had reached a crossroads and made a choice. Rather than face financial ruin, he'd chosen theft and murder.

'So many men came out of the trenches with their minds twisted.' Lisette looked up at Gray. 'And it's happening again. Another war, and more damaged people. I wish I knew what I could do, but we cannot make it stop.'

'We cannot,' confirmed Mr Gray. 'But we can do something to make the lives of our boys a little happier. Mademoiselle, Mr Churchill has very much enjoyed hearing you sing in the club, as have I, and we would like to put a proposition to you.'

'I didn't know you had been in the club!' Lisette chuckled. She looked at Wyngate, and he gave her that little smile of his, the one he so rarely shared with anyone. 'What proposition do you have?'

'We would like you to undertake a tour of the United Kingdom,' said Mr Gray. 'Entertaining the troops and civilians, building morale. What do you say?'

Lisette tried to stifle her gasp. She knew singers and actors toured around the country, and yet she'd never thought for a moment that she'd be offered the opportunity. It could open so many doors; she might even release a record, go on the radio, who knew what else.

But as she pictured herself singing in front of a huge audience, the lights above her imaginary stage went out one by one, and she was plunged into the darkness of the blackout.

She couldn't do it.

Lisette shook her head. 'It is such a wonderful opportunity, Mr Gray, but I can't. I need to stay in London.' She reached across and took Wyngate's hand. 'Those six children living on St Joseph's Terrace don't have anyone in the world, except for Wyngate and myself. They've lost everybody they've loved, and the very people who should have looked after them let them down. I cannot do that to them as well, Mr Gray. It wouldn't be fair.'

And she couldn't leave Wyngate either.

Mr Gray nodded. 'I understand,' he said with a sigh. Then he seemed to brighten, and flipped up a monocle to his eye, regarding her through it for a moment, before he let it fall again on its blue ribbon. 'Perhaps we might still come up with a scheme. London has plenty of opportunity for entertainment too, eh?'

Wyngate smiled as he squeezed Lisette's hand. 'And Lisette deserves every one of them,' he said.

SIXTY-EIGHT
LISETTE

Lisette was happy with her little world. There was a reason she'd stayed at Jasper's for so long; it was where she was happiest. Would she have been content touring around the country, staying in different digs every night? She would've had to pretend to be glamorous on stage every evening, but it was a dingy and uncomfortable life on the road.

She stood to one side, watching the audience settle at their tables in the smoky room, the candles casting shadows on their faces. The police raid, which had ended with three arrests, could've spelled the end for Jasper's, and yet the little nightclub carried on. Tiny, the gentle giant, would be upstairs on the door, welcoming the guests. Jasper was sitting at his place at the bar, his boyfriend, Edgar, beside him as they gossiped with Lillian. Ruby and Andrea were leaning against the piano as Lucien played a medley of Noël Coward songs. Sitting at a table in front of the stage were Jack and Ned, Susan and Ben, drinking bottles of ginger beer.

They were all waiting for the debut of two brand new performers. Lisette sensed movement beside her and became aware of a tall figure in a heavy overcoat and fedora at her side.

Wyngate slipped his arm through hers and whispered, 'I thought I'd missed it.'

'You're just in time.' Lisette greeted him with a kiss to each cheek. 'I've got butterflies in my stomach, and it's not me that's going to sing!'

'Tomorrow—' Wyngate took a breath. 'I have to go away. But it won't be for long.'

Lisette studied his gaze. His eyes glittered in the darkness. He couldn't leave. What would she do? 'Oh... I hadn't expected you to... but I understand. It's your job.' And he wouldn't be able to tell her where he was going, either. He would've signed a document just like the one she'd put her name to. 'You will take care, won't you, mon cher? I'll-I'll miss you. And the children will, too.'

'I'm coming home.' He sounded so sure of it, leaving no room for the alternative. 'Soon.'

Before Lisette could reply, three figures walked onto Jasper's small stage. The sequinned flapper dresses two of them wore sparkled in the stage lights, and the audience gasped before bursting into rapturous applause and cheers. The third was wearing a sparkly dog collar.

Elsie and Connie beamed at their audience, Connie more bravely than Elsie, who was grinning as if she might get a fit of the giggles, while she tightly clutched Pippa's lead. The dog wasn't nervous at all; her tail was wagging as she stared at the audience, her head tipped to one side. As Elsie ran her gaze across the front row of the audience, Lisette knew she'd see all her friends there, and Jack, the proudest brother there could be. And Lisette watched Elsie's nerves fall away.

Standing at the microphone that Lisette had sung at so many times, Connie said, 'Evenin', everyone, you might've heard of the Blitz Kids. Well, we just happen to be two of them. I'm Connie, and this is...'

She gestured to Elsie, who stepped forward, bringing Pippa

with her, and went up on her tiptoes to say, 'Elsie! And we're going to sing to you!'

Lucien started to play Noël Coward's 'A Room with a View'. Lisette rested her head against Wyngate's shoulder as she listened. The two girls – one who had been silent for so long – filled the nightclub with their sweet voices.

They had found a room with a view; in fact, they had found a whole house, where they could escape from cruelty, where they could be children but live on their own terms.

Each night, when the sirens sounded, the Blitz Kids went out into the darkness as bombs fell around them. They were the bravest children Lisette had ever known.

It was difficult prising the girls from the stage – the audience wanted more and more – but eventually they went off into the wings to huge applause, and the other Blitz Kids followed, with Lisette and Wyngate too.

Backstage, there were hugs and laughter, then Lisette sat the children down.

'Wyngate has something to tell you,' she said. She didn't trust her voice not to crack with emotion.

Six pairs of eyes looked up at Wyngate.

'I have to go away for a while on business,' he told them. 'It won't be for long. I'm counting on all of you to look after each other. Lisette too.'

'Don't worry, we'll look after each other, we always do,' Connie assured him, and Susan nodded in agreement.

Elsie's forehead furrowed as she fussed Pippa on her lap. 'Don't go far, will you?'

He shook his head and settled on the arm of Elsie's chair. As he did, he took a paper bag from his pocket and held it out to the little girl.

'So you never lose your voice again,' he said. 'And so you'll be able to tell me what I've missed.'

Elsie took the bag, her eyes wide with wonder. 'Thank you,

Mr Wyngate!' She reached inside the bag, and drew out a notebook with a red leather cover. Embossed on the front in flowing gold letters surrounded by flowers it said, *Journal*. The other children crowded around her to look. Elsie clutched it to her as if it was the most precious thing in the world, besides her brother and Pippa, and the stack of letters from their father, which the Red Cross had finally been able to forward to them. 'I'll write down *everything*, I promise!'

And Wyngate smiled the rarest smile of all, open and bright. He would come home, Lisette knew, if he possibly could. He would never let her or the Blitz Kids down.

EPILOGUE
ELSIE

Us Blitz Kids have been busy! The other night, we helped put out fires down by the docks, and last night we helped a lot of people who were in a shelter that fell down on their heads. Connie's doing a first aid course and she practises her bandages on us.

Me and Jack write to Dad. It's almost like talking to him, only we have to wait a while for him to reply. Whenever I see a Red Cross envelope on the doormat, I smile all day long.

I've taught Pippa a trick. She sings along to the piano! Everyone laughs down at the club. And I've started lessons with Lucien. I'm not very good yet, but one day I'll play when Connie sings.

We got new shoes from Mr Sharp the other day. I got nice red ones, and Lisette said she was jealous because she'd like red shoes too. Esther got Ned a job, and now he runs messages for her. He knows all the news in London.

Susan makes clothes for her doll out of material that no one else wants, but then she realised that meant she could make baby clothes. Ern and Agnes find people for her to give them to. And Agnes is teaching me and Susan to knit.

We still have our lessons, and Ned and Ben still hate them. But even they like our lessons from Mr Gray when he comes to visit us. He teaches history and languages, and the other day he made us act out the Battle of Agincourt.

I better go. Dinner is nearly ready. Au revoir, Mr Wyngate, until we see you again. I know you're busy being a hero, but please come back to London soon.

Wherever you are, I hope you are taking care of yourself, just as you took care of us.

A LETTER FROM ELLIE CURZON

Did you know that Ellie Curzon is in fact two authors writing as one? Both of us would like to say a huge thank you for joining us and the Blitz Kids in wartime London. This is just the first of many adventures – we look forward to seeing you for the next. Sign up to our newsletter or follow us on social media to hear all the latest Blitz Kids news!

www.bookouture.com/ellie-curzon

www.elliecurzon.co.uk

facebook.com/elliecurzonauthor
x.com/MadameGilflurt
goodreads.com/ellie_curzon

ACKNOWLEDGMENTS

We couldn't have written this novel if it hadn't been for a brave band of returned evacuees, the Dead End Kids who risked everything to help London in its darkest hour.

And as ever, great big thanks to Rhianna, our editor at Bookouture, for her enthusiasm and guidance. You've really helped to shape our ideas and hone our stories. We couldn't do it without you.

PUBLISHING TEAM

Turning a manuscript into a book requires the efforts of many people. The publishing team at Bookouture would like to acknowledge everyone who contributed to this publication.

Commercial
Lauren Morrissette
Hannah Richmond
Imogen Allport

Cover design
Eileen Carey

Data and analysis
Mark Alder
Mohamed Bussuri

Editorial
Rhianna Louise
Ria Clare

Copyeditor
Jacqui Lewis

Proofreader
Elaini Caruso

Marketing
Alex Crow
Melanie Price
Occy Carr
Cíara Rosney
Martyna Młynarska

Operations and distribution
Marina Valles
Stephanie Straub
Joe Morris

Production
Hannah Snetsinger
Mandy Kullar
Jen Shannon
Ria Clare

Publicity
Kim Nash
Noelle Holten
Jess Readett
Sarah Hardy

Rights and contracts
Peta Nightingale
Richard King
Saidah Graham